A PRIVATE SORROW

It's been just over a year since the opening of McQueen's Agency and already Molly is expanding the business. She's determined to move forward with her life, renovating the flat above the agency and putting last year's traumatic events behind her.

But trouble seems to follow Molly and when a client's friend approaches her about helping discover the truth behind her daughter's disappearance, she sets out to unravel a web of lies twenty-five years in the making.

A PRIVATE SORROW

A PRIVATE SORROW

by

Maureen Reynolds

Magna Large Print Books
Long Preston, North Yorkshire,
BD23 4ND, England.

British Library Cataloguing in Publication Data.

Reynolds, Maureen
A private sorrow.

A catalogue record of this book is available from the British Library

ISBN 978-0-7505-3598-4

First published in Great Britain in 2011 by Black & White Publishing Ltd.

Published in Large Print 2012 by arrangement with Black & White Publishing

Magna Large Print is an imprint of Library Magna Books Ltd.

Printed and bound in Great Britain by
T.J. (International) Ltd., Cornwall, PL28 8RW

Ann
for all her support

PROLOGUE

Confession is good for the soul. Now where did that thought come from? Long forgotten Sunday school lessons, or maybe from one of the wayside posters that used to be found on noticeboards outside churches? Witty little sermons aimed at people passing by on their way to the shops? However, it was strange that this thought should appear now. It was almost as if the nightmares weren't bad enough – the endless agony of terror before finally waking up in a cold sweat and the prospect of another long night without sleep. Confession is good for the soul. Now there was a thought.

1

'This is déjà vu,' said Molly, speaking out loud to the stepladder. 'In a moment, Ronnie will appear.'

Two minutes later, he did. Molly was amazed by this spooky, familiar feeling. It was almost identical to starting her agency fifteen months ago but now she was overseeing renovation, which would turn the upstairs rooms into a flat, instead of painting the front of the shop. Once again Molly gazed around with a feeling of pride. The only job left was the painting of the walls, hence the reason for Ronnie's presence. Ronnie looked just the same as he had fifteen months ago. His overalls were the same paint-spattered ones he had worn on that occasion and they hung from his thin body. He still had bad acne, red raised spots erupting on his neck and chin but he was just as cheerful as always.

'I'll finish the bedroom walls then make a start on the bathroom,' he said, laying a large groundsheet on the floor and placing a selection of paint tins and brushes on it.

Molly took one last look around before leaving him to his job. She was pleased with the final result on these two previously unusable rooms. The large room had been turned into a kitchen and living room while the smaller one was the bedroom with the addition of a small shower room. When completed, it would save her the long, tedious journey to Newport every night. Also, it was her own private place and she almost hugged herself with delight. The feeling of déjà vu still persisted when she went downstairs to the office. Like the day in June last year when she opened the agency and had interviewed Edna and Mary, it was strange to be interviewing more staff today. Molly was nervous about this. Initially, the agency had been a secretarial venture but recent enquiries had indicated the need for domestic help and the three women coming today fell into this category.

The first two to arrive were punctual – a good sign. Mrs Watson and Mrs Charles also looked apprehensive, which amused Molly because that made three of them unsure of what lay ahead. Molly glanced again at the applications. Alice Charles was a young woman and although her letter said she was twenty-four, she looked older; a plain looking girl, tall and thin with a red, raw looking face that appeared as if she scrubbed the skin every day with a Brillo pad. Her companion, Maisie Watson, was much older. Her letter said she was fifty but she was thin and wiry and looked as if she had spent her life doing hard work.

Molly liked to be honest with her staff. 'This is a new venture for me because I started this agency as a secretarial business but I've had lots of requests for temporary cleaning and household work. I'm not sure how many hours I can guarantee. It may vary each week so if you both need regular hours then I'm not sure if I can give you that.'

Maisie spoke first. 'Well, I'm looking for work but would like some days to myself so I thought this job would suit me.' She turned to Alice. 'Alice and I are neighbours and she feels the same.'

Alice nodded. 'I only got married two months ago so I'm looking for work that will tie in with my husband's job. He works in the Caledon shipyard and he likes me to have his tea on the table when he gets home at six o'clock.'

Molly nodded. She was quite out of her depth with the thought of having to be home every night to get the tea on the table but she knew a lot of married women were in the same situation. 'I expect any work you do to be of the highest standard and if you can't do any day for some reason I would need to know in advance. You will also have to wear the agency overalls and treat the client's home with respect. The work will be just the normal cleaning but should a client want a proper spring clean then I would send two of you to do this.' The two women nodded eagerly. 'If you leave me your dress sizes I'll get the overalls ordered and if you would like to start next Monday at nine o'clock, hopefully I'll have work for you both.'

After they left, Molly looked at the small pile of business cards on her desk. She had ordered more and they now advertised her as a Secretarial and Domestic Agency. Edna and Mary still worked for her and her friend Jean was now on the reception desk. Molly was very pleased with how busy the past fifteen months had been and she now hoped that with this new addition to the workforce she would be even busier.

The next interview wasn't for another hour. After that she planned to phone Hamilton Carhartt's factory to order the overalls. They had an industrial workwear factory at Carolina Port. She wanted royal blue overalls with the agency name on the pocket. Ronnie was still busy upstairs so she stayed in the reception to help Jean make out some invoices. Jean had started work last year, doing a few hours to help Molly out but she now liked the idea of having some extra money. Her husband gave her a generous household allowance but it was lovely to have something to spend on herself so she had taken on the job full-time.

At eleven o'clock sharp the door opened and a young blonde woman entered. Once again, Molly experienced that spooky feeling of déjà vu. It was as if she was looking again at Lena Lamont. Then the feeling disappeared when the woman spoke. Her voice was husky and slightly out of breath. Molly could also see that she was much younger than Lena.

'I have an interview at eleven o'clock,' she said.

Molly smiled. 'Miss Dunn?'

'Yes, Deanna Dunn.'

Molly was confused. The interview was for a domestic cleaner and not a look-alike film star. Jean left to post the invoices so Molly ushered the woman to the chair by the window and she sat behind the desk.

'I'm looking for someone to fill a post in our domestic side but perhaps you were looking for a secretarial job?' Molly had noticed the well made-up face with bright red lipstick and matching polish on her nails; nails that looked as if they had never been contaminated by hot soapy water.

The woman laughed, a funny sounding deep chuckle that belied the exquisite creature. 'I can't do any office work, Miss McQueen. Not unless you want me to sit on a desk and do some photographic work. I'm an actress but I'm resting at the moment.'

She stopped to explain. 'That means I'm between jobs in the theatre. I saw your advert for domestic work and I thought this would help me until I get another job and even when I do, I can still work during the day except if there is a matinee on a Wednesday and Saturday.'

Molly was still confused. 'Is Deanna Dunn your stage name?' The initial interview had taken place over the phone and Jean hadn't got anything but the bare details.

'No, it's my real name. My mother was a great fan of Deanna Durbin when I was born in 1936 but I love it and hope one day to be as famous as her.'

Molly explained the work and the overalls and to her surprise Deanna sounded eager. 'That sounds great. Does that mean I've got the job?'

Molly said, 'Yes. Start at nine o'clock next Monday.'

After she left, Molly wondered if she had done the right thing. Deanna was only eighteen and an actress, so how would she manage cleaning dirty and dusty houses? She decided to give her a chance and if it didn't work out then she could always tell her there was no work for her. Maybe the part of a lifetime would appear on her doorstep and she would be too famous to need this work.

Edna and Mary were due to check in

much later in the day but as Molly had a lot more invoices she could be doing at home, she decided to leave in the early afternoon. Ronnie said he would lock up and bring the key back tomorrow when he was likely to finish the painting.

She made her way to the ferry and home to her parents' house in Newport. When she arrived, her father was pouring over travel plans. Her parents were going to spend the winter months in Australia.

'We're planning to travel up the east coast and see some of the country before going to visit Nell, Terry and Molly.' Nell was Molly's sister and she had had her baby last year. A girl called Molly. 'Why don't you come with us? It would do you good to have a holiday and see Nell and Terry again ... and the baby.'

Molly had been down this road before, 'I can't. I've just started this new domestic side to the business and I have to be here to see it goes smoothly. Maybe some other time.'

Her father looked at her over the top of his glasses. 'Mmm maybe,' he said before gazing back at the tour book.

Her mother appeared from the kitchen. 'It's macaroni cheese for tea,' she said. Molly looked at her in alarm. Once more the feeling that she had done all this before struck her as curious.

Later, as she lay in bed, she recalled what a strange day it had been. It was almost a carbon copy of her first day at the agency in Coronation week last year. She hoped it wasn't going to be an omen of bad luck.

2

Edna was on her last day at Albert's store. For the past few months she had been doing three days a week there. In a way, she was sorry to be leaving but she had other jobs to go to and she looked forward with pleasure to being at John Knox's house next week.

Dolly Pirie came in with her friend, Mrs Little – or, as she was better known by her nickname, Snappy Sal. 'I hear yon Nancy's coming back,' said Sal.

'Aye,' said Dolly. 'Her job at Butlin's holiday camp seems to be over.'

'Albert, what was it she was doing in yon holiday camp?' asked Sal, trying her best to be all sweetness and light.

'She was working as a Redcoat,' said Albert. 'She had the job of entertaining the campers but the season is over and she's coming back to work here until next year.'

Sal turned to Dolly. 'A Redcoat! She's

more like a red nose with all the colds and flu she's aye getting.'

Dolly gave her pal a quick dig in the ribs. 'Shush, you better no let Albert hear you running down his niece.'

Edna was amused by all this banter and she knew she would miss it. Later, when she went round to Dolly's flat for her dinner-time bowl of soup, they both had a laugh at Sal's accurate description of Nancy.

Dolly said, 'I heard she wasn't a Redcoat but was working in the dining hall, serving the meals and clearing up the dirty dishes. The couple from the next close went to Butlin's at Ayr and they told me. But I've never mentioned this to Sal because you know what she's like.'

Edna laughed. 'My lips are sealed, Dolly.'

'Now tell me what's on the agenda for you now,' said Dolly.

'Mr Knox, you remember I mentioned him, well he's writing another engineering book and I'm going to be working for him again, plus other jobs that come in. Molly has added a domestic side to the agency so I hope it's successful.'

Dolly gave Edna a shrewd look. 'You like this Mr Knox, don't you?'

Edna tried hard not to blush. 'We're friends and we've been out quite a lot over the year. I think he just likes company.'

Dolly gave her another cool look. 'Well

you watch your step young Edna. You never know what it will lead to. Have you heard anything about Eddie now that he's running Albert's new shop on the Hawkhill? Do you ever see him these days?'

Edna shook her head. 'I haven't seen him for a few weeks. I'll always be grateful to him for saving my life and I did hear he's making a grand job of the new shop.'

Dolly nodded. 'Aye, I heard that as well.'

On that note, it was time to go back to work.

Sal appeared back in the shop a few minutes before closing time. Albert gave her a big smile. 'Mrs Little, what can I get you?'

'Two ounces of tea and a quarter pound of butter and I'll maybe treat myself to a half pound of biscuits in yon box over there. Make sure none of them are broken.'

When she came to the cash desk to pay for her purchases she said, 'I thought I'd better get my messages today instead of next week because I don't like that Nancy.' She leaned closer to Edna. 'I heard she was just a glorified dishwasher at Butlin's. I mean I ask you – can you see yon streak of misery entertaining holidaymakers?'

Edna very wisely said nothing but she felt a pang of sorrow that she probably wouldn't see Albert, Dolly, Sally or any of the customers for some time. She had grown fond of them all. They had become good friends and she knew she would miss them all very much, especially Eddie and Dolly.

3

Molly was pleased with her flat. Ronnie had made a good job and all the woodwork was freshly painted and the walls papered. The small kitchen area with the new sink, cooker and cupboards was partially hidden by a room divider with shelves that held her favourite books, photo frames and ornaments. The new studio couch, which folded down into a bed, and the two comfy armchairs had arrived yesterday and the large colourful carpet had been laid earlier this morning. The new bed, sideboard, table and four chairs would be coming later from Henderson's furniture shop at the top of the Wellgate, and the flat would be complete.

She had been very lucky with the couch and chairs. She had seen them advertised in the *Courier* and they had been a bargain, especially as the owner had hardly used them. Molly was grateful to her parents for helping her out financially. Living above the office would save long hours travelling back and forth across the river. Just thinking about the river made her shiver.

There was one small surprise with the flat. When Ronnie was painting the cupboard in what was now her bedroom, he discovered it led to another door, which opened onto a narrow stone staircase that led onto Baltic Street. The key had been hanging on a hook in the cupboard but Molly, apart from using the place as a staffroom, hadn't really looked at the two rooms above the office and this had been a huge surprise. 'This must have been the main entrance at one time,' Ronnie had said. Molly was delighted with this extra entrance; it would save her opening the office door every time she wanted into the flat. She was looking forward to the small party tonight when she planned to show off her new home to her family and friends.

She went downstairs. Jean was busy behind the desk and she knew Mary would be finishing her job later. Edna was starting back with John Knox on Monday while Mary had another two weeks with her placement in a city centre office. As for the three new cleaners, well, it was fortunate that there were jobs waiting for them. Thank goodness. She sincerely hoped this new venture would be profitable and successful.

She smiled to herself as she thought about Edna and John. Was there a romance there she wondered? Then there was Deanna.

How would such a glamorous creature cope with the hard domestic work, which was part and parcel of this job? The sight of Henderson's delivery van brought these thoughts to an end and she led the way back to the flat as the two men expertly manoeuvred the furniture up the stair.

Later, her mother and father arrived with their neighbour, Marigold, followed soon after by Mary, Edna and her mother Irene, and a few of her friends who worked part-time when they were needed. Jean couldn't manage because she had a prior invitation with her own family; a twenty-fifth wedding anniversary party.

Molly had organised a small buffet with sandwiches, sausage rolls and crisps with tea and coffee. Everyone was complimentary about the flat. 'It looks so cosy,' said Edna. 'It hardly looks like the two rooms you had last year and I like the way you've decorated it.'

'Well I had to warm the rooms up because I hardly get any sunlight in here as this window looks onto the Wellgate and the bedroom looks onto Baltic Street. I'm glad your mum could come with you, Edna. Did you get someone to look after Billy?'

'John is looking after him. Billy loves going to his house because John has kept all his toys from when he was a boy and you should see them Molly – all pre-war. He's got loads of Dinky cars with a super wooden garage, toy soldiers and a marvellous train set, plus lots of books and jigsaws.' She laughed. 'I might not manage to get him away from all those toys.'

Molly said, 'He seems to be getting bigger every time I see him.'

Edna agreed. 'He's coming up for seven now and I think he's going to be as tall as his father.' Molly nodded. Edna was barely five feet in height but she had heard that Edna's late husband Will had been almost six feet tall.

Marigold came over. 'You've transformed this place, Molly, but I'll miss you when Archie and Nancy go away back to Australia. But I do understand your reasons for not wanting to cross the river every day. This will be really handy for you.'

Molly was pleased by all the compliments. 'If you want to come over to do any shopping or whatever, Marigold, you can stay here for the night. The studio couch makes a grand bed.' She turned to Edna. 'I've got Marigold to thank for the lovely wallpaper.'

'Well,' said Marigold. 'I've had it in my cupboard since 1932. There was never enough to do my own rooms but I'm glad to see Ronnie has had enough to do all the walls in here.'

Edna was impressed with the quality. 'It's lovely and expensive looking. I like the creamy background with those bright gold leaves, and the narrow border at the top matches the colour. You can't buy wallpaper like this nowadays with everything still having the quality control mark.'

Mary came over with Irene. 'I hear you've hired an actress on the domestic side,' said Irene. 'Is she very glamorous?'

Molly said she was. 'Her name is Deanna Dunn and she just wants some work in between looking for her next big part in the theatre.'

Mary looked impressed. 'Imagine, a real-life actress working alongside us.' Molly just smiled and hoped she had done the right thing adding this domestic side to the agency. Still, time would tell.

Archie and Nancy came over to say goodbye. 'We've got to catch the last ferry, Molly. The place is looking great and we hope you settle in.' Nancy turned as she was putting her coat on. 'Mind and come over for your dinner tomorrow, Molly, and you can maybe stay for the afternoon.'

Marigold was leaving as well. She laughed. 'You had better come over to see Sabby. She's missing you.' Sabby was the McQueen's cat and it was a family joke that she had never taken to Molly.

With the departure of her parents and Marigold, the other guests slowly dispersed and by half-past ten Molly was clearing up the plates and cups. She was tired and ready for her bed. The noise from the street carried up to her window and she found it hard to go to sleep in spite of her weariness. Her bedroom in Newport looked over the back garden and everything was silent at this time of night. Still, this was her home now and she would have to get used to it.

The next day turned out to be quite warm and sunny. Molly loved autumn. She loved the trees when they were beginning to turn to gorgeous shades of brown, russet and gold and, although winter wasn't far away, on a sunny day like today it felt as if summer was still clinging on.

Thankfully, the river was calm and she found her parents sitting out in a sheltered spot in the garden. Marigold was tidying up a huge mound of leaves and she called out over the garden fence, 'I hate all these leaves, they get everywhere.'

'The dinner won't be long,' said Nancy. 'I've made a steak pie and rice and stewed apples for pudding.' Molly, who had made a cup of tea and a slice of toast for her breakfast, was starving as the aroma of the cooking wafted out. Suddenly she felt bereft. Her parents were leaving for Australia in ten days' time and although she had planned this move to the new flat and, indeed, had been looking forward to it, she now realised how lonely she might be living all alone. She was going to miss her parents very much and for one brief moment she wished they weren't going away but were staying to look after her and protect her. Feeling childish and silly, she put these thoughts out of her mind as they went in to have their dinner. Sabby was sitting on the window seat in the sunshine but she turned her back and swished her tail as Molly passed by. 'Hello, Sabby,' said Molly sweetly. 'Still as snobby as usual.'

4

Molly was pleased to see the three new cleaners were all on time and waiting for their instructions. Deanna looked a bit sleepy and Molly hoped she would be a good timekeeper. Standing beside her, Alice still had the raw looking face and in the early morning light she looked years older than her age. Molly saw Deanna glance at Alice then quickly look away in case she noticed the scrutiny. Alice was going to do some housework for a family in Blackness Road. It was just for the morning and then she had another assignment for the afternoon. Molly had said she would give them all their tram fares in order to move around the different jobs. Deanna was going to a Professor Lyon, who lived in Windsor Street, and Maisie had drawn the short straw with Mrs Jankowski, who lived above the ice cream shop on Constitution Street. Before Molly had decided on starting this new venture, Mrs Jankowski's neighbour had been in the shop almost every day looking for some help for her. Molly got the impression the woman was run off her feet by her neighbour.

They all looked so smart in their new blue overalls with the agency crest on the breast pocket and Molly was amused to see that Deanna had customised hers with a thin silver belt. It looked very fetching, but Maisie just glowered at it.

Deanna and Alice made their way to the tramcar stop at the top of the Wellgate steps as they were both going in the same direction. A few men who were seated in the tram turned round to admire Deanna as she climbed the stairs, followed by Alice who would rather have sat downstairs.

Deanna took out her cigarettes and offered Alice one. 'I don't smoke,' Alice said, then turned to look out of the window. Deanna shrugged her slim shoulders and lit her cigarette. 'I really should give up as well and I'm going to make it my new year's resolution to stop.'

Deanna glanced at the woman beside her. She had never seen such a plain looking woman, she thought, but she could improve herself if she wore some powder and lipstick and got her hair cut and styled. Alice's straight brown hair looked clean but it was limp and dull looking.

Deanna said, 'Did you start at the agency this morning as well?' Alice nodded and Deanna smoked her cigarette in silence until the tram reached the stop on Blackness Road. Alice looked at her slip of paper with her address and Deanna set off for Windsor Street. The house lay at the bottom of the road and she discovered that Professor Lyon lived in the top floor flat.

When he opened the door, Deanna was surprised to see a very old man. He was smoking a pipe. 'Ah, come in, come in,' he said, looking quite astounded at the pretty young woman standing on his doorstep.

'I'm from McQueen's Agency,' said Deanna, in her sweetest voice.

The flat felt stuffy with the smoke from the man's pipe. Professor Lyon led the way into the living room. 'I'm just finishing my coffee. Sit down and have a cup before you start work,' he said, leading the way to a table by the big window.

When they were both sitting down on the comfy sofa, he said, 'What's a pretty young girl like you doing in a cleaning job like this?'

'I'm really an actress but I'm resting at the

moment. Still, I'm hoping to get an audition soon.'

'Well, I hope you do,' he said. Deanna asked him what work needed done. 'Oh, just a general tidy up. The kitchen needs some cleaning and this room needs dusting.' He led the way into the kitchen and Deanna saw that it did indeed need some cleaning. The basin in the sink was full of dirty dishes and the entire room was untidy.

'I'll tell you what we'll do,' said the professor. 'I'll wash up if you dry the dishes and we'll tidy up the room together.' Deanna wasn't too sure about his arrangement. Surely she was meant to do all the work and she said so. 'Rubbish,' he said. 'We'll get the work done quicker if I help.'

Later, Deanna went around the living room with a feather duster while the professor cleaned the bathroom and at dinner time he made another cup of coffee before she finished her shift. When she was leaving, he said, 'I'll speak to Miss McQueen and book you every Monday morning to give the house a clean.'

As she waited at the tram stop, she was bemused by the morning's events. She hadn't even got her hands wet and if this was all there was to this job, then she was well pleased.

Maisie climbed the stair to Mrs Jankowski's

flat. A large bell was situated by the side of the door and when she rang it, it emitted a shrill noise. It seemed ages until the door was opened but she heard loud mutterings long before the occupant appeared: 'I come, I come. Wait till I come.'

When the occupant opened the door, Maisie saw an elderly woman leaning heavily on a thick walking stick. Maisie held out her card. 'McQueen's Agency cleaning service.'

The woman moved aside with difficulty. 'Ah come in, come in. I expect you.' Maisie was ushered into a large living room with a bay window which overlooked the street. Mrs Jankowski inspected the card. 'Mrs Watson.'

'Yes, Maisie Watson.'

Mrs Jankowski hobbled towards the window. 'Now, Mrs Watson, I need these curtains down and clean curtains put up. You find small ladder in lobby cupboard.' She pointed her stick in the direction of the lobby cupboard, which Maisie thought wasn't needed as she had just passed through the lobby.

However, she wasn't sure which door housed the cupboard. Mrs Jankowski hobbled towards one door and opened it. 'Ah, here is ladder.' Maisie pulled the step-ladder from the deep depths of the cupboard, dislodging an assortment of household items and what looked like a collection of boxes that had been stuffed away.

'Next week I get you to clean out this cupboard.' Maisie, who usually wasn't afraid of work, was dismayed but she carried the ladder to the window. The curtains were heavy brown chenille ones and they hung from a thick wooden rail. The minute Maisie touched them, a thick cloud of dust made her sneeze.

'You have flu?' asked Mrs Jankowski, looking a bit alarmed.

Maisie assured her she was well. 'It's just the dust from the curtains.' This statement was borne out when the first curtain landed on the floor in a dusty pile, throwing up thousands of dust motes that hung in the light of the pale morning sun. After a great deal of pulling and tugging the hooks from the rings, the second one followed, which made things worse. Maisie noticed a thick film of dust on the windowsill and she realised the floor would be as bad.

Mrs Jankowski pushed one of the curtains with her stick. 'I not know where all dust comes from. The curtains just up for two years.'

Maisie was astonished. 'Two years?' she said as she climbed down from the ladder.

Mrs Jankowski pointed her stick at the lobby cupboard again. 'Clean curtains in there.' Maisie hadn't noticed any but Mrs

Jankowski bent down to pull a brown paper parcel from the detritus around it. Maisie took some time to undo the string from the parcel but when it was finally opened she saw a carbon copy of the curtains she had just taken down. 'I buy four pairs before war. They a bargain.' Maisie groaned inwardly. Where were the other two pairs she wondered?

Still, after a bit of a struggle, the new curtains were up. Although they looked the same, they were at least clean.

'I help you fold old ones up,' said Mrs Jankowski.

When this was done, Maisie was instructed to put them in the brown paper and tie them up with the string. 'Take to Stevenson's dry cleaners on Hilltown.'

Maisie struggled down the stairs with her burden and she had to stand in a queue when she reached the dry cleaners. When it was her turn, the woman behind the counter smiled. 'Ah, Mrs Jankowski's famous curtains. Tell her they will be back in a week's time.' Maisie almost said it didn't matter since they were to lie in the cupboard for the next two years.

When she got back, she had to clean up all the dust. As she was cleaning the windowsill, she thought what a great view there was of the Empire picture house. She said this to Mrs Jankowski. 'Yes, I like to sit and watch people queuing and waiting for picture house to open. It helps me forget about my arthuritis. Now, Maisie, we have some tea and sandwiches and there will be some work in afternoon. I have my bridge club but when they come, you go.'

Maisie was getting used to her employer's way of speaking. She had almost corrected the woman when she mispronounced arthritis but stopped in time. She was here to clean, not to teach Mrs Jankowski the English language. In the afternoon, when her bridge partners arrived, Maisie's first stint in this new job would be successfully over. They sat in the kitchen with a large brown earthenware teapot and a plate of thick-cut sandwiches. Maisie took a bite from hers and almost choked on the pungent filling.

'Polish sausage,' said Mrs Jankowski. 'I buy it from the shop on Victoria Road. Reminds me of home.'

Maisie nodded as she caught her breath. 'Quite strong but tasty.' This seemed to please her employer.

Maisie had almost finished cleaning the kitchen when the doorbell shrilled its strident note. Mrs Jankowski made her way to the door. 'Ah come, come Vera, you are the first to be here.'

Five minutes later, two other women arrived. By this time, Maisie was carrying the plate of sandwiches through to the living room. The women obviously stopped for refreshments during their game.

Mrs Jankowski was perplexed by the newcomers. 'Maria, good to see you.' She glanced at the stranger who stood beside Maria.

Maria explained, 'Teresa couldn't come today so I brought my friend Anita.'

Mrs Jankowski ushered them into the room. 'Thank you for coming, Anita. I am Gina and here is Vera.' Vera was sitting by the fire but stood up when the women entered.

Anita smiled when she saw Vera. 'It's Mrs Barton, isn't it?'

Vera looked cautiously at the stranger. 'Yes, I'm Vera Barton.'

'I don't expect you remember me. I was living at 96 Hilltown many years ago and you were one of my neighbours.'

Vera said, 'Ah, yes, I remember you. You were the young married woman who lived in the building in front of us. I can't remember your married name.'

'It's Armstrong. My father-in-law owned a large hardware shop in Dundee but he branched out with another business in Glasgow. My husband went to manage it and we stayed there for years. We've come back to live here now and my new neighbour is Maria. I love playing bridge so she persuaded me to come along in place of Teresa.'

Mrs Jankowski was anxious to stop all these

recollections and get on with the game. 'All sit here,' she said, leading them to the card table at the window.

But Anita wasn't finished. 'How is your husband Dave? And your daughter Etta will be grown-up and married. Perhaps you're a grandmother?'

Vera went quiet and pale. 'I...' Suddenly she burst into tears, loud sobs that left her gasping for breath.

'Maria, get Maisie from kitchen. Tell her to bring glass of water and make some hot sweet tea,' said Mrs Jankowski. Anita stood dumbfounded, wishing she hadn't mentioned Vera's family. She had never learned to hold her tongue and was forever wading in with her constant chatter. Now look what she had done.

Maisie, who had been putting on her coat, hurried through with the water. She took in the dramatic scene but had no idea what had caused it. Surely they hadn't fallen out over a game of cards, she thought. 'I've put the kettle on and the tea won't be a minute,' she said, glancing over at the woman who was still crying, before scurrying back to the kitchen.

Vera had been helped to a chair by the fire and Maria was trying to comfort her by rubbing her hands and making soothing noises. Then Maisie arrived with the tea. 'I've put three spoonfuls of sugar into it, Mrs Jankowski.' She handed over the cup to Maria who tried to get Vera to take a sip. 'Just a few sips, Vera. It'll calm you down.' Vera looked at Maisie who nodded encouragingly. 'Drink up, love. You'll feel better after it.'

After drinking the tea, Vera felt so embarrassed. 'I'm so sorry about spoiling the bridge afternoon but I want to go home.'

Maria and Anita jumped up and went to get their coats but Vera said she could manage. Maisie said she was going down the Hilltown and if Vera wanted, she could walk with her until she reached home. Vera nodded. 'That will be fine.' She turned to Mrs Jankowski. 'I'll see you next week, Gina, and I'm sorry for this awful scene.' She said goodbye to the other two women and left with Maisie.

Anita, who had said sorry to Vera ten times, was now silent. Mrs Jankowski said, 'Please get bottle of sherry out of sideboard cupboard, Maria. I think we all need a wee drink.'

Anita suddenly said, 'What did I say that upset her so much?'

'Vera's husband Dave was killed in accident in 1930 but that's not what brought on crying. It was mention of daughter Etta, who disappeared day after accident and not seen since,' said Mrs Jankowski. 'Vera spend years trying to trace her but there is no word. Not from that day till this.' Anita and

Maria were saddened but as Mrs Jankowski said, 'It was all so long ago and you not know anything about it so not to feel upset.'

Anita twisted the stem of her sherry glass and felt more than upset. She felt devastated as she recalled Etta who would have been fifteen in 1929 – the year she and her husband had left 96 Hilltown to go to Glasgow.

Maisie saw Vera to the end of her close but she had said she was feeling better and would manage fine. Later, as Vera sat in the darkness of her kitchen, she racked her brains to remember where she had seen the logo on Maisie's overalls. McQueen's Agency. Then, at two o'clock in the morning, she remembered. It was that case in the papers last year when Molly McQueen had been involved in that mystery. Before she fell asleep, she made a mental note to visit the agency the next morning.

5

Vera was waiting for the office to open. Molly came downstairs and was surprised to have a customer so early in the morning.

'I want to thank Maisie for helping me yesterday,' said Vera. She explained the incident and Molly was pleased that one of her staff had made such a good impression, especially on her first job.

Vera sat in Molly's chair, quietly twisting the handle of her handbag. The office door opened and Jean arrived. She glanced at Molly and Vera but made straight for her desk just as the phone rang. Vera seemed ill at ease as Jean quietly dealt with the inquiry.

'I wonder if you can come to see me later today at my house?' She wrote down her address and Molly said she would come at one o'clock.

'I have work to do this morning but I'll see you then.'

Vera made her way home. Her mind was so totally confused that she passed a couple of her neighbours without noticing them or hearing their greeting.

Later, Molly made her way to the house. Maisie had put her in the picture when she had turned up for work but Molly had no idea what Vera wanted her to do. 96 Hilltown was more of a pend than a close and she passed a few buildings before coming to the last tenements, which faced a grassy area bordered by a wall. Vera lived on the top floor. There were three houses on the plattie and Vera's had a colourful striped canvas curtain to protect the woodwork from the warm sun, but now it was pulled to one side. A window box filled with a few withered pansies was a reminder of the summer.

Vera must have been looking out of her window because the door opened before Molly could knock. She was shown into a cosy kitchen, which had a brightly lit fire warming the room.

'Thank you for coming,' said Vera, ushering her visitor into one of the chairs that flanked the fireplace. A kettle began whistling on the gas cooker but Molly declined a cup of tea. Vera moved swiftly over and switched the kettle off, leaving the room with a quiet hush.

Suddenly she spoke, her words tumbling out as if she had to let the whole story out in case she forgot any of it. 'My husband died in an accident in October 1930 and the next day my daughter Etta disappeared. I haven't seen or heard from her since.' Vera's voice broke but she continued. 'I would like you to take on this case and look for her.'

Molly was taken aback. 'Oh, I'm sorry Mrs Barton but I only take on secretarial and domestic work. Don't you think you should get the police to try and trace her?'

Vera shook her head. 'They investigated Etta's disappearance at the time but because she was sixteen they said she was an adult and had probably ran off with some boyfriend. They did question some of her friends but nothing came of it and they just dropped the case.'

'But it was so long ago. I wouldn't know where to begin,' said Molly. 'What made you come to me instead of the police?'

'I saw your picture in the paper last year when you solved that mystery and I thought you could help me find Etta.' She looked at Molly as she wiped away tears. 'I'm not getting any younger and this is my last chance to find out what happened to my daughter.' She went over to the sideboard and returned with a cardboard folder and a large photo frame, which she handed over to Molly. 'This is our wedding photo taken in 1914. I was only seventeen and Dave was eighteen.'

Molly looked at the photo, which showed a very young couple standing with their backs to a picturesque scene of snow-covered mountains. The bride was dressed in a simple shift dress with a huge fox fur around her shoulders and an even larger bouquet of flowers and trailing ivy, while the groom, who looked like a schoolboy, wore his army uniform with pride.

'We only spent two weeks together before Dave was shipped off to France. He knew I was expecting a child but she was five years old when he finally came home. In 1915, I got word that he was missing presumed dead and it was a dreadful time in my life. I had no money but my family tried to help me out and I managed to get some part-time jobs. I also took in a lodger to help with the bills. Then, in 1919, Dave reappeared. He had been injured, he said, at the Battle of Loos and had been taken prisoner. He was then taken to a German military hospital before being sent to a prisoner-of-war camp.' Vera opened the folder. It held a few newspaper cuttings and another photo. 'This is the only photo I have of Dave and Etta. It was taken not long after he came home.'

She handed the folder to Molly. The man in the photo looked much older than in the previous one, but then he had just experienced a dreadful war. Molly gazed with interest at Etta. A plain looking child with large ribbon bows in her hair. Both figures posed for the camera with serious expressions and Molly suddenly felt sad at the loss of Mrs Barton's entire family.

The cuttings were old and yellow with age. They nearly all told the same story…

MAN DROWNS

There has been a dreadful accident in Arbroath. Mr David Barton, a native of Dundee, was presumed drowned yesterday as he walked along the clifftop path. It is thought he took a bad turn and tumbled into the sea. No body has yet been found although the search continues.

MAN'S BODY FOUND

A man's body has washed up on a beach near Stonehaven. It is Mr David Barton from Dundee who fell from the clifftop path in Arbroath a few weeks ago. Positive identification has taken place today.

Molly noted the first date was 6 October 1930 and the second one 5 November. The next cutting dealt with Etta's disappearance.

YOUNG GIRL DISAPPEARS

Miss Etta Barton (16), who lived with her parents at 96 Hilltown, has gone missing from home. She was last seen on Saturday, 4 October. Miss Barton's father, David, was the victim of an accident in Arbroath when he slipped from the cliff path and fell into the sea. So far his body has not been recovered. It is hoped Miss Barton will get in touch with her mother and that they will soon be reunited.

The date on this cutting was 7 October 1930. Molly placed the cuttings back in the folder and returned it to Vera. 'It's a very sad story but I can't see how I can help.'

Vera put the folder on her lap and wiped her eyes with her handkerchief. 'I've tried searching for her before but I must have one more try before I die. Please let me hire you for one month to see what a fresh pair of eyes can find out.'

Molly was still not convinced she could shed any more light on this disappearance. 'It all happened so long ago. Where can I find former friends of your daughter after all this time? Their memories will have faded by now and if the police had no luck then what do you think I can do?'

Vera leaned forward in her chair. 'Just try. For one month. After that, if you haven't found anything out, then I will just have to forget it all.'

Very much against her will, Molly said she would look into the case. For one month. 'Do you have any names from those days that I can contact?'

Vera went over to the sideboard again and brought out an old address book. 'Some of Etta's friends have kept in touch over the years. Sometimes with just a Christmas card but I've got a few of their addresses in here.' She handed the book to Molly. 'Can you copy the addresses and give me the book back?'

Molly took the book and put it in her bag. 'The cutting said that the last time Etta was seen was on the Saturday at work. Where was that?'

Vera suddenly looked annoyed. 'She had a great job in Marks & Spencer in the Murraygate. It was well paid and I thought she loved it. That's why I could never understand why she just threw it all away and vanished.'

'Did she take her clothes and money with her?'

'She didn't take all her clothes but she almost emptied her savings book account, which had about three pounds ten shillings in it. She only had five shillings left.'

Molly was perplexed about Etta and the last sighting after work on the Saturday. 'Didn't you worry when she didn't come home?'

Vera shook her head. 'Oh, I'm sorry but I should have said. I was in the infirmary, having had an operation on the Friday, 3 October.' She stared into the fire. 'It was a major bladder operation. I think it was called a Manchester Repair but I've no idea why it's called that. The doctor didn't tell me about Dave until the following week and by then Etta had gone. It was a very stressful time for us all.' She burst into tears. 'That's what made it so hard for me because I wasn't there when Dave had his accident, nor was I there for Etta when she went away. I'll always blame myself. Maybe if I had been at home they would both still be here.'

There was something else bothering Molly. 'After twenty-four years, it's strange that Anita Armstrong recognised you right away.'

'Gina Jankowski told me that Anita had been chatting to Maria about the other bridge players and Maria had said who I was and where I lived. Maria didn't know about all this family history and Gina only knew part of the story.' She gave a strangled laugh. 'It's not something I advertise about myself and, as you say, after all these years it's ancient history. Now, of course, after my exhibition the other day, everyone will know.'

'You said the police thought Etta had gone off with a boyfriend. Did she have a boyfriend? One that was serious enough to make her leave home, especially when you were ill in hospital?'

Vera shook her head. 'I never heard her speak of any boy but she did go dancing every Saturday night, so maybe she did have one.' She started crying again. 'I have to tell you that Etta was never very close to me after her father came home. They were almost joined at the hip those two and I always felt like an outsider.'

A couple of things were niggling in Molly's brain. 'Why did the newspaper know that it was Mr Barton who fell from the path if his body wasn't found until November? And didn't you wonder why your husband and daughter never visited you after your operation?'

Vera tried to wipe the tears away. Molly

hated to have to interrogate her like his but she had to know the whole story. 'Etta and Dave came to see me on the Wednesday evening, just before my operation, and Dave came to see me on Saturday afternoon during the visiting hour. Etta couldn't manage, he said, because she was working. I can't remember much about that visit because I was still sedated. The reason his identity was known so quickly was because the police found his jacket on the path and it had his wallet in the pocket. The police thought he had been carrying it but dropped it as he slipped and fell. It was lodged in a small bush at the edge of the path.'

'Did anyone see the accident?'

Vera said, 'According to the police, there were no eye witnesses but some people thought they heard a scream.'

Molly had noted all this down and she got up to leave. 'Will you be all right, Mrs Barton? Is there a neighbour or friend who can come in to keep you company?'

Vera shook her head sadly. 'No, I'm fine, but do try and find Etta for me.'

Molly felt so sorry for this sad, lonely woman who still had a vestige of beauty in spite of her traumatic life. As she made her way back to the office, she felt so angry with Etta. What kind of daughter would abandon her poor mother after all the tragedy and illness she had suffered? Molly thought about her own mother and couldn't understand the reason behind the girl's disappearance. Halfway down the Hilltown she stopped. Of course, it all made sense if Etta was also dead. Perhaps, overcome with grief about her father, she had decided to end it all. Yes, Molly thought, that could be the reason. But why was her body never found?

6

Edna couldn't remember when she last felt so happy. She was back working three days a week at John Knox's house. His first book had been a success and he was busy writing a second one. They sat in the cosy lounge with all its disorder but, strangely, he could always produce whatever he was looking for.

'Another five minutes, Edna,' he said. 'It's almost dinner time and I've put the soup on.'

Edna nodded and gazed around the room. She loved this house, especially this room which overlooked the garden that was now a lot tidier since John employed a man for two afternoons a week. She smiled when she remembered her first visit last year. She had been afraid that the thorny bushes that edged the path would tear her treasured nylon stockings.

John had stopped speaking and he was looking at her. Edna felt herself blush at the intensity of the stare. 'I like it when you smile, Edna,' he said.

Edna became flustered. 'Oh sorry, I was just thinking about something from our first meeting.'

'I often think about that as well,' he said. He stood up. 'Time for something to eat.'

As Edna tidied her notebook away, her emotions were all over the place. Often, before she went to sleep at night, she pondered what she would do if he did propose to her. He was twenty years older than her, which didn't matter now, but what about the future? The good points were he adored her son Billy and Billy returned this adoration. Perhaps because his marriage had been childless, he liked having a boy about the house and Billy loved all the toys that John and his brother had kept since their childhood. Irene, Edna's mother, also liked him – another feeling which was reciprocated – and as for herself, well she was sure she loved him. He was like a warm security blanket after all the trauma of last year.

With her head in a whirl, she went into the kitchen where he had set the table. A strange feeling came over her as she sat down. We're like an old married couple, she thought and smiled again. John had his back to her so thankfully he missed this. I just hope nothing comes along to burst my happiness balloon, she thought. It was three o'clock and the lamps were already lit because of the growing darkness outside.

Edna normally finished at four and she was busy typing up her notes when the doorbell rang. John looked at her in surprise. 'Who can this be? I'm not expecting anyone.' For a brief moment Edna experienced a small flutter of fear. Please don't let it be something wrong with Billy, she thought.

While John went to the door, she glanced out of the window. Car lights were shining in the street and a man was busy lifting a few suitcases from its interior. It was a taxi. She was still standing by the window when she heard John's raised voice. 'For heaven's sake, Sonia, you should have written or phoned me.'

A pleasant female voice answered back. 'I didn't know my plans until a day or two ago, John.'

The door opened and a tall elegant woman swept through in a cloud of expensive perfume. She was beautifully dressed and groomed with white upswept hair and a handsome face. She stopped dead when she saw Edna and turned to look at John, an expressive enquiry on her face. John said,

'Edna, this is Sonia, my sister-in-law. Edna is my secretary. She's doing all my notes and typing.'

Sonia moved over to say hello. 'How lovely to meet you, Edna.'

John seemed flustered, which was so unlike him. 'What's brought you here, Sonia?'

'Oh, I'll tell you all about it later, John.'

Oh yes, thought Edna, after I've gone.

John came over. 'I think we'll call it a day, Edna. I'll see you on Friday.' He went to get his coat because he always walked her home during the dark nights.

Edna held up her hand. 'I'll manage, John.'

He made a protest but Sonia was sitting by the fire. Looking, as John said much later, like an elegant Rock of Gibraltar. Still, he saw her to the garden gate, which took some doing as they had to manouevre around four or five suitcases in the lobby.

'I'm sorry about all this, Edna. I had no idea she was coming or what she wants. She's Kathleen's younger sister. She has a successful career in Edinburgh.' He held her hand. 'I'll see you on Friday.'

Edna walked swiftly away down Constitution Road. She had a worrying frown between her eyes and the terrible gut feeling that her happiness balloon was about to be pricked by an enormous drawing pin.

After Edna left, John sat down facing Sonia. 'Now what's this all about?'

Sonia looked hurt. 'I thought I'd get a better reception than this, John, and not even a welcoming cup of tea.'

John stood up and went into the kitchen with Sonia following behind.

'It's quite simple,' she said. 'I've sold my flat and gave up my job and I'll be looking for somewhere to stay in Dundee. I won't be staying here for long.'

'What made you sell up so suddenly? I thought you loved your work.'

'Well, I don't. I thought it was time to make a new start and as I'm the only family you have on Kathleen's side, I thought I would like to be living near you.'

Like Edna, John's heart sank at this very unwelcome news but, as she said, she was family and he would have to put up with her until she found somewhere else to stay. Hopefully that wouldn't be too long. He had lived on his own for some time now and he didn't relish having a permanent lodger in the spare room. But it was just like Sonia to act like this. She had always been a wilful and headstrong person, even as a girl. He went upstairs as she drank her tea and made up the bed in the spare room with his emotions growing stronger by the minute. What was her game, he wondered. Well, judging by the amount of luggage she had, it looked as if he had lots of time to find out.

7

Molly decided to go and see Mrs Jankowski. She was annoyed with herself for taking on this hopeless job and she had tried hard to dissuade Vera from this course of action. After so many years, Etta, if she was still alive, had made no attempt to contact her mother, so it was a bit of a lost cause. Molly also hated having to charge the woman but she seemed quite happy to pay for a month's work and Molly had to charge for her time. Like Maisie, Molly had to wait while Mrs Jankowski made her way slowly to the door with her sing-song voice calling out, 'I come, I come.'

When they were sitting in the living room, Molly explained her mission. 'Mrs Barton says you know some of her story about her late husband and missing daughter.'

Mrs Jankowski said, 'Please, call me Gina.' She gave a loud sigh and looked at Molly. 'Yes, I know some of it. I first knew Vera in 1932 when I arrive here in Dundee with my husband Eric. We come over from Poland for my husband's job and we start a bridge club in the evening. Vera likes playing bridge so we become good friends. When Eric dies in

1938 I am overcome with grief as it was an accident. Vera is good to me but all she said was that her husband had also died in an accident and that her daughter went missing at the same time. But that is all I know. I never mention it to anyone and Vera stopped speaking about it as well. But now you tell me that she wants you to find Etta.' She shook her head and her fleshy cheeks wobbled. 'It's not good to – what is it you say – rake up the past.'

Molly silently agreed with her but said nothing, put her notebook in her bag and stood up. 'Thank you for seeing me, Gina, and if you remember anything else please let me know as it's going to be difficult prodding people's memories after so long.'

Molly didn't add that it was also going to be difficult finding the names in Vera's address book. They could all be living in different places now. There was also the problem of her parents leaving for Australia tomorrow. She would take them to the train at Wormit and see them off. Her mother had been going on and on at her for not going with them and quite honestly she now wished she was – then she wouldn't be lumbered with this difficult job now. Still, it was only for one month and she couldn't see Vera having the financial means to prolong the search. She would have the use of their car again and she planned to park it in Baltic Street, just under her bedroom window.

As she was leaving, Gina said, 'I got the impression that the marriage wasn't a happy one but I could be wrong. Vera certainly never said this.'

As Molly walked down the Hilltown, she wondered if this opinion was significant. She wasn't an expert on married life and for all she knew, loads of married couples were living unhappily together. She thought of her own parents – they seemed happy together but what deep emotions lay underneath daily life?

Back in the office, Jean was arranging work for the next week and Molly noticed that Mary had been allocated a month's vacancy in the quality control department of Keiller's sweet factory. There was also work for Edna, plus her three days every week with John Knox. What a good customer he had turned out to be and she smiled at the thought that it had to be Edna he requested. She wondered if love was in the air.

She had copied all the names from Vera's address book into her own and asked Jean to type them up and put them in the filing cabinet. The address book had been a bit chaotic, with names and addresses scored out and others pencilled in. Molly hoped she would be able to speak to some of these people and try to get some idea what kind of girl Etta was.

Later, she made her way to Craig Pier to catch the ferry to Newport. She was staying with her parents tonight as they were leaving on an early train in the morning. Darkness had fallen and the river was a mysterious black stretch of water. The lights and smoking chimneys of Dundee slowly receded as the ferry chugged its way to the opposite shore. It had turned colder and the stars looked icy and bright in the dark sky. Molly loved the stars and her eyes traced the Plough with Polaris the Pole Star, Cassiopeia, and the great hunter of the cosmos, Orion. In a few weeks, her parents would be looking at the Southern Cross, which was a constellation that Molly had loved when she had been in Australia. Then she suddenly thought of Tom and Kenneth and she began to cry softly into the night sky.

After tea, still feeling depressed, she went next door to see Marigold. Molly knew the garden was a riot of colour, with the trees and bushes a delight to look at with their various shades of autumn colours. There were also a few containers with blue and yellow winter pansies competing with the russets, reds and browns. But in the darkness, everything was shadowy with small golden shafts of light from the roadside lamps.

Marigold was delighted to see her and

ushered her into the lounge where a fire was blazing in the grate. Sabby was curled up on a small chair but she totally ignored Molly. Molly suddenly felt homesick for the warmth of her parents' house and their wonderful neighbour. Her flat was functional but it lacked the homely touches. Still, she dismissed this thought as it had been her decision to move above the office.

Marigold poured two glasses of sweet sherry. 'Here, drink this. It'll warm us up on this cold night.'

'Marigold, did you ever read about a man, who died in an accident in Arbroath, and his daughter, who went missing in Dundee in October 1930?' asked Molly. 'I've been hired to trace the girl.'

Marigold sipped her sherry and looked astonished. 'Disappeared in 1930? Heavens, that was twenty-four years ago.'

Molly, of course, was already aware of this but Marigold had a fantastic memory for all sorts of strange news items and bits of gossip. Marigold went over to the cupboard in the corner of the room, rummaged around the shelves and appeared with a thick book in her hands. 'I like to keep scrapbooks with interesting bits of local news. Now let's see.'

Molly moved over to sit beside her and she watched as Marigold turned the thick pages that were covered with cuttings from the newspaper. 'Ah, here it is,' she said, passing the book to Molly. Molly was disappointed to see that they were the same cuttings that Vera had given her.

'Yes, I remember the accident,' said Marigold. 'At the time, I felt so sorry for Vera Barton, his wife. She was in the hospital having a major operation and she had to also contend with her husband's death and her daughter clearing off.'

'Do you think Etta, the daughter, is still alive, or what did you think of at the time?'

Marigold gave this some thought. 'It's just my opinion, of course, but I thought she must be a selfish girl to put her poor mother through all that torment. But whether she's alive or dead, I couldn't say.'

Molly had to agree with her. 'Yes, I think the same. I could never do that to my parents.'

Marigold patted Molly's hand. 'No, but you're a good, sensible, truthful girl with high morals. I'm afraid some people are quite able to do these things without a second's thought.'

Molly sighed and drained her glass. 'I'd better be off. Mum and Dad have an early start tomorrow and I've got to try and make a start on finding Etta Barton.'

As they went to the front door, Marigold became serious. 'Be careful, Molly. This Etta has never contacted her mother during all these years and there must be a reason for that, so please be very wary what you discover. Uncovering dark secrets can be like lifting a wet stone. All manner of creepy crawlies try to scuttle out of view and some can give you a nasty bite.'

As Molly hurried down the dark garden, she shivered suddenly. Heavens, she thought, I'm letting Marigold's warning frighten me.

The next morning, they all piled into the car with their luggage. Because it was still dark, Molly drove carefully. The train pulled into the station on time and with a flurry of goodbyes, her parents were on their way. Her mother had said, 'This will be our last trip for a while and I wish you were coming with us to see Nell, Terry and the baby, Molly.'

'Give them all my love and I'll write soon,' she had replied.

As the train pulled out of the station, Molly experienced again the feeling of déjà vu. It was so strong that, should the train have still been in the station, then Molly would have been tempted to jump on board. She walked away to the car, mentally chastising herself. 'I'm a big girl now,' she said aloud, her words echoing in the empty darkness.

8

Edna walked to John's house on Friday with a feeling of trepidation. Her stomach was churning and she wished now she had eaten some of the breakfast Irene had made for Billy. The house looked the same and all was quiet as she knocked at the door. John had given her a key but for some reason she didn't want Sonia to know this.

Suddenly the door was yanked open and John stood on the step, his face red with annoyance. He strode ahead of her and when she reached the lounge she saw the reason for his anger. The room had been cleaned thoroughly. All the papers and books had disappeared, the carpet had been vacuumed and the smell of lavender polish was explained by the shining furniture.

'I'm sorry, Edna. We can't do any work today because all my notes have been tidied away. I'll have to search for everything and that will take time.'

Edna was appalled. 'Let me help you, John. Surely they'll be in some cupboard.'

John's face was still red. 'No, Sonia can't remember what she did with them. She thinks she threw them out as they looked like a pile of rubbish. No, Edna. I don't want you to be here when I have strong words with her.'

Just then the door opened and they heard the sound of the vacuum in the lobby. Sonia poked her head around the door. 'Good morning, Edna. I'll put the coffee on when I finish this.' She looked at John. 'Do you know, John, that your house is so untidy and dirty that it's a disgrace?' She stared at Edna as if she was the cause of all this untidiness.

John put on his jacket and walked Edna into the garden. 'I'm so sorry,' he said, 'but don't come back for the next two weeks, Edna. I have to sort this mess out and I hope to be rid of her soon. I'll still pay the agency so you don't lose out financially but I'll see you a fortnight on Monday.'

Edna was upset. 'But what about your notes and papers?'

'I don't know but hopefully she hasn't thrown them out and I'll find them.' He looked at Edna. She was almost crying.

'I'll see you soon then, John. Goodbye.'

He walked with her to the garden gate and suddenly put his arms around her and kissed her. 'Don't worry. It'll all be sorted out soon. I promise.'

Edna was filled with a mixture of emotions, and happiness at his kiss was uppermost. However, the figure at the window that witnessed the tender moment was filled with fury. 'So that's how the land lies,' she said. 'Well we'll see about that.'

Alice was over the moon with her week's wages in her pocket. She would now be able to have a treat and buy some things that were badly needed, like a new pair of stockings, for example. She hated lying to Victor but she had told him she only worked for two hours on two mornings a week. She knew he earned a good wage as a welder at the Caledon shipyard but he only gave her £2.10s. a week to pay for everything and he ate like a horse. She was always scrimping by Wednesday, no matter how hard she tried to make the money last.

It had been Maisie who had told her to keep back most of her wages and that she would look after the money for her in case Victor raked around the house, as he often did on a Thursday, even having the cheek to ask her if she had anything left from her 'generous' household allowance. These were his words, not hers, but she learned to keep her purse empty, as he would grab it and search for coins.

'This is a terrible house when a working man can't have a drink or two with his mates at the end of a hard day,' he would shout when his two closest pals came calling at night. She would sit and hear them calling at the door. 'Are you coming out for a pint,

Buffo?' That was another thing, that ridiculous nickname and God only knew where it came from. He never explained. In spite of having no money, he would still join them and she suspected he borrowed money from them. She could just hear him complaining to them: 'It's all right for you two. You don't have a wife like mine who takes all my wages.'

But now she was financially self-sufficient and she hoped this job would last because she enjoyed meeting all her families who needed help with their cleaning. She stopped at the butcher's shop on Princes Street and bought a steak pie for the tea and hurried up the stairs to her flat in Arthurstone Terrace. There was just time to put the potatoes on and set the table before Victor arrived home. When he came in, his face lit up at the aroma of steak pie. 'Oh good, I'm starving,' he said, taking the pie out of the oven.

Before she could cut it into two portions, he scooped the whole pie onto his plate and added most of the potatoes. He also put the bread on the table and cut four slices, which he proceeded to dunk in the thick, rich gravy. Alice put the couple of potatoes onto her plate and added the dregs of the gravy from the dish. Victor, being the kind of man he was, never made the least comment on his wife's meagre portion.

When he was drinking his mug of tea, he

put her housekeeping money on the table. Alice saw it was ten shillings short. 'You've just given me two pounds,' she said.

'Aye, I have. Now that you're earning ten bob a week at your job it's time for you to help out with the bills.'

Alice was angry. 'That's not the point, Victor. My money is to be used for some extras for us both. I couldn't afford the coalman last week and I owe him for a bag of coal.'

But Victor wasn't listening. 'I'm away out of here. I can't stand a woman nagging me all the time.'

'I thought we might go to the pictures tonight,' she said.

'No, you better keep the picture money and pay for that bag of coal with it.'

Alice was almost crying as he sauntered out the door but as soon as she was sure he was gone, she wiped her eyes and went down to the chip shop where she bought a haddock supper with a pickled onion. As she sat at the table with a large pot of tea she was so thankful that she had kept quiet about her true hours. Later, she went with Maisie to the Broadway cinema, which was a few hundred yards from the house, and they had a bag of sweets between them.

Meanwhile, Victor made his way to Gussie Park where the carnival had arrived a few days earlier. He wasn't interested in all the flashing lights of the fairground attractions but made for the perimeter of the ground where the large boxing booth was situated. He did, however, cast an appreciative eye on the two pretty girls who were advertising some Hawaiian event. Dressed in skimpy grass skirts with flowers around their necks, their orange-toned faces, legs and arms were covered with goose pimples due to the cold wind. But they never looked at him. They were probably wishing they could be on some warm, sun-kissed South Sea island or at least at home with a good book and a cup of cocoa.

Inside, the boxing booth was heaving with scores of men standing around the boxing ring that took centre stage. Thick blue cigarette smoke filled the tent but no one seemed to notice. Then the star boxer arrived in the ring and the scrawny looking referee began shouting that a prize went to any man who could last a couple of rounds with the boxer. Victor wasn't tall, just five feet six inches tall, but he kept himself fit. He eyed the boxer as various men climbed into the ring and left without the money. The man was tall and broadly built but he was getting old. Victor noticed the roll of fat around his waist and the way he shuffled around the ring. But he still packed a mighty punch.

Victor stayed in the tent for a couple of

hours and then went to meet his two pals in the pub. The carnival would be there for a couple of weeks and Victor promised himself he would climb into that ring and show the old bruiser that a new young king was in town. King Victor.

9

Molly had spent a sleepless night after her parents had left thinking about the problem of this new assignment. At 3 a.m., she made up her mind to go and see Vera Barton and tell her she couldn't take on this job. She was a secretary, for goodness sake, and not a detective, even though Christie had joked about starting a joint agency with her in Canada. She wondered what he was doing tonight. He wrote frequently and was still running his antiques business with his father.

However, when she woke up, the morning was fine with a hint of the sun on the eastern horizon. After a pot of tea and toast, she felt ready to tackle the world. She took her notebook with the names and addresses and studied it again, along with the newspaper cuttings. The last girl to see Etta alive on the Saturday night wasn't named in the cutting but Vera said her name was Frances Paton. She had married and was now Mrs Flynn and, according to the new address in the book, lived in Kirkton, the new housing estate that was being built on the edge of the city. As she crossed the river with the car, she recalled the depression she had felt in the darkness and throughout her sleepless night, but now everything was bright and the river shimmered in the watery sunlight. She felt so much better.

However, when she reached the office, Edna was waiting for her and explained her situation with John Knox. Molly felt so sorry for her as it looked as if she was never going to have a simple, happy life. She always seemed to land in some drama or another that was not of her own making. She sympathised with her and told Jean to reorganise the schedule. Thankfully, there was work that she could do for two weeks.

Vera had told Molly that the number eleven bus left from Victoria Road and went straight into Kirkton, so she made her way up the Wellgate steps and stood at the stop right beside the Ladywell Tavern. There was a large queue ahead of her but she managed to get a seat and she spent the journey rehearsing what she would say to Mrs Flynn. After all, it's not every day someone turned up on your doorstep asking about the past.

Molly was amazed to see the large housing

estate taking shape. These new houses would be home to the hundreds of families living in cramped and unsanitary conditions in the multitude of crumbling tenements that were now due for demolition. Mrs Flynn lived in the row of houses by the side of a line of brightly lit shops that were busy with people buying groceries, milk, rolls and papers.

Molly hadn't had time to let the woman know she was coming, so she was unsure of her welcome as she rang the bell on the brand new door. It was eventually opened by a young girl in her teens. A voice called out from the interior of the house, 'Who is it, Maggie?'

The girl yelled back, 'It's a woman wanting to speak to you, Mum.'

Molly hoped the entire interview wasn't going to be conducted like this. If that was the case, then the whole street would hear. Thankfully, an older woman arrived at the door and the girl disappeared back into the house. Mrs Flynn was smoking a cigarette and due to the smoke, gave Molly a squint-eyed look. 'Aye, what do you want?'

Molly's heart sank at this stern welcome but she held her head up and said, 'I would like to talk to you about a girl called Etta Barton. I got your address from her mother.'

Frances Flynn stared at her and held onto the handle of the door. For a brief moment, Molly thought she might faint. Then she stood aside and said, 'Well, you better come in.'

She was ushered into a well-furnished living room. Everything looked brand new. Frances said, 'We only got this house six months ago. We used to live in Carnegie Street, just off Ann Street. We got our house all newly furnished because our old stuff looked so shabby,' she said proudly. 'We've even left the plastic cover on the settee and chairs as we don't want to get it dirty.'

'Your house is lovely,' said Molly, and she meant it.

'Aye, it's great to have a kitchen and bathroom, especially with the family. I've got my husband and two boys who are working while Maggie is still at school. She's off sick today. Still, I miss the noise and neighbours from Carnegie Street. It's like living in the country out here and it costs a fortune for buses into the town.' She lit another cigarette and looked at Molly. 'You said this was about Etta Barton? That's going back in history. So what do you want to know? Oh and by the way, call me Frances.'

Molly explained her mission. 'According to the newspaper, you were the last person to see her after work on the Saturday. Is that right?'

'Yes, I think I was. But maybe she was seen on the Sunday but I don't think anybody came forward at the time.'

'How was she that night?' asked Molly. 'Did she seem happy or unhappy or worried about anything?'

Frances gave this a bit of thought and shook her head. 'I think she looked just the same as usual. We weren't really friends. It was just that we sometimes met on the Murraygate when we finished work – Etta worked in Markies and I was a junior saleswoman in Grafton's clothes shop, which was directly across from Marks and Spencer.' She glanced ruefully at Molly. 'You wouldn't think I was once a fashion lover, would you?' she said, fingering the sloppy, worn-out looking cardigan and shabby skirt. 'But I loved clothes away back then and I dressed really well. Not like Etta, she always looked old-fashioned. As I said, after work, if we met in the street, we would walk up the Hilltown together as she lived just a few yards away from me.'

'Did she ever mention she had a boyfriend or someone she was fond of?'

'I don't remember a boyfriend but I do know she was very close to her father. She adored him. She once told me that her mother had said he was dead. That's when he was in the army during the First World War. I believe he was missing but he turned up after the war was over and she said she never forgave her mother for telling her lies. I said, "But your poor mother was told he was missing presumed dead, so it wasn't her fault."' Frances leant forward and looked at Molly. 'Do you know what she said when I said that?' Molly shook her head. Frances whispered, 'She told me she wished it had been her mother who had been missing presumed dead and that she would never ever forgive her for lying to her. Aye, she was a queer lass now I come to think of it.'

'Did you think her father tried to tell her the truth about the war and defend his wife?'

'Yes, I know he did because I overheard him one day. He said, "It's not your mum's fault, because she couldn't help it."'

'When was this?'

Frances rubbed her nose and lit another cigarette. 'I think it was just before his accident and her disappearance. I think it was the week before. He came to meet her at work just as I arrived and she was angry about something and he said it wasn't her mum's fault. She never mentioned anything to me about it, not then and not on that last evening.' She looked at Molly in despair. 'I told the police all about it. They questioned me so much that my parents had to put a stop to it. They said I had told them all I knew but the police thought I might remember something, but I didn't.'

'And have you remembered anything, however small, after so long?'

Frances laughed. 'Aye, just that Etta's disappearance was a bloody nuisance. My manageress in the shop wasn't very pleased with my involvement, so that's why my parents had to put a stop to the questioning. They told the policeman that my job was at stake and that I was being treated as if I was some sort of criminal. Then, after a few weeks, everything died down. There must have been some other story for the papers to print and my life went on as usual. I sometimes wonder what did happen to her, whether she's alive or dead, but to be honest, I don't really care that much. I found her a strange girl with an intensity that I'd never seen in other pals of my age.'

Molly stood up and thanked the woman for her help.

'So do you think you'll find out what happened?' asked Frances.

'I don't know,' said Molly truthfully.

While she was sitting on the bus on her way back, Molly decided to go and see Mrs Jankowski again. When she was back in Gina's house, she apologised for bothering her. 'I wonder if you have the address for Anita Armstrong?'

Gina said she didn't but she could give her Maria's address and she would know where the woman stayed. 'After all, she bring her here to play bridge so she must know where she stays.'

Maria Janetta lived in Hill Street, so Molly

made her way there. Maria was surprised to see this stranger at her door but she knew Anita's address. It was two closes down from hers. Molly hoped Anita would be at home and was relieved when the door was answered. 'Can I have a word, Mrs Armstrong? It's about Vera Barton.'

Anita almost fell over her feet to let Molly in. 'Oh yes, come in, come in.' She led the way through a long lobby to the living room. Molly noticed it was very comfortably furnished with thick velvet curtains at the window, comfy chairs and a sofa. There was also a small television on a table. Molly realised that money was no object in this household.

She declined a cup of tea, getting straight to the point, 'You were a neighbour of the Bartons in 1929, I believe.'

'Oh yes, we were. Bill and I were just married and we managed to rent this small house at 96 Hilltown. Not in the same block as the Bartons but we knew them by sight.' said Anita. 'I remember Vera very well, as she was a beautiful woman. She must have been in her early thirties then because Etta would have been about fifteen. Poor Etta. She didn't inherit her mother's good looks. In fact, she was a very plain looking girl and always seemed to have a surly expression. Not like her mum.'

'What about Dave Barton? What was your

impression of him?'

Anita's chatter seemed to dry up and she looked pensive. 'I didn't know him so well. He worked in a foundry somewhere but sometimes, on a Sunday, I would see him and Etta going for a walk. She adored him. I could tell by the way she looked at him. My elderly neighbour next door said she'd known him and his family for years and he was a very moody man. He hadn't always been like that but the war changed him, she said, just like it changed hundreds of men who came home traumatised or injured. I felt sorry for them. Then after six months, Bill's father opened another hardware shop in Glasgow and we went to live there. We've moved back here because Bill's dad died this summer and Bill manages the shop here while our two sons run the branch in Glasgow.'

Molly put her notebook away and thanked Anita for her help. When they reached the door, Anita said, 'Oh, I forgot to mention the lodgers.'

Molly said, 'What lodgers?'

Anita became flustered. 'Well, they weren't really lodgers, but mainly young people who needed accommodation when they were at the Technical College in Bell Street or the university. When Vera's husband was missing during the war, she registered with the education department and said she was willing to put up one person at a time in her house. It was to earn money for Etta and help her pay the bills. She didn't have people all the time, just when someone needed accommodation, and she continued to put students up even after Dave returned.

'When we were living in our house, I remember Dave and Vera had a young girl staying with them. She was a very pretty girl who was studying at the university. The rumour was that Dave fancied this girl very much and that Etta didn't like it one bit. My neighbour, the one I mentioned earlier, told me that Etta's nose was put out of joint.' Suddenly she laughed. 'It was just a rumour put about by this neighbour, who was a terrible old gossip, and probably wasn't true. Some of the stories she told me would make your hair curl.'

This was just the sort of person Molly needed. 'I don't suppose she's still alive?'

Anita shook her head. 'I don't think so, she was about eighty years old away back then.'

'What was her name?'

Anita had to think about this. 'It was Mrs Pert. Nosey old besom if you ask me.'

'Can you remember the name of the student?'

Anita looked doubtful. 'It was such a long time ago and I don't think she was there for very long.'

Molly was disappointed but she smiled and walked to the door. 'Thank you so much for all your help and if you remember anything else, let me know.' She handed Anita a card. 'My telephone number is there or you can call at the agency.'

10

Molly went straight to the office. She had to sort out the jobs for Mary and Edna. This trouble with John Knox had thrown the work schedule into disarray. Mary was due to start at Keiller's sweet factory on Monday, so maybe Edna could fill in the last week of Mary's assignment at a city office and then, if this stalemate lasted any longer, then she would have to reorganise everything.

Molly felt tired. It was all this questioning and, although she was getting a better picture of Dave and Etta, she was no nearer to finding the girl. Jean was busy on the phone about a cleaning job that had come up. At least the cleaners were all kept busy and Mrs Jankowski had booked Maisie for the next few Monday mornings.

'I like Maisie,' she had said. 'She do what I tell her and not stand around doing nothing. Not like the last young girl I had. She was lazy and hopeless.'

Molly was pleased at the praise and she hoped that Alice and Deanna were also making good impressions. It was almost four o'clock and Molly decided to go upstairs and check through all her statements. She would also look through the addresses from Vera's book again. There were quite a few and she didn't know which ones were relevant to Etta.

She had just gone upstairs when Jean called up. 'Molly, there's someone here to see you.'

Molly was surprised to see Anita. She was dressed in a cosy checked coat with a brown scarf, hat and gloves. She looked like she was going to a wedding or some other grand occasion but no, she had only popped down to Woolworths for a look around and the Home and Colonial shop in the Wellgate for her groceries. All this information tumbled out like bullets from a machine gun. Jean looked amused.

'After you left, I thought so hard to remember the student's name. Then it came to me. She was called Sasha but I can't remember her second name. I think I recalled her first name because I always thought it was exotic.'

Molly could have kissed her. 'Thank you, Anita. You've been a great help with your fantastic memory. I wish everyone could remember things from so long ago.'

Anita's face went pink with pleasure. 'Well, I was just married and interested in everybody who lived around me. And I had Mrs Pert. What she didn't know wasn't worth bothering about. I once said to my husband, "That woman would make a great blackmailer." Jean gave a gasp and Anita looked guilty. 'It's just that I had been reading a great murder mystery and the victims were being blackmailed and then bumped off. But everybody knew about Mrs Pert and they used to laugh at her gossip.'

Molly managed to say 'cheerio' to Anita after half an hour and even then she stood at the window and waved. 'For heaven's sake,' said Jean, 'I thought she would be here all night.' She became serious. 'You don't think there could have been any truth in her blackmail suggestion do you?'

Molly laughed. 'Oh, I shouldn't think so.'

Jean was quiet. 'That Anita is a sharp little madam. She's observant and she notices and listens to all sorts of stories.'

But Molly wasn't listening. The name Sasha rang a bell and she hurried upstairs to look at the address book. Yes, there it was. Dr Sasha Lowson, Beach House, St Andrews. Vera had written a small note beside the name. 'Sasha has sent a lovely letter about Dave and Etta. I heard from her last year, and she is still in St Andrews.' Molly would go and see Dr Sasha Lowson on Monday. As she would be driving, she decided to spend Sunday night in Newport and she could make an early start the next morning. She was hoping to see Marigold and discuss the case with her. Maybe she would see something that Molly was missing.

When she arrived and stood in the living room of her parents' house, a feeling of loneliness suddenly overwhelmed her – it was a true saying that it was the people who made a home and, if they weren't there, then it was just a pile of bricks and mortar. She quickly went over to visit Marigold, who was delighted to see her and she insisted that Molly stay for her tea. This was an invitation that didn't need issuing twice because Molly wasn't in the mood to cook for one in her parents' quiet, empty house.

After tea, Molly took out her notes and they both settled down beside the blazing fire. Marigold asked how the investigation was going. 'I'm not sure,' said Molly. 'I've spoken to three people who knew the family but I've still no idea what happened to Etta. Vera was in hospital before and during the accident and she never saw Etta again. It's a complete mystery. Still, I'm going to see someone who lodged with the family in 1929 and hopefully she can help me. She's a doctor who lives in St Andrews.'

'There's one thing that bothers me,' said Marigold. 'Why was Dave Barton in Arbroath that Sunday, especially as his wife was in hospital? And where was Etta? Was she with him or did she stay at home or go out with a friend?'

Molly could have kicked herself for overlooking this important fact. It was easy to see that she wasn't an investigator. 'I've no idea, Marigold. I'll go and see Vera tomorrow, after I've seen this Dr Lowson. I don't know where Etta was but the newspaper cutting said the last known sighting of her was on the Saturday night after work.'

Marigold laughed. 'Don't believe everything that you read in the papers. They sometimes get it wrong.'

'Well, I've taken the job on for one month and I've told Vera not to get her hopes raised as it's been so long ago. I didn't take the job under false pretences. Thank goodness, as I'm not getting anywhere fast.'

The two women settled down to listen to the radio while outside a storm had blown up. Rain rattled against the window and gusts of wind blew hot specks of ash into the hearth. Marigold looked out as she went to make cups of cocoa. 'What a night! The rain is lashing down and that tree in the garden is almost bent double under the wind.'

As she handed a cup to Molly, she said, 'Why don't you stay here tonight? Your house will be cold.' Molly was grateful for the offer and this was the second invitation she didn't turn down.

Later, as she lay in bed and listened to the wind and rain, she tried to make sense of all the information she had so far and wondered if she had missed something. But tomorrow was another day and another interview, she thought, as she snuggled down in the warm bed. Within a few minutes, she was fast asleep.

The delicious smell of bacon woke her up. Marigold was busy in the kitchen, wearing an apron with large red roses splashed all over its surface. She looked like she had brought the garden indoors. Sabby was purring around her feet and Marigold was putting warm milk in her bowl. Molly didn't say anything but she was amused by the wonderful life the cat led. No wonder she didn't want to go home. The storm had abated slightly but the rain was still as heavy. Large black clouds made the morning murky and dark but Molly hoped the weather would improve as she set off in search of the good doctor.

An hour later, she was on her way. Marigold stood at the door as the car drove out of the drive. 'Watch the road, Molly. There might be floods after last night.'

As she waved back, she thought that was all she needed, but thankfully, although there were lots of deep puddles at the side of the road, she managed to make good time and she drove into St Andrews at around 10:30 a.m. She found a car park just off the main street and hurried to the shops. She planned to find the post office and ask the way to Beach House. Presumably it overlooked the beach but it could be anywhere along the coastline.

The rain had stopped when she was halfway through her journey but it was still grey and dismal. She soon found the post office and she waited in the queue until she reached the counter. The assistant was very helpful but she probably thought Molly was in need of medical help. Fortunately, the house was near the town. 'Doctor Lowson's house? Yes, go to the end of the street and if you follow the road you'll come to Beach House.'

Molly followed the directions but it took longer than she thought. When she came to the end of the street, she had to go along another couple of roads but when she turned the corner, the beach lay before her. On this dreary morning, the wet sand looked drab, with clumps of seaweed lying in a line at the high watermark, while the sea rushed to the shore in large waves. There was no sign of anyone on the wet, pristine stretch of sand and the beach looked forlorn and uninviting, like an alien patch of land from some uninhabited part of the world. Yet how different it would be in the height of the summer, she thought, with holidaymakers making patterns with their footprints.

Molly turned her attention to the row of villas that lined the road and she made her way along the pavement, searching for Beach House. It was situated half way along the street and had a sign outside that stated it was a doctor's surgery. She walked up the brick drive to an extension on the side of the house, which had another sign saying 'Surgery'. Inside was a small hall with two doors and Molly decided to open the one nearest to her. She found herself in a medium-sized room with chairs along three walls and a long coffee table that held glossy magazines. There were four people waiting and Molly sat down. A couple of the women gave her a scrutinising look. They were obviously long-term patients and they knew a stranger at a hundred yards. Molly gave them a smile and they returned to reading their magazines. Molly was hoping she wouldn't have too long to wait as she wanted to visit Vera this afternoon. She had no sooner given this a thought when the door opened and one of the women went in, followed quickly by the other three patients.

When it was her turn, she was ushered into a small cosy room with a large desk at the window. Dr Lowson was tiny, just about five feet and very slim. She had dark shiny hair, cut in a neat bob, and lovely grey eyes. Molly could well imagine how Dave Barton had felt with this gorgeous creature living in his house.

The doctor looked surprised to see a stranger. 'Are you on holiday?' she asked.

Molly was unsure how to broach the subject of Etta. 'I'm sorry to turn up on your doorstep like this, Dr Lowson, but I got your name and address from Vera Barton's address book.'

The woman raised her eyebrows in surprise. 'Vera Barton? How can I help you with her?'

Molly explained the situation and said, 'I'm trying to find out all I can about Etta Barton and I wondered if you could help me in trying to find her.'

The woman gave a nervous cough. 'Yes, I stayed with the Bartons for a few months in late 1929, while I was at medical school in Dundee, but I've no idea where Etta went, or where she is now. I'm sorry.'

Molly decided to be blunt. 'I have a witness who says there was a rumour Dave Barton fancied you and that Etta didn't like it.'

The doctor burst out laughing. 'Oh, I know he did, but it wasn't anything to be worried about. It was more a liking he had for me and we used to have long talks about medicine and books, and things like that. Vera was a lovely woman and I liked her very much. I wasn't so fond of Dave, but it was nothing to do with his behaviour as he was always the perfect gentleman. No, I left after a few months, but not because of the rumours. I told Vera that I had to go and live with an elderly aunt who needed someone to be with her at night, which was a lie. I got accommodation elsewhere and I never saw them again.'

'But you did write to Vera twice. She noted it down in her book.'

'Yes, I did. I saw the article about Dave's accident in the paper and then about Etta's disappearance and I wanted to send my condolences to Vera because, as I said, she was a lovely woman and didn't deserve the life she had. I also sent a Christmas card last year.'

'Was there any reason to send a card? Had you heard from any of them?'

'No, I was clearing out some old correspondence and I came across an old letter from Vera. I just sent her my best wishes and hoped she was keeping well. It was a spur of the moment thing.'

'Was there a reason why you left after a few months?'

She looked out of the window at the grey sea and sky and sighed. 'I'm a doctor and I can never be judgemental about anyone but if you must know, I left because of Etta.'

Molly was surprised. 'But Etta was only fifteen years old. Why?'

'Yes, she was four years younger than me... I guess it can't do any harm now to tell you why. One day I was leaving to go to the college when she followed me out. As you probably know, their house is up the two stairs with the plettie outside. This particular morning, I was running late and didn't see Etta till she came right up beside me. She said, "What a long drop it is to the ground," and she leaned right over. "It must be twenty feet or more and you could have a nasty accident if you fell over." With that, she gave me a push. I managed to shove her back and run down the stairs but I was frightened and said that night that I was leaving.' She leaned on her desk and looked Molly straight in the eye. 'I will never forget the gloating look she gave me when I told them. It was malevolent. So I don't care what's happened to that child and if Vera had any sense she wouldn't either. Still, I suppose it's all to do with motherly love. Not that Etta loved her mother, it was her father she adored.'

Molly realised she wouldn't get much more information from her but she asked, 'Did you know if Etta had a boyfriend?'

Dr Lowson shook her head. 'If she did,

then no one would have known. She was a secretive one that Etta.'

Molly was still wondering about the scene of Dave's death. 'Do you have any idea why Dave would have been in Arbroath that day, Doctor Lowson?'

The doctor looked troubled. 'No, I'm sorry. I'm not going to wish you good luck in finding Etta because I think it will bring more pain to Vera. I think she couldn't live without her father after his death and I think she killed herself. Sorry to be so blunt, Miss McQueen, but that's my theory.'

Molly thanked her and made for the car park. A watery sun had come out and a couple with three dogs were marching across the sand, spoiling the perfect surface. It was a bit like people's lives she thought: perfect on the surface until footsteps marched all over your soul.

Molly made her way back to Dundee but it was 4:30 p.m. by the time she arrived at Vera's house. She looked pleased to see Molly but the hope died in her eyes when she realised there was no news about her daughter. Molly told her all the people she had seen and what she had learned, keeping back the bit about Etta's unpopularity or, in Sasha's case, her malevolence.

'I went to see Sasha Lowson this morning, Vera–'

Before she could finish Vera butted in.

'Oh, how is she? We all liked her when she stayed here. She's a doctor now but she was just a wee slip of a lassie away back then. I thought she would become friends with Etta, but I suppose she was too busy with her medical studies.'

'Yes, she told me you made her very welcome and that she had long conversations with your husband.'

Vera burst out laughing. 'Oh, I know there were rumours about her and Dave and I used to tease him about it, but there was no truth in the stories.'

'Yes, that's what she said, but she didn't stay long with you.'

Vera stopped smiling and she became serious. 'She said she was going to live with some elderly aunt but I knew it wasn't true. Still, I pretended to believe her and she left almost overnight.'

'Why do you think she left so suddenly?'

Vera became angry. 'It was because of the rumours, wasn't it? She didn't want to put me in this position because we got on so well. She wouldn't have wanted people to think my husband was serious about her.'

Molly stayed silent. So Vera didn't know about Etta's threats. Or did she? 'You didn't think it was anything to do with Etta?'

Vera looked astonished. 'Etta? Why would she leave because of Etta?'

Molly had to backtrack. 'Oh, I just thought,

with two young girls in the house, perhaps they had a falling out.'

Vera gave this idea some thought. 'No, I don't think so. As I said, Sasha was too busy with her medical books and she never socialised with Etta. I often suggested they should go to the pictures together but they never did.'

'Did you get another lodger after Sasha left?'

'Yes. We looked after four young men after that but I had to stop taking anybody else after the last one left because I had to have this operation.'

'Have you got their names and addresses, Vera?'

'No, I don't have their addresses. Robert McGregor stayed for six months and he left in the spring of 1930. Then Michael McGregor arrived for a few weeks, he was Robert's brother. Lenny Barr stayed for two months but he left to go to a job in England, while the last person was only here for a few weeks because of my ill health. I couldn't ask Dave and Etta to look after him and cook for him, so he left.'

'I was talking to Anita Armstrong and she told me that a Mrs Pert was the source of the rumours about Sasha.'

Vera screwed her face up in disgust. 'Mrs Pert was usually the source of all rumours and gossip. I always thought she never had enough to do with her life, that she had to meddle in everybody else's affairs. I expect she's still at it.'

Molly looked surprised. 'Is she still alive? Anita said she was about eighty years old in 1929.'

Vera laughed again. 'Isn't that typical of a young, newly married bride of nineteen? They think all elderly people are ancient. No, Mrs Pert was only about sixty when she lived here, but now she lives with her sister and her niece in Clepington Road. I mean, she'll be really old now, but she's not dead and buried like Anita seems to think.'

Molly jotted down her address. She would go and see the woman tomorrow. She hoped that this old woman, with the sharp eyes and even sharper tongue, would help in this case where there were scores of facts and theories but nothing that could be pinned down to the truth. So many people who knew Etta had their own impressions of her, which didn't help in piecing together her last few days living with her mother.

'I've just one more question, Vera. Have you any idea why Dave went to Arbroath on the day he died, and do you think Etta went with him?'

Vera said, 'That's something I've often wondered and I can't think why he would go. As for Etta, well, she was never seen again after the accident, so I don't know.'

She stopped speaking and looked unhappy. 'When we married in 1913 we were too young. Then Etta was born and when Dave didn't return from the war until she was five. We had a hard job readjusting to one another and I have to admit we didn't really succeed. Dave was very moody and he had a bad temper at times. I felt I had to walk on eggshells all the time. He would go on long walks, either by himself or with Etta, and I felt left out of that arrangement. I guess it makes sense that they would both leave me at the same time, not giving me any clue as to what happened.'

Not knowing how to reply to Vera's melancholy, Molly simply said, 'Well, I'll get back to the office and type up all my notes.' She left Vera sitting by the fire with an empty plate and cup beside her on a small table. She felt such a pang of sympathy for the woman that she had to hurry out the door and down the stairs in case she burst into tears.

11

Mary turned up for work at Keiller's sweet factory at 7:15 a.m. and joined the throng of people who were making their way into the Albert Square factory. This noisy group filtered into various departments and she was soon the only person left at the small office by the front door. An older man appeared and scrutinised her work slip. 'It's the quality control department you're looking for, lass,' he said. 'I'll show you where it is.'

They walked through a lot of the departments, which even at this early time of the morning were hives of activity. In contrast, the quality control office was a quiet haven. A plump woman came forward and introduced herself. 'I'm Miss Whyte and I'm in charge of this office.' She looked as if she was ready to burst out of her skirt and Mary wondered if part of this job meant having to taste all the sweeties.

Standing at a desk was a young man who came over. 'Hi, I'm Phil. You will be working with me most of the time.'

Mary could only stare at him. He was the most handsome man she had ever seen outside of the Hollywood films. His black hair was slicked back and his eyes were deep brown. She had often read in her *True Romance* magazines about people with limpid, luscious eyes but she had never believed it ... at least not until now. Then he smiled, showing the whitest teeth. He was perfection from head to foot. She wished now that she had taken more care over her appearance. Not that she was badly dressed, but her work suit and white blouse looked frumpy next to this gorgeous man.

He started to explain what the work entailed. 'We go round all the departments and take samples so we can analyse them, to make sure they are the best quality because the factory take their quality satisfaction very seriously.'

Mary was issued with a white overall and set off with the Greek god. 'We've got the enrobing department this morning,' he said.

Mary was alarmed. It sounded as if she would have to take her clothes off but when they reached it, Phil explained. 'This is where all the soft centres are coated in chocolate. That's what *enrobing* means.'

'Oh,' said Mary, suddenly feeling relieved.

Phil strode over to the large vats of chocolate that lay at the edge of the floor and took a small ladle and metal container out of his bag. One of the men in charge of the vat took a small sample of chocolate and handed it over. Then it was over to a large conveyer belt, where the fruit centres slowly marched under a stream of chocolate before disappearing into a tunnel. Mary was then taken into a cold room next door, where the sweets were deftly taken off the belt by a bevy of women and packed into wooden trays. Mary was quite overcome by the sweet, hot smell of chocolate. Another thing she noticed was the looks the machine girls were giving Phil. They obviously found him as handsome as she did.

At dinner time, Phil said, 'We have a good canteen here with hot meals at reasonable prices. I always go there, so I'll show you the way.'

They reached the canteen, which was warm and bright and filled with workers. Mary chose a steak pie and mashed potatoes and a cup of tea from the self-service counter and was amused to see Phil had chosen the same thing. They managed to get an empty table by the wall and Phil pointed his knife at her plate. 'Great minds think alike,' he said with a laugh.

Mary could barely eat her dinner because the eight girls sitting at the next table kept looking over and making eyes at Phil while giving her some hard stares.

One of the girls, a very pretty blonde, said, 'Are you going dancing tonight, Phil?'

He smiled at her. 'No, I never go on a Monday night, Linda.'

'Well, I'll be out on Saturday at the Palais. I'll maybe see you there.'

Phil said. 'Do you go dancing, Mary?'

She nodded. 'I go to Kidd's Rooms with my chum every Saturday.'

He gave her a look with his limpid eyes and Mary felt herself blush. 'To change the subject,' he said. 'How long have you been hired for?'

'Two weeks, with an option of another week in case your colleague hasn't been replaced by then.'

He gave her another look. 'Well, let's hope she isn't.'

Mary asked him, 'Why did she give up such a great job?'

Phil smiled. 'She left to have her baby and the job has been advertised in the *Courier.* I think the interviews are at the end of the week. Then they'll have to advertise my job.'

Mary was surprised. 'Are you leaving as well?'

He shrugged. 'I have to do my National Service soon. I'm expecting my call-up papers in a month or so.'

'Oh, I see,' she said. 'What branch of the Services will you be in?'

'I would like the RAF, but I suppose it'll be the army.'

They had each finished their meal so they got up and walked towards the canteen door, followed by the eyes of the eight girls.

Mary overheard one saying to Linda, 'You'll have to work fast before he goes away. Just think of all the good looking *fräuleins* and *señoritas* abroad.'

'Oh, just shut up,' said Linda crossly.

Edna was unhappy. It had been a whole week since she had left John's house and she really thought he would have come to the house to see her and explain this strange situation. However, there had been no word from him and she had to stay away another week before going back to work at the house. She was enjoying working in the large office in town but she missed John so much that it felt like an ache. At night she would toss and turn, wondering if and when he would deal with this mess. Sometimes she would wake up at 3 a.m. with the thought that it would never be sorted out, and she couldn't get back to sleep again. Still, there was only one more week to go and everything would hopefully be back to what it was.

In the morning, after Edna had left for work, Irene took Billy to school and she made a detour after dropping him off at Rosebank Primary. Instead of heading back to Paradise Road, she walked up Constitution Road and slowed up when she reached John's house. The house looked deserted and no lights shone in the front rooms. Irene stood for a moment, unable to decide what to do. Should she walk up to the front door and tell John she was just passing or should she walk on?

After a few moments' hesitation, she retraced her steps and went home. She hated seeing Edna so unhappy and she was also a bit annoyed at John for this high-handed treatment. He had made his intentions very clear and now it looked as if he had changed his mind. He was quite entitled to do that, Irene thought, but he should have been honest with her daughter.

As she turned and walked away, Irene hadn't noticed the figure standing in the darkness behind the curtains, but she had seen Irene. 'Well, well, what was that all about?' she said out loud. But there was no one to answer her and she moved into the kitchen to make some tea and toast.

12

Molly wanted to make an early start. She wasn't sure how long it would take her to reach the house where Mrs Pert was staying with her sister. Clepington Road was long and Molly wasn't sure where to begin looking. She decided to take the bus to the top of Caird Avenue then get her bearings from there.

As it turned out, she had made the right choice because the flat was in a well-kept, stone-built tenement a few hundred yards away. Vera had said the sister's name was Isa Young and Molly soon found the flat. It was on the ground floor and the wooden door looked quite substantial, as if it would have been able to withstand the onslaught of an invading army. The brass bell and name-plate were shiny and fingerprint free. They looked as if they were well buffed up every day with Brasso, and Molly felt guilty for having the cheek to ring the bell.

It took a few minutes for someone to come to the door but Molly knew the two ladies who lived here must now be in their eighties. That was why she got a surprise when a smart looking woman, who looked to be about fifty years old, opened the door. Slightly taken aback, Molly asked if she could see Mrs Pert.

It was the woman's turn to look surprised. 'Can I ask what it's about?'

Molly didn't want to discuss it on the door-step but it looked as if the woman wasn't going to let a complete stranger past the fortress of the door. Molly handed over her card and said. 'It's about an old neighbour of Mrs Pert. A girl called Etta Barton. I'm working for her mother, trying to trace her.'

'Wait there a minute, while I check if she

wants to talk to you.' With that curt sentence she turned on her heels and disappeared into the dim lobby, but not before making sure she closed the door first.

Molly felt a fool standing in the close. She should have made an arrangement to see Mrs Pert in advance and not pounce on people like she had been doing. Suddenly, the door was opened and the woman said, 'Come in.'

Molly followed her through the lobby to a bright living room, which had too much furniture in it; large solid pieces that looked antique and well cared for. A fire was blazing in the grate and two women sat in comfy armchairs at either end. Molly could tell they were sisters because they resembled each other very much. Both were thin with short, grey hair and sharp, enquiring eyes that gazed at her with anticipation. 'Sit down. Sit down. I'm Isa and this is Mabel Pert.'

Molly sat down on a large armless chair, which was surprisingly comfortable and wished she had something like it in her own flat. The young woman came back into the room and Isa introduced her as her daughter Moira.

Mabel said, 'Sorry you had to wait outside but we've had a bit of trouble with people coming round the doors, wanting to buy furniture and ornaments. The woman up the next close let a couple of men into her house and they robbed her.'

Molly was alarmed. 'That's terrible. Did the police catch the thieves?'

'No, no. They weren't burglars,' clarified Mabel. 'They bought a few of her lovely things from her display cabinet and a footstool and small table. They paid her two pounds for the lot but when her son came to see her, he was furious because they were antiques and worth a lot more. So we've all been warned not to let any strangers in.'

Molly was quite bemused by all this drama. She had come here to question Mrs Pert and here she was, listening to what sounded like an episode of *Mrs Dale's Diary*. She decided it was time to mention why she had come. She explained her part in the search for Etta. 'You stayed in the same close as the Bartons. Can you tell me anything about them, especially Etta?'

Thankfully, Isa and Moira stayed silent. 'I remember the family very well. It was a small community in that close and we all knew one another's business.' Molly knew this wasn't totally correct, as she knew Mrs Pert was the main gossip, but she stayed silent.

Mabel continued. 'The father was a strange man. He would take off at weekends and go for long walks, and Etta was like him. I used to see them sometimes going off together and I felt sorry for his wife. He may have had his job in the foundry but she worked hard with her lodgers.'

Molly mentioned Sasha Lowson. 'There were rumours about a relationship between Dave Barton and her.'

Mrs Pert drew herself upright and said. 'They were not rumours. They were true.'

'I spoke to her yesterday and she said there was nothing true about the gossip.'

Mrs Pert laughed. 'Oh, she'd say that, of course. A young girl of nineteen and a man in his early thirties. But he was a good looking man and he certainly fancied his chances with her. And she left very suddenly. One day she was there, the next she was gone. Now why is that we ask ourselves?'

'She said it was because of a threat from Etta.'

Mrs Pert laughed again. 'Oh, I can well believe that, but I think it was because of him.'

Molly was getting a bit tired of all this rumour and conjecture with no proof to show of any wrongdoing. She said as much to Mabel Pert.

'Oh, but I've got proof,' she said. 'There used to be a small woodshed at the end of our houses and I caught them twice coming out of this shed late at night and they weren't carrying wood. Then there was the fact that her parents lived in Arbroath at the time – could that have been the reason why he was there on the day he died? I think they met up and something happened. Perhaps she told him it was all over and he threw himself off the cliff in despair, because let me tell you he was in love with her.'

'And what about her? Was she in love with him?'

Mabel made a rocking motion with her hand. 'I'm not sure. I think she was flattered that an older man fancied her, but she wouldn't have wanted it to go any further.'

'What did Etta think about all this? When he went off to Arbroath to meet Sasha, she must have known about it.'

'Oh, she did not like having Sasha as a lodger and what a noise she made about it. We could hear her shouting at her mother so much that Vera used to put her coat on and clear off out of the house.'

'I think it's a pity that Etta didn't have a boyfriend to take her out and about. It couldn't have been a great life for her, only having her father to talk to.'

Mabel's eyes lit up. 'What makes you think she didn't have one?'

Once again Molly was surprised. 'Everyone I've spoken to said she didn't.'

'Oh, she was a fly one all right. I used to see her sneaking into the backgreen with a young man. I almost knocked them over one night when I was putting my ashes in the bin.'

Molly almost groaned with disapproval. Mrs Pert seemed to spend her nights either beside the woodshed or the ashbin. Still, it was something new in this tangled story. 'Did you recognise the young man?'

Mabel looked disappointed. 'No, he turned his head away and it was dark, but I recognised her.'

'I've talked to the young woman who was the last to see Etta on the Saturday.'

'Well, that's rubbish for a start because I saw her on the Sunday evening, which was the day of the accident. Of course, I didn't know about that until the next day when the police came to see her. By then, she was gone. Never turned up for work on the Monday. I never saw her again and I don't think the policeman saw her either. Goodness only knows where she went. I thought she had maybe run off with the boyfriend.'

Moira spoke. 'Can I say something? I worked in Marks and Spencer's shop the same time as Etta and it wasn't common knowledge, but she was going to be sacked from her job. There had been lots of complaints about her being rude to the customers. Still, with her disappearance, nothing came of it.'

'Was there anyone else who worked with her who could maybe remember the name of this boyfriend?'

Moira thought for a moment. 'I don't

think she was very friendly or popular with any of the staff. She seemed to think she was superior to the rest of us. There was one girl who used to share her table in the canteen. Maybe she can help you. Her name was Davina McDonald, but she's now a Mrs Foster. She lives at the top of the Hilltown but you will have to go and see her at night because she works in the SCWS shop on the corner of North George Street. I used to go in there quite a bit and I'm sure she's still there.'

Molly couldn't think of anything else to ask, so she thanked the three women for all the help and got up from the super chair, ready to leave. 'Come back and see us if you solve this mystery,' said Mabel. 'I'd love to hear what happened to Etta.' Wouldn't we all, Molly thought, but she smiled and said she would.

Mabel continued, 'Now remember, rumours are only rumours if they're not true. People lie for all sorts of reasons and getting to the truth isn't easy.' Molly said she would heed that good advice and made a mental note to go and see the evasive Sasha Lowson again, and see what she had to say about Mabel's story. If it was true that Sasha's parents had lived in Arbroath at the time of the accident, was Dave on his way to see her there? Perhaps they had arranged a meeting and she wasn't as immune to his charms as she had said.

She hated digging up all this past history, especially since it was all in the hope of finding an obnoxious girl who had made up her mind to disappear from the planet, and had successfully done so for the past twenty-four years.

13

Molly made her way up the Hilltown. She was going to the SCWS shop to see Davina Foster. She didn't want to appear at the woman's door in the evening, so she thought she'd have a quick word with her at her work.

The shop was busy with customers and Molly waited until she reached the counter. There were three women and one man serving but it was the man who was cutting the bacon and cheese, while the women quickly gathered the items requested by the customers. The woman in front of Molly had obviously just nipped out from a nearby house because she wasn't wearing a coat but she looked warm enough in a bright red jumper, black skirt and floral apron. She was also wearing her slippers. When it was her turn to be served she said, 'Twenty

Craven A and a pan loaf.' After paying for her purchases, she darted out of the shop, clutching her bread and cigarettes.

The assistant looked at Molly. She was so plump that her overall was straining at the seams and some of the buttons were unfastened, but she had a smiling face. 'Can I have a word with Mrs Foster, please?'

The smile grew wider. 'I'm Mrs Foster.' For what seemed the hundredth time, Molly told her the reason for the visit. Mrs Foster glanced towards the man who was now slicing cold meat. He was obviously the manager and Molly was worried the woman would get into trouble. Molly said, 'I can come and see you tonight if that's all right?' Mrs Foster nodded and it was settled that eight o'clock was the best time to call. The manager looked over and Molly asked for a half-pound of biscuits. As Mrs Foster put an assortment of biscuits in a bag, the manager turned his attention to another customer's request for six rashers of Ayrshire bacon.

Molly went back to the office and placed the biscuits on the desk. 'Something for your tea break,' she told Jean. She took out her notebook to look again at the statements and she noticed it was almost full. Putting it back in her bag, she went and got a new notebook from the desk drawer.

At 7:30 p.m., she was walking back up the

Hill. Mrs Foster lived near the top. Her close lay between a jeweller's business and a small grocer's shop. The stairs were well lit and she found the flat on the first floor. Mrs Foster opened the door and ushered Molly into a small kitchen where she had been preparing sandwiches. 'If you don't mind I'll finish these off before we sit down.' The sandwiches looked tasty and substantial with boiled ham on some and cheese on the others. Molly suddenly felt hungry as she still hadn't had her evening meal.

'I've got extra pieces to make just now. Some for my husband and the rest for my daughter who's tattie-picking this week with the rest of her class in school.'

When everything was neatly packed away in brown paper bags, Mrs Foster showed her to the living room. Although the wireless was on, the room was empty. 'Bob's gone to his domino match in the pub and Barbara's gone upstairs to her pal's. No doubt to moan about their sore backs with the tatties.'

'Mrs Foster…'

'Please call me Vina,' she said, as she moved a bundle of knitting from one chair and placed it on the floor. She chased a big ginger cat from the other chair.

'Vina, I've been told that you used to work with Etta Barton, that you both sat at the same table in the canteen.'

Vina nodded. 'That's right. It all seems so long ago but we were about the same age and I think we may have started work together at the same time. I worked in the children's section and Etta was in the women's wear department.'

'How did you get on with her?'

'To be truthful, I felt sorry for her. Although I have to say it was her fault, because she always seemed to rub people up the wrong way, but I still thought she was a sad case.'

'What did you talk about with her?'

Vina had to give this some thought. 'Oh, just the normal things young girls think about. I think I did most of the talking, if I remember it right.'

'Did Etta ever mention how she got on at home?'

'No, not much. I got the impression she didn't get on with her mum but she mentioned her dad a few times. Said they went to lots of places together, which I thought was odd because I hardly ever saw my dad. He was always at work, but I got on great with my mum and my sister and brother.'

Molly was getting the same information about Etta and it wasn't bringing her any nearer to finding out what happened to her. 'Do you think she had any other friends or a boyfriend?'

Vina gave a deep chuckle. 'She used to

boast about all her boyfriends, but not to begin with. Like I said, when we first got to know one another, I usually did most of the talking. One day, I was going on about a family wedding I had been to and I kept mentioning the handsome Best Man and how I fancied him. I told Etta this was my very first romance and she told me she had had lots of romances, most of them with her mum's lodgers. There was a Robert and I think she mentioned a Michael and a Pedro.'

Molly couldn't believe her luck. She was now getting somewhere with Etta's love life, and it might hold the clue to her whereabouts. 'There was also a Lenny Barr who was a lodger. Did she mention him?'

'Yes, I think she did, but she said he was an older man and she only liked the young students.'

'How did she seem on those last few days before she disappeared? Was she happy or sad, or was she worried about anything?'

'She stopped speaking about her boyfriends. I think Robert had left and she never heard from him again and she never mentioned this Pedro again either. I think she made it all up and that no one had ever gone out with her on a date. As I said, I felt sorry for her, but she looked much the same as usual. Only more withdrawn, if that was at all possible.'

Barbara came in and her mother told her it was bedtime. 'You've to be up early tomorrow to catch the tattie bus.'

Molly smiled at the youngster who looked so much like her mother except for the weight. 'Are you enjoying the tattie picking, Barbara?'

Barbara made a face. 'Not really, but I like the money. So does my chum upstairs. We're saving up for some new clothes. Also, we like the farmer, Len Barr. He doesn't give us big bits to pick.'

Molly said, 'Len Barr?'

Barbara looked at Molly as if she was daft. 'Yes, his farm's called Sidlaw Farm and we've been there all this week, but tomorrow is our last day.' She went over to fill the kettle. 'But maybe it's Ben Barr.'

Vina was curious. 'Do you think it's the same person?'

Molly didn't think so. 'It's a common enough name and Vera's lodger went off to England a month or so before all this happened.'

'Still, I suppose he could be back living here,' said Vina. 'I mean, if he left Dundee in 1930, he could be living anywhere now.'

'Yes, he could.' Molly put her notebook in her coat pocket and thanked Vina and Barbara for all their help.

Afterwards, as she walked quickly down the Hill, she decided she would go to Sidlaw

Farm tomorrow. It was probably a wild goose chase but she had no leads yet in this baffling case and maybe it was the same Lenny Barr who had been the one-time lodger of Vera and Dave Barton. Before she went to sleep, she reviewed all the interviews in her mind. Was there something she was missing? Mabel Pert had hinted that not everyone had told the truth. But the problem was recognising the lies.

14

Molly had found out from Barbara that they stopped for a break – she called it 'piecie time' – at about ten o'clock and Molly planned to be at the farm at that time. The temperature had dropped during the night, so she had to scrape a thin film of ice from the car's windscreen before setting off. But by the time she reached the road that led to the farm, the sun had come out and was shining pleasantly.

Barbara had given her some rudimentary directions. She said the farm was near Auchterhouse. Again, Molly had the feeling of déjà vu. It was like the time she had visited Clifftop Farm but the circumstances were different now. She was searching for a missing girl and the way things looked, if she didn't get any more leads in the next two weeks, then that was that. The job was finished.

The road had narrowed as she left Dundee behind and there were a few farm roads but so far, not the one she was looking for. The sun was in her eyes and she had to squint at the signposts. Then a couple of miles along a road that looked like a track, she saw the name at the foot of an even narrower road: Sidlaw Farm. She drove slowly as she didn't want to damage the car with some large potholes that were filled with water and looked innocuous enough until the wheels plunged into them. 'The things I do to run a business,' she said out loud.

The road ran for a half a mile or so before she came into a clearing. A small grey building seemed to snuggle up against the hill and Molly parked in front of it, scattering hens in her wake. A thin wisp of smoke drifted lazily up into the blue sky but there was no sign of life. As she got out of the car, she heard voices and, a few hundred yards ahead of her, she saw a tractor chugging up a field followed by another smaller tractor pulling a wooden bogey. There was a straggly line of figures filling metal baskets with potatoes and a young man was busy lifting them and throwing the potatoes into the cart.

Molly walked towards the field and stood watching. The elderly man driving the tractor saw her and made a sign for her to wait. Barbara, who was dressed in a warm jacket and hat, saw her and waved. Then the tractor stopped and the man stepped down and walked towards her. He was heavily built with a well-trimmed grey beard and a woollen hat pulled down almost to his eyes and a thick waterproof jacket and trousers. 'Can I help you?' he said. 'Have you lost your way?'

Molly said no and she handed him her card. 'I hate to bother you but I'm looking for a Lenny Barr.'

'Better come down to the house,' he said, before turning to the man who was driving the bogey. 'Better have our piecie time now, George.' George waved and all the tattie pickers made a beeline for their bags, which held their sandwiches and drinks.

The man walked ahead into the house. Molly had to walk between Wellington boots encrusted with inches of dried mud and jackets that seemed to take up one entire wall. The kitchen was basic with a large table and a few assorted chairs but it was warm because of the Aga cooker. A kettle was boiling on the top. 'Do you want some tea,' he pulled out a pair of reading glasses and squinted at her card, 'Miss McQueen?'

Molly said no, that she didn't want to

hinder him in his work. As they sat down at the table, she looked at him more closely and suddenly had a niggling feeling that she recognised him from somewhere. 'I've just got a few questions,' she said. She mentioned Vera and Etta. 'I was wondering if you were the same Lenny Barr who used to lodge with Mrs Barton. This would be in about 1930.'

He made a deep, gravelly sound and Molly realised he was laughing. '1930? Heavens, that's a long time ago, and you say this girl Etta disappeared then?'

'Yes, just after her father's accidental death.'

'Oh, I'm sorry to hear that. What a tragedy. But I'm not the man you're looking for. My name is actually Eck Barr and not Lenny. Eck is short for Alexander. In 1930, I was working on a farm in England and, in 1938, I married the woman who owned the farm. Sadly, she died last year and I moved here with my stepson George. We've never been to this part of the world before but we saw this farm advertised in the *Farmers Weekly* and we thought we'd give it a try. My wife had been ill for a few years before she died and we thought the farm held too many sad memories for us.' He looked ruefully around him. 'Still, one farm is much like another but we're going to sell up here as it's got too many hilly fields. It's not good for my old legs.'

There was a sound in the lobby and a figure passed the open door. 'That's my stepson.' Molly saw a hefty figure with short grey hair. He was dressed in dark dungarees, a thick polo-neck jumper and wellington boots. Pulling on a woollen hat, he nodded as he went back out.

Eck said, 'I'd better be getting back. We're hoping to finish the lifting today while the weather's good.'

As Molly got into the car, the two men strode out towards the field. By the time she reversed, she heard the sound of the tractors. Molly was depressed as she made her way back along the road. This case was going nowhere and except for some snippets of Etta's personality, she was no closer to finding her. In a way, she would be glad when the month was up. The agency needed her and she realised she hadn't seen Edna, Mary or any of the cleaners for days.

She decided to go and see Anita again to see if she could remember any of the lodgers and if she'd seen them out with Etta. When Anita opened the door, she looked delighted to see her. Once again, Anita was dressed in the height of fashion. She wore a pink woollen cardigan with a black, full-skirted dress.

Molly apologised for bothering her again. 'I won't keep you long, Anita, as I see you're going out.'

'No, I'm not, so don't worry about asking me more questions.'

'I've talked to someone who told me Etta had loads of boyfriends who were mainly the young students who lodged in the house. Do you remember if you saw her with any of them?'

Anita shook her head. 'She was always on her own every time I saw her or else she was with her father.'

'Does the name Pedro ring a bell?'

Anita looked doubtful, then shook her head again. 'Sorry.'

'Oh well, it doesn't matter.'

'I don't think Etta had any friends, boys or girls.'

'Mrs Pert says she saw her with a young man in the backgreen on one occasion at least.'

Anita almost choked. 'Mrs Pert? Surely she's not still alive?'

Molly smiled. 'Yes, she is. She lives with her sister and niece. At the moment, they are busy hiding from unscrupulous antique dealers.'

'Well, all I can say is that doesn't sound like the Mrs Pert I remember. The old Mrs Pert would have dealt with anybody in those days, regardless of whether they were unscrupulous antique dealers or the Archangel Gabriel.'

Molly was still laughing as she made her

way back to the office. She liked Anita. She was sharp-witted and funny and she had the most marvellous clothes. Business must be booming in the hardware trade she thought. Still, if Anita ever needed a job, then Molly would snap her up immediately.

15

Deanna hurried into the office on Friday morning, her face pink with pleasure. Molly and Jean, who were dealing with invoices and bookings, looked up as she breezed in. She sounded a bit breathless. 'I've got a part in a play.'

'That's great news, Deanna,' said Molly, secretly hoping she could still count on her to do some of the bookings that were coming in. Molly had a few friends who helped out when needed but they were all on the secretarial side. She couldn't imagine any of them taking on cleaning chores. But if need be, then she could always ask.

'Where will you be acting?' asked Jean.

'I'll be at the Dundee Repertory Theatre in Nicoll Street. It's just a small part, but I'm hoping it will lead to more work and, hopefully, larger parts.' She suddenly looked anxious. 'I hope I can still work here, Molly, in between rehearsals and the two matinees.'

Molly couldn't answer her at this point because she didn't know which days she needed off. 'If you can give me a list of the days you can't do, then we'll try and work something out.'

Deanna looked pleased. 'Oh, thanks. Thank you.' She didn't dance around the office but Molly got the impression she would have liked to. 'My professor in Windsor Street says he doesn't mind what days I work, so I can always manage to work for him. He's a darling. In fact, it was him who got me this part because he knows someone who knows the director.'

Molly and Jean looked at each other, smiling. It was hard not to feel Deanna's joy or amusement about the fact that the client was now 'Deanna's professor'.

Jean asked, 'What's the name of the play?'

Deanna came down to earth and put on a sober face. 'It's a serious historical play called *Glencoe's Tragedy* and it's all about the Macdonald massacre.' Well, it's not a bundle of laughs, Molly thought. 'The Rep is putting it on in two weeks' time and I want everybody here to come and see me.'

Molly said she could count on herself but Deanna would have to ask the others. On that high note, Deanna departed with her day's assignment.

Molly was planning to go to St Andrews

again to see Sasha Lowson. The doctor had given her the surgery's telephone number and Molly had phoned last night. Sasha didn't sound pleased. In fact, she was almost downright rude and told Molly that she hoped she wasn't going to have to put up with this questioning forever. Molly assured her it was just a small thing she wanted cleared up. She was hoping to get the truth out of Sasha regarding her relationship with Dave Barton. Mrs Pert was a nosy neighbour but Molly believed her story. There was something not quite right about the doctor and her so-called platonic friendship with Dave.

Molly caught the mid-morning ferry and was soon on her way. Sasha had said to come at about midday. There wasn't a lot of traffic on the road, so she made good time, parking the car overlooking the beach. She checked her watch – it was only 11:30 a.m., so she sat looking at the sea. Noisy squawking gulls flew overhead and the sea looked rough. It was a grey cloudy day but there were quite a few people out, either walking along the beach or on the road. Molly was wishing she had brought sandwiches and a flask of tea, but maybe she would go to the small café on the High Street after speaking to Sasha.

At twelve o'clock she was sitting not in the

surgery but in the kitchen where Sasha was busy making coffee in a blender. The smell was wonderful and the cup of steaming black coffee tasted delicious. Molly never normally drank coffee, much preferring tea, but she didn't want to antagonise the woman even more.

Molly decided to leap right in. 'I've spoken to someone who saw you and Dave Barton coming out of the woodshed in the close on two occasions at least. Is it true you were having an affair with him?'

Sasha gave Molly a long cool look. 'Actually, it's none of your business.'

'I know it isn't and I'm not trying to rake up old gossip. Nothing you tell me will go any further. The only thing I'll tell Vera is that I spoke to you in the hope you remembered something about Etta. Do you think Etta knew about you and her dad? I'm just trying to find a reason for her disappearance.'

Sasha cradled the cup in her hand and looked out of the window at the well-tended garden at the back of the house. 'It's true what I told you before. Dave and I were just friends; at least that was how I felt. I think he was more serious about me and that, along with Etta's threat, made me leave. We used to go to the pictures now and again and before going home we would sit in the woodshed. There was a small bench in there and we would smoke a cigarette and just talk. Dave always said we couldn't have a decent conversation in the house because Etta would sit and listen to every word.'

'Did he come through to Arbroath to see you?'

She nodded. 'I suppose your numerous informers told you that my parents used to live there. Sorry to not have told you myself, but I just couldn't stand the thought of Vera thinking I would betray her in any way. So yes, if you have to know, he came twice but by then I didn't want to see him and my parents were also planning on moving here by that point, so that put an end to it.'

'Did you see him on the day of the accident? Maybe you told him you didn't want to see him and he jumped from the cliff path?'

Sasha was outraged. 'He didn't jump deliberately. It must have been an accident because he once told me he would never leave Etta. I didn't see him that day but I wish now that I had. Maybe he would still be alive. Poor man.'

Her story was convincing but as Mrs Pert said, even the most innocent of people had an absence of truth in what they said. However, Molly couldn't see how this friendship had caused the events that followed.

Sasha saw her to the door but there was no social conversation on the step. The minute

Molly stepped out onto the front path, the door was firmly and noisily slammed shut behind her. Oh dear, she thought, I wish I hadn't taken this job as it's making people angry. Also, there was the fact she had an agency to run and she couldn't afford to make enemies.

When she got to the ferry, she sat in the car. The sky was dark with thick, black clouds and the rain was heavy. She could hear it on the roof but it was a therapeutic noise and took away the thought of the rough crossing as the small paddle steamer thrashed its way through large waves. Molly had not recovered completely from last year's trauma but as she sat in the confines of the car, her mind was going round in circles. After two weeks, she still had no idea what had happened on that fateful day and afterwards.

As the Fifie neared Craig Pier, she made up her mind to see Vera next week and tell her not to waste any more money on the search. After all, if the police couldn't find the girl, then what chance did she have? However, by the time she reached the Wellgate, she decided to go and see Frances Flynn in one last attempt to uncover any missed details.

Luckily, a number eleven bus drew up as she reached the stop, which she saw as an omen, and by the time she stood outside

Frances's door, the rain had stopped. She knocked loudly twice and Maggie appeared – did this girl never go to school? Maggie shouted up the lobby, 'It's that woman again.'

Frances appeared and she looked flustered. 'I've got a visitor.'

'It's just a couple of final things I'd like to ask you. It won't take a minute.'

'Oh well, you better come in,' she said. 'But it's not convenient.'

When Molly went into the living room, she saw a woman sitting at the fire. It was obvious Frances had been smoking because of the blue haze that lingered near the ceiling and the overflowing ashtray on the small table by the chairs. 'This is an old neighbour of mine,' said Frances, but she never gave the woman a name. The woman was plump but not fat and it was her face that Molly noticed. Her dark hair was set like a helmet that was very unflattering to her round face, which held a sullen expression. Deep lines ran down from her nose to her down-turned mouth and there were also deep frown marks between her eyebrows. She looked as if a smile had never crossed her face.

Molly was unsure about asking any questions but Frances said quite crossly, 'Well, what do you want now?'

Molly tried to put a brave face on but this was another unfriendly welcome. 'I wondered if you remembered anything else about Etta?'

Frances lit another cigarette, totally forgetting a half-smoked one still sitting in the ashtray. The woman looked scornfully at Frances, while screwing her eyes up at the smoke, but she didn't budge from her chair. 'No, I don't. I told you everything when you came here and I won't remember anything else now after all this time.'

Molly's eyes were beginning to smart with all the smoke, so she decided to finish up and clear out into the fresh air. 'There's just one more thing. Do the names Robert and Michael McGregor mean anything to you? Or Pedro? These were apparently Etta's boyfriends and some were lodgers at her house.'

Frances coughed loudly. 'Etta's boyfriends? I don't believe it. She never had any friends, I told you that.'

She didn't get out of her chair when Molly left but Maggie saw her to the door. Before she left, she heard Frances complaining to the nameless woman. 'Etta, Etta, Etta. I'm sick of hearing her name. She was trouble then and she's trouble now.'

Maggie shrugged her shoulders in embarrassment. 'Sorry about that.' Molly smiled at her. She seemed a nice girl but it was a pity she was losing so much schooling. 'I'm leaving school soon and I wondered if you were taking on any staff in your agency. I would love to work as a secretary.'

Molly handed her a card. 'It all depends on your school grades, Maggie, but call in any time and have a chat.'

16

Mary was getting ready to go out with her friend Norma. It was the usual Saturday night dancing at Kidd's Rooms. Norma had recently moved into the next close at Moncur Crescent and Mary was pleased to have her as a pal because Rita, who used to go out with her on a Saturday, had started to go out with a new crowd – people she worked with at the Vidor battery factory at the Industrial Estate.

Norma had bought a new dress and she looked great in it. It was a full-skirted, woollen one with autumn-coloured checks and a black velvet collar, but Mary wasn't envious because she was wearing her favourite black taffeta skirt with a black and white blouse. Her flat ballerina shoes and belt were red and she always felt confident when wearing this outfit. She would have a laugh with Norma, saying they were the Rock 'n' Roll Generation and the world was their oyster.

Norma worked in Birrell's shoe shop in the Overgate and she was complaining. 'What a day I've had. The amount of women who come in asking for size four shoes when they need a size six. They looked at me as if I'm to blame. One customer told me that the shoe shop was making the shoes far smaller than before the war. No wonder I need a night out.'

The dance hall was busy by the time they reached it. In fact, they were no sooner in the door when they were both whisked up for a dance. The two young men were regulars and knew Mary well. Although Norma was a newcomer, she had soon got to know the crowd. At the end of the dance, Mary made her way across the floor to where a crowd of people were standing on the fringe of the dance floor. The young men were pulling out cigarette cases and lighting up their Senior Service cigarettes. In their sharp suits or new sports jackets and corduroy trousers, they thought they were men of the world instead of being barely out of their teens. It was a heady atmosphere and one that Mary and Norma loved, feeling comfortable with the surroundings. In fact, Mary often thought it was like being with a big familiar family.

Then, out of the corner of her eye, she spotted Phil and he was making his way over to her. Quite a few of the girls turned around to look at him and Mary noticed some of the lads were also following his movements. He looked even more handsome in his dark-coloured suit and Mary was both delighted and apprehensive.

In all the time she had worked at the agency, there hadn't been a job she disliked. Oh, there had been some that were boring and others that were hectic, but this past week at the sweetie factory had been an unhappy experience, all because of Linda and her pals. Not to mention the effect Phil was having on her emotions.

When he reached her side, he asked her for a dance and soon they were sweeping across the floor in a quickstep. He was an accomplished dancer and not for the first time did she wonder if there was anything he wasn't good at. 'I didn't know you liked coming here,' she said, raising her voice against the music from the band.

'No, I usually don't but I came here to see you. I didn't see much of you yesterday and you had gone when I got back to the office. So here I am.'

Mary knew that was true. She had worked all day in the office, typing up all the quality reports from the past week, while Phil had accompanied the new arrival for the job. A young and good-looking woman called Beth. 'How did you get on with the new woman?'

Phil grinned. 'Oh, she's all right I suppose.

She talks all the time, which is a bit of a nuisance. I much prefer you.' Mary felt like turning somersaults but she didn't know how to deal with this devastating man. She had only known him for a week but he had turned her world upside down and inside out. She kept this warm feeling as the dance ended.

Phil still had his arm around her waist when, out of the fringe of onlookers, appeared Linda and two chums. They all glared at Mary while Linda went up to Phil and put her arm through his. 'I was looking for you at the Palais, Phil, but I couldn't find you.'

Phil disengaged her arm. 'That's because I wasn't there, Linda.'

By now, Norma had joined them and Mary introduced her. Phil was charming to her and Norma was almost goggle-eyed over him. 'I came here with someone and I better find him. He only came as a favour, so I don't want to abandon him,' he said, leading Mary by the hand, while Norma tagged along behind. 'Ah, here he is. This is Stan.'

Mary and Norma said hello but when he spoke his voice was very quiet and Mary thought he was shy. He was taller than Phil and although he was nice looking, he wasn't in the same league as his friend. He had a shock of blonde hair that looked a bit unruly and his eyes, which were shielded by a pair of gold-rimmed glasses, were blue. He was dressed in a grey sports coat with navy blue corduroy trousers and he looked so out of place in the hall. Mary thought he should be working in a library or studying at the university, but apparently he didn't as he said he worked in a quantity surveyor's office.

The four of them went to sit down. 'Stan has just finished his National Service and I'm waiting for my call-up papers.'

'Service life isn't too bad, Phil,' he laughed. 'The first six months are the worst but after that, it's all right and you get to see a bit of the world. I was in Hong Kong.'

Mary and Norma said in unison, 'Hong Kong!' But Stan just smiled shyly.

'I'll probably get sent to Germany if I have to go into the army,' said Phil, but he didn't seem concerned about it. 'Let's have another dance, Mary.'

After they were on the floor, Stan turned to Norma. 'I'm sorry but I can't dance so please go and join your usual crowd.' Norma was hesitant. Good manners said she shouldn't leave him sitting all alone but the decision was taken out of her hands when a young man asked her to dance and she leapt up.

Mary had kept a beady eye out for Linda but they were nowhere to be seen, so she began to relax. Then it was the last dance and Phil said, 'Can I see you home?'

Mary said no. 'I've promised Norma's mum that we'll stay together and come home on the same bus. She's a bit younger than me.' But she made it sound like a regret and not a relief.

'Well, can Stan and I walk you both to your bus?' That was fine by Mary. After all, the Shore Terrace bus stance would be crowded with people and she could say goodnight surrounded by the crowds.

A short while later, she was standing outside with Norma, waiting for Phil and Stan to emerge when, suddenly, Linda and her two pals appeared. 'Just you keep away from Phil,' said one of the girls. 'He's been going steady with Linda and he just wants to make her jealous.'

'And another thing,' said one of the other girls, 'if you think you're something special, think again. You better watch out for Beth. We've seen how he looked at her yesterday.'

'That's right,' Linda said, finally breaking her silence. 'His tongue was nearly hanging out of his mouth.'

Norma had moved slightly behind Mary while this was going on, but Mary was annoyed by all this drama. Fortunately, the two men appeared on the pavement and the girls disappeared into the darkness like surly ghosts. At the bus stance, Norma and Stan tactfully stood a few feet away from Mary and Phil.

'Next week will be your last week with us. What about coming with me to the pictures next Friday night?' Phil asked.

'I can't. I've to go with my parents to my Gran's house as it's her birthday. We always go at this time of year.' Once again Mary felt relief and disappointment and wondered what was wrong with her.

'You haven't been coming in to the canteen. Is something wrong?'

Mary was going to tell a lie but then decided the truth was better. 'I can't take all the glares and comments from Linda and her gang.' She turned and looked him straight in the eyes. 'Tonight one of her pals said you were going steady with her. Is that true? Because if it is, I don't want to stand in the way if you've both just had an argument and you're trying to make her jealous.'

Phil gave a huge sigh. 'Yes, we did go out for about three months in the summer, but I found her too bossy and possessive. I mean, she was looking at engagement rings after a few weeks of just going out to the pictures or the dancing. Then there were those pals of hers. No matter where we went, they would be there, sitting at the back of us in the cinema or mooching around the Palais. And she told them everything we talked about. It was like I was dating a mass band.'

Mary gave him a sympathetic look. 'Oh, I see.'

Thankfully the bus appeared. 'Well, I'll see you on Monday, Phil. I've enjoyed tonight and I'm sorry about next Friday.'

'I can't make it next Saturday or else we could have gone out then,' he said sadly.

The two men stood at the stance until the bus moved away, then made their way to catch their own bus for Barnhill. 'Two nice girls,' said Stan.

'Yes they are.'

All the way home, Norma had gone on and on about Phil and how good looking he was but Mary had just nodded. When she was in bed, she mentally kicked herself for acting like a wee naïve girl. She was a bit frightened of getting too close to him but also a bit exhilarated as well. She had stopped using the canteen on the Wednesday because of Linda and her chums. Instead, she had taken sandwiches and a flask of tea with her to work and had sat on the cold bench in the museum gardens. The week had been cloudy and grey with cold winds and she missed the warmth of the bright canteen. Before she fell asleep she thought, just one more week, then she would be on a new assignment and everything would be back to normal. After all, he was going away for two years with his National Service training, so that would be the end of all these stomach churning feelings. Wouldn't it?

17

Molly was waiting outside the SCWS shop, hoping to catch Vina when she finished work. She didn't want to bother the woman again especially as she would have to get the evening meal ready for her family. Molly looked at her watch. Just five minutes to go, thank goodness. It was a cold day as the wind whipped around the corner of North George Street and whistled into all the open shop doors on the Hilltown. The shop was busy with last-minute shoppers buying their groceries for the weekend and a stream of people, mostly women dressed in thick coats and wearing headscarves, hurried into the wind with their message bags.

A few minutes later, Vina appeared. She looked surprised when she saw Molly standing there. 'Hullo, are you waiting for me?'

Although she smiled, her voice sounded harassed. Molly said, 'I'll walk with you as far as your close. Here, let me carry one of those bags.'

Vina gratefully handed over a heavy bag, which seemed to be filled with tins. 'I like to stock my cupboard up every month. What a difference it makes now that we don't need our ration books. Bob and Barbara eat like horses, so you wouldn't believe the amount of food I buy every week now. Thank goodness I've got my job in the shop.'

Molly explained the reason for standing waiting on her. 'I just wanted to tell you that the farmer at Sidlaw Farm is called Eck Barr. Apparently it's short for Alexander but please thank Barbara for telling me, I was hoping it was the man I was looking for but it isn't.' She sighed. 'This case won't be solved I'm afraid. I keep coming up with dead ends.'

Vina sympathised. 'Etta, if she's still alive, could be anywhere and Vera will just have to accept that. She obviously doesn't want to contact her mother.'

They were almost at the close. 'Vina, have you thought any more about this Pedro? Any clues that will help me find him?'

Vina shook her head. 'No, I'm sorry. Etta just called him Pedro but she never mentioned a second name or anything about him. One small thing, though, that I've remembered. At the time, I got the impression that Robert and Michael McGregor had never been Etta's boyfriends, but this Pedro certainly was. The look on her face when she mentioned his name was enough to convince me she was in love with him.'

Then why had she not mentioned his full name or where he lived, Molly wondered, but she remained silent. 'Well, I'll say cheerio, Vina. Remember and thank Barbara.'

Vina laughed. 'She'll be thrilled to think she's helped a wee bit in a mystery. She used to love reading the *Famous Five* books when she was younger.' She became serious. 'You'll let me know how things go, won't you? I mean, if you do succeed in finding Etta?'

Molly promised she would but said it looked highly unlikely. She wasn't looking forward to going back to her flat. She never realised how much she missed Marigold's company ... and her parents. They would be basking in the warm sunshine in Australia with Terry, Nell and Molly. She was a year old now and Molly had only seen photographs of her. But then she realised that was her own fault. She could quite easily have gone out with her parents. Feeling a bit sorry for herself, she let herself into the flat, walking through the empty office. Jean had left all the invoices on the desk but Molly thought she would deal with them tomorrow.

Upstairs, she put on the electric fire and the table lamps and everything suddenly looked cosy. In the kitchen, she opened a tin of soup and carried it over to the armchair. She had toyed with the idea of buying fish and chips when she passed Dellanzo's chip shop on the Hilltown but hadn't felt that hungry then. Now she wished she had but thought she could always nip out later and get something. She switched the wireless on and looked at the *Radio Times.* There was a dance band playing on the Light programme or a play on the Home Service. She settled for the play but half way through, she fell asleep. Outside the wind strengthened and it started to rain heavily.

Vera stood outside her door, immediately regretting accepting the invitation. Last Monday, Mrs Jankowski had sent a letter to her via Maisie, saying two new neighbours would like an evening playing bridge and she hoped Vera could manage on Saturday night. Gina had said they couldn't manage in the afternoon because they both worked, so the regular afternoon session would still be held.

Vera had her umbrella but the wind kept turning it inside out, so she rolled it up and pulled up the collar of her coat. It was all right for Gina Jankowski, she thought bitterly, she was in the cosy house and didn't have to climb the Hill in this awful weather. Water was running down like a miniature river and her shoes were soaked long before she reached Ann Street. The Hilltown, which was normally abuzz with people, was deserted, although the low murmur of conversations was heard as she passed the brightly lit pubs.

Yet, in a way, she was looking forward to her evening. Bridge was one of the pleasures of her life and she knew she didn't have many of them in her lonely existence. Another thing she liked about playing at Gina's was the fact that it didn't cost money. Gina was most insistent that it was just a game and not a gamble. Vera hoped she had explained this to her new friends because she had heard hair-raising stories about women getting into debt with their bridge-playing friends.

Vera didn't have a lot of money and what extra she had, she was using to hire Molly, so she had to be careful. Dave had carried a life insurance policy, which at the time had taken her by surprise at the amount. She had saved most of it but after all these years, it was dwindling. It was all right when she was working and had her lodgers but after her operation, she hadn't been able to do a lot. That and the fact she had almost lost the will to live after Dave's death and Etta's vanishing act.

By now she had reached Gina's door and was surprised it was opened almost at once. A small woman in her fifties stood inside. She was pretty in a faded kind of way but Vera thought that was because she was wearing a grey dress that matched her straight grey hair. 'I said I would open the door and save Mrs Jankowski's legs. Come in – what a night. We got soaked and we only live in the next close.' She took Vera's coat and hung it on the hook in the lobby. 'I'm Una and my husband is Harry.'

Inside the living room, Harry and Gina were sitting by the fire, which cast a cosy glow over the room. 'Come in, come in, Vera, and have a glass of sherry before we start our game,' said Gina.

Vera sat down and warmed her feet at the fire. She loved this room, especially when the curtains were shut and everything was warm and homely. It put her in mind of her childhood when she would sit with her mum and dad. They would drink milky cocoa by the fire before going upstairs to the chilly bedrooms. But her bed always had a hot water bottle in it, which she hugged until she fell asleep.

Gina had set the small side table with her favourite cups and saucers and the teapot ready to be filled later. A plate of sandwiches and a plate of tiny cakes sat beside it. In spite of the rotten start to the night, Vera enjoyed herself. Gina was in sparkling form because she won the first two games, while Una and Harry were good company.

'Yes,' said Una. 'Harry works in the NCR and I work in a baker's shop at the top of the road. We just moved here recently from Strathmartine Road. Our three boys are all grown up and work away from home so we decided to sell our large house and move into a smaller flat and we love it, don't we Harry?'

'Yes, we do. I enjoy having no garden. Our last house had a huge garden and it was too much work. I'd rather play bridge than do gardening,' said Harry with a laugh. At the mention of Una's family, Vera caught Gina's eye and got a sympathetic look in return.

At ten o'clock it was time to go home. Vera had settled down in the cosy house and didn't relish the thought of the journey home. The storm was still blowing outside and Gina suggested that Vera stay the night. 'I have two beds in my room,' she said. 'Why not stay here with me?'

Vera said no, thank you, she would be fine and it wasn't very far to walk down the hill. Harry said, 'I'll walk down with you, Vera. The walk will do me good.'

By this time Vera was mortified by all this concern for her welfare. 'No, honestly, Harry. It's not late and there's always people about. I'll be fine.'

'Are you sure?' said Una, looking unconvinced.

'Yes. But thank you.'

So it was settled. Vera said goodnight and walked into the darkness and the rain. At the foot of the close, she stopped. She thought of going straight down the hill but the pubs would have discharged their customers and there might be a few drunk stragglers. She made up her mind to turn left and go down Rosebank Road, Tulloch Crescent and along McDonald Street, where she would only have to walk a few yards to her close. These were streets with houses so it wasn't as if they would be deserted at this time of night.

She put up her umbrella and marched off resolutely into the darkness. She had brought her large handbag with her, the one that was all soft and squashy like a message bag, and she held both the bag and umbrella in front of her like two shields. The street was deserted but most of the houses were lit up as she hurried past deep pools of water.

She was almost at the foot of Tulloch Crescent, just by the entrance to Rosebank School, when she thought she heard the sound of a car. The noise sounded muffled because she had wrapped her large woollen scarf around her head, so she didn't turn round. That is why she was so surprised when it hit her. She didn't actually see the vehicle or its headlights and had thought she was imagining the sound, but after the impact she went sprawling on the pavement, landing on her bag and umbrella.

She must have screamed, although she couldn't remember doing it, because the curtain moved in the window of the janitor's house in the school playground. A man hurried out and picked her up. 'Are you all right, missus?' he asked. 'Better come inside and the wife will call a doctor.'

'Oh no, please, I'm fine and just a bit shaken up by the fall. I must have tripped over the pavement.'

The man looked dubious but said, 'Well, if you're sure, but let me walk you home. Where do you live? Just let me get my jacket.'

Vera told him and they walked along McDonald Street. At her close she said, 'Thank you very much.'

'Now mind, missus. If you need medical treatment, call the doctor out.'

Vera said she would as she hurried through the close, glancing fearfully at the dark shadows and almost flying up her stairs. When she reached the door, her hands were shaking so much that she couldn't put the key in the lock but she made herself take a deep breath until, finally, she practically stumbled into the kitchen and fell into a chair.

Her stockings were ripped, the umbrella was broken, there was wet mud on her coat and gloves, but apart from that, she seemed to be all right. When she took off her gloves, her knuckles were bruised and covered in blood and also her knees. She had a dull pain in her left hip and when she looked at it, there was a large bruise. She realised how lucky she had been. Her large bag had cushioned her fall, which meant she wasn't as badly injured as she might have been.

She put the kettle on to boil some water to wash her wounds and to make a cup of tea but when she tried to spoon the tea into the pot, her hand shook so much that the tea leaves scattered all over the table. Instead, she swallowed two aspirin tablets with a large glass of water, which she gulped down like a drowning man. Later she climbed into bed with a hot water bottle but she couldn't sleep. It must have been a car, she now thought. She tried to think if she had accidentally been walking on the road instead of the pavement and maybe the driver had not noticed her. There had been no sign of lights, of that she was sure. It was just the darkness, the rain and wind she remembered. She fell asleep at two o'clock, finally convincing herself it had been an unfortunate accident.

18

On Sunday morning, after a restless night, Molly decided to go and see Vera and give her an update on the case so far. Not that there was much to report, but after a quick breakfast, she set off.

The storm had left heaps of litter blowing about in the street and deep puddles everywhere. Molly had looked out her winter boots and she was glad she had, otherwise her feet would have been soaked long before she got to Vera's house. The Hilltown was busy as people hurried out to the shops for milk and Sunday papers but they didn't linger long on the street for their usual chats as the wind had turned very cold. The sky was a dark brooding mass of clouds.

Molly had planned to go over on the Fifie this afternoon to see Marigold but she didn't relish the thought of crossing the river on such a wild and windy day. But maybe it will brighten up, she thought optimistically. When she got to Vera's house, she was dismayed to see the curtains were closed and it looked as if Vera was still asleep. She stood at the door, uncertain whether to knock or go away. However, as she was on the verge of turning away to go down the stairs, the curtains were pulled back and Vera noticed she had a visitor.

Molly was shocked when she saw the woman. Vera had pulled a dressing gown over her short nightdress, but Molly could still see the deep grazes to her hands and knees, which looked worse in the early morning light. Vera almost pulled Molly into the house. Molly noticed the muddy coat and shoes and bag, the broken umbrella and the basin in the sink with its pink stained water. The room was also icy cold.

'What's happened, Vera?' Molly said, quite alarmed by the grey pallor of Vera's face and the mess all around the usually immaculate kitchen.

Vera burst into tears and Molly made her sit down while she put the kettle on to make her some hot tea. She also went to clean out yesterday's ashes from the fire but Vera said to leave it. 'I'll get the electric fire.' She went into the lobby and brought out a small, one-bar fire from the cupboard, which she plugged in beside the chairs. It didn't give out much heat but it was better than nothing.

When Molly had made her comfortable with a cup of hot sweet tea and a rich tea biscuit, she asked again, 'What happened?'

Vera's hands were shaking as she told her story. 'I thought I heard a car but now I'm not so sure, although I felt something hit my side. I've been wondering if I maybe wandered into the road and the driver might not have seen me. It was a terrible night. Then I think I might just have tripped and the muffled sound I heard was maybe a vehicle further down the road because I didn't see any lights.'

'Did you see a car when you left Mrs Jankowski's house?'

'No. I would normally have walked down

the hill but I decided to take the quieter road because of the pubs coming out. Now, when I think about it, I should have kept to my original plan.'

Molly was worried by this turn of events. 'Who knew you were going to be out last night? Don't you normally play bridge on a Monday afternoon?'

Vera explained the reason for being out on a night when most normal people were tucked up indoors. 'Maisie knew. She brought the letter here last week. I haven't been back to the bridge afternoon since that day when Anita came. Harry and Una knew, but he had offered to see me home. I wish I had taken up his offer,' she said bitterly.

Molly put the kettle back on. 'I'll bathe those cuts for you, Vera, they look inflamed. I can go down for my car and run you to the accident and emergency at the infirmary because I think you need a doctor to check you over. You could have some broken bones.'

But Vera was insistent that she was all right. 'I'll be fine once I get dressed. Now, Molly, what news have you got for me?'

Molly wished she could bring some good news to this poor woman but she didn't have any. 'I've interviewed a few of Etta's acquaintances and workmates but I'm no further forward, Vera.' If Vera had noticed she hadn't used the word friends, she didn't say. 'I've spent the last two weeks checking out names, but there's nothing to bring me any closer to the reason behind Etta's disappearance.' She leaned closer to her. 'I don't want to spend any more of your money because I think there won't be any more news.'

Vera fished a handkerchief out of her pocket and blew her nose. She looked worse than ever. Her face was pinched and it was obvious she was in pain with her hip. 'I'd like you to do the next two weeks, Molly, and if nothing new turns up, then I'll just have to forget it.'

Molly nodded. 'At least let me call the doctor for you.'

Vera said no, promising she would go to her doctor tomorrow morning.

'Well, can I ask you some questions?'

'All right. Go ahead.'

'When you identified your husband, the paper said he had been in the water for some weeks. I'm sorry to be so blunt, but was he recognisable?'

Vera shivered and sat closer to the meagre heat from the little fire. 'I didn't really look at him. Just a quick glance but I recognised his watch. It was strange but it was still strapped to his wrist.' She got up and hobbled over to the sideboard drawer, coming back with a grimy looking wristwatch. The leather strap was hard and brittle and it had long since given up ticking but it was a watch like Molly had never seen before. 'Dave loved that watch. He said he got it from a German soldier in the Great War but I suspect he took it from a dead body. It was made in Germany and it has these little dials inside the face. As I said, Dave never took it off, except when he went to bed, but it was one of the first things he put on in the morning. So that's how I recognised him. By a dead soldier's watch – how ironic is that? Almost like it was cursed.'

Molly handed it back and Vera placed it in the drawer. 'Did Etta ever have any boyfriends? Like the Robert or Michael McGregor who lodged with you, or someone called Pedro?'

Vera looked shocked. 'I don't think my lodgers would have had any romantic feelings for Etta. She was just fifteen or sixteen when they lived here. Michael was Robert's brother and he came after Robert left. I don't know anyone called Pedro. Do you think Pedro is Spanish? I never had any Spanish lodgers.'

Another brick wall, thought Molly. There were just a couple more queries. 'When I looked at your address book, I saw a name that had been scored out. It looked like Ruby or something similar.'

Vera went very pale and her ravaged hand flew to her mouth. 'She won't be able to help you.'

'Vera, I have to try and speak to anyone who knew Etta. Maybe she can help.'

Vera was clearly very agitated now and Molly wondered why. 'No, she won't be able to help and I don't know where she lives now.'

'Alright then. When Dave died, you were in hospital. So did the police come and tell you? And did you not wonder why Etta didn't come to visit after the tragic news came to light?' Molly hated having to question her, especially when she was clearly ill and upset.

'Well, the police told the doctor and he was so kind when he told me. I was put in a small side room until I got home the following week. I never saw Etta again. The last time she came to the hospital was with her dad on the previous Wednesday night visiting hours. Dave came by himself on the Saturday afternoon but I knew Etta would be at work. Then, after the accident, I just assumed Etta was too upset to visit, until others confirmed she was missing as well.'

'Did Dave mention he was going to Arbroath the next day?'

'No, he didn't and that was a strange thing because he always mentioned what he would be doing while I was in the ward. He would tell me what he cooked for their meals and what film they'd seen when they went to the pictures together. Etta never said much, but that was just Etta. She would sit and gaze all around the ward or read one of my magazines.'

It was time to go but Molly hated leaving Vera alone. 'I can easily stay here with you and take you to the doctor tomorrow,' she said.

Vera said she would be fine. 'I'm feeling a bit better now. I'll get dressed and just lounge around.'

Molly was worried about her but there was nothing she could do. She had offered her help and it had been gently rejected. As she walked towards the agency, her mind was going around in circles. Who was the woman in the address book, the one that Vera so clearly didn't want to be found and questioned? Also, what had made Dave Barton suddenly go off to Arbroath on the Sunday when he was obviously going to visit his wife on Sunday afternoon? Molly looked at the ever-darkening sky and decided to forego her trip to see Marigold. Like Vera, she would just work from home today and try and make sense of everything.

After Molly left, Vera sat for a long time. There was so much she could be doing, like lighting the fire and tidying up from last night, but she felt unable to move. She was regretting starting this quest for Etta – too many old memories were being reopened and once they were out in the open, it would be impossible to thrust them back into that part of her life labelled 'forgotten'. Yet Molly had offered her the chance to stop now, she had said there seemed no point in going on, so why had she not grabbed the chance to push everything back into the past where it would remain hidden forever? She had no answer to that thorny question except to wonder if she was on a self-destruction mission.

She rose stiffly to her feet and began clearing out last night's ashes and putting a fire on. Perhaps, she thought, she would feel better with some warmth and a good programme on the wireless. Then she would lie down on the settee and have a nap.

19

Peter Walsh was a worried man as he set off on his bike on the Sunday morning. He'd had a row with his wife at breakfast time and he could still hear her sharp words as he made his way through the deserted early morning streets. The bike wheels swished through the deep puddles but he barely noticed them because his mind was on more serious matters.

He knew he should never have taken the works van yesterday and now there was a huge dent in one of the wings. He was on his way to see Jimmy Flynn, his colleague at Milton's joinery firm. Jimmy was the registered driver of the van and he would be in deep trouble as well. His only hope was Jimmy's mate, Alex, who had a small garage in the back courtyard of his house. Peter was hoping and praying that Alex would be able to repair the dent.

Jimmy was waiting for him and he wasn't pleased. 'I told you to be careful with the van, didn't I?'

Peter was ready with his story. 'It was the heavy rain that caused it. The windscreen misted up and I went off the road and hit a fence.' He made it sound as if the fence was the culprit. Almost as if it had jumped out and hit him.

Examining the damage, Jimmy said, 'Well, we better get it over to Alex's workshop and see what he can do.' He turned to Peter. 'And you're going to foot the bill.'

Peter became more depressed. The argument this morning had been about money, or the lack of it. His wife had shouted at him, 'I've not got enough to pay the electric bill and I'm two weeks in arrears with the rent.' His two teenage daughters had sat silent at the table with their bowls of sugar puffs topped up with almost a pint of milk.

No wonder money was tight in this house, he thought.

'Well, I can't help it if there's been no overtime for weeks and that I had to stay off work for two weeks after I cut my hand,' he shouted back in his defence. However, his wife was not listening to his side of the story. She had started her ranting and she intended to continue until she spelled out the entire financial pressure they were under.

Jimmy drove carefully from Kirkton to Muirhead. Alex lived in a lovely detached house on the outskirts of the village and he was already in his workshop. 'Hullo guys,' he said cheerily. 'What brings you two out here so early on a Sunday morning?'

Jimmy showed him the dent. 'Can you fix this right away, Alex? We'd be very grateful.'

Alex squatted down beside the damaged wing. 'I think so. Luckily the paintwork's not damaged so I'll try and knock it back into shape. I'll be about an hour, so just go in and Jackie will make you both a cup of coffee.'

Jackie was Alex's wife and the fantasy of both Jimmy and Peter. She was beautiful with long black curly hair and she always had a golden tan. She also had some fabulous clothes. The two men sat in the kitchen while she moved around like a golden goddess, stretching up to reach the cups from a row of hooks under the wall cupboard. Peter couldn't help but compare her to his own wife, Donna, with her white, pinched looking face and sharp tongue.

Within the hour, Alex appeared and went to wash his hands. 'That's the job done. Hopefully nobody will notice it's been damaged. Who do I give the bill to?'

Jimmy pointed to Peter, who felt like giving up on everything. He worked like a navvy all week and what had he to show for it? Sweet nothing, that's what.

When they were leaving, he said to Alex, 'Do you think I can pay this bill a bit at a time, Alex? We're short of money just now.'

Alex agreed but he said, 'Now I want something every week without fail. Give it to Jimmy and he'll pay me.'

As they drove away, Peter said, 'What does Alex do apart from that garage?'

Jimmy tapped the side of his nose. 'He's an entrepreneur. He does a bit of this and that.'

'Well, he must be making a fortune with his bit of this and that. I mean, look at his house and that gorgeous wife. Her clothes weren't bought with the Co-op dividend.' But he felt better now that the damage to the van had been repaired. If he cut down on his cigarettes for a few weeks, he could pay the bill off without Donna finding out.

As he hadn't slept last night, he almost nodded off in the van until Jimmy nudged him. 'On your bike, Peter,' he said with a laugh.

'Look, Jimmy, I'm really sorry about all this.'

'Get away home. That's what colleagues are for. I don't want to know what you were doing last night, as that's your business.'

Peter pedalled away back home, back through the deep puddles, but he noticed them this time and it brought back the memory of the storm last night.

20

Edna was pleased that the fortnight's absence from her job with John was over. It was still dull and overcast but the rain had stopped as she hurried up the road and arrived just before nine. She had taken more care than usual with how she looked and had even gone to the hairdresser on Saturday to get a new style. Irene, her mum, had said it suited her and she hoped John would like it as well. She had been pleased when her mum said that and she knew she was acting like some young girl on a first date, instead of a widow with a young son.

As she approached the house, her stomach did a somersault. The house looked to be in darkness but she was relieved when she saw the faint fanlight above the door. She knocked and waited. Something wasn't right. She knocked again, a bit louder this time, and she also pressed the bell. Suddenly, the door was yanked open and a sleepy-eyed Sonia gazed at her with annoyance. On seeing Edna, she pulled her dressing gown around her. 'What do you want?' she said.

By this time, Edna was also annoyed that she was still standing on the doorstep. 'I've come to work for Mr Knox. He knows I'm starting today.'

'Didn't my fiancé tell your agency that you were no longer needed?'

Edna was confused. What did Sonia's fiancé have to do with her employment with John? 'Your fiancé, I don't think I know him?'

Sonia took two steps towards her. 'John is my fiancé. Oh, don't tell me he didn't let you know. What a forgetful man he is.' She had her left hand on the door and the light from the hall caught the sparkle of a beautiful engagement ring. 'Never mind,' said Sonia. 'I'll phone your agency this morning to cancel your contract so just you run off home again.'

Edna was furious at her condescending tone but she tried hard not to show it. 'I'm afraid you can't do that. It has to be the person who hired me and that person is Mr Knox, so if you let me see him I think we can get this problem sorted out.' Edna wasn't sure if this was true or not but she wasn't going to let Sonia tell her what to do.

'He's not here. He said to tell you and I doubt if it matters who hires or fires. Your agency will be paid for all the work you've done.'

So she wasn't an empty-headed woman, thought Edna. She knows I've been bluffing. 'Well, I have some of my things still in the house. They will be in the lounge where we did all the work.'

Sonia stood for a few minutes, undecided. 'Oh, I suppose you better come in, then. Mind you, I've tidied everything away. I'll be doing John's shorthand and typing from now on and I can't work in that dreadful untidy mess.'

Edna walked through the quiet house. Was John still asleep upstairs? Then why didn't he come down and face her himself? The lounge was like an advert from a glossy *House & Garden* magazine. All the wonderful clutter and homeliness of the original room was gone. She looked around but her small bag with her new notepads and pencils was nowhere to be seen.

Sonia sighed. 'I put everything in a cupboard. Wait till I have a look. What is it you've left?'

Edna told her and she listened as the woman trotted off to the lobby. A minute later she came back, empty-handed. 'I'm sorry but I can't find it. I think it must have been thrown out along with my fiancé's rubbish.'

Edna was speechless. John's rubbish, as she called it, was years of work he had done in preparation for writing his books. Edna stood for a few moments glancing around the room. She had loved this job and this room, and she now realised she loved John but it was too late. Perhaps if she had let him know, it would have turned out better but she still couldn't understand where he was. As if reading her mind, Sonia said. 'He's gone to see his publisher and he won't be back for another week or so. Then we'll set the date for the wedding. At our age, we don't want to hang about, do we?' She made John sound like a ninety-year-old decrepit.

Edna had to leave, she had no choice, and as she walked away down the path, she realised she hadn't given her good wishes to the bride-to-be. 'Well, I don't wish her any happiness,' she muttered to herself and then suddenly felt guilty. 'Yes, of course I wish her and John a happy life.'

When she reached Paradise Road, she felt on the verge of tears. Not wanting to face her mother and upset her, Edna retraced her steps and went to the agency. After all, she was now finished with this job and she would have to be allocated something else.

Molly was in the office and she looked up in surprise when Edna entered. She took one look at her face and ushered her upstairs to the flat. When she was sitting down, Edna burst into tears. Molly was at a loss at this sudden emotion. 'What on earth has happened, Edna?'

Edna took some time to tell the story but when she was finished, Molly said, 'That's not like Mr Knox. He wouldn't leave someone else to give you this news, Edna, especially as he told you to start in two weeks' time while he sorted this mess out.'

'That's what I thought, Molly, but she's wearing a lovely engagement ring and she's still living in the house, and running it by the look of things.'

Molly was firm. 'I still don't believe it. If she cancels your contract, I'll tell her it must be done by Mr Knox and until that time we'll still be billing him. That'll put her wind up and he'll have to appear or phone here, so maybe you can get to the bottom of this whole mystery.' This cheered Molly up slightly, especially imagining the look on Sonia's face when she realised the bills would still be coming in. Molly fully intended to refund this money if it was John Knox's decision, but not until she heard from him.

'All the jobs have been allocated for today, Edna,' she continued. 'Mary is finished with her assignment at Keiller's sweet factory and she is out on another job now. Just go home and come back in tomorrow.'

Edna didn't look too happy with this suggestion. 'I can't face my mum. At least not until this evening, so I'll just go somewhere and have a coffee and maybe have a look around the museum or something like that.'

Molly said, 'You can come with me if you like. You know the job I'm on and maybe another pair of eyes and ears will help me make some sense of this mystery.'

Edna was surprised but pleased. 'Is it not a confidential matter between you and Mrs Barton?'

'Well, I wouldn't go around mentioning it to everyone but I don't think she'll mind. Anyhow, I'm just going to see how she is today. She had an accident on Saturday night and she thinks a car hit her.'

Edna was shocked. 'Is she badly injured?'

'No, she was lucky, but now she's not even sure if there was a car or not. She's a bit confused about it but before we go to see her, I want to speak to the janitor of the school. He found her lying in front of the school gate.'

The two women made their way to the Rosebank School and Edna said, 'This is the school Billy goes to.'

'It looks like a good school,' said Molly. 'I expect the janitor will be working this morning but maybe he can give us a few minutes of his time.'

When they arrived at the school, they were lucky. The janitor was in the playground. He came over when Molly called and he took them into the house. His wife looked surprised when the trio entered but he told her, 'It's about that poor woman who had the accident on Saturday night, Morag.'

'Oh, I hope she's all right,' the woman said. 'She looked terrible when we found her and Norman was going to call an ambulance but she wouldn't hear of it. But he walked her to her close and saw she got home safely, didn't you, Norman?'

He nodded. 'I wasn't happy leaving her. Is she all right?'

Molly said she was still a bit battered and bruised but otherwise she had been lucky. 'Did you hear a car going past at the time of the accident?'

Norman put his hand over his mouth and gave this a bit of thought. 'We had the wireless on and I can't say I heard anything until the scream. I went outside and she was lying there. Quite honestly, I thought she was dead because she didn't answer me right away. If there was a car, I didn't see any lights. Mind you the rain was pouring down and the wind was strong. I doubt if anyone would have heard anything with the sound of the storm. What on earth was she doing out on a night like that?'

Molly said, 'She was playing bridge with her friends.'

Morag looked at her husband and mouthed silently, 'Bridge?'

Molly knew she wouldn't get anything else from the couple but as she was going out, she had a sudden thought. 'I'm looking for a girl called Etta Barton – the woman you picked up on Saturday is her mother – I think she would have been a pupil here in the late 1920s. I don't suppose you have any knowledge of her?'

'No,' said Norman. 'We came here to work after the war. I got the job after coming home from the army in 1946, but maybe the school register will have her name on the list.'

Molly hadn't thought of that but decided to go and talk to the headmaster. The school was quiet, as all the children were in their classes. The milkman was delivering crates of milk in small-sized bottles for the pupils to drink at the mid-morning break.

The headmaster was busy but a very charming woman called Mrs Chambers helped them with their enquiries. 'Yes, Etta Barton was a pupil here from 1919 to 1926 when she left to go to the Morgan Academy. She won a bursary which allowed her to attend that school and I believe she did very well in her exams there, as she did here.'

'What was she like as a pupil, do you

know?' asked Molly. The woman said, 'I don't have that information here, just her school and exam marks and where she went after leaving here.'

'Would there be any teachers left here that maybe taught her?'

'Well, Miss Kidd came here in 1925, so she maybe remembers her but she's teaching at the moment and you won't be able to speak to her until dinner time, or after school.'

Molly said, 'I would be grateful if you could speak to her and tell her I'd like a word at dinner time if that's convenient for her. We'll come back then.' She turned to Edna and said, 'I'd like to go see Vera now. She looked terrible yesterday and I just want to check she's all right.'

As they walked away, Edna said, 'Would the police be able to give you some idea about this case?'

Molly looked doubtful. 'I'm not sure if they are allowed to discuss a police matter with a member of the public.'

'What about the newspaper office? Surely they would have reported on the story of the accident and the disappearance.'

'Vera showed me three cuttings from that time. Do you think there might have been more newspaper coverage other than the ones I saw?' Edna said it was worth a try. 'Right then, we'll go and see Vera and Miss Kidd, then in the afternoon we'll go to the

Courier office.

When they reached Vera's door, Molly was pleasantly surprised when Vera opened it. She was dressed in her coat and furry hat. 'Come in,' she said. 'I've just got back from the doctor's surgery.'

The kitchen was clean and tidy and a bright fire was burning. Thankfully, there was no sign of the broken umbrella, muddy coat and shredded stockings. Molly introduced Edna and asked Vera how she was feeling. 'The doctor examined me and I've got a bruise on my hip, but thankfully no broken bones and my cuts and grazes will clear up in time. He's given me some pills to take away the pain, plus some sleeping pills to let me get a good night's rest. I haven't slept since Saturday. I keep remembering the accident and how I could have been killed.'

'At least you've seen a doctor and there's nothing seriously wrong, which is a blessing,' said Molly. 'Vera, we've been to Rosebank School to speak to the janitor and he didn't hear the sound of a car, but he did have the wireless on so that doesn't mean there wasn't one.'

Vera suddenly looked tired. 'The more I think about it, the less I remember. Maybe I imagined a car, I just don't know. The doctor said the bruise was caused by something hitting me but he said it could have been the way I fell. Maybe I hit my side on the pavement.'

'There's just one thing, Vera. The school secretary said Etta was a very clever girl and that she won a bursary to go to the Morgan Academy. You and your husband must have been very proud of her.'

Vera seemed a bit agitated. 'Yes, we were in the beginning, but she didn't like the secondary school, so she left when she was fifteen. We had high hopes that she would stay on until her sixth year and maybe go to the university, but she didn't want to do that,' Vera said. 'I'm going to fill a hot water bottle and lie down for a wee while.'

It was time to go.

When they were outside, Molly asked Edna if she had any thoughts on Vera.

'I feel very sorry for her,' said Edna. 'Just one thing – why did she become edgy when you asked her about the school?'

Molly said she had noticed that as well. 'She also became agitated when I asked her about a name and address in her book that had been totally scored out. I could only make out the name Ruby. I thought she looked scared when I mentioned it.' Molly sighed – she seemed to be uncovering more questions than answers.

21

Back at the school, Miss Kidd was waiting for them. She was a very tall woman in her fifties with a gaunt looking face, limp brown hair and clothes that were entirely brown. She knew why they were here and she held a large ledger in her hands. 'I taught Etta Barton when she was in primary six, right through to primary seven. A clever girl who, as you know, won a bursary to the Morgan.'

Molly repeated her statement about how pleased her parents must have been.

Miss Kidd looked thoughtful, as if trying to recall those far off days when she was a young teacher. 'Yes, they were, but the strange thing is that Etta totally ignored her mother's praise. I remember how happy her parents were when we told them of the award, but when Mrs Barton went to give her a hug, Etta kept her arms at her side and went rigid, yet when her father did the same, she went wild and threw her arms around him. I remember the hurt look on her mother's face. I've never forgotten it and, of course, when she disappeared after her father's tragic death, I can't say I was surprised. I thought then that she had also died, and I still think that.'

'What about friends in the school? Did she have anyone special she played with or hung around with?'

Miss Kidd suddenly looked stern and unhappy. 'I shouldn't mention this but it is all so long ago. She didn't seem to have any friends but there was a girl in the class she particularly didn't like and one day she hit her with a wooden club that was used for PE classes. The girl wasn't badly injured and thankfully she recovered. There was a bit of a hoo-ha over it but Etta was almost on her last few days here, so it was dropped. Then, when she was fifteen, she did a similar thing to a girl at the Morgan Academy and her parents took her away from school. I believe she started work that year in Marks and Spencer and I often saw her when I went in there.' Molly and Edna were speechless at this revelation. 'I'll tell you this, Miss McQueen, Etta may have had a clever brain but she wasn't a nice girl. Oh no, not at all.'

As they walked down Dallfield Walk, Edna said, 'What a terrible girl. If she was my daughter, I'd be grateful that she'd disappeared and left me in peace.' Then she thought of Billy and knew that no matter what he did with his life, she would always be there for him. Just like Vera. He had been in the dining hall when she was in the classroom with Miss Kidd. He used to come home for his dinner but now all of his pals went for school meals so he wanted to join them. It was a blessing for her mum, who now only had to take him to school and pick him up.

'I think we'll have something to eat before we go to look at the old newspapers,' said Molly. 'Do you fancy going to Wallace's restaurant, Edna?'

Edna, who hadn't eaten much breakfast and was now feeling very hungry, said that would be fine. The restaurant was busy when they arrived but they were soon seated at a small table up beside the kitchen door. 'I'll have some potato and leek soup,' said Molly and Edna said she would have the same.

When they were eating the soup, Molly said, 'What do you make of this case, Edna?'

'Well, it's such a long time since the girl went missing and she could be anywhere. She might even be living in Dundee, a happily married woman with a family. Or she could be dead. I just don't know, Molly.'

Molly sighed loudly, 'Neither do I.'

The two women then settled for fish and chips and two cups of tea. 'I didn't feel hungry until I passed the dining hall at the school,' said Molly.

Edna laughed. 'No, neither did I. To change the subject, Molly, what did the newspaper cuttings say? The ones that Vera showed you.'

'She just had three: one about the accident; another about Etta going missing; and the third one about Dave Barton's body being found.'

Edna looked thoughtful. 'You would think that the papers would have reported these twin incidents more thoroughly wouldn't you?'

'Maybe they did, but Vera just kept the three cuttings.' By now they had finished their meal and Molly insisted on paying for it. 'You've been a great help coming along today, Edna.'

Although Edna didn't say anything, she was pleased with this praise. They made their way to the *Courier* office and asked if they could see some back issues. The girl smiled when they came in but seemed taken aback when Molly mentioned 1930. They were soon seated in a small room with a few copies of the *Courier* and the *Evening Telegraph*. Molly soon found the relevant dates and was disappointed to see the same cuttings that Vera had shown her.

Edna pointed out, 'There must be some others that explain who found his jacket and why the police assumed he had fallen into the sea?'

Then, tucked away on page four of the *Courier* dated 8 October 1930, was another bit of news.

MAN'S DEATH

The body of Mr David Barton, who was the victim of a tragic accident on Sunday, 6 October, still hasn't been found. Two women who were out walking on the cliff path on Sunday afternoon found a jacket and wallet belonging to Mr Barton. They handed these items into the police station and they were put into the lost property.

Then a report also came on Sunday afternoon that a young couple who were sitting on the clifftop on Sunday morning at about eleven o'clock said they heard a scream but because they couldn't see the path from where they were sitting, didn't know what had happened. They also thought the scream came from further along the path. After discussing it with their parents, the pair contacted the police and a thorough search was instigated.

At the spot where the jacket was found, the police noticed the path was broken at the edge and it seems likely that the unfortunate man lost his footing and fell over. The police also discovered a fragment of blue fabric, which was found a few feet down from the path. Mrs Barton identified this fabric scrap as belonging to a shirt owned by her husband.

Molly and Edna scrutinised the rest of the

papers and it wasn't until 12 October that the *Evening Telegraph* had an article about the missing girl.

GIRL STILL MISSING

The police are becoming increasingly worried about a missing girl. Miss Etta Barton hasn't been seen since Saturday, 5 October. Miss Barton is the daughter of Mr Barton who was tragically killed in a fall from the cliff path at Arbroath on Sunday, 6 October. Miss Barton's mother is beside herself with worry and she appeals to her daughter to get in touch, as she's worried her daughter doesn't know about her father's death.

There was no more about either case. 'Well, that seems to be all the papers said about the events,' said Molly. 'I wonder why Vera didn't cut these out and keep them?'

'Maybe she didn't see them. You did say she was in hospital and when she came home perhaps the doctor gave her some sedatives and she never saw these two editions.'

'Yes, that's probably the reason. I'll ask her the next time I see her.'

As they walked towards the agency, Edna said, 'Will I come in tomorrow, Molly?'

'Yes, of course. I'll speak to Jean now and any job she was thinking of giving to the temporary staff, I'll give to you.'

Edna was amused. Molly's temporary staff was a group of her friends who liked the odd few days of work but didn't want to be employed full-time because they were married and had husbands and homes to look after.

At the agency, Jean was taking down the details of a fortnight's work and Molly handed over the job sheet, saying, 'There you go, Edna, and don't worry about John Knox. It'll all work out, you'll see.'

As Edna walked home, she wished she had Molly's confidence but there was nothing she could do. If John had become engaged to his sister-in-law then that was that. She walked along the road with her head held high, silently rehearsing what she would say to her mother.

22

Sonia arrived at the agency before it opened on Tuesday. She hung around outside in the cold for twenty minutes until Molly came downstairs and opened up. Sonia was furious as she glanced at her watch but sensibly remained quiet, at least until she was in the office. 'I want to make a complaint about Mrs McGill. She came to the house yesterday and demanded to be let in. I told her that John no longer wanted her to work for him but she didn't believe me.'

Molly knew who she was but still asked her, 'Excuse me, but can you give me your name?'

Sonia glared at Molly. 'My name is Sonia Simpson and I am the sister-in-law and fiancé of Mr Knox who, until lately, employed one of your girls to do his secretarial work for him. I happen to be a trained secretary and I will be doing this work for him and, I may add, at no extra cost to him. Not like your outrageous charges.'

By now, Molly was angry with this woman who had stormed in and tried to slander one of her staff. 'Let me put the record straight, Miss Simpson. Mr Knox entered into a contract with Mrs McGill to come and work for him on three days a week. The agreement stated that should he wish to terminate his contract, he could do so at any time by coming here or writing a letter signed by him. He can't send you. He must come personally or, as I said, write a letter confirming the termination.'

Sonia was outraged. 'I've never heard such nonsense in my life and John won't be sending another penny here to keep that upstart of a secretary in a job.'

'That is where you are wrong. Until we hear personally from Mr Knox, we will continue to expect payment as agreed in the contract.' By now, Jean had arrived and she stood inside the door in silence.

Sonia glared at them both and pushed Jean out of the way as she made for the door. 'John is out of town just now but I assure you, he will be in touch after I tell him about this ridiculous, so-called contract.'

After she was gone, Molly let out a deep breath. 'Well, she's got the message I hope.'

'I wonder what Edna has let herself in for this time. She always seems to have man trouble.'

Molly sighed again. 'I really don't know what's behind all this drama, Jean, but it's not Edna's fault. John Knox wouldn't behave like this even if he has fallen madly in love with the obnoxious Miss Simpson. No, he would tell Edna face to face and not do this disappearing act.'

She stopped and suddenly saw the irony of this. Surely one disappearance was enough. Life was hard enough trying to find the obnoxious Etta without a client doing a vanishing act. It was only 9:30 a.m. and already Molly felt drained. She had sat up till one o'clock that morning, going through her notes, trying to find hidden meanings behind the answers she had been given, but there was nothing. Edna had said that Etta could be living anywhere, maybe as a happily married woman with a family, and if she had wanted to contact her mother, to give her the good news about her happiness and let the woman know she was a grandmother, then she had had ample time over the past twenty-four years.

Molly decided to go and see Mrs Pert again, even if it did mean running the gauntlet past Moira's blockade. To her surprise, when she got there, the door was answered by Mrs Pert. 'Are you not worried I was the bogus antique dealer?' said Molly with a smile.

'No, I was at the window and I saw you coming into the close. Moira and Isa have gone to the shops and I promised them I wouldn't answer the door, but I like living dangerously,' she said with a twinkle in her eye. 'Now, what can I do for you this time?'

Molly didn't know where to start. 'On the Sunday Mr Barton disappeared, he went to Arbroath. Do you think he took Etta with him?'

'That I don't know,' she replied truthfully. 'I'm normally up early every morning but on that particular weekend I had a bad cold, so I stayed in bed until the middle of the morning and didn't see either of them. I did see Etta in the early evening, but she was on her own and going towards the house.'

'Do you think she went out again?'

'Well, unless I was out with the ash bucket, I wouldn't know. The curtains were drawn because it was dark and I would probably have settled down to listen to the wireless.'

'And you didn't see Mr Barton at all that day?'

Mrs Pert shook her head. 'No, sorry, I didn't. I wish now I had gone outside, but I knew Mrs Barton was in hospital and I just assumed they were visiting her.'

'What about the police, did you see them?'

'Yes, they came to see me the next day. It was in the morning and they were questioning all the neighbours but, like me, they hadn't seen anything. The policeman told me that they had arrived at the house late on the Sunday night but there was no sign of the daughter and they were anxious to see her. Then, of course, they had to go to the infirmary and give Mrs Barton the bad news. It must have been a terrible shock.

'I mentioned that I had seen Etta on the Sunday evening. About six o'clock it was, but the police told me the house was locked up. Mrs Barton had to stay in the hospital until she recovered but when she got back there, the house was just as she'd left it. Then she noticed some of Etta's clothes had gone, along with her post office savings book. Well, I don't need to tell you what a state the woman was in, I offered to stay with her but her young neighbour from next door went in and helped.'

Molly said, 'It must have been a great

talking point in the close. Did anyone have their own ideas about what had happened?'

'It was just the usual gossip, that she had ran off with a boyfriend or else she had been kidnapped by some unknown gang. Most of us knew about Mr Barton's moodiness and how he often went on long walks, not only at the weekends but often in the evenings as well. Sometimes he went with Etta, but not always.' She tapped the side of her nose. 'When he went to the pictures he often went alone.'

Molly sat silent for a moment. How could a girl of sixteen vanish off the face of the earth? Where would she go? Why would she leave her beloved father, unless she already knew he was dead? But surely if she had been with him that day she would be so overcome with grief and horror that the last thing she would want to do was disappear. Another thought – what if she didn't know? Her father often went off on his own, and she would assume he was visiting the hospital. Vera had said that Etta hadn't come to see her that day nor Dave, but Etta wouldn't know that. Had she waited in the house until early evening then gone to look for him? Had she also seen the police at her door? If so, why hadn't she answered it? Molly had the beginnings of a headache. 'Did you ever hear of someone called Ruby who was friendly with the Barton family?'

Mabel Pert looked dubious. 'No, I can't say I have. There was a Ruby who used to live in the close but she was an old woman away back then and the poor soul was a bit wandered in her mind. She used to forget where she was at times and some relative took her to stay with them and she never came back.'

Molly had no more questions. Mabel saw her to the door. 'I won't have to tell my sister or Moira that I answered the door. It'll save me getting a telling off from my niece, as she's so protective of us.'

Molly walked briskly back to the Wellgate, hoping the fresh air would get rid of the headache. There was one small niggling worry that wouldn't go away. Who was the woman with Frances Flynn? The one who hadn't been introduced except as an ex-neighbour. Frances had said she had lived in Carnegie Street before moving to Kirkton and Carnegie Street was not far from 96 Hilltown. Perhaps this unnamed woman with the surly, unsmiling face would be able to help in her enquiries. Molly would have to go back and ask Frances for her name, but not today. Her plan was to go back to the agency and get Jean to make out an invoice for Edna's wasted days at John Knox's house. When he got in touch and explained the situation, then Molly would cancel these charges, but it would give her great pleasure to send this bill to Miss Sonia Simpson. She knew she was being childish but the woman had annoyed not only Edna, who had simply turned up for work as arranged, but also herself.

23

Alice was running late. Her last job in the afternoon should have finished at 4:30 p.m. but the client, who had three small children, had asked Alice to stay on for another thirty minutes because one of the children had spilled a bowl of rusks and warm milk all over the floor and had then promptly run through the mess, taking all the debris into the living room carpet. It had taken Alice some time to clean it up.

She was still desperate not to let Victor know that she was working full-time because she knew he would dock even more house-keeping money from her. Maisie was still looking after her small nest egg and Alice had bought new stockings and also a new skirt and jumper. She was careful not to splash the money about in case he sussed it out, but she got a great deal of pleasure from knowing she had some extra money at her fingertips. Maisie had also advised her to have her tea before he came home and that way she would get her fair share of the evening meal. She had been doing this for a while now but it looked as if it wasn't going to happen today.

As luck would have it, the butcher's shop was busy and one customer was dithering about buying a lamb chop or a half-pound of mince and taking an age to make up her mind. Then she had to go to the baker for bread and the grocer for butter, cheese and milk. She was on the verge of leaving the butcher's shop when the woman made up her mind and bought half a pound of corned beef. Alice quickly asked for two pork chops and hurried out into the street.

The tramcar seemed to take ages to arrive, then it trundled up Princes Street and up past Arthurstone Terrace where she got off. By the time she reached her house, she was panting so hard she wondered if she was having a heart attack. Luckily, she had set the fire in the morning and it was soon alight. Shoving the chops into the frying pan, she set about cutting potatoes for chips. Suddenly, the frying pan caught fire and she realised she hadn't turned the gas jet down. The chops looked black but she scraped away the burnt bits and decided to put an egg on the plate to disguise the charred edges.

The tea was just ready when Victor sauntered in. He sat down at the table without a word and began spreading his usual pile of bread and butter. Thankfully, he didn't notice the charred chops because he had propped the evening paper up in front of him.

Alice sat down with a cup of tea and realised she had nothing in the house for herself except the bread and cheese, but she would need these for his work pieces. She wasn't sure if he was going out tonight, as it was a Wednesday, but he began to get dressed after his meal and his three pals arrived a few minutes later. She was actually glad when he left. She had no illusions about her marriage and she longed to have a house and life of her own.

Maisie had said to save up as hard as she could and then make her escape. Maisie also said she had known Victor when he lived at home with his widowed mother. He had treated her the same way, handing over a pittance from his pay packet and expecting to eat and live like a lord, with his meals all on the table when he came in and his shirts all washed and ironed. Before he married Alice, his mother had put him out of the house and told him to get lodgings. That was when Alice had met him, when she was not long out of the orphanage where she had been brought up. Victor had seen in her someone who would be grateful for the small scraps of affection and money he doled out and they had married quietly in the Registry Office with just two of his workmates, a married couple who witnessed what she had then thought was a happy occasion.

After the men were gone, Alice went next door to see Maisie and told her the whole unhappy episode of her job. 'That family are terrible for letting their children run riot. The mother shouldn't leave a bairn with a bowl of rusks and hot milk. It's just asking for an accident,' said Maisie, who had worked a couple of shifts with the family.

Maisie was concerned about her neighbour. She was thin and gaunt looking and her face looked grey with worry and tiredness. 'I'm just about to have my tea. Why don't you join me? It's soup and stovies, but it'll be filling and tasty.' Alice was about to say no when Maisie insisted. 'As usual, I've made loads and there's plenty for the two of us.'

While the two women were eating and having a great blether about the joys and tribulations of cleaning other people's houses, Victor and his pals were making their way to the carnival. This was the last week and Victor was ready to face the opposition in the boxing booth. 'Do you think you should take that guy on, Buffo?' said one of his mates, a thin-faced, scrawny youth who looked as though a gentle breeze would blow him over.

Victor puffed out his chest. 'Of course I'm

taking him on. He's past his best and it's about time someone showed him the ropes. Aye, after tonight, the boxing promoter will be looking for a new boxer.'

Sandy, another one of his pals, said, 'Aye, he might be getting on but he's got a great punch and he's had years of experience in the boxing ring. He hasn't always worked in the carnival booths. He was once a heavy-weight champion, I believe.'

Victor gave a humourless laugh. 'When was that? Away back in the war?'

Although it was midweek the boxing booth was full and, as the evening wore on, it became busier. The action was all in the ring in the centre and Victor watched with satisfaction as one after another, unsuccessful challengers were led out of the ring. 'When are you going to go in?' asked one of the pals.

Victor didn't answer. He was busy judging when he thought the boxer would be feeling his legs and arms tiring. Twenty minutes later, his moment of glory had arrived. With cheers from his pals and a loud round of applause from the onlookers, he stepped into the brightly lit ring and viewed the boxer with disdain. He really looked ready to be knocked out and Victor was the man to do it.

The referee shouted out the rules of the match then Victor was on his feet. He managed to put a couple of punches into the face of his opponent and he was feeling good about his chances. Suddenly and without Victor seeing it coming, the man threw a hefty punch that knocked Victor clean off his feet. He tried to get up but his legs wouldn't let him and he sank back onto the canvas as the referee counted him out. His pals tried hard not to laugh, especially when it was clear he was hurt, but he staggered away from them into the night, leaving the jangle and noise of the carnival behind.

He ended up in a pub in Victoria Street, feeling so humiliated that he sat at a table on his own, even when a few regulars spoke to him. He was in a very bad temper and an hour later, after eight pints of beer, he staggered home.

Alice was reading a book by the dying embers of the fire when he almost fell through the door. She stayed silent as he barged into the room and she could tell his mood was ugly, so she decided to get ready for bed. As she stood up, he grabbed her and gave her a punch in the face that knocked her to the floor. 'That's all you're good for, you lazy cow. Sitting burning coal that we can't afford and buying books.' He grabbed the book, tore pages out of it, then threw it in the fire.

As she tried to stand up, he hit her again and pulled her across the floor by the neck of her new jumper. 'I don't know why I ever married you, when I think of the lovely women that I could have had instead of you.'

This riled her. 'Lovely women? You? Your own mother threw you out because she couldn't stand you. You pathetic wee man.'

Anger exploded in him and he began to punch her over and over again, finally stopping when he had to rush to the sink to be sick. Alice made it out of the house and banged on Maisie's door. Maisie had been in bed but when she saw her neighbour, she rushed her inside. Alice's new jumper was streaked with blood and her face, arms and legs were covered in bruises. She also had a deep cut at the corner of her mouth, which was the cause of all the blood.

Maisie was furious. 'I'll have to phone for the doctor, Alice love.'

Alice was mortified. 'No, don't do that. What will he think?'

Maisie was adamant. 'Stay here and I'll lock the door behind me so he can't get in. I'll phone from the box at the corner of the street and I won't be long.'

Alice sat down wearily in the fireside chair and began to cry. As Maisie hurried downstairs, she heard the sound of furniture being smashed in Alice's house and shook her head in anger. As it turned out, the doctor sent an ambulance because of the injuries Maisie described on the phone and Alice was taken away to the infirmary with Maisie in tow.

It was midnight when Maisie got back home. All was quiet next door. Alice had a couple of stitches in her mouth wound but thankfully no bones were broken. The bruises looked awful but they would disappear in time. However, she was being kept overnight for observation. She had tried to tell the doctor she fell down the stairs but he knew better. Before she left, Alice had grabbed Maisie's hand and said, 'What will I do about my job tomorrow, Maisie? I really need the money and what if Molly tells me not to come back?'

'Just you get better, Alice, and don't worry about anything. I'll explain everything to Molly. Everything will turn out all right. Now I'll come to see you tomorrow and if you get home, then you're staying with me. I think you should get the police on to him.'

Alice was weary. 'The police don't do anything when it's a domestic row.'

Sadly, Maisie had to agree with her but what was her future? Living with that sadistic thug? Oh, she knew how he'd got his nickname and why he hated it. When he was at school, he had to wear a large pair of bathing trunks, as they were the only ones he owned. When he went swimming at the pool, every time he got out of the water, he always showed his backside, much to his pals' mirth and the attendant's annoyance.

After that, he started wearing a belt with the trunks, which solved the problem, but the nickname remained.

The next morning, when Maisie left for work, Alice's house was still in darkness. When she arrived at the agency, Molly and the rest of the staff were appalled at what had happened. 'Alice is scared about losing her job as she really needs her own money.'

Jean, who was normally a mild-mannered woman said, 'What a pity she didn't hit him with the frying pan.'

Molly was left with a whole day's work and no cover but she said, 'Maisie, can you and Deanna manage do some of Alice's work as well as your own?'

Maisie said yes and Deanna also agreed. 'I've no rehearsals this week so I can work really late if that's a help to you.'

Edna and Mary were out on their assignments, so Molly said she would do the first two jobs of the morning and Jean would phone around to see if some of the clients were willing to reshuffle their times. Actually, Molly was pleased to have a break from her job as private investigator, but she hoped Alice would soon get better. She knew most marriages were happy but she was also aware how much domestic abuse went on, often unnoticed by the world.

Maisie went to collect Alice after tea and when they arrived back home, the house was still in darkness. The door was unlocked but there was no sign of Victor. Alice started to cry when she saw the devastation of smashed furniture and ripped curtains. 'Nip down to the house factors tomorrow, Alice, and get the house changed to your name, and change the locks so he can't get back in. If he comes back, call the police.'

'I don't need to change the tenancy, Maisie. The house is in my name. I got it before we were married.'

Maisie was amazed. 'That wee thug has certainly been pushing his luck. You could have thrown him out at any time.'

Alice was worried. 'Do you think I brought all this on myself?'

'No, you didn't. I'm afraid Victor has always been a bully with the knack of hitting other women. But, like the bully he is, he hates it when someone gets the better of him. You mark my words, someone got the better of him last night. That's what all this is about. Now, I want you to stay with me for a few days to get everything sorted out and to deal with him when he comes back.'

But he didn't come back that night or the next. Much to Alice's relief he stayed away and she was grateful for that. At the end of the week, there was still no sign of him. Deanna came to see her with her case of cosmetics and showed Alice how to disguise her facial bruises with foundation and face powder. 'That will let you get back to work, Alice.' She added, 'With a small plaster over your stitches, you'll look fine and with your overall on and your stockings, no one will see the bruises on your arms and legs.

On the Friday night, Sandy, one of Victor's mates, came round to the house. The room was almost empty of furniture, as Maisie had taken all the broken stuff down to the bins. The bed was the only item left virtually untouched and Alice had borrowed a table and chair from neighbours. Everyone had been so kind.

'We heard what happened, Alice, and we wanted to say how sorry we are for all this.' His hand swept around the room. 'I always thought Buffo was an idiot, but to treat a good looking wife like that is terrible.' He looked quite embarrassed as he handed her an envelope. 'The rest of the lads and me had a whip round and we want you to have this, to help with whatever you need.'

Alice was so touched by this act of kindness that she had tears in her eyes. 'Oh Sandy, there's no need to do this. I've still got my job and I'll get by, but Victor better not come near me or this house or I'm going to the police.'

'Don't worry – I don't think you'll see him again. There's a rumour going around that he's joining the army and that's the best place for him. At least his enemies will give as good as they get. Now take this wee gesture from us and use it for yourself.'

'Okay, I will. Thank you.'

After he left, Alice opened the envelope and found four pound notes inside. She was so overcome that she burst into tears, then she remembered how Sandy had called her a good looking woman and she smiled.

24

Maggie Flynn was in the town to buy new shoes. She had passed the agency on her way to Birrell's shoe shop and had hesitated. She would love to work in the agency when she left school and Miss McQueen had been helpful, but she wasn't confident enough to go in.

As luck would have it, on her way back to catch the bus, she met Molly going into the office. 'Maggie, how are you?'

'Good – I'm back at school next Monday. I've been off with a bad dose of tonsillitis but I'm better now.'

Molly was pleased there was a genuine reason for her absence at school. It wasn't right for a young person to miss their education. 'Come in and have a look around.'

Maggie almost leapt through the door. 'As

I said, Miss McQueen, I would love a job here when I leave school next year.'

Molly said warily, 'I did mention it all depends on your school exam results, Maggie.'

'I've brought them with me,' she said, pulling a brown envelope from her handbag. 'These are my last three report cards.'

Molly was amused by the way she had nonchalantly produced them and guessed Maggie had been debating about coming in to see her. Taking the cards from the envelope, Molly sat down and studied them, fully expecting them to be mediocre, but she was astounded to see that Maggie's marks were very high, except in science, a subject she had barely passed in, but her attendance at school was also very good. This dose of tonsillitis was genuine.

Maggie pointed this out. 'I'm hopeless at science. I just can't get my head around all those Bunsen burners and chemical things.'

Molly laughed. 'You won't need any Bunsen burners here, Maggie. Your marks are excellent, so I'll expect to see you nearer the time when you leave school and we'll discuss a job here.' Maggie was pleased and glad she had seen Molly. 'How is your mother?'

Maggie shrugged. 'She's fine. I just wish she would give up smoking. She's always worse when that horrible Miss Price comes around. Dad calls her "Vincent", after that spooky film star in *The House of Wax.*'

'Is that your ex-neighbour?'

Maggie's lip curled in disdain. 'She's not an ex-neighbour. Mum just says that because she's scared stiff of her. She used to be mum's teacher at school and she is always spouting on about hellfire and damnation. No wonder mum smokes like a chimney when she visits, because she knows Miss Price hates it. She calls it a sin but it doesn't stop her visiting us.'

'So why does she come round so often?'

Maggie laughed with such pleasure that Molly had to join in. 'Mum say it's because she fancies my dad and always has.' Maggie could barely contain her glee. 'Imagine anybody fancying an old man like Dad.'

By Molly's reckoning, if Frances was the same age as Etta, then she would be about forty years old and her husband maybe a year or two older. He was hardly an old man and maybe not too young for Miss Price if she had been a very young teacher back in the late twenties.

Molly suddenly thought of something. 'Have you ever heard of anyone called Pedro?' Maggie frowned with concentration.

'Pedro? Now I've heard that name somewhere but I can't remember where I heard it.'

Molly said, 'Would it have been someone your mother mentioned?'

'It could have been but I can't remember. I think I only heard it the once. I'll tell you what, I'll think hard about it when I go home and can I come and see you if I remember?'

'Oh yes, please, Maggie. It's very important.'

Maggie looked pleased at maybe having some important information and she promised she would do her best to try and recall where she had heard it. Molly was glad it was Saturday. Some of the cleaning jobs had been hard, especially the one with the unruly children. One of them had thrown a plate of toast and beans at her. It had landed in an orange mess all over the floor but Molly had made the child pick it up and place the debris in the kitchen bin. Then she had a word with the mother, saying if this was a common occurrence then the cleaning rate would have to be increased. Molly wasn't going to have Alice treated like this and, if she started work on Monday, she would ask her to tell her how often this happened.

Before she climbed the stairs to the flat, she was delighted to see Marigold coming through the door, wearing her cream waterproof coat and black leather gloves. She was also carrying a basket with three jars of jam, a home-baked cake and some mail. 'I've just come for a short visit, Molly,' she said, handing over the letters and postcards. 'These are from your parents and I hope you like my homemade jam.'

'Marigold, it's great to see you.' Molly missed her neighbour but she had been so busy these last few weeks with Etta's case. Marigold cut the cake into portions while Molly put the kettle on for tea. The room felt cold because it had been empty all day but the electric fire soon warmed it up. Molly quickly read through the mail and was delighted to get three photographs of Nell, Terry and wee Molly, plus one of her parents standing in Nell's backyard with the sun beating down. Her parents were both in short-sleeved shirts and shorts. Marigold laughed at Archie's knees. 'It's a good job he's not competing in Butlin's holiday camp knobbly knees competition.'

'How is Sabby?' Molly asked, suddenly feeling a pang of longing for the cat.

'She's still the same. Thinks she's the Queen of Sheba.'

When they were sitting down with a pot of tea and a huge slice of Victoria sponge cake, Marigold asked how the case was coming along. Molly would gladly have not mentioned it as this case seemed to be taking over her life but she knew Marigold would be curious. 'It's not coming along very well. I'm stuck at the moment and can't see a way forward. Quite a few people who knew the family at the time all say the same thing:

Etta was not a nice child. But that doesn't explain her disappearance. The only conclusion I can reach is that she killed herself after hearing of her father's accident. That would make sense. Still, I have one more week to make enquiries and then I have to tell her mother I can't do anything more to help her.'

'I've been thinking about it as well, Molly, and I have to agree with you. She was a young sixteen-year-old girl with no known relatives and her mother ill in hospital. Maybe she thought her mother was going to die as well. Girls of that age can have a vivid imagination. She took her post office book with how much money?'

'She had £3-10/- but she took most of it out. All except five shillings. It would be worth a lot more back then but it wasn't a fortune. Not enough to run away with and keep yourself in food and lodgings for very long.'

'Did the police ever find out if any money was taken out of the account after she left home?'

Now there was a thing, thought Molly. 'I'm not sure. I'll ask Vera on Monday. If she did go away somewhere, then maybe she cashed the money in another town and that would prove that she had run away.'

'Well, I wish you luck with it.'

At 7:30 p.m. Marigold said she had to

leave. 'Why not stay the night here?' suggested Molly.

'I would but I've got to be at the church early tomorrow, then we have a meeting about next week's sale of work and I don't like leaving Sabby. She misses me when I'm not there.'

Molly stayed silent but thought to herself, Sabby was one clever cat that had Marigold wrapped around her striped, furry paw. 'Let me run you to the Fifie. It's dark outside and I think it's starting to rain again.'

The two women hurried out to the car, which was parked in Baltic Street. The rain was quite heavy and Marigold was grateful for the lift. The town centre was busy with people going out for the evening and the lit shop windows reflected off the wet pavements. 'I wish you didn't live on the other side of the river, Marigold,' said Molly.

'But you like living in your flat, don't you, Molly?'

Molly said she did but it was a bit lonely in the evenings. Marigold had a suggestion. 'Is there no place you can go to? Like an evening class or something like that?'

'If there was an evening class for sleuths, then I'd gladly join that,' said Molly, laughing.

Within five minutes, the car drew up at Craig Pier. The two women noticed the boat had already docked and Marigold quickly made her way down the walkway and on to the Fifie. Marigold stood on the lower deck and waved until the paddle steamer began to slip away from her moorings and headed for Newport. Molly was glad she wasn't on it as the sight of the dark water made her shiver. She stood until the ferry was almost in the middle of the river before she turned the car around and made for home. Molly felt another familiar pang of loneliness but she decided she'd spend the evening reviewing the case again.

A white envelope was lying on the mat as she opened the office door. It was addressed to Miss McQueen and had obviously been delivered after she'd left with Marigold. Wondering who could have left it, she carried it upstairs to the flat. Inside was a single piece of paper from Maggie Flynn.

Dear Miss McQueen
I hope you don't mind me delivering this letter. I thought I would leave it with you when I went to the pictures with my friend. I've been thinking all day about the name Pedro and I've remembered where I heard it. My brother Jimmy has a workmate called Peter Walsh who lives at 28 Alexander Street. A couple of years ago, I heard someone call him Pedro but he said not to call him by that name as his wife Donna didn't like it. He said it made him sound Spanish and that annoyed her. I hope this is a

help to you and thank you for being so kind to me today.
Yours sincerely,
Maggie Flynn.

Molly almost danced with joy. This could very well be Etta's one-time boyfriend. If it hadn't been so late she would have gone to see him tonight but she planned to go tomorrow. Hopefully he would be able to add some sense to this mystery. She was so glad she had made a friend of Maggie and she would tell her when she saw her next.

She wondered what this Pedro looked like. From what Vina had gathered, Etta had gone out with him for a few weeks but then the relationship, if that was what it really was, had finished. Did they have an argument? Or was it just a youthful flirtation that ended when one of them had a change of heart? Or perhaps it turned out to be more of a friendship? Hopefully all would be revealed tomorrow and this case might get solved. Maybe this Peter Walsh had kept in touch with her and knew her address. But if that was the case why hadn't he come forward when she disappeared? He must have seen the news of her father's death in the papers, followed by Etta being reported missing.

According to Vina and Frances, Etta had been a master of keeping secrets. Whether it was to protect her boyfriends from scrutiny or to keep her lies from being detected, there was so much secrecy here that Molly didn't think she would be able to get to the bottom of it. She would give it her best try though.

Marigold would be landing on the jetty by now and heading for her home. Molly was starting to wish she had gone with her.

25

Molly was unsure when she should go and see Peter Walsh. According to Maggie, he worked with her brother Jimmy, so maybe he liked to stay in bed later on a Sunday. She also didn't want to go at dinner time. After a great deal of thought, she decided to go around one o'clock in the afternoon and if that wasn't suitable, then she could always return at another time. Her desire to see this man was intense. After so many blanks in the story, she had at last found the elusive boyfriend that Mrs Pert had glimpsed that night twenty-four years ago.

It was a dreary wet day when she set off for Alexander Street. The tenements huddled in the rain like grey, stone ghosts and few people were out on the street. A couple of brave souls, wrapped up in their thick coats, were coming out of the little grocer's shop on the corner of James Street but apart from them, even the children, who normally would be playing in the streets, had decided to stay indoors.

Peter Walsh lived on the second floor of number twenty-eight. A shabby looking door bore a tiny brass nameplate. However, before she reached the door, it was yanked open and a young girl who looked about fifteen rushed out. She had no coat on and was wearing a pair of scuffed slippers on her bare feet. 'Get a *Sunday Post* and *The People* and don't forget my twenty Capstan cigarettes,' an irate male voice shouted loudly.

This was followed by a shrill female tone: 'Janey, put on your coat and shoes and don't go out in the rain with your baffies.'

Janey paid no heed to this advice and proceeded to run down the stairs. Molly went to the still open door and knocked. A thin woman with dark curly hair appeared. She was still dressed in her pyjamas with a cardigan buttoned tightly over the top. Molly felt overdressed when faced by this morning ensemble but she was soon brought back to the reason for her visit when the woman spoke. 'What are you wanting? I hope you're no selling anything.'

'Can I speak to Mr Peter Walsh, please?'

The woman's eyes narrowed and she

swept her hair back from her face with a thin hand. 'What do you want him for?'

'I'm looking into the disappearance of Etta Barton and I think your husband knew her.'

The woman gawped at Molly. 'You're joking. Etta vanished over twenty years ago. What's Peter got to do with it?'

By now, Molly was getting tired of conducting a conversation on the doorstep. 'Can I please speak to Peter?'

The woman went to close the door. 'No, I don't think so. He won't even remember Etta Barton.'

No, but you do, Molly thought. Just then, Janey came rushing back upstairs and her mother was annoyed that she had run out in the rain with no proper shoes. 'Didn't I tell you to put on your coat and shoes?'

'Just let the lassie get in the house with my cigarettes and papers for God's sake Donna,' said the man's voice. 'Who's that at the door? The one you're busy yapping with.'

Before Donna could answer, Molly said loudly, 'Can I have a word with you, Mr Walsh?'

Peter came to the door. He was dressed in his pyjama bottoms and a vest. He also had dark curly hair and his face was unshaven. He looked very tired. 'What do you want?' he said, repeating the same words his wife had used.

'Can I come in?' asked Molly.

He looked at Donna and she looked dubious but he said, 'All right but make it snappy.'

Molly was shown into the kitchen and she was glad that she hadn't come earlier because it looked as if the family had just finished breakfast. The table, with its oilcloth covering, held plates with congealed egg and bacon fat on their surfaces and half-full cups of tea. The room was quite small with a sink at the window and the frying pan and kettle on the cooker. The fireplace still held the ashes from the day before.

A young girl of about eighteen years was sitting at the table. She was also dressed in a short nightdress with a thick woollen cardigan over her shoulders. She had the same black hair as her parents and had been wearing mascara at some point because she now had two black-rimmed eyes, like a panda. She barely looked at the visitor but concentrated on eating her toast. Molly was fascinated by her behaviour because she held the slice of toast in her hand and slowly rotated it, taking delicate little bites from the edges. Molly quickly reviewed her first impression of a panda and now thought she looked more like a squirrel.

The other girl, Janey, sat beside her mother and stared at Molly. It was very off-putting but Molly was determined to know if this man was Pedro, the one-time boyfriend of Etta. 'I'm really sorry to bother you so early on a Sunday morning,' she said, feeling a bit ridiculous since it was only a couple of hours until teatime. 'I wanted to ask you, Mr Walsh, if you can give me any information on a girl called Etta Barton?'

Peter almost choked on his cigarette. He had a deep hoarse cough that spoke of too many cigarettes. He gulped down a swig of tea while Donna glared at her. 'Etta Barton? Is that what this is all about?' he said in disbelief.

Molly wanted to know, 'Is your name Pedro?'

Before he could answer, Donna began to shout, 'Don't call him that. I hate that nickname. You would think we were bloody *Spanish* or something.' She stressed the word Spanish and made it sound derogatory.

Molly silently thought that the Spanish might be annoyed that Peter was one of them. She decided to be extra polite. 'Mrs Walsh, I've been hired by Etta's mother to try and find out what happened to her. Now, you're a mother yourself. Wouldn't you want the same for your girls if this happened to you?'

Donna gave Molly a look that said, at that particular moment, she would be glad of a rest from panda eyes and Janey, who ran out in the rain in her slippers.

Peter said, 'When I was about sixteen and an apprentice joiner, I went out with Etta for a few weeks. It didn't last long, as I wasn't really keen on her, but we went out to the pictures. It wasn't serious, at least not on my part.'

'I have spoken to someone who says Etta was in love with you and that she took your relationship very seriously.'

Panda eyes stopped eating her toast and looked at her father in total disbelief. He noticed the look and said crossly. 'Don't look at me like that, Andrea. I happened to be a great looking lad when I was young.' He shrugged. 'Well, she might have been serious, but I wasn't and she knew it.'

'Did you tell her it was over?'

He looked guilty. 'No. I'd met Donna by then and I dropped Etta. I just stopped seeing her and I think she got the message.' On seeing Molly's look, he said, 'That was what we used to do when we were young – have lots of girlfriends before settling down and getting married.'

'I never liked that Etta,' said Donna. 'I mean, she wasn't pretty and she had a funny nature.'

'Do you think the fact that you left her made her run away, Peter?'

He lit another cigarette and blew the smoke up to the ceiling. 'No. We split up a few weeks before that all happened.' He leant his arms on the table. 'Look, I was very sorry when I heard about Etta and her dad. In fact, I still feel sorry for Vera Barton, but nothing good comes from digging about in the past. Will you tell Vera that?'

Molly said, 'I think she knows that but she wants to know the truth, regardless of what might come up.' Molly couldn't think of any more questions, so she thanked them and said, 'I'm sorry I disturbed you on a Sunday.'

Donna stood up to show her to the door. 'It doesn't matter. Sunday, Monday, Tuesday – they're just days to me.' She stood on the stair landing. 'Look at this dump. Trying to bring up a family in this house is terrible. We all live on top of one another. We're waiting for a key to a new house in Kirkton and then we'll all have our own room, plus a kitchen and bathroom. The girls keep asking when they'll be able to have a bath. Janey's even bought a jar of bath salts. Oh well, maybe next month we'll hear from the Corporation.'

Molly suddenly felt a wave of sympathy for the woman. For all her bravado, she was only wanting the best for her family, just like Vera had wanted for Etta. Molly handed her a card. 'If you can think of anything else about Etta, please get in touch with me.'

Donna looked at the card and said, 'All right.'

Molly took hold of Donna's hand. 'I hope you get your key for the new house soon and

I really mean that.'

Donna nodded as she went back inside her house and Molly descended the stairs to the street. The rain was heavier than ever and Molly pulled up the collar of her coat before hurrying away down the Hill to her own flat, which was about the same size as Donna and Peter's house. Her flat had one occupant while the other had four. She felt disappointed and deflated. She had pinned so much hope on finding Pedro and now it turned out that he didn't know what had been in Etta's mind. It was another blank wall.

26

The woman was almost incandescent with rage. It burned like a fire in her heart and she could barely hide her hatred. That nosy woman, Molly McQueen, was the cause of her anger. Why was she raking up all this old muck? Etta Barton was truly in the past and that's where she should stay. Not picked over like yesterday's dinner. Of course, it was all the fault of Vera Barton. Why didn't she let the past stay hidden? Trying to find out the truth would be like facing the jaws of hell. Well, there would be tears soon or even worse, she thought. Oh yes, she would make sure of that. Vera Barton and Molly McQueen had better watch their steps.

27

Phil had received his call-up papers and was leaving on the Monday night. When he had met Mary at Kidd's Rooms on Saturday night he had said, 'Will you come to see me off at the station, Mary? My train leaves at half past six.'

Mary had said she would and now she stood on the platform along with Stan, Phil's parents and his two sisters. The two girls, who were younger than Phil and still at school, looked like they had been crying. The conversation was a bit stilted. Mary and Phil were friends but they hadn't known each other for long. Mary had never stood on a railway platform to say goodbye to anyone and she didn't know what to say. Also, the fact that his family were standing beside them made her feel shy and tongue-tied.

Stan said, 'I'll go and let you all say goodbye.' He spoke to Phil. 'Cheers, Phil. We'll meet up when you get home on leave.' Then he turned towards the entrance.

Within five minutes of Stan walking away

down the platform, the train came in. Mary asked him, 'Will it be a long journey, Phil?'

'Yes, I have to report to Aldershot Barracks and I've no idea what else lies ahead.' He sounded apprehensive about what the future might hold. 'Will you write to me, Mary?'

'Yes. Let me know your address and I'll keep in touch. Look after yourself.'

Then his parents and sisters wanted to say goodbye, so Mary left. Stan was standing at the entrance to the station. 'Would you like a cup of coffee before you catch the bus?' he asked.

It was another cold, wet night and Mary had come to the station straight from her job in one of the departmental offices in the council building. 'I'd love one, thank you.'

Stan suggested the Chrome Rail coffee bar, which was a few hundred yards from the station. It was quiet at this time of night but according to Stan, it normally got busy later as people made their way out for the evening. When they were seated at the counter in the American-styled restaurant with its shiny chrome fittings and mirrored wall, Stan said, 'It won't take long to pass, Mary. Phil will get some leave after his training, or the dreaded "square-bashing" as it's called, and if he's stationed in this country, then he'll get home quite often. It's amazing how fast the time goes by, especially after the first year.'

Mary nodded. 'Yes, I suppose so.' She felt

dejected. Although she had only known Phil for a few weeks, she had enjoyed his company and the fact that he was gorgeous was a bonus. She had grown used to the looks of envy from other girls and no doubt there would be plenty of pretty girls in Aldershot.

'Where are you working now?' Stan asked, bringing Mary back from her reverie.

'I'm filling in for someone in the council offices. She's got the flu. I don't know how long I'll be there but that's the best thing about this job – the variety. What about you, Stan, do you like your job?'

'Yes, as a matter of fact I do, but I loved my time in Hong Kong. It's a wonderful exotic place with super people. They are so hard-working. Do you know, you can go in for a suit in the morning and the tailor will have it ready by evening.'

Mary was impressed. 'Maybe you'll go back sometime.'

Stan took his glasses off and wiped them with his handkerchief. Mary noticed how blue his eyes were. He laughed. 'Yes, maybe. Shall I tell you my little secret, Mary? When I get married, I want to take my wife there on our honeymoon.'

Mary felt a strange pang of disappointment. 'Are you getting married soon?'

Stan roared with laughter and the waitress turned to look at them. 'I haven't even got a girlfriend yet. But that's my dream.' He looked at his watch. Mary thought he was embarrassed by his confession. 'I'll walk you to your bus.'

They walked in companionable silence to Shore Terrace and had to wait a few minutes for Mary's bus. When it came, he said cheerio and stood waiting till the bus set off.

The woman in the council office wasn't the only one with flu. Edna was back in Albert's Stores because Nancy had Asian flu. She was grateful for this opportunity to meet her old friends and it helped her cope with the upset over John. A typewritten letter had arrived at the office at the end of last week and the signature was John's. Molly had asked her if it was genuine and she thought it was. What she couldn't understand was the way he was acting now. It was so out of character but maybe his love for Sonia had overcome all his good manners and he was embarrassed by the suddenness of it and didn't want to face her. Yet, he had seemed so annoyed when she arrived without warning ... but it just went to show you that you could never anticipate human nature.

Whatever the reason, she had to try and forget him. Eddie was still doing well at the branch shop and Albert was, as always, his cheery self. Oh yes, it was good to be back. In a way, she hoped Nancy's flu, Asian or otherwise, would last another couple of weeks. Edna would have gone to see Eddie but Albert had given her all the news since her last stint in the shop and Eddie was going steady with one of the assistants he worked with. She didn't feel up to meeting both of them.

Snappy Sal came in with a face like a sour lemon. 'I've brought back this cheese, Albert, because it's mouldy. I've only had it for a fortnight and it shouldn't have turned green like this, and then there's this bag of biscuits; half of them are broken.' She dumped the two items on the counter with such force that it was a wonder the biscuits weren't in crumbs.

'Now what have we here, Mrs Little?' said Albert. Trying hard to smile through gritted teeth, he picked up the piece of cheese, which resembled a matchbox. He then marched over to the cheese and butter counter, where he carefully cut a minute piece of cheddar and wrapped it in greaseproof paper. He then chose six rich tea biscuits from the tin and placed them in a bag. 'There you are, Mrs Little. Service is my policy.'

Snappy Sal's face was a picture of disbelief. 'But I bought a half-pound of cheese and a half-pound of biscuits. All you've given me is this wee amount back.'

'Yes, Mrs Little, but you've eaten the rest.' He turned to serve another customer and she left the shop, muttering that she would take her custom to Lipton's grocery in the future. Later, he said he would pay Lipton's to take her on.

Then Dolly Pirie came in and she was so different from her pal, Mrs Little. 'Are you coming up for some soup at dinner time, Edna?'

Edna said she couldn't, as she had to go home. This wasn't really true but she couldn't face Dolly's questions about John and how the relationship was going. 'Still, it's great to see you back. That Nancy and her Asian flu. Why can't she be like everyone else and get the common cold bug? But no, it has to be some exotic disease she's got!'

At dinner time, Edna was wishing she had gone to Dolly's house because it began to rain again and she had to wait ten minutes for the tramcar. While she was waiting, her mind wandered back to John and his upsetting behaviour. He had terminated his contract and Molly had sent out the bill for the work covered, including the two weeks when Edna wasn't working for him. She had said to Edna how sorry she was but Edna had her pride and said it didn't really matter that much. However, no one in the office was fooled by that dignified answer.

28

Like Mary and Edna, Molly was also depressed – she had learned so little from Peter Walsh. During these last three weeks, she had pinned her hopes on being able to solve the case when she finally managed to find him, and now that she had, she still had nothing to show where the girl had gone.

To make matters worse, it was another horrible night, with thick fog that hit your face like a wet clammy glove. When the office closed, she decided to stay indoors with a hot cup of Ovaltine and have an early night. She was sound asleep by eleven o'clock. The book she was reading had been boring and she could barely keep her eyes open, so she switched off the bedside lamp and snuggled down in the cosy bed with her hot water bottle. Before she fell asleep, the thought crossed her mind that she was living her life like some aged spinster: *sans* man, *sans* marriage and *sans* finding Etta Barton.

It was the sound that wakened her. She looked at the alarm clock with its illuminated hands, which showed it was 1:15 a.m. The noise came again but she realised it wasn't coming from the flat, but from outside. She slipped out of bed and peered through the curtains, but she couldn't see a thing because of the fog and the fact that the streetlight was broken at her end of the street. The noise had sounded like something metallic, as if a metal door was being opened. She tried to see her car but it was impossible to see anything. She was afraid that someone was damaging her father's car, so decided to go down to the street and investigate. If it were some youngsters, then she would call the police. Only stopping to put her coat on over her nightdress, she slipped through the door in the bedroom and down the stairs.

As she reached the end of the close, someone had left a bottle sitting at the entrance and she knocked it over. The noise seemed so loud in this fog-bound world, that it took away the chance of spying on the culprit without being seen, so she marched boldly out into the street to find it silent and deserted. The car was still parked in its usual spot and she went up to check it out. Everything seemed fine until she came to the passenger door, which was ajar. Someone had used some kind of tool to force the lock. Molly could have cried because she hated the thought of any damage being done to her father's pride and joy. It then struck her as odd that anyone would break into a car parked so near a busy street. Baltic Street was quiet but the Wellgate still had people walking through it on their way home.

She glanced at the street again but there was no movement, so she made her way back upstairs. Luckily there hadn't been any valuables in the car. In fact, there hadn't been anything worth stealing, so the person with the tool had had an unfruitful night. It wasn't until she was back in bed that she remembered the bag with her notebooks had been in the car. But why would anyone want a couple of notebooks with addresses and statements written in shorthand? She didn't want to go downstairs again, back out into the foggy night, and maybe the books were still in the car. She would check in the morning. She found it hard to go back to sleep again, so she picked up the book with the boring plot and read it until her eyes closed with either boredom or tiredness.

When she woke at nine o'clock after a restless night, she felt she had gone ten rounds with Joe Louis. The first thing she did when she was dressed was to go and investigate the car break-in. The fog still lingered but she saw the lock had been forced and her bag with the notebooks was no longer on the back seat. This wasn't a big deal because she had a copy of all the statements in the office. She had typed them out after each visit to the witnesses' homes along with their names and addresses.

She would go and see Vera later and ask her

about Etta's post office savings book but, no doubt, like everything else in this case, it would turn into another dead end. Then she thought, stop being so pessimistic, something might turn up.

She thought again about the name Ruby in Vera's address book but she hesitated to ask her, as she had looked so terrified by the mention of the name the last time. Still, this was the only name not accounted for and she didn't like overlooking it.

29

The woman had had a scare. She hadn't known about the back entrance to the agency flat, thinking it was only accessed from inside the office. Thank goodness for that bottle, otherwise she would have been caught red-handed. She had had time to step into the doorway of Kerr B. Sturrock's shop-fitting business that was across the street from the car. She was also grateful for the broken street lamp and the fog – it seemed as if divine providence had been working in her favour. No doubt Molly McQueen would report the incident to the police but she had nothing to worry about. No one could pin this robbery on her. Once again, the hatred sprang up in her head, so much so that her hands were shaking when she finally emerged into the foggy night, but not before she saw the light go on in the flat's window. She quietly walked away, keeping to the shadows until she reached Meadowside. She carried the bag with the books and now she would be able to see what Molly McQueen had found out. She suspected precious little but she couldn't be sure.

30

Molly was in two minds about going to the police station to report the break-in but instead she took the car to the garage in Seagate Lane and they said they would fix it. The garage mechanic looked at it and gave his opinion. 'It'll need a new door lock but we'll have to order it. You can either leave the car here for a couple of days or take it home and bring it back in when the part comes in.'

Molly said she would leave it with the garage. She didn't want it sitting in the dark street with a broken door where anyone could gain access to it and maybe steal it. It was bad enough losing her notebooks. If she was in two minds about going to the police, she was also in two minds about who to see next. She had planned to see Vera this morning and ask about the post office savings book but during her restless night she had suddenly thought of Anita.

She set off for Hill Street, hoping Anita wasn't out shopping or browsing around Woolworths, and was pleased when the door was answered after the initial knock. Judging by her dress, Anita was in the throes of housework. She wore a very fetching floral apron, had a scarf around her hair and her face was flushed. She seemed pleased to see Molly. 'Oh, come on in. I'm dying for a cup of tea and now I have the excuse to stop for a while.'

She led Molly into the living room. All the pictures were off the walls. The ornaments were huddled on the table and a large tin of polish sat on the sideboard next to a duster. When they were seated with their tea, Molly said, 'Do you remember anyone called Ruby who used to visit the Bartons?'

Anita frowned in concentration. 'I don't think so. There used to be an old woman called Ruby who lived in the close but she was a bit wandered, I think. She used to go out to the grocer's shop in her nightdress with a woollen hat on her head. When the shop owner asked her why she hadn't got dressed, Ruby would say that she was dressed and she would point to her hat.

"I'm wearing my hat," she would say. Poor old soul but she was the only Ruby I knew.' Anita put her cup and saucer down on the table, where it competed for space with the ornaments. 'Is this Ruby woman important?'

Molly sighed. 'Oh, I don't know, Anita. It was just a name in Vera Barton's address book.'

'Can you not ask her about Ruby?'

'She doesn't want to say who it is and I can't force her.' Molly said truthfully.

'I wonder if it's a relative or someone Vera doesn't like…' Anita stopped. 'I've suddenly remembered a woman, but her name wasn't Ruby, it was Robina. She was Vera's sister.'

Molly almost choked on her tea. 'Her sister? But Vera said she had no family.'

Anita laughed. 'I don't think she would want everyone to know about Robina. It was early one Monday morning. My husband had left for work very early because he was stocktaking and I had run out for the paper. When I came back in the close, there was this strange looking woman standing at my door. At first, I thought she was a nun because she was dressed all in black but when I got closer, I saw it was a black coat and long skirt with a black headscarf over her hair. I remember she had a very fierce looking face. I asked her if I could help her and she said she was looking for her sister, Mrs

Barton. Well, I showed her the way but then I never saw her again.'

Molly was grateful that, once again, Anita's sharp observation and memory had uncovered a crucial new piece of the puzzle.

'Then later,' Anita continued, 'when I met Dave, I asked him if his visitor had found the house and he just grunted.'

'Did any of the neighbours, like Mrs Pert, ever say anything about Vera's sister?' Molly asked.

She gave this some thought. 'No, but I got the impression then that the sister had been away somewhere because she didn't know where Vera and Dave were staying.'

Molly wanted to know more about Robina. 'Did Vera ever mention her to you after that? Maybe to say thank you for showing her the way to their house?'

Anita shook her head. 'No, she didn't, and I haven't thought about that incident until now. Not until you mentioned the name Ruby.'

'This happened about a year before Dave's accident and Etta's disappearance?' asked Molly.

Anita nodded. 'Yes. It was a wee while before we moved to the west coast, so it must have been in the summer of 1929.'

She looked puzzled. 'Why didn't Vera tell you about her? I mean, she did ask you to try and find her daughter. Why be so secretive about her own sister?'

That was something Molly was going to find out when she met up with Vera later. She thanked Anita. 'You've been a great help with your memories. It's a pity you had left the close before all this happened, as I'm sure you would have seen or heard something.'

Once again, Anita looked pleased. She picked up one of the ornaments and gazed at it. 'I suppose I'd better put these all back and get on with my housework.'

Molly decided to go and see Vera to find out what she had to say about Robina and the post office savings book. She was getting used to going through this close now and she wondered what the neighbours were thinking. Perhaps they weren't interested in observing who came and went and maybe they liked to keep their lives private. Not like years ago, when Mrs Pert and Anita had been so good in knowing a bit of what went on. However, it was a pity Mrs Pert hadn't seen Etta leave with a young man or a suitcase.

As it turned out, it was a wasted journey, as Vera wasn't in. Had she gone to play bridge at Mrs Jankowski's house? Molly walked towards the office and made a plan to return later tonight.

31

Vera hadn't gone to play bridge. When Molly was climbing her stairs to question her about her sister, Vera was hurrying into the town. She didn't normally go near the city centre, except on the rare occasion when she needed something out of one of the department stores like G.L. Wilson or Smith Brothers. She tried to walk as fast as she could. Her hip was still a bit sore but excitement made her hurry past pedestrians who were thronging the Murraygate.

She had the letter in her pocket and she couldn't believe the good news she had received by the post this morning. Her destination was the DPM tearoom in Reform Street. She glanced at her watch and saw that it was almost eleven o'clock – the time the writer had said to meet. There was a crowd standing on the kerb at H. Samuel's clock, waiting for the traffic to pass before crossing to the Overgate. Vera couldn't understand why the town was so busy on a weekday but as she hadn't shopped here for a while, maybe it was always like this.

She joined the crowd at the kerb, impatient to cross over. She was looking up the street to see if there was a break in the traffic so she could hurry across when she felt a huge fist at her back. Someone had pushed her and she landed on the road. As if from a distance, she heard the screams from the onlookers as an oncoming bus tried to screech to a halt. She could feel the heat from the engine and smell the fuel as she lay terrified on the tarmac but the bus managed to stop inches from her.

The bus driver jumped out, his face white with apprehension and fear while a few of the pedestrians also hurried over and helped pick her up. Vera was so shocked that she could barely stand and the pain in her hip had intensified. The passengers in the bus were all agog and looking with stretched necks out from the windows. The driver said, 'Are you all right, missus?'

By now, Vera was horribly embarrassed and said she was fine thank you. The driver got back into his cab and drove like he was going over eggshells while his passengers, now sensing the drama was over, gave Vera one last look and settled back in their seats. Vera was almost in tears. Her coat and skirt were streaked with dirt and one of her stockings had a huge ladder in it. An elderly woman who had witnessed the near accident came over and took her arm. 'Let me take you for a cup of tea, my dear. You're in shock and need to sit down.'

Vera then remembered her appointment. She was dismayed to see it was now ten past eleven. 'I've got to get to the DPM tearoom across the road to meet someone.'

'I'm going there as well, so let me help you.'

Vera didn't want anyone with her but it would have been impolite to turn the old woman down, so she let herself be led away towards the tearoom. As she walked, she tried to brush the dust from her coat.

When they reached their destination, the tearoom was almost full with customers and it looked like there were no empty seats left. A waitress appeared and she found them two seats in a corner of the room. The woman ordered tea and scones for the two of them and she said, 'Do you see your friend?'

Vera was vexed by the crowd of customers and she shook her head. What she didn't tell her was that she had no idea if the writer of the letter was a man or a woman but he or she said they knew Vera and they would come and speak to her. After scanning the crowd anxiously for half an hour, Vera knew her contact wasn't coming. Or else they had left when she didn't show up at eleven. The woman had introduced herself as Bella. 'Now tell me, my dear, why you almost got killed trying to cross in front of all those buses?'

Vera almost told a lie but somehow Bella's

gentle gaze made her tell the truth and she said, 'Someone pushed me.'

Bella looked shocked. 'Pushed you? But why?'

That was something Vera was asking herself. This was the second accident and it had all started with the enquiries into her daughter. She wasn't going to burden the old lady with all that drama but she said quite simply. 'I'm trying to trace my daughter who disappeared in 1930 and I got this letter that said the writer knew something about the disappearance and to meet here.' Vera put her hand in her pocket but the letter was gone. Frantically, she searched every pocket but the letter wasn't there. 'I've lost the letter. It must have fallen out when I landed in the road. I must go back and look for it.'

She jumped up as Bella quietly paid the bill. 'Let me help you.'

They made their way to the junction, this time waiting patiently until the traffic had passed, but there was no sign of the letter on the road or on the pavement. 'Maybe the wind has blown it further along the road,' said Vera, but in spite of searching all the length of Reform Street and both sides of the pavements, there was no sign of it.

Vera felt like crying but she knew that wouldn't help, so she said she wanted to go home. 'Thank you for helping me, Bella, but I'll manage to get home now.'

'I live in Victoria Road so let's walk together.'

Vera would have liked to be alone but again, she didn't want to be rude in the face of Bella's kindness. When they reached Molly's agency, Vera decided to go in and see Molly. 'I've a friend who works here. I'll go in and see if she's around.'

Bella put her hand on Vera's arm. 'Please watch out for yourself, Vera. Someone tried to kill or injure you today and if it hadn't been for the skill of the driver and the good, strong brakes on the Corporation bus, they would have succeeded. I don't want to alarm you, my dear, but do take care.'

Vera knew this but she said she would be careful and she watched as Bella made her way up the Wellgate steps towards Victoria Road.

Molly was in the office and was surprised to see her. She noticed the laddered stocking on the usually immaculate woman and had a spasm of fear. Vera seemed on the verge of collapse. Molly and Jean helped her up the stairs to the flat where Jean put the kettle on to make a hot drink. Vera began to tremble and tears rolled down her cheeks. Downstairs, the phone was ringing and Jean hurried back into the office to answer it. Molly was almost frightened to ask her what was wrong, as it was clear Vera was in a state of shock. 'Tell me what's happened, Vera.'

Molly tried to keep her tone soothing.

'I ... I got a letter this morning...' She broke off, unable to continue.

'Who sent the letter?'

Vera wiped her eyes. 'I ... got a letter this morning. It said to go to the DPM restaurant in Reform Street to meet the writer of the letter. I went but they weren't there.'

Molly had to try and calm her down. 'Show me the letter, please.'

Vera let out a loud sobbing wail that brought Jean hurrying up the stairs but Molly told her everything was fine. Vera began to shake uncontrollably. 'I almost got killed by a bus. Someone pushed me and I was almost killed.'

By now Molly was really alarmed. She hurried to the cupboard and found the half-full bottle of brandy that she had bought for the housewarming party. She poured a large measure into a glass and placed it in Vera's hand. 'Drink this, it'll help to calm you down,' she said, hoping it would.

Vera's teeth chattered against the side of the glass but slowly she relaxed.

'Are you able to speak now?'

Vera nodded. 'I went into the town this morning. I was to meet this person at eleven o'clock.' For a moment, she shuddered before she told of her near escape with the bus and how the person didn't come when she got to the café.

'Have you got the letter with you?'

'No. I had it in my pocket but when I went to look for it, it was gone. Bella and I searched the entire street but it wasn't there.'

By now Molly was confused. 'Who is this Bella?'

'An old woman who helped me to the café and she walked with me as far as here when she left to go home to Victoria Road.'

Molly took hold of Vera's hands. They were icy cold. 'Tell me what the letter said.'

Vera sat up and frowned, as if trying to remember the contents. 'It was written with a pencil. It said: "Dear Mrs Barton, It's come to my knowledge that you are looking for your daughter Etta. Meet me this morning in the DPM Restaurant in Reform Street at 11 a.m. as I have some important news regarding your daughter. A well-wisher."'

'Have you any idea who could have written this letter?'

Vera shook her head. 'No. That was what I was hoping to find out.'

Although she sounded calm, Molly was very worried about this new turn in the case. This second attempt confirmed that someone was trying to seriously harm Vera and she felt it was time for some action. 'Vera, listen to me, you have to go to the police about these accidents. They will find out who is behind them and you'll be safe because they will look after you.'

'No, I can't. I don't want to involve them. If you find out what happened to Etta, then I'll drop the case.'

'You hired me for a month, Vera, and there're only a few more days to go. I haven't had any success in finding where Etta went to on the day your husband was killed, never mind finding out where she is now.'

Vera looked down at her glass, surprised to see it was empty. She had never drunk a full glass of alcohol in her life and here she was, slurping down brandy.

Molly didn't want to tell Vera about the break-in with her car but she had to get her home, quickly and discreetly. 'My car's at the garage and I have to pick it up. Wait here and I'll take you home when I get back. If you don't want to stay here you can go down and sit with Jean. I'll be about half an hour. Have you any food in your house? I'll make you some dinner when we get you home.'

Vera was now sounding tired. 'Yes, I've got eggs, bread and some spiced ham.'

'Well, I'll cook something when I get back.'

After Molly left, Vera settled down on the studio couch and fell fast asleep.

Molly hurried along to the garage in Dock Street, hoping the lock had been repaired. She was very worried. Marigold had warned her about lifting stones and how all sorts of horrible things would be uncovered. She wondered who this letter writer could be. It must be connected to the people she had questioned. Someone knew about her investigations. Who was hiding something?

Molly loved reading detective stories and if she had a true investigator's mind like Miss Marple, Hercule Poirot or her favourite American private eye, Philip Marlowe, she would have known she was being watched, but she was a secretary and she was oblivious to her stalker. Thankfully, the garage had repaired the car and after settling the large bill, she set off for the agency.

Getting Vera home took some time because Molly didn't want to wake her and it was after three o'clock when they finally reached the Hilltown. Vera looked ill. Her face was pinched and grey and as she threw away her new stockings, she gave a huge sigh. Molly made scrambled eggs and toast for them both and although she ate hers with relish, Vera barely ate more than a few mouthfuls. 'I can stay here with you for a few days if you like, Vera.'

Vera tried to smile and failed. 'No, it's all right. I'm a big girl.'

Yes, thought Molly, a big girl that almost got run over by a huge bus. She wanted to ask Vera about her sister and the savings book but was unsure if the woman could stand more questioning. Still, it had to be done at some point and there was no time like the present. 'Vera, did you ever find out anything more about Etta's savings book?'

Vera's eyes looked dazed, as if tiredness was her only hope of salvation after the trauma of the day. 'Etta's post office book?' She made it sound like this was the first she had heard of it.

'Yes, did you ever find out if any of the money was taken out in some other post office? Maybe it would show where she went to.'

Vera lay back in the chair and closed her eyes. When she spoke, her words sounded dreamy. 'The police investigated it. Apparently Etta had been withdrawing money for a few weeks before she left and there was hardly any money left in the account. I think it was five shillings but she never withdrew that. The police said it looked like she had been planning to go away all along.'

Molly was slightly put out that Vera hadn't given her this information earlier but it did confirm what she had been thinking – it looked like it was a determined getaway. 'Do you still see your sister Robina?'

Vera sprang up, the tiredness was gone and her body stiff with indignation. 'Robina? Who told you about her?'

Molly wasn't going to divulge Anita's name. 'It came up in my investigation.'

Vera now looked even more frightened than

before. 'It wasn't Robina who pushed me.'

Molly was surprised. She hadn't considered this but why was Vera so sure? 'Do you think she's capable of doing this to her sister?'

Vera sat down again, all the fight slowly leaving her rigid body. 'Robina and I haven't seen each other since before Dave died. She was a strange child and she grew up with a strong religious sense of right and wrong. Dave and I weren't married when I was expecting Etta but we were by the time she was born. Robina started ranting to my mother and father about sin and hell, and the damnation of the soul. One day, she attacked me with an old cricket bat and my parents banned her from the house. She was away at training college at the time and she never came back home. Not until one morning, when she came to see us. I was mortified to see how much Etta resembled her and then she started ranting on and on about her religious beliefs and how we should go to confession for our sins. Etta was quite taken with her aunt but Dave put her out of the house and we never saw her again. Sadly, Etta became fixated on this idea of punishing those she thought were sinful and I could have killed Robina for coming that day.'

'Do you know where she is now, or have you heard from her over the years, maybe by letter?'

'No, I've no idea where she is and to tell the truth, I don't want to know. I had an ideal childhood spoiled by her. The time she hit me, when she was banned from the house, wasn't the only time she had done something like that. I suffered years of abuse from her. She would smack me hard if I didn't say my prayers right or kneel properly in church. I never told my parents but I was glad when she never came home again. I told her that on the day she came to see us but I wish I hadn't – she gave me a look of pure hatred and I know her ... she thrives on revenge.'

'But you don't think it was her who pushed you?'

Vera looked puzzled. 'I would have recognised her, wouldn't I?'

Molly wasn't so sure. 'Do you think it's possible that Etta went to stay with her when she went missing?'

Vera was positive. 'No. Robina was living in a training hostel, so it wouldn't have been possible for Etta to go there.'

'What was she training to be?'

Vera said she was unsure. 'Something to do with the church, I think. Probably to be a nun but she didn't say.'

Molly had to go but she was worried about Vera. 'Is there anyone who can come and stay with you? Or maybe you can go for a few days to Mrs Jankowski's house?'

Vera said no, she would be fine. She would lock the door after Molly left and go straight to bed. She certainly looked exhausted.

Molly drove away in the car, her head spinning with the day's events. This sister seemed to be the ideal candidate for the accident today but did she own a car? Vera was sure she had heard a vehicle on the night of the first accident.

If Vera wasn't going to go to the police then Molly made up her mind she would think about consulting them. This case was getting more dangerous by the minute. Molly had obviously opened old festering memories with her questions, but who was the culprit?

32

The woman was feeling pleased with herself. So pleased, in fact, that she could barely contain it. She wanted to jump out and shout, 'Look at me!' She had watched the devastation she had caused but cursed the bus driver. What a pity it was a fit young man and not some old guy with slow reflexes. Still, there was always another day.

She had also seen Molly go for the car and had watched with satisfaction as she had paid what looked like a large bill. Maybe this was the road to go down with nosey parker McQueen: keep damaging the car and make her pay dearly for all her questioning about something that had nothing to do with her. Yes, that's what she would do. Make her pay through the nose for her part in this. She had gained a lot of knowledge from the stolen notebooks, but she would deal with that later.

33

Molly parked the car in the dark street after she had taken Vera home. She felt uneasy walking away from it. The street lamp was still broken and there were deep shadows where anyone could lurk without being seen. She glanced up and down but the street wasn't a busy thoroughfare, merely a quick way to reach Meadowside. It was used quite a lot during the day but by nightfall it was deserted.

She decided to go for a fish supper at the nearby fish and chip shop, and carried the hot meal up to the flat. She felt exhausted and puzzled by the day's events and, to make matters worse, she had a terrible headache. This case was proving to be far more complicated than she thought, and she was now wishing she had been more firm in turning it down. Who could have sent that letter to Vera? It must have been someone who wanted to harm her, but why? Why was keeping the truth hidden about Etta's disappearance worth killing for? There was also the worrying thought that someone must be watching Vera, and that maybe the anonymous someone was also watching her. She had to be on her guard and if she saw one of the people she had talked to, then she had better take care.

Another thought slipped into her mind. It might not be someone from her interrogations. Suppose they had talked about the case and a neighbour or even a member of their families had overheard them. It could be anyone, but why was this person taking the case so seriously? It had been twenty-four years ago and the chance of finding her was very slim indeed.

The car was still on her mind. She put the light out and opened the bedroom curtain. The rain had come on and there was a strong wind. It looked like it would be a stormy night. She knew she couldn't stand all night at the window, much as she would have liked to. It would give her great pleasure to discover the culprit who had damaged her father's car. After an hour gazing out at the darkness, she got ready for bed, but she still kept the light out.

She awoke suddenly from a restless sleep. The alarm clock said 2.20 a.m. Was it a noise she'd heard through her subconscious that had wakened her? She peered down but everything seemed peaceful. A cat wailed in the distance but there didn't seem to be anything human lurking around. However, she decided to go down and look.

Making sure there were no bottles or other obstacles in her way, she made her way out into the cold wind – thankfully the rain had stopped. She had brought a small torch with her and she circled the car. It was just as she had left it.

Back in bed, she made her plan. By seven o'clock she was up, dressed and in the car, on her way to the first sailing of the Fifie. She reckoned if someone was watching her, then maybe they started later in the day.

Marigold was surprised when the car drew up at the door. She was still in her dressing gown when Molly knocked at the door. 'What's happened?' Marigold sounded worried.

Molly explained about her suspicions that someone was watching her. 'I want to leave dad's car here because I think whoever broke the lock and stole my notebooks will do something more serious to it next time.'

Marigold was shocked. 'You have to go to the police, Molly. There's someone very dangerous out there and I don't want you getting into trouble like last year.'

'I'm hoping to be back at the agency before my stalker gets wind of this.'

Marigold began to prepare breakfast but Molly just wanted tea and toast. 'I've got to catch the next sailing back to Dundee, and don't worry, Marigold, I'm going to see that policeman from last year, DS Johns. I thought he was very kind and helpful.'

Within an hour, Molly was back on the ferry and when it docked at Craig Pier, she made a detour so as not to take the usual route of the Fifie passengers. If someone was watching, then they wouldn't know where she had gone.

By 10:30 a.m. she was back in the office, looking as if she had just arrived for work. She had warned Vera to stay indoors and not be fooled by another letter. This was a precaution until she contacted the police.

34

Peter Walsh hated the dark mornings, especially when the clocks changed to wintertime. To make things worse, the weather was awful with wind and heavy rain. He got his bike out of the shed in the backgreen and went back upstairs to get his piece bag and flask. He wished he had the use of the van to go to work but Jimmy Flynn was the driver. Life would be easier when they got the key to a new house in Kirkton. Then he would get a lift to work with Jimmy. Donna was getting depressed living in this house and he didn't blame her. Still, the girls were growing up and would soon be moving on. Andrea was working as a junior assistant in D.M. Brown's department store, while Janey was almost done with school.

Milton's joinery business was named after the street where it was situated. Milton Street was a small narrow street that branched off from Byron Street and although it wasn't that far from his house, it still meant he had to make the steep incline of the Hilltown. He hoped he wasn't going to be late but he was wary of pedalling too fast because the road was slippery with the overnight rain. There were a few people about the Hilltown and Strathmartine Road but, when he turned into Harcourt Street, the houses all looked dark and quiet. He passed the playground of St Peter and Paul's red-bricked primary school but it was too early for any children to be out and about.

He saw the car without really noticing it but when it pulled out in front of him he tried to brake. To his intense surprise, the brakes didn't work. The last thing he remembered was hitting the pavement and the surge of pain that shot through him before he lapsed into unconsciousness.

Jimmy Flynn was also rushing to work but he had the comfort of the work's van. He was feeling cheerful, owing mainly to his impending date with the lovely Gemma who worked in the joinery office. After trying to wangle a date with her for ages, she had finally succumbed to his charms and he was taking her to the pictures tonight. Hopefully it would lead to more times together. He had been infatuated with her for months. She was in her twenties, just a couple of years younger than him. Small and slim, with jet-black hair and large brown eyes, she was a magnet for all the other joiners at the work but she had consented to go out with him. He couldn't believe his luck.

He was whistling when he turned the van onto Harcourt Street and saw Peter lying on the road with the twisted bike beside him. His good mood vanished as he rammed on the brakes and ran out. 'Peter, what happened?'

Peter let out a yelp of pain. 'A car... My brakes didn't work.' He then lapsed back into silence.

Jimmy rushed into the joinery yard and thankfully the office light was on. Gemma, who lived in Strathmore Avenue, must have come into work from the other end of the street and hadn't seen Peter. Michael was out of breath when he pushed the door open. 'Gemma, phone for an ambulance and a doctor. Peter's had an accident.'

Gemma quickly dialled 999. By now, Jack Cooke, the boss, had arrived and the two men went back to the scene where Peter still lay unconscious. Jimmy went to lift him but Jack Cooke said, 'Leave him where he is. Let the ambulance men deal with him because he might have internal injuries that could be fatal if he's moved.'

The two men knelt down and Jack put his overcoat over the inert body. Jimmy could hardly speak for shock. 'He said it was a car and that his brakes didn't work.'

Jack gave him a queer look. 'He spoke to you?'

Jimmy nodded. 'Just for a minute, then he became quiet again.'

By then, the rest of the workforce had arrived and pedestrians were also out on the street. They stood in a silent bunch until the siren from the ambulance was heard. A doctor had also arrived in his car and he knelt down on the wet road and quickly examined the patient. He then spoke to the ambulance men and Peter was gently lifted onto a stretcher and whisked away.

Jack Cooke took charge of the situation. 'Right then, Peter is in the best of care at the infirmary, so we'll all get back to work. I'll keep you informed of his progress when I get it.'

Jimmy went to go into the factory but Jack said. 'I think you should go and see Peter's wife and family, then go with them to the infirmary. Keep me in the picture.' He picked up Peter's bike and carried it back to the yard.

Jimmy was just getting into the van when he heard Jack call out. 'Jimmy, come and see this!'

Jimmy went towards him and they both looked at the mangled bike, which had had its brakes neatly cut. Jack looked wordlessly at this for a moment, then said, 'I think I'll call the police. This looks like someone wanted Peter to have this accident.'

Jimmy nodded. He couldn't get his head around this deliberate sabotage. Everyone liked Peter. He had his problems like everyone else, but this was something serious and not some practical prank.

'And Jimmy,' warned Jack, 'I don't think Peter is going to make it but don't tell his wife that.'

As he drove towards Alexander Street, Jimmy was crying, but he had to put on a face for poor Donna and the girls.

Janey answered the door. 'Dad's away to work, Jimmy, and Mum's getting ready to go to her work at the baker's shop.' But something in his face gave him away and she backed into the flat, her face white with fright. 'Muuuuum, Muuuum,' she wailed and Donna and Andrea rushed to the door, fearful that she had maybe fallen down the stairs.

Jimmy held Donna's hand when he told her. 'I'll take you all up to the infirmary in the van.'

It was a terrible journey. Donna wanted to know what had happened and he told her about the accident, keeping back the information of the cut brakes and the fact that Peter might be dead. He parked in the car park near the front door and they all hurried into the accident and emergency department. There was no sign of Peter or the ambulance but when Donna asked the nurse on the enquiry desk, she quickly summoned the doctor. He took Donna into a small side room while Jimmy sat with the girls. Janey was sobbing loudly while Andrea was almost rigid with shock.

The doctor was sympathetic and quiet spoken. 'Your husband has had a very bad accident with his pushbike. He has two fractured legs, a dislocated shoulder and broken wrist and a bad cut to his head. He may also have some internal injuries. He is in the theatre now and we won't have any news till the operation is done. You can wait here if you like but you won't be able to see him till later. I suggest your two girls go home with you and you all come back in the afternoon.

We should have news of any other injuries then and his broken bones will be set.'

Donna was distraught when she came out and Jimmy steeled himself for the news of his friend's death but when he heard he was still alive he let out a huge deep breath. 'The doctors will do their best for him. Let me take you all home and we'll come back in the afternoon.'

Donna said, 'What about your work?'

'Jack said to take all the time off I needed to see you and look after you all.'

When they got back to the flat, he made them all some hot sweet tea and spread some bread with strawberry jam, but no one felt like eating. Donna sounded weary. 'I better nip down to the baker's and let them know why I'm not in and maybe they'll phone Andrea's work to tell them.'

Janey had stopped crying but her face was all blotchy and her eyes red and swollen. Jimmy had never felt so inadequate in his life and he was glad when Donna appeared. 'One of the girls in the shop said they would phone D.M. Browns and let them know, Andrea.'

Jack had said to let him know about Peter's injuries so he said, 'Donna, I have to go back and report to Jack but I'll be back in an hour.' The three white, pinched, haunted faces looked at him numbly but Donna nodded.

When he got back to the yard, Jack was in

conversation with a man in a grey overcoat and a young looking policeman. 'Jimmy, this is DS Johns and Constable Williams.'

'So you found Mr Walsh?'

Jimmy said he had. 'I came round the corner and he was lying on the road, with the bike wheel all twisted.'

DS Johns said it would be better if they moved into the office. 'Was he conscious when you found him and did he say what had happened?'

'Yes, he came to briefly and said it was a car and his brakes didn't work.'

Charlie Johns looked out of the office window. A few of the joiners were moving about in silence. The usual banter was gone. 'Could he have made any enemies here?'

Jack said no, he had loyal and hard-working employees who all got on with one another. The detective decided to take this statement as gospel, at least for now. He looked at Jimmy. 'Are you friendly with him?'

'Yes, I am. Even although he was older than me, we got on great.'

'Do you know if he had fallen out with anyone, maybe over a gambling debt or something similar?'

In spite of his distress, Jimmy laughed. 'Peter didn't gamble. For one thing, he never had the money to spare. His one addiction was his cigarettes but he was even finding these hard justify with the rising prices. He was saying just last week that he was giving up...' He stumbled to a halt, unable to carry on.

'Where would he keep his bike when he was working?'

Jack pointed to a corner of the yard where there were four bikes lined up. 'Just over there.'

'Mr Flynn, do you know where he kept it at home?'

'Yes, there is a small shed in the back-green, but sometimes he kept it on the landing by his door.'

The two policemen thanked them. 'Mrs Walsh lives at 28 Alexander Street, is that right?'

'Yes,' said Jack, 'But do you mind if Mr Flynn goes along? He promised the family he would take them back up to the infirmary this afternoon.'

Charlie Johns said that was all right with him. Jimmy managed to reach Alexander Street first but just by a few minutes. 'Donna, there are two policemen coming to see you about Peter's accident. They want to ask some questions.'

Donna was puzzled. 'But what do the police want to know if it's just been a road accident? I don't understand.'

He took half a crown from his pocket. 'Andrea and Janey, go down to the shop and get some biscuits in case the police want a cup of tea.' Janey jumped up but Andrea gave him a strange look. However, she did as she was told.

After they left, Jimmy said, 'Donna, someone cut Peter's brakes on his bike. It was a deliberate thing to do and the police want to find the culprit.'

Donna was shocked and she had to sit down. 'I don't understand, Jimmy. Who would want to hurt Peter?'

'I don't know but tell the police everything. Any little incident that happened might have a bearing on this.'

There was a loud knock on the door and the police, Andrea and Janey all arrived together. The officers didn't want tea but they sat by the unlit fire. 'Mrs Walsh, have you any idea why someone would harm your husband?'

She shook her head and started to cry. Constable Williams shifted slightly in his chair. This was one part of the job he didn't like; having to ask questions when someone was anguished and distressed. 'Did he have any worries, or was he maybe frightened of someone?'

Donna shook her head again. 'Oh, we had the usual worries about money and bills coming in, but there wasn't anything unusual in that.'

'Have there been any strangers or has he mentioned meeting with someone he doesn't know well?'

Donna said no, life was just the same as it always was. Then Janey piped up, 'What about that woman who came to see Dad?'

Donna said, 'But surely a woman didn't do this.'

'Do you know who it was who came to see him?'

'Yes, she left a card.' She went over to the sideboard and brought back the small card. For a moment, Charlie Johns thought he would explode. However, when he spoke he sounded quite normal. 'This Molly McQueen, what did she want?' It was now the turn of the constable to look up from his notebook with a sharp look of surprise.

'She said she was looking into the disappearance of a girl called Etta Barton who vanished from home in 1930 and has never been found. Peter once went out with Etta when they were teenagers, but it only lasted a few weeks. Peter hasn't seen or heard from her in all these years so he couldn't help. Still, we were pleased to help her as she was very pleasant and sympathetic.'

Charlie Johns said, 'I think that's all for now, Mrs Walsh. We'll have to speak to your husband but not until tomorrow and see if he's able to help us.'

When they reached the car, the constable asked, 'Is this the same Molly McQueen who was involved in that strange case last year?'

Charlie Johns looked grim and very annoyed. 'Yes, it is. What has she got into this time? That woman seems to invite trouble. Right, let's go and pay her a visit.'

Back in the house, Donna and the girls got ready to go back to the infirmary. 'I've got the van outside, Donna,' said Jimmy, going ahead of them and hurrying down the stairs.

Although they looked calm, it was clear that tears weren't far away. Jimmy drove carefully and they reached the infirmary just as the clock was striking twelve. They sat in a corridor for what seemed ages but only an hour had passed. Every time a nurse or a doctor appeared, they raised hopeful faces to the passing staff, but no one came to tell them how Peter was.

Just before two o'clock, the doctor arrived and took Donna and Jimmy into his office. 'The good news is that your husband has no internal injuries but he has two bad leg fractures, a broken wrist and dislocated shoulder, plus a deep cut on his head which we've stitched up. He's sleeping now and I expect he'll be very sore when he wakes up, but we'll control his pain.'

Donna cried out, 'I thought he was dead.'

'No, he isn't. He's a strong young man and he'll take a while to recover, but he'll be fine.'

'Can we see him?'

'Well, just for a few moments.'

Donna, Jimmy and the two girls crept silently into a side room. Peter was lying pale and still on the crisp white bed, wrapped in white bandages, his legs and arm in a stookie. Donna gave a small cry and sat down beside him, taking his good hand in hers. 'Oh Peter, who did this to you?'

Peter was lying motionless and sound asleep. The doctor did say that the anaesthetic hadn't worn off yet, so they sat for a few moments more. The girls said a quick cheerio to their dad while Donna promised to come later that night.

When they were outside, Jimmy said, 'You haven't had anything to eat. Put the kettle on, Donna and I'll go and get some pies from the baker's.'

He arrived back a few minutes later, carrying a bag with four hot pies, and in spite of saying they weren't hungry, the three women ate every crumb and drank the hot tea. 'I have to get back to work, Donna, but I'll come back tonight and take you all up to the ward.'

Donna was flustered. 'We'll manage, Jimmy. I don't want to put you out.'

But he was adamant. Later, as he drove away, he suddenly remembered Gemma and his date with her that night. Hopefully she would understand and go out with him another time. When he reached the yard, Jack Cooke came out. His face was grey with worry. 'What's the news?' he asked.

Jimmy told him and Jack's face lost its worried frown. 'That's good news. I really thought he was dead when I saw him lying there.'

Jimmy mentioned the policemen and Jack said the same thing as Donna. 'Who could have done this to Peter? I mean he's an inoffensive, hard-working guy. A man that I would say doesn't have an enemy in the world.'

Although Jimmy stayed silent, he remembered the dent in the van. Peter hadn't told him how it happened and he wondered if he had got himself mixed up in something.

Later, when they all went back to see him, he was still sleepy but he was able to whisper, 'I think I've been dropped from the top of the Law Hill.'

Now that they knew he was going to be all right, the girls were amused to see his dark hair had been shaved to let the doctor put five stitches in his head wound. 'You've got a baldie spot, Dad,' said Janey.

No one mentioned the sabotaged brakes.

35

Molly had two places to go to this morning. Her first call was Vera's house. Vera was still in bed but she got up to answer the door. The room was untidy and last night's dishes were still in the basin. The room was cold, so Molly began raking the ashes from the fire while Vera gazed at her with a blank look. Once the fire was lit, Molly said, 'Are you getting dressed, Vera?'

She shook her head. 'What's the use of getting dressed when I'm afraid to go outside?'

'We'll both go out and get some food in the house for you.' Molly looked in the cupboard but it was almost bare. The bread looked like it had shrivelled up and died, while the milk lay congealed in the bottle.

Vera eventually made the first move to put on her clothes. Molly was dismayed to see her jumper had a large stain on the front. She leant over and took it from her. 'Where do you keep your jumpers, Vera?'

She pointed listlessly to a chest of drawers in the bedroom. Molly found a reasonably clean one and handed it to her. Molly couldn't help comparing the Vera who had initially hired her to this pathetic, unkempt woman who now sat opposite her. 'Put your coat on and we'll go out to the grocer's shop across the road and get some fresh milk and bread.'

Vera was like a small child. She stood up and put on her coat and waited until Molly found the message bag. Once outside, she walked by Molly's side and she stayed silent in the shop, much to the owner's curiosity. Filling the bag with some essentials, Molly paid for them from her own purse while Vera gazed into space. The shop owner could contain her curiosity no longer. 'Are you feeling ill, Mrs Barton?' Vera simply smiled and walked out of the shop, followed by Molly.

Back in the house, where it was much warmer now that the fire was lit, Molly asked her, 'I hate to question you when you're not feeling well, Vera, but there's something I should have asked you earlier. What was your maiden name?'

Vera seemed to come out of the stupor and looked surprised. 'My maiden name? What's that got to do with anything?'

'Well then, what's the surname of your sister Robina?'

Vera looked really annoyed and Molly realised she must have taken a sleeping pill last night that made her act like a zombie. 'Look, Vera, I wouldn't ask if it wasn't important.'

The annoyance disappeared and was replaced by a stubborn, sulky look. 'I don't like to talk about my sister. I haven't seen her in years and good riddance.'

Molly lost her temper. 'Fine, but just tell me her surname.'

'If you must know, it's Price, Robina Price.'

'Thank you. Now, Vera, I have to go. Will you promise me you'll cook some breakfast for yourself? I'll come back later, so don't go out on your own.'

Molly hurried down to catch the Kirkton bus. She had to see Frances Flynn immediately. The bus seemed to take forever as it drew into every stop but soon she was making her way to the house.

Frances opened the door right away. 'Oh, I was expecting my son Jimmy. His boss phoned the shop next door to tell me one of his colleagues had been injured in an accident and he would be home late.'

Molly wasn't listening to this story. She wanted Miss Price's address. Frances was still going on. 'Poor Peter Walsh, he fell off his bike at work this morning and he's badly injured.'

Molly stopped dead. 'Did you say Peter Walsh?'

'Yes, I did.'

Molly had to sit down on one of the new chairs in the living room. This was terrible news. She was hoping it was a simple accident but a small voice in her head said it wasn't. What was going on, she wondered. Who was doing all this? She had taken a simple case of a disappearance and now people were being hurt.

Molly realised there was something different about the room. She sniffed. There was a fresh smell of polish and no overflowing ashtrays. Frances noticed this. 'I've given up the cigarettes. It's a mug's game wasting money on blowing smoke into the air.'

Another omission was Maggie. Molly asked after her. 'She's away back to school. Her tonsillitis has cleared up.'

Molly came straight to the point. 'Have you got the address of your ex-neighbour, Miss Price?'

Frances stared at her. 'Miss Price? You mean Vincent?'

'Yes, I know that's what your husband calls her but I think her name is Robina and she's Vera Barton's sister.'

Frances laughed out loud. 'Don't be daft. Miss Price was my teacher at primary school. I hated her as she would hit you if you did anything wrong.'

'What school did you go to?'

'I went to convent school in Ireland. My parents came over to Dundee when I was twelve. One day I bumped into Miss Price. She had recently moved here and I invited her to come and visit as I thought she was a lonely person.'

'So when you came here to live it would be about 1926?'

'No, early 1927.'

'Was Miss Price still at the school when you left?'

'Yes, she was and to be frank I was glad to be away from her but I find her company all right now.'

'Do you have her address, Frances?'

'Yes, she lives at 10 Elizabeth Street.'

Molly thanked her and said, 'Good luck with your no smoking regime.' She was going to mention her thanks to Maggie but thought it better to leave it, just in case Maggie hadn't told her mother about her visits to Molly.

As she sat on the bus, Molly tried to make sense of Frances' statement. If Robina had been in Ireland in 1927 then she must have come over to see her sister in 1929. That's if Anita's memory was correct. What did she do then? Stay here or go back to the convent school? Was she still in Dundee when Dave Barton had his accident, and could Etta have gone to see her aunt and maybe travelled with her back to Ireland? That would make sense and explain why Etta had disappeared so suddenly. Had she heard about her father's death and gone to see Robina and her aunt had suggested moving away with her?

When she got off the bus, she made her way to Elizabeth Street, a narrow street of houses that lay between Ann Street and Alexander Street. Number ten was on the left and the houses looked different from their neighbours, mainly because they had narrow gardens between the street and the closes.

Molly scanned each door and found Robina's flat on the first floor. She knocked but everything was quiet. No one answered, so she knocked again. Still no answer, so she had no choice but to walk away. Before she did, she took a card from her bag and wrote that she would like a few words with Miss Price and that she would be in the office. A single-decker bus turned the corner and stopped outside the close but no one got off or on. She looked up at the windows but most had net curtains screening the view and there wasn't the slightest twitching from any of them. Only once she had turned to head back did the curtain on the first floor move but by that point Molly was already walking away.

She decided to go see Vera again before going to the office. Molly was dismayed to see Vera hadn't washed the dishes or made herself something to eat. 'Vera, did you know your sister lived in Ireland and taught at a convent school there?'

Vera didn't seem interested and Molly

wondered how many sleeping pills she had taken. 'Vera, did you hear what I said?'

Vera waved her hands in front of her face. 'Oh, just go away.'

Molly was alarmed by this attitude. 'Yes, Vera, I'm leaving and the case is closed as far as I'm concerned. I'm sorry I didn't find your daughter but I'm now going to go to the police about the attempts on not only your life but on another witness's as well.'

Vera looked at her. 'Another witness? What witness?'

'A man called Peter Walsh, who went out briefly with your daughter before she disappeared.'

Vera laughed harshly. 'Etta never had any boyfriends. I would have known.'

'Well, she went out with this lad when they were both sixteen. It only lasted a few weeks before he said he had another girlfriend and he says she was devastated by this.'

Before leaving, Molly asked her, 'What's the name of your doctor, Vera?'

'Doctor James. He has a surgery in Garland Place.'

'Well, please get him to come and see you, as you need help with all this trauma.'

Vera nodded but, again, she didn't seem interested.

Molly made a detour to Garland Place to see Doctor James. Luckily he wasn't busy, so she was able to have a quick word with him and tell him her worries over Vera. He said he would make a house call that afternoon.

Feeling slightly better, she finally reached the office and was taken aback to see DS Johns sitting in the visitor's chair. Jean was quietly answering the phone and trying hard not to notice him. Mary was just leaving. She had also been waiting to see Molly about a new assignment but she recognised him from last year and said, 'I'll come and see you tonight, Molly.'

DS Johns stood up when he saw her and said, 'I'd like a word with you, Miss McQueen. Somewhere private if that's possible.'

Jean looked alarmed but stayed silent. 'Come upstairs to the flat.' Although she sounded confident, her heart was beating wildly. She hadn't seen him since last year and the sight of his official manner brought it all back to her.

His gaze took in the entire room. 'You've done it up great,' he said.

Molly said she liked living here. 'It's strange that you should be here,' she said. 'I was just going to contact the police about this job I've taken on. It's turned very dangerous and I don't know what to do about it.'

'I think you should start at the beginning, Miss McQueen.' Charlie Johns sat back in his chair and made himself comfortable. He was expecting to be here for some time. 'I've just come back from the infirmary where a Peter Walsh has just come through a very serious operation after a particularly nasty accident.'

Molly butted in. 'Yes, I heard.'

Charlie looked surprised. 'How did you hear about it? It only happened this morning.'

Molly explained her connection with Frances and her son Jimmy. 'I went to see Frances Flynn about another person. I wanted her address and Frances told me about Peter. How is he?'

'Well, he'll live but I expect the person who cut the brakes on his bike was hoping he wouldn't.'

'Cut the brakes?' Molly was shocked. She had hoped that it had been an accident and not this premeditated act. 'Vera Barton, the woman who hired me to try and find her daughter, has also had two accidents and I've had my father's car broken into and my notebooks stolen.'

Molly told him all she had found out so far. 'I'll type up my notes along with the names and addresses and if you wait for half an hour I'll give them to you. Or maybe you would like to come back later?'

Charlie looked at her as she went over to the desk where the portable typewriter was sitting. Although he was upset that she hadn't come to the police with this case earlier – she could have got herself hurt – he was glad that they had been thrown together again. She was a good-looking woman with great stamina. He had admired her last year after her traumatic time and he noticed she had got on with her life and even turned the two dingy rooms into a lovely flat. Now it looked like she had got embroiled in another nasty incident and he hoped he could solve it before there were any more accidents. 'Can I make a cup of tea, Miss McQueen?'

'Oh, for goodness sakes, call me Molly, and you can make me one as well.'

'All right, but only if you call me Charlie.' He pottered around the tiny kitchen area and soon found all he needed, even a tin of biscuits. He carried the tray over to the coffee table. 'Tea's ready when you are,' he said.

Molly joined him with a thick bunch of typed paper, which she had put in a cardboard folder. She had even put a sticky label on the front, which stated it was a report on Etta Barton. 'You should be in the police force, Molly. I've never known anyone to type as quickly as you,' he said, while eating a custard cream biscuit.

He laughed when she winked and said, 'That's why I've got a secretarial agency with my name above the door.' She became serious. 'As I told you, this case began in 1930 and all the people I've interviewed have been great in telling me their thoughts on Etta, but no one has any idea where she went. But now with these accidents it seems I've uncovered something but I've no idea what. Maybe one of the people I talked to has mentioned it to someone else, and then they passed it on to someone else. It's endless.' She smiled at him. 'I'm glad to be finished with it, to tell you the truth, and I hope you get to the bottom of it.'

Charlie thought she'd got a lovely smile. 'I hope so and we'll do our best.'

They sat with their tea and Molly asked. 'How are Tam and Rover?' Molly had met them last year.

'Tam's fine and Rover still likes his walks every day. I go and see him every two or three weeks and have a drink with him on my day off. He loves his rum and a chat. He's a marvellous old man and, of course, Rover has to have his dog biscuit when I visit them. His neighbour next door, Ina, is still very good to him and he says she's like the daughter he never had.'

'I'm glad. Give him my regards when you meet him again. Now, back to this case. I couldn't get an answer from Robina Price's address but I'm sure she was in. She's the only one I haven't talked to and if I had to suspect anyone, I would say it was her.'

Charlie stood up reluctantly. He was enjoying his chat with Molly. He was amused by this because earlier today, he had been furious when he knew she was involved with another mystery, and he had intended to give her a good talking to and now, here he was, having a cosy chat and tea, not to mention on first name terms.

'One more thing, Charlie. Can you keep an eye on Vera Barton, please? I'm really worried this person will attack her again and maybe succeed next time.'

He promised he would. 'I think now that the police are involved, this person might be frightened to carry on. It's one thing dealing with two women and a man who doesn't know why this has happened to him, but another thing when the police force is involved.'

As they walked down the stairs together, Molly asked him, 'Will you keep in touch with me over this?'

Charlie, who had been wondering how to see her again, said, 'I'll do that and if you give me a card, I'll phone, just to make sure you are all right.'

As he left, Jean raised her eyebrows, a question forming on her lips. 'He'll phone you?' Molly felt her face turning red and she bolted up the stairs with Jean's laughter following her.

Mary turned up after work. Molly was

pleased to see her as she had lost touch with the staff because of this case, but she knew Jean was capable of dealing with the day-to-day running of the business, at least for a short time. Mary was apologetic. 'I need to have next Monday off, Molly. My uncle has died and we are going to the funeral. I'll still be in Watt's office until the end of that week and I'm not sure if you'll have a replacement for me. I did ask Jean, but she said to talk to you.'

Molly went and looked at the work's roster. 'I see Edna is still at Albert's Stores but she finishes at the end of next week.' She laughed. 'Providing Nancy gets over her Asian flu and doesn't fall foul of the dreaded Scottish cold. That girl is a young hypochondriac but it gives us some work, so we'll not wish her a speedy recovery. Still, I'll be able to take over that day for you, Mary, and I'll give you a letter to take to the office to explain everything.'

'That's fine, then,' said Mary. 'Mum wasn't sure if I could but she'll be pleased that we can all go as a family. He is my dad's oldest brother.'

'How are you getting on with this job? Is it a pleasant place to work?' Molly didn't want to keep Mary from getting home but she was glad of the company as she didn't relish another night on her own.

'Yes, I enjoy the work. It's a small office but

the two women who work there are very friendly. Their colleague has been off with the flu, but I'm not sure if it's the Asian kind.' They both laughed. Mary seemed to be in chatty mood. 'I got a letter from Phil yesterday. He says the square-bashing is tough and the sergeant keeps shouting at them, but he hopes to get home on leave soon.'

'Do you miss him, Mary?' asked Molly. She had heard loads of stories of sweethearts, wives and husbands being parted by National Service commitments and how tough it was on them.

'He's just a friend but I like him. We have a laugh together when we go to the pictures, but to be honest, Molly, I'm not sure I could cope with all the attention he gets from other girls. I'm not a jealous person, at least I don't think I am, but I could easily feel like that if we were serious about one another.'

'Well, there's no need to be serious yet. Just enjoy his company when he comes home and then see how it goes.'

'That's what I thought I would do.'

'Will you stay for something to eat, Mary? I could easily rustle up a simple meal.'

Mary was apologetic. 'I'd love to stay but Mum always has my tea ready when I get home.'

After she left, the flat was quiet and Molly wondered how she would spend the long evening alone. She was glad to be back in the middle of running the agency and tomorrow she would see Maisie, Alice and Deanna and find out how their jobs were coming along. She would also make a point of seeing Edna, and although she wouldn't ask about John Knox, she hoped it had all been sorted out.

It had only been a month since she had met Vera but it seemed much longer. However, she was glad it was all over, at least for her. She wished she could pop in and see Marigold but it was getting a bit late to catch the Fifie and then get home again, so she settled down with the evening paper and a cup of cocoa before going to bed early with her mystery novel. Before falling asleep, she thought about Peter Walsh and hoped that he would soon be out of hospital.

36

Dolly Pirie was annoyed. Edna had never mentioned John any of the times she had come to Dolly's house for a bowl of soup at dinner time. She thought Edna was her friend but she had stayed silent about the man. Well, she thought, if Edna can't speak about him, then I'm not going to say anything.

Snappy Sal had invited herself in for a cup of tea and she sat while Dolly took the cups out of the cupboard. 'I hear Nancy has recovered from the Asian flu but has now come down with pneumonia. I suppose Edna will be kept on for another couple of weeks,' said Sal, who was a bit jealous of Dolly's friendship with Edna.

Dolly sniffed. 'I suppose so.'

Sal's antennae quivered. Did she sense a split in the friendship? If so, she was delighted; like a lot of lonely elderly women, Sal liked nothing better than a good gossip – or even better, a bit of drama or scandal – to bring a bit of colour to her dull life. 'I think Edna's not looking well, what do you think, Dolly?'

Once again, the sniff. 'I've never noticed.'

Sal could hardly conceal her pleasure. Yes, there was a definite cooling of the friendship, but what had brought this all about, she wondered. When Dolly began to pour the tea, Sal tried to bring the subject back to Edna. 'I really thought she would get together with Eddie but I hear he's now going out with a girl from his shop. I wonder what Edna thinks about that? I bet she feels rejected.'

Dolly realised that Sal was just fishing for information and although she felt annoyed with Edna, she wasn't going to indulge in any backhanded gossip with Mrs Little. She changed the subject. 'How is that sore leg you had last week? Is it any better?'

'It is and it's not,' explained Sal. 'I can hardly sleep some nights with the pain, but then during the day it seems to get better. I'm really fed up with it, Dolly.' She quickly drank her tea and made a quick exit. 'I almost forgot, I have to buy some tea from the shop. I've only a couple of spoonfuls left in the caddy.'

Dolly knew she was only rushing out to the shop to check on Edna. Her pleasure would be brimming over if she could catch Edna with tears in her eyes or a deep mournful look on her face. But Dolly knew Edna wasn't like that. She would keep any hurt or misery hidden, and that's why she had never mentioned John. She decided to go to the shop as well. She didn't trust Sal not to come out with something hurtful or stupid.

When she got there, Sal was trying to strike up a conversation with Edna and Dolly could see Edna wasn't pleased. 'That's a quarter-pound of tea, Mrs Little. Is there anything else?'

'Now, let me see.' She glanced around the shop then said, 'No, I think that's all I need. Will you be going up to see Dolly at dinner time?' Edna said she probably would. 'It's just that I got the impression she was annoyed at you for some reason, Edna.'

Edna was amazed. In spite of herself she said, 'Why would Dolly be annoyed at me, Mrs Little?'

Sal gave an exaggerated shrug. 'Beats me, but that's what I thought.'

Sal saw Dolly and said, 'Here she is. She'll tell you herself what's bothering her.'

Dolly ignored her and told Edna she would see her at dinner time. Edna couldn't think what she had done to annoy Dolly but no doubt she would find out later. Meanwhile, Sal ventured forth from the shop with her bag of tea and a smile on her face.

Albert was watching while this exchange was going on and he said to Edna, 'Never mind Snappy Sal. She likes making mischief.'

Edna was glad when it was time for her dinner break and she hurried up to see Dolly. She was stirring a big pan of broth and the table was set for two but before she sat down, Edna asked, 'Have I said something to annoy you, Dolly?'

Dolly sat down beside her. 'No, of course not, Edna, and as I've told myself, it's your own business and nothing to do with me.'

Edna was puzzled. 'What's my own business?'

'Well, I thought you might have mentioned John.'

Edna had to compose herself for a minute. 'I didn't mention him because I haven't seen him for over two weeks. He's seemingly engaged to his sister-in-law and doesn't want to see me again.'

Dolly was surprised. 'What?' Edna repeated the story. Dolly said, 'I saw him in the infirmary a couple of nights ago; he's in the men's surgical ward. There was a blonde woman and another man visiting him and I just thought, as you never mentioned he was ill, you didn't want me to know.'

'John's in the men's ward? I didn't know that.' Edna was shocked that Sonia couldn't even drop her a line about him. She quickly put Dolly in the picture and she told her how unhappy she was over the whole thing. 'I must get up to visit him. Are there visiting hours tomorrow?'

'Yes, in the afternoon.'

'How did you see him, Dolly?'

'My cousin's husband is in the same ward and I recognised John, although he didn't see me.'

Edna was so worried she ate her soup without tasting it and was glad to get back to the shop. When she got home, she told her mother what Dolly had said and Irene said that Sonia was a wicked piece of goods.

Saturday morning seemed to drag. Edna took Billy to the barber for a haircut, then into the town to let him buy a toy from Woolworth's. Then, in the afternoon, she set off for the infirmary. There was a large queue and Edna joined the end of it. It seemed to take forever to move but once it did, she was soon heading for the ward. A young nurse sat at the entrance to the ward, a small table with visiting cards in front of her. Edna approached her. 'I've come to visit Mr John Knox.'

The nurse glanced at the cards and said, 'Mr Knox has got his two visitors. You'll have to wait downstairs in the waiting room for one of them to come out and then you can go in.'

'Is it not possible to have a few moments with him?'

The nurse shook her head. 'No, sorry. We have a strict rule of two visitors for each patient.'

Edna was so disappointed she almost burst into tears but she had no choice but to go back to the waiting room. She waited until the visiting times were up but no one came out. Then she spotted Sonia and John's brother James. She jumped up but a wave of people suddenly appeared in the doorway and when she managed to get out, they were gone. Edna was furious with Sonia. She had told her John was away on business and all the time he was lying ill in the infirmary. She didn't feel like going home and telling her mother that she hadn't been allowed to see John. Irene was already furious with Sonia and this would make her worse. On the spur of the moment, she decided to go and see Dolly.

Dolly had been out but she was just opening her door when Edna arrived. Like Irene, she was angry when Edna told her the story. Then she had a brilliant idea. 'Tomorrow, I'll borrow my cousin's two cards and we can go in and see him. Then, when the nurse isn't looking, you can pop over and see John.'

Edna could have hugged her. 'That's a wonderful idea, Dolly. I'll meet you at the gate tomorrow afternoon.' As she went back home, she felt a lot happier. Even if John didn't want to see her, then at least she would have the chance to see him.

On the Sunday, she felt nervous. Dolly clutched the two cards in her hand and they made their way to the ward. 'What if the nurse recognises me from yesterday?'

Dolly said not to worry. 'It'll probably be a different nurse today.' And it was. The two women walked quickly over the highly polished floor to a bed situated halfway along the large ward. The man looked puzzled when he saw Edna but Dolly said she was her friend. As the two of them had a great conversation, Edna scanned the rest of the ward and it was Sonia she saw first. John's bed was only a few yards away. Then James arrived but, thankfully, he didn't look at the rest of the patients and their visitors. Edna could hardly breathe and she listened with half an ear to Dolly asking if the food was good.

'Aye, it's not bad but it's a bit tasteless, Dolly. Not like your homemade broth.'

A bell sounded and Dolly said that this was the first warning that visiting times were almost over. Sonia and James looked like they had taken root and Edna began to despair. Then, suddenly, Sonia and James stood up. 'We'll be back in to see you tomorrow, John,' she said in her breathless voice.

Edna turned away as they passed and the minute they were out of sight, she darted to John's bedside. He looked pale and listless but the minute he saw her, his eyes lit up. 'Edna, I've been waiting for you to visit but Sonia says you didn't want to come.'

As quickly as she could speak, she told him the whole story and he became angry, especially when she mentioned his engagement to Sonia. 'What happened, John?' asked Edna.

'Peritonitis. I'd been suffering severe pains for a while after you left and my appendix burst and that is why I'm in here.' He held her hand tightly. 'I'll be getting home in a few days and I want you to come to the house. I'm going to sort Sonia out once and for all. My fiancée, indeed! There's only one woman I'm in love with and it's you.'

The bell sounded for the second time and

Edna said, 'I have to go but let the office know when you're home and I'll be there to see you.' She gave him a quick kiss. 'Oh, I've missed you so much, John.' She hurried back to Dolly and they made their way out of the ward, but not before Edna turned and waved to John and he blew her a kiss.

When they reached the street outside, Dolly said, 'Well, are you happier now?'

Edna's eyes were shining. 'Oh, much happier, Dolly, and thank you so much for all your help. I wouldn't have been able to see him if it hadn't been for you.' Dolly looked pleased.

37

Charlie Johns was outside Robina Price's close. He gazed up at the windows before climbing the stairs and knocking loudly on the door. No one answered and he rapped even louder. He was getting fed up with this case. This was the second time he had been here and he was getting nowhere. He had left a note last time requesting a word with her. He went and knocked on the other door, which was immediately opened by an elderly woman. 'Yes, what do you want?'

'I'm trying to see Miss Price next door.

Do you know when she'll be in?'

'Oh, I don't think she's gone out as I haven't seen her waiting for the bus. I always look out of my window.' She smiled. 'It passes the time for me.'

He thanked her and went back to knock again. However, this time he looked through the letterbox and said, 'It's the police. Please open up.'

The door was yanked open and a fierce looking Miss Price glared at him while the next-door neighbour peered out. 'Can I come in or do you want to conduct the conversation on the doorstep?' he said.

She grudgingly told him to come in but she was still furious. 'How dare you shout out like that about being the police. I'm a respectable woman and I don't want all my neighbours to know my business.'

'Well, you should have answered the door. I did leave a note the last time I was here, saying I would be back today,' he answered. He wasn't in the best of humour himself.

'Well, you better come through to the kitchen.' Although she didn't say it, Charlie just knew she was thinking 'and don't expect a cup of tea'. The room was like a cell: white painted walls with no pictures and the furniture consisted of a simple wooden table and chair, plus a lovely desk that sat by the window. The floor was covered in brown linoleum and the only concession to comfort was a colourful crocheted blanket, which was placed on the back of the chair. A kettle stood on the cooker while the fire was barely visible, and it certainly didn't throw out any heat. He got straight to the point. 'I'm investigating two attacks on your sister, Mrs Vera Barton, and another on a Mr Peter Walsh, and I would like to know your movements on...' he glanced at his notes and mentioned the dates.

She sat quite relaxed with her hands in her lap. 'I can't tell you what I was doing on the first two dates but when you say this man was attacked, I was in church. I was probably in church on the other occasions as well.'

Charlie Johns didn't believe her. 'What, at ten o'clock at night? That's the first time your sister was almost run over.'

'If it was as late as that, then I would be in my bed. I go to bed every night at nine.'

'When you go to visit Mrs Frances Flynn, have you ever met her son Jimmy's work colleague, Peter Walsh?'

'No, I haven't. And I have to tell you that I have had no contact with my sister since 1929 when I went to see her and her husband. They didn't make me welcome then and I've never repeated the impulse to see her.'

'What about Etta, her daughter? Did you see her before she disappeared or did she come to see you after her father died in the accident?'

'No, she did not. I knew retribution would come to Vera and Dave for their sins.'

Charlie was shocked by this statement. 'Retribution? What do you mean by that?'

'They were having a child before marriage. That's a sin. I told my parents that at the time and, on my last visit, I told Vera and Dave as well.'

'What did they say to that?'

'They practically threw me out, but I was right. Retribution came to Dave Barton and it will come to my sister.'

Charlie felt he was being battered by dogma. 'When did you leave Ireland?'

'I came back a year ago but I plan to return.'

'And you've no idea where Etta might have gone?'

She shook her head and the dark eyes glared at him. 'No, I don't. She didn't come and see me then, nor have I seen or heard from her since my visit in 1929.'

'One other question, Miss Price. Do you have a job?'

'No, I don't. I've saved my money over the years and I live a very simple life. I go to see Frances now and again as I was her primary teacher when she was a child in Ireland, and I go to church. Apart from people I meet there, I have no other friends.'

Charlie couldn't think what else to ask her. He knew she would deny anything he said, so he stood up. 'I might have to come back, Miss Price, and be sure to answer the door if you're in.'

When he got outside, he was glad to be in the fresh air. In one way, she was a very intimidating woman but, on the other hand, he felt a bit of sympathy for her. She was a woman of strong religious principles, but to have her family throw her out must have hurt her a great deal. He wondered if there was more to the family feud than what she had told him.

His next visit was to the infirmary. The doctor had said he could have a word with Peter. The patient was in a small side room and he seemed to be a mass of white bandages. Whoever had cut his bike brakes had almost killed him and that's what they would be charged with ... when they caught them. As well as his injuries, Peter had a lot of bruises to his face where he had hit the edge of the pavement.

Charlie pulled over a chair and sat close to him. Peter was finding it hard to speak because of a cut lip, which had needed a couple of stitches. 'Mr Walsh, can you tell me what happened?'

Peter sounded tired but he said it was the medicine. 'I got on my bike, as usual, and cycled to work. I didn't use my brakes as I was going uphill and it wasn't until the car pulled out right in front of me that I put on the brakes but they didn't work.'

'Can you describe the car and the driver?'

'It was a small black car, like a Ford or something similar. I didn't see the number plate or the driver.'

'You know someone cut your brakes deliberately. Have you any idea who would do this? Do you have any enemies who might want to harm you?'

Peter shook his head. 'I did borrow some money this year from a friend but I've paid it all back, plus a bit of interest. Apart from that, I haven't done anything wrong or got on the bad side of anyone.'

Charlie was interested in the bike. 'Do you keep it locked up in that shed in the drying green?'

Peter tried to shake his head but it was too painful. 'I normally do, but sometimes I leave it on the landing by our door. There's room for it and it means I can get to work quickly if I sleep in. No one has ever touched it before.'

'Going back to Etta. You went out with her years ago, is that right?'

He groaned out loud. 'Bloody Etta. Everything seems to have gone wrong since that woman came to see me. I don't know how she found me because I used to be called Pedro in those days. I went out four times with Etta, mostly to the pictures, but we were both only sixteen. She was a very serious girl. I was serving my apprenticeship as a joiner and had little money, but I liked to have a laugh so we stopped seeing one another. I got the impression she had met someone else but I'm not sure.'

'All right, Peter, I'll let you get some sleep.' Charlie looked at the list of addresses that Molly had given him. His next call would be at 28 Alexander Street to see Mrs Walsh.

Donna had just finished her shift at the baker's shop and was sitting with a cup of tea and a cheese sandwich. The letter lay on the table. She was feeling depressed and she didn't want to break the news to Peter when she visited him later. Charlie apologised for interrupting her dinner break. 'That's all right,' she said, 'I'm finished for the day.'

'The morning of your husband's accident, did you see anyone hanging around?'

'No, I never went outside and neither did the girls. Sometimes Janey runs down to the shop, but she didn't go that morning. Peter had a quick cup of tea and toast, then grabbed his pieces and flask and hurried out. He was hoping to work some overtime so he had extra pieces with him.' She stopped and began to cry.

Charlie went to the sink and came back with a towel. 'I'm so sorry to have to question you, Mrs Walsh, but we think this person has attacked another person and damaged a car.'

Donna's eyes widened with fear. 'Will they try and hurt Peter again?'

'No, he's in the best place for getting better. Now, can you remember if Peter had his bike at the door or was it in the shed?'

Donna rubbed her eyes. 'I'm sorry, I can't remember. What did Peter say?'

'He thinks he went to the shed for it but he's not sure. I just wondered if you had seen it before he set off.'

'I wish I had, then maybe I'd have seen who cut the brakes,' she said angrily.

'Is there anything else you remember about that morning?'

She shook her head. 'No, it was just the same old routine. Peter and I had been rowing the day before about living in this tiny house with our girls getting bigger. I was depressed about not hearing from the Corporation housing department about a new house in Kirkton, and Peter said we would just have to wait our turn as hundreds of families are waiting for a key to a new house.' She held out the letter. 'Now we've been allocated a house, but I'll have to turn it down because we can't afford the bigger rent now that Peter's not working, and goodness only knows when he'll ever get back. I'm so relieved he's still with us, but it'll be a long time before he gets better from his injuries.'

Charlie felt so sorry for her. The room he was in was tiny and he couldn't imagine four people sharing it. 'Why don't you go to the housing department and tell them about the accident? Peter will get his sickness giro every week and could you maybe work a few more hours every day? It's none of my business, but if I were you, I would take the house and maybe everything will fall into place.'

She tried to smile but failed. 'Like maybe winning the football pools?'

Charlie shrugged. 'Well, someone's got to have eight draws on a Saturday.'

Donna said she would take his advice and hope for the best. It would certainly make a difference to their lives. The two girls would have a bedroom each and the bathroom and kitchen, complete with hot water, would be bliss.

As Charlie descended the narrow stairs, he hoped that life would get better for them. He went out to see the shed in the drying green. This was just a small patch of dried-up grass with a row of ramshackle wooden sheds along one wall. He inspected Peter's shed and saw that, even when locked, it would be easy to open the door and tamper with the bike.

Before going back to the police station, he decided to drop in to the agency to see if Molly was around and was pleasantly surprised to find she had just returned from a job. 'I can't wait long,' she said. 'I'm filling in for Mary. She's away to a funeral.'

Charlie said he wouldn't keep her for more than a few minutes. 'I've caught up with Miss Price and I'm not sure if she's involved. She said her sister and her husband threw her out when she visited in 1929 because of her religious views, and that she hadn't seen them or Etta since.'

Molly was doubtful. 'Vera did say that Robina had hit her with a cricket bat and that's what made their parents put her out of the house, but you would have to ask Vera about that.'

Charlie stayed silent. A cricket bat, now that's worse than a rant about sin, he thought.

38

Well, well, well, she thought, the police are now on the case. She knew she would have to be more careful now that Mr Plod was walking all over the evidence with his size-twelve boots. She had hoped to be more successful with her exploits but she was still pleased with the way things had turned out so far. So the nosy McQueen woman had handed all her findings over. The woman knew McQueen would never have solved the mystery, but it had given her some satisfaction to muddy the waters. Clever clogs McQueen had moved her car and had been devious in hiding it but never mind, maybe something else would happen to her to make her realise that she should keep her nose out of affairs that were no concern of hers. That thought pleased the woman. You reaped what you sowed.

39

Alice looked around her small living room with pleasure. She had just bought a new three-piece suite on hire purchase. She would manage the payments of five and six pence quite easily, especially as Molly had increased her hours. Maisie had left a few minutes earlier after coming in to view the new furniture. 'Good for you, Alice. You deserve something nice.'

Alice had also purchased a new winter coat. It was black with a velvet collar and she loved wearing it. When she saved up some more money, she would treat herself to some new clothes and shoes as well. Life was much better now that Victor had gone for good. He had come round one Saturday morning but she had kept him on the doorstep, ready to slam the door if he became aggressive.

His friend Sandy came around quite often and they sometimes went out together to the pictures or a sit down fish and chip meal in the tiny sitting room of the chip shop. However, Alice wasn't keen on another commitment and she told Sandy they were just friends and he had accepted that.

Victor hadn't joined the army as had been rumoured after he left and he was still working at the Caledon shipyard. His mother had taken him back, very reluctantly, if the story was true, but she had insisted on a fair amount of money for board and lodgings. He wasn't a happy man but the memory of his humiliating night in the boxing booth was slowly fading. As he had found out soon after the event, it was a seven-day wonder and most people had enough to worry about without dwelling on his failures. What his mother didn't know was that he was planning on asking Alice to take him back. He had tried before but she hadn't let him over the doorstep. Still, with his charm, he reckoned she wouldn't hold out forever. It was a great annoyance to him that she was the tenant of the house, otherwise it would have been her out in the cold and not him.

He still had the swaggering manner of

thinking he was better than most men. Sandy, who also worked in the shipyard, couldn't stand him now. Not after what he had done to his lovely wife. Victor met up with him one day at breaktime. 'I never see you now, Sandy. What about coming out for a few pints tonight?'

'Sorry, Victor, I'm doing something else tonight.'

Sandy had kept very quiet about seeing Alice as he didn't want Victor hassling her again and Victor didn't know a thing about it. If he had, he would have kept his plans to himself. 'Sandy, I'm thinking of giving Alice another chance at making a go of our marriage. In fact, I'm going round there tomorrow night and if I'm lucky, maybe she'll make my tea and ask me to stay.'

Sandy had almost choked on his tea. After work, he hurried around to see Alice as he felt he had to warn her. She was surprised to see him. 'Alice, Victor is coming round tomorrow night to see you. He wants you to take him back.'

Alice had to sit down, as she was frightened she might faint. 'I don't want anything to do with him, Sandy. What am I going to do?' The thought of sharing the same house with Victor filled her with revulsion.

'We were going to go out tomorrow night, so you won't be here when he comes.' He stopped, unsure how to carry on. Ever since he had started seeing her, he hadn't mentioned Victor because he wasn't sure how she still felt about him. He had heard how abused wives had taken their husbands back time after time, despite suffering the same treatment. 'Why don't you put in for a divorce and that way he can't touch you?'

Alice's face showed relief. 'I was hoping to do that but I don't know where to start. Do I need a solicitor and will it cost a lot of money?'

'Never mind the cost,' said Sandy. 'I want you to go and see a solicitor next week. Ask Miss McQueen to help you, she will know of someone.' He was also feeling a sense of relief that it looked like Alice had no feelings left for her husband.

Alice planned to see Molly at work the next day and ask her advice. Molly was organised and she would know where to send her. She arrived early for work the following morning. She had been doing some of Deanna's jobs because the play had started at the theatre and she needed time off for the Wednesday and Saturday matinees. Still, Alice didn't mind because it gave her extra money. Molly was in the office when she arrived. Alice was a bit shy about asking her boss for help but the thought of Victor worming his way back into her life gave her courage. 'Molly, can I ask a favour?' she said.

Molly looked surprised but said, 'Of

course, Alice. What can I do for you?'

Alice hesitated. She hated discussing her private life with anyone but she had no choice. 'I want to divorce my husband and I need a solicitor. Do you know anyone who'll help me?'

Molly was taken aback by the request but she had heard the stories of the husband's ill-treatment. 'Good for you, Alice. I know a firm of solicitors in Union Street who can help you. They're called Gilchrist, Gilchrist and Preston.' She wrote this down and handed the note to her. 'Do you want me to phone and make an appointment for you?'

Alice felt so grateful. 'Will you? That'll be a big help. I've never been to a legal office before and I'm scared.'

Molly felt so sorry for her. She was a lovely, hard-working woman who had had the misfortune of marrying a domineering bully. 'Alice, would you like me to come with you?'

Alice nodded. 'Would you? I'd be so grateful.'

Molly made the phone call and said, 'Mr Preston can see you at four thirty on Monday. Is that suitable for you, Alice?' She nodded and Molly made the appointment. 'That's the first step made, Alice, and I think you're making the right decision.' Alice said she thought so as well and she left for her first job of the day, the family with the badly behaved children.

Later that evening, Sandy arrived and they both went out to the pictures. Meanwhile, Victor was in a bad mood. His mother had asked for extra money because he had such a huge appetite and he had had a row with her. He was standing in the pub, nursing his sixth pint of beer and becoming angrier by the minute. He should still be living at home with his wife and she should be looking after him. The more he thought about it the angrier he became and by closing time he was like a smoking volcano of anger and self-pity.

He staggered to the flat at Arthurstone Terrace and hammered on the door. The window was in darkness and this fuelled his fury. So she was out gallivanting and not giving a toss about his needs. He gave the door a mighty kick but ended up with bruised toes for his trouble, so he used an empty milk bottle that was lying at the door to smash the window. Maisie was coming up the stairs at the time and she wondered what on earth was going on. She saw Victor aim another blow at the window. 'What do you think you're doing? I'm going to call the police.'

She set off down the stairs again but Victor staggered after her, shouting, 'What's it got to do with you, you old bat? I know you're Alice's mate, so tell her from me that I'll be back and I want to be admitted to my marital house or else she'll end up with a bashing that'll put her back in hospital.'

Maisie stood at the end of the close as he staggered away, hoping and praying that he wouldn't meet up with Alice and Sandy. But as it turned out, they had been warned of Victor's whereabouts and had stayed away. Alice was upset when she saw the two broken panes of glass in the window and she began to sweep up the debris that had landed on the coalbunker. Sandy was furious and Alice had to stop him going after Victor and sorting him out. 'I'll stay here with you tonight and tomorrow night, Alice, just in case he comes back. I'll sleep on your new settee and when you see the solicitor on Monday, mind and tell him about this and how scared you are of him.'

This was true because she was shaking with nerves. Maisie came in and said she had witnessed it but Alice mentioned the appointment and Maisie said it was the best thing she could do. 'That lad is a bully and a wife-beater. I just hope he gets his come-uppance,' she said.

But Victor didn't come back that weekend and at 4:30 p.m. on Monday, Alice found herself in the office of the solicitor, Mr Preston. She was surprised to see he was a young looking man with a fresh complexion and sandy coloured hair. He looked like he enjoyed being outdoors. Alice had imagined him to be about eighty with a wrinkled face, gnarled hands and a slow way of walking. Instead, he bounded up and pulled a chair over to his desk for her. 'Now, you want to discuss starting divorce proceedings, Mrs Charles?'

Alice said she was and she told him the entire story of her marriage to Victor, including the broken windows on Saturday night. He wrote everything down and said, 'The infirmary will have a record of you being admitted with injuries sustained in his attack on you?'

Alice said, 'Yes, it will. He has hit me lots of times but I didn't go the doctor. I just tried to live with it.'

'Well, it's a pity you hadn't looked for medical attention earlier, as the more evidence we have of his physical cruelty, the better it will be for your case. However, we seem to have enough to start the proceedings.' He asked for Victor's address and she gave it to him. 'We'll make another appointment for next week at the same time.' He stood up and Alice thanked him.

Molly was waiting in the outer office. She couldn't help thinking about the lottery of marriage. It could be heaven or hell depending on the person you chose to be your life's companion. Alice looked a bit happier now she had set things in motion and, although she knew it would take some time for it to be finalised, at least she had taken the first step.

40

Charlie Johns was having no more luck with this case than Molly had. He had interviewed all the people on Molly's list but their stories were exactly the same as they had told her. He had looked at the old case sheets in the police archives but although it had been properly investigated at the time, the problem was the girl had gone missing before anyone could question her about her whereabouts at the time of her father's death.

The police had asked around the shops in Arbroath that day but no one could remember seeing either her or her father. It wasn't very clear if she had even been there, as Mrs Pert had seen her on that evening in the close and walking to the house. Where had she gone after that? According to the testaments of the witnesses, she didn't have any friends apart from one work colleague and one neighbour she sometimes walked home with. She had gone out with Peter Walsh for three weeks but they had broken up some weeks before her disappearance. So why had he almost been killed? Charlie had delved into his background and found nothing. He had borrowed money from a colleague but he had repaid it weeks ago and the man had said there had been no animosity. 'He paid me back regularly every week until it was cleared,' he said.

At first, he had suspected that Etta had gone with Robina to Ireland but checks on the convent said Miss Price hadn't travelled anywhere on those dates. She had taken some leave the previous year but nothing in 1930. Charlie knew about the visit to Vera and Dave Barton in 1929, so it all checked out. Still, she was a strange woman, full of sermons about retribution and sin, and having to pay for human foibles.

Then there were the two attacks on Vera and he wondered if she had just fallen the first time and imagined the hand on her back the second. If people had been milling around the junction waiting to cross the road, then it could have been an innocent nudge. He thought that this would be another unsolved case and if it hadn't been for the attacks, he would have shelved it without a qualm. But something was nagging him and he couldn't figure out what it was.

He was almost back at the police station when he remembered – the elderly woman who befriended Vera after the bus incident.

Molly hadn't gone to see her and there had been no name or address except that she had gone in the direction of Victoria Road. He made a mental note to see Molly and ask her about this.

Back at the station, he sent for PC Williams. The young constable was having a tea break but he quickly went to the office with his notebook. 'Did you get anything from the house-to-house enquiries?' Charlie asked him.

'No, not very much. Most people still had their curtains shut due to the rotten weather. One woman,' he studied his notes, 'a Mrs Roberts from Byron Street, said she saw a small black car driven by an elderly woman heading towards Rockwell School. It was going quite fast and that made her wonder, as elderly drivers usually drive like snails. However, she didn't get the registration.'

Charlie's antennae twitched. This was another sighting of an elderly woman. It could be coincidence but he had to try and trace the elusive good Samaritan that had escorted Vera Barton back to the agency and had also been a confidante of Vera as they sat in the restaurant.

He also had another niggle that was hanging around on the edges of his brain – he hadn't yet visited Frances Flynn. 'I want you to drive me to see a witness, Constable.'

'Yes, sir,' said the policeman as he hurried

off to get the car. It took him some time to drive to Kirkton, as he hadn't been in the new estate before, but once he found the street, it was easy to get a parking space. Mrs Flynn was worried when the two men knocked at her door. 'Has something happened to Jimmy?'

'No,' said Charlie. 'I just want to ask you some questions about Etta Barton.' As they were shown into the pristine living room, Charlie asked her, 'Are you worried about your son Jimmy, Mrs Flynn?'

'No, not really, but this business with Peter has upset us all. It must be some maniac that's going around tampering with people's bikes, and it might be work vans next.'

'We're doing all we can to trace the culprit. That's why we're here. You told Miss McQueen that you were born in Ireland and left when you were twelve.'

Frances nodded. She suddenly felt the need of a cigarette, which was her normal crutch during stress.

'Miss Robina Price was your teacher at your school?'

'Yes, and a right rotten beggar she was then. I didn't like her but thankfully I only had her for a year and then we left to come to Dundee with my father's work.'

'But you still see Miss Price from time to time? She comes and visits you?'

Frances looked unhappy. 'Yes, she does,

but I don't particularly like her coming here. It was just that I met up with her in the street one day in the summer and she seemed to have changed. She sounded lonely, so I asked her to come and see me. We lived in Carnegie Street at the time and she said she had rented a flat in Elizabeth Street, which was only yards away from us. When we got this new house, I hoped she would stop but no, she comes every few weeks. But I have to say, she doesn't stay long.'

'You know she's Vera Barton's sister?'

'I do now, but I didn't know that when I first met her. Etta never mentioned she had an aunt living in Ireland. In fact, Etta hardly said anything about her life.'

'Well, that's all Mrs Flynn. Thank you for your time,' said Charlie.

When they were in the car, he asked the constable, 'What do you make of her?'

'I think she's telling the truth, sir, but she doesn't like this woman coming to see her and the family, and I wonder why.'

Charlie laughed. 'If you had someone who continually warned you about the sins of the flesh, well, that can hardly be a cheerful conversation.' He told him to drive to the Hilltown, as he wanted to see Vera.

Once again, it was easy to get a parking space and as they went through the close, a few of the curtains twitched. Vera was looking a bit better. She had stopped her sleeping pills and was feeling more like her old self. Charlie began by asking if she could remember anything about the woman who had helped her. 'Did she look familiar? Like someone you might have known at some time?'

Vera shook her head. 'I'm sorry, but I hardly took any notice of her. I was still shaking after my accident and then I was agitated in the café because I was looking for the writer of the letter. The woman's name was Bella, she was quite plump, her coat looked too tight for her and she wore a woollen hat and a scarf, but that's all I remember. She didn't take the hat or scarf off at the table but we were only there for a short time.'

'You were looking for the writer of the letter that got lost?'

Vera's face went red. 'I know there're some people who think I imagined the letter and that I fell in front of the bus by accident, but I didn't. I felt someone push me quite hard and the letter was in my pocket. It must have fallen out.'

'Please don't get upset, but I do have to ask you these questions. I've spoken to your sister Robina.'

Vera interrupted him. 'You managed to call her in Ireland?'

'No, she's living in Dundee and has been here for a year.'

'Well, she's never come to see me. I

thought she was still at her convent school in Ireland.'

'Did the woman mention where she stayed in Victoria Road? Try and think back to that day and see if anything made you suspicious of her.'

'Suspicious? Why would I think she looked suspicious? She was just an elderly woman who helped me.'

Charlie said, 'Yes, she more than likely was, but she was a witness to the accident and I'd like to talk to her. Maybe she saw someone acting strangely behind you.'

Vera looked doubtful. 'I don't think she did because she would have said. She paid for my cup of tea and then walked back with me to the agency as I had to see Molly. I mean Miss McQueen. She told me to be careful because someone had tried to kill me and that frightened me. Then she walked up the Wellgate steps and headed right, as if going further along Victoria Road. I'm sorry but I didn't really look at her even when she put her hand on my arm and was so sympathetic. You'll be thinking I'm odd that I didn't really look at her, but I think I was still suffering from shock and then searching for the letter made me more anxious than ever. To tell you the truth, I was wishing she would go away and leave me alone. I wanted to search further along the road but she said it had obviously blown away.'

The two men stood up to go and Vera went to the door with them. Charlie put his hand on her arm and said, 'Please be careful while we try and catch the person responsible for your attacks.'

Vera gasped. 'That's odd. I must have noticed it at the time but I didn't take it in. When she put her hand on my arm, she was wearing nail polish. Still, maybe she likes keeping her nails nice.'

When they were walking back to the car, Charlie said, 'We'll have to find this woman because she's becoming more dangerous by the minute. Miss McQueen seems to have stirred up a hornet's nest. She's spoken to all these witnesses and they've probably mentioned it to family and friends and it's alarmed someone. Someone who doesn't want the past brought up.'

41

Jimmy Flynn planned to go and see Peter that night. He was worried about the dent in the van and now the police were asking questions about Mrs Barton being run down by a vehicle on the same night Peter had borrowed it. Jimmy was furious that he had given him the keys but he had seemed desperate and he had felt sorry for him. He was an old friend of his mum and dad. They had been youngsters together away back in the early thirties and they had remained friends all these years. In fact, it had been Jimmy who had got him the job with the joinery when Peter's last employer gave up his business.

However, he didn't want to get a row from Mr Cooke. There was a strict rule about who drove the three vans and Peter wasn't one of the drivers.

He was busy at work when Mr Cooke came to see him. For a brief moment, Jimmy thought he had found out about the van but no, he wanted to go and see Peter as well. 'I thought of going up tonight, Jimmy, and I wondered if you would like to come with me?'

Actually, Jimmy would rather have gone alone but he couldn't turn down his boss's request. He smiled. 'That'll be great, Mr Cooke. I'll meet you at the infirmary door.'

It was a cold blustery night when the two men met up but the hospital was warm and bright inside. The nurses swished past with their starched aprons and Mr Cooke said, 'A lot of nice looking lasses work here, Jimmy. Don't you wish they were looking after you?'

Jimmy laughed. 'Yes, I do, Mr Cooke.'

'Call me, Jack,' he said. 'About Peter's

accident, do you think someone has a grudge against him? I mean, cutting someone's brakes is a nasty thing to do. He hasn't been seeing another woman on the sly and the husband has got wind of it?'

Jimmy said no, Peter was loyal to Donna and had been for over twenty years. 'I think this all started when that woman began looking into that missing girl case from years ago. Don't ask me why Peter got hurt, because I don't know, but I'm sure it has something to do with that case.' Although he sounded confident, he hoped that Peter hadn't got mixed up with something illegal.

By now they had reached the side room and Jack Cooke was shocked when he saw Peter lying with only his face showing. 'My God, lad, I knew you were badly injured but it is still horrifying to see you like this.'

Peter tried to smile but failed. 'I'm getting better, Mr Cooke, and hopefully I'll get home soon.'

Jimmy couldn't ask him about the van with his boss sitting across from him so he was reconciled to coming back in on another day. 'Jimmy tells me you've got the key for a new house in Kirkton, Peter.'

Peter looked annoyed. 'We've been waiting for ages for it and now we'll have to turn it down because we can't afford the dearer rent on sickness benefit. The wife and girls are heartbroken. Still, we'll maybe get another chance when I'm better.'

'Well, that's why I'm here. I want you to take it and I'll make up your wages to what you were earning before.'

This bit of kindness overwhelmed Peter. 'Oh, I can't let you pay out every week, Mr Cooke. It might be weeks before I can get back to work.'

'You let me worry about that, Peter. You can tell your wife and daughters to go ahead with the house and it'll be ready for you when you come out of here.'

'I can only say thank you very much. The two girls were dreaming of having a bedroom each and Andrea just loves the bathroom. You know what young girls are like.'

'When you do come back to work, you can travel with Jimmy in the van. I don't want any more cycling to work.'

During all this conversation, Jimmy had hardly said a word but he was really pleased for Peter's family. The bell sounded for the end of visiting time and Jack stood up. 'Hurry up and get well, lad,' he said as he made for the door.

Jimmy saw his chance. 'I'll see you in a minute, Jack. I just want a quick word with Peter.'

Peter gave him a puzzled look. 'The night I lent you the van, Peter, and you got that dent in it – did you knock someone down with it?'

Peter looked confused. Jimmy was going to explain when a nurse came bustling in. 'Visiting time is over.' She didn't exactly push him out but the threat was there. He had no option but to leave, which meant another sleepless night worrying over this.

42

Mary and Norma were going to Kidd's Rooms. She half expected Stan to be there but she felt guilty about her feelings for him, especially with Phil away in the army. She knew Phil was just a friend but it seemed so disloyal somehow to have these feelings for his friend.

Stan wasn't there when they reached the dance floor and she was disappointed. Norma had made loads of friends at this Saturday night dance and she was asked up to dance almost immediately. Suddenly, a voice at her shoulder said, 'Hullo, Mary.'

Mary was dismayed to see it was Linda but she seemed to be alone. She smiled. 'Linda, how are you?'

'I'm fine. Have you heard from Phil since he went into the army?'

Mary wasn't sure about answering this but she said, 'Yes, I have. He writes every week and he should get a leave soon.'

Linda looked wistful. 'I wish he would write to me and give me all his news.'

Looking at her sad face, it suddenly struck Mary that she was really in love with him, not just full of petty jealousy. 'I can give you his address if you would like to write to him, Linda.'

Her face brightened. 'That would be great.' Then she became downcast again. 'He'll not want to hear from me. He stopped seeing me, and after I thought we were getting on great.'

Mary made up her mind to tell the girl the truth. 'Linda, send him a letter with all the news of the sweetie factory, all the little bits of gossip. Keep it simple. You can say you are all missing him around the factory. If you keep it light and nothing dramatic like undying love, he will want to answer and then when he's due home, you can say how great it would be to meet up for a coffee and a chat about his army experiences. Make it a date for two and don't invite all your pals along. I think if you play a bit hard to get, he may be interested in starting a relationship again.'

Linda was puzzled. 'But what about you? Won't you be jealous?'

Mary thought, oh yes, I would, but only if I was in love with him, which I'm not. 'We're just friends, Linda. I'm not in love with him but you are, so best of luck.'

'Thanks, Mary. I'll write to him tonight.'

Norma, who had overheard most of this conversation, said, 'You sounded like Evelyn Home's agony aunt column in the magazine.'

Mary laughed. 'That's where I read about a similar case and that was the reply she gave to the lovelorn lass who wrote in.'

'But are you going to give up a gorgeous guy like Phil without a fight?'

'Good looks aren't everything, Norma. I like Phil very much but not in that romantic sense.' She smiled. Stan had just walked in.

On Saturday, Molly had had a very busy day in the office, dealing with invoices and the roster for next week. Jean had wanted the day off, so that meant she was in the office on her own.

Deanna had come in earlier that morning. She was bursting with joy at how well the play was going. 'The newspaper critic has said it is a wonderful performance and all the actors have been praised as well.'

Molly was very pleased for her although she could have done with Deanna being able to help out with some of the jobs that were coming up. If the work was going to come in like this, then she would have to hire another woman, but she decided to leave it till after the new year. Thankfully, she had Maisie and Alice who were quite eager to take on extra work. It would soon be November and Molly recalled how the jobs had slumped a bit at that time last year, so she would wait a few more weeks and see how things were going.

One bit of good news was the new contract with John Knox. He had been discharged from hospital a few days ago and one of the first things he had done was to reinstate Edna. Molly didn't know all the details of this rift but she was glad to have him back on the books. Edna was overjoyed at this news and planned to start work on the Monday morning. She had been apprehensive to begin with when Molly told her about the new contract. 'I don't know how he'll get rid of Sonia. He says he can't throw her out, but he's hoping she'll find another place to stay.'

'Everything will be fine, Edna. He must have made up his mind how to deal with this while he was in hospital and look how quickly he wants you back.'

Alice and Maisie had come in early that morning before setting out for work. They collected their wages and Molly asked Alice how things were at home. 'Victor hasn't come back since the night he broke the window, so hopefully he'll stay away for good now,' she said. 'Is it all right if I run across to Henderson's furniture store to pay my weekly payment for my three-piece suite?' Molly said that was fine as the shop was only yards away and the new job didn't need Alice until 9:30 a.m.

Molly wondered how the case was coming on. Charlie Johns hadn't come back to see her but she knew he would be busy with other cases, not just Etta's. That was why she was surprised when he appeared at tea-time. She was just thinking of closing up when he came in, his overcoat wet with the rain that had started to fall in the afternoon. 'I was wondering if you could make me a cup of tea while I bring you up to date with the case,' he said.

Molly quickly closed and locked the door and as they climbed the stair to the flat, she turned out the office light. 'I'll make you something to eat if you're hungry,' she said, looking hesitantly at the packet of bacon and six eggs that she had bought that morning.

'That would be great, but only if it's not a nuisance.'

She put on the frying pan and began to cook the bacon. 'Do you want me to set the table?'

She nodded but kept her face turned away from him. The flat had warmed up with the electric fire and by the time they were sitting down to the meal, everything was cosy.

Later, when they were drinking their tea on the couch, he said, 'I haven't made much headway with the case. I keep going round in circles with the people you've interviewed and I suppose they've mentioned it to other people. Yet, however the information reached them, we have a dangerous person in our midst. These weren't coincidental accidents – they were deliberate attacks. The day Mrs Barton had her accident with the bus, she came here afterwards in the company of an elderly woman. Did you see her before she went along Victoria Road?'

Molly said she hadn't. 'The first thing I knew about the accident was when Vera half stumbled into the office. She said someone called Bella had helped her.'

'I'd like to trace this woman but we've no idea where she lives. We have a witness who saw an elderly woman driving a small black car after Peter Walsh's accident, and then we have an elderly woman who was around when Vera almost landed under the bus. It could mean nothing at all but I'm not sure about this Bella. Vera remembers that she wore nail polish and I'm not sure if older women paint their nails. What do you think, Molly?'

Molly wasn't sure. 'I suppose she could be a woman who likes to keep herself looking good. Did Vera say how she was dressed?'

'Yes, a coat that looked too tight for her, a woollen hat and scarf, which she didn't take off in the café, and red polished nails.'

Molly looked doubtful. 'It doesn't sound like a woman who takes care of her appearance. Did Vera describe anything else about her?'

Charlie said, 'No. She says she was in too much shock and then agitated at not finding the letter writer or the letter.'

'Well, that makes sense. Vera looked totally shocked when she came here. She didn't even notice her stocking had a large ladder in it and her coat was all grey and dusty. I think she's been taking sleeping pills for a while now and she probably felt groggy that morning.'

'It makes you wonder if it was just a genuine accident but she swears she felt a big push from behind. I've been checking up on some of the women you interviewed. Anita wears red nail polish, Vina wears pale pink and Frances didn't have any painted nails but she did have the traces of red at the edges of her nails. It looked like she had used remover but didn't get into the corners. Oh, and by the way, you'll be pleased to know Vera's not taking the pills any longer.'

Molly was relieved by this news. She had switched the wireless to discover it was a music programme. Charlie settled back on the couch with his cup in his hand and sighed. 'You've made this place look really fantastic. I suppose I'll have to make a move and go out in the storm.'

By now the wind was blowing rain on the window. For one out-of-character moment she thought of asking him to stay. After all, he could easily sleep on the couch, but then he stood up and put his coat on. 'Thanks for the meal and the company, Molly. I'll be back when I have more news, but please watch out for yourself. I don't like the way this case is going.'

Molly was going to let him out by the street door but that meant taking him through the bedroom, so they went downstairs and through the darkened office. At the door, Charlie shook her hand. 'Thanks again.'

He made his way down the Wellgate to wherever he lived. Molly had no idea where that was, but maybe he was going back to the police station. It was only eight o'clock and the Wellgate was busy with people hurrying to the cinema, the pubs or the dance halls. She shivered in the cold night air and locked up. The flat seemed empty and quiet now that he was gone. She thought about the evening and smiled. Last year, he had been furious with her over her involvement in a case and she hadn't really cared for him. But now he was showing a different side to his character and she blushed when she thought about how much she liked him.

43

The woman was fed up with waiting in the rain. What did the policeman want now with McQueen? Well, it certainly wasn't to question her, as the woman saw her locking the door and putting the light out. So he was invited up to the inner sanctum was he? Wonders would never cease. She reviewed her plans. There was still quite a bit to deal with but she would manage it. Once again, she was furious that all the memories had been brought to the surface, but these people would pay for their interference. Oh yes, there was no doubt about that. Here he comes, looking like he wanted to stay, but the upright Molly McQueen wouldn't have had it. Actually, the woman quite fancied him for herself and one never knew how things would pan out. Maybe if he got to know me better, she thought, he would like me. But there wasn't going to be a chance for that.

44

Molly finished some more work and then decided to have an early night after Charlie had gone. She thought about her impulse to ask him to stay but she was glad it had come to nothing. He was just doing his job and because she was involved, it was natural for him to visit every now and again.

She tried to read her book but it was another boring tale and she couldn't be bothered with it. She lay for a long time listening to the people pass by on the street but soon she was fast asleep. A fit of coughing woke her up and she couldn't get her breath. Wide awake now, she was horrified to see the room was thick with smoke and she stumbled and struggled to get out of bed. Her eyes were stinging and her throat felt on fire but the worse thing was she couldn't make out where the door was. Stay calm, she thought.

Finding the end of the bed and then the cupboard, she managed to make her way down to the outside door but as she went to unlock it, she realised the key was hot. The fire must be outside this door, she realised, so she retraced her steps and found the stairs into the office. She half stumbled down the stairs and found the office was also starting to fill with smoke. By now she was almost collapsing but she managed to crawl to the front door and unlock it.

She sprawled like a wet fish on the rain soaked pavement in front of a group of young lads who were on their way home. Molly could only whisper that there was a fire at the side door. One of the lads draped his coat around her while the rest hurried along Baltic Street. They found a fire was built up outside the door, mainly with rubbish and some wood, but there was a small burning tyre on top. The thick wooden door had managed to keep the fire out and the lads tried to kick the burning debris away from the door, dispersing the fire's fuel into the street where it fizzled in the rain. 'We'll have to get the doctor and the police,' said one lad.

'I don't think we'll need the fire brigade because the fire's almost out.'

'What if there's also a fire inside?' said his pal. 'Maybe we should investigate.'

By now, Molly was propped up in the doorway. She was still unable to speak. While two of the lads went inside, another one ran to the phone box but he met a policeman on the beat. The policeman said, 'Where's the fire, son? Where are you going in such a hurry?'

'There is a fire, constable, down there.' He pointed to the Wellgate.

They both ran to the agency and the constable hurried back to the police box at the foot of the Hilltown to report it. They all managed to get Molly back inside the office, which was now reasonably clear of smoke. She was shivering in her wet nightdress and the jacket wasn't much warmer.

Within half an hour, a fire engine and an ambulance had arrived. Molly protested she was feeling better but she was whisked off to the infirmary. The policeman promised to lock up the office and the lads stood around looking helpless with their faces, hands and clothes blackened by the fire. Before she went away, Molly tried to thank them but they said they were only glad they were able to help.

On their way home, they joked about what their mothers would say when they saw the state of them but one of the lads said, 'That fire was started deliberately. If that woman hadn't had another door to escape from, she would be dead by now.'

That stopped all the jokes, as they had to agree with their pal.

Molly couldn't stop coughing and her chest felt as if it was on fire. The doctor at the infirmary gave her oxygen to help her breathing and although she was wrapped up in a warm blanket, she was still shivering. 'I'm going to keep you in here overnight and check you're all right. Maybe you'll get home tomorrow but we'll see how you get on,' the doctor said.

He was a tall, thin man with a shock of red hair. He turned to the nurse who was in attendance at the casualty. 'Take Miss McQueen to the ward, please, nurse.'

Molly tried to protest but by now she was exhausted and the tears weren't far away. Another spasm of coughing shook her body and she ached all over. She was worried about the agency but she trusted the policeman to make sure it was all locked up. During all this time, never once did she think the fire had been started deliberately.

She didn't get much sleep that night, as she was aware that the doctor and a few of the nurses checked on her regularly, so she was glad when she heard the ward start to wake up. When breakfast arrived, she gulped down the tea and then noticed the jug of water on the bedside locker. She drained that and felt a bit better. She didn't eat anything, as she was sure her throat would be raw with the smoke and the coughing, but she managed to get a nurse to bring her more water. The cold water helped her and she fell into a deep sleep.

It was almost dinner time when she awoke and she was surprised to see Charlie sitting beside the bed. He looked grim. She held out her hand. 'Charlie, what are you doing here?'

'I got the report of the fire this morning.' He leaned over her so he wouldn't be overheard. 'I want you out of that flat, Molly. That fire was started deliberately and it was a nasty and dangerous one. Whoever started it had put a small bicycle tyre on top and that made the smoke even more noxious. You were lucky you weren't killed by it and if those lads hadn't managed to put it out then the whole flat and office could have gone up in flames.'

Molly was so shocked she couldn't speak.

'Can you go home to your parents' house where Marigold can keep an eye on you? I have to find out who is doing all this before someone is killed.'

Her throat felt like sandpaper. 'Charlie, I can't think straight at the moment. I don't know what to do. Is the flat badly damaged?'

'There's a lot of smoke damage and you'll need a new door. It was badly burned, but because it was so strong it saved your life.'

'The doctor said I could go home today. Did he tell you that?'

'Yes, he did, but as I said, I don't want you going back to the flat. The fire didn't reach the inside but everything will have to be cleaned and repainted.' He saw the tears in her eyes. 'I'm sorry, Molly, but at least you are all right.'

She suddenly remembered she had been wearing her nightdress when she was admitted last night. 'I haven't any clothes to go home in. Can you go to Edna's house in Paradise Road and get her to bring me up something to wear?'

He stood up. 'I'll be about an hour and that will give the doctor time to check you over to see if you can go home.'

He had no sooner left the ward than the doctor appeared. It was a different one from the Casualty. 'How are you feeling now, Miss McQueen?' he asked, glancing at his notes.

Molly tried hard not to sound so croaky, just in case he kept her in another night. 'I feel a lot better, doctor. I've sent my friend to get my clothes for getting out.'

The doctor peered at her over the rim of his glasses and Molly's heart sank. He glanced at the notes again, then went to see the ward sister who was busy at the bottom of the ward. She saw them having a talk and then he came back. 'We'll let you go home but you must stay somewhere else, as I believe your house is still smoke damaged.'

Molly would have agreed to go and live on the moon just to get out and she said, 'I'm going to my parents' house in Newport, doctor.'

'That's good. Well, as soon as your clothes arrive, you can go.'

Charlie hurried to see Edna. He wasn't sure which house was hers but Molly had told him the number. It was Edna's mother Irene who opened the door and she looked surprised to see a strange man on the doorstep. He showed her his warrant card and her hand suddenly flew to her mouth. 'It's all right, Mrs McGill; I've come to see Edna.'

He quickly explained the situation to her. 'Is Molly going to be all right?'

'Yes, she is. She inhaled a lot of noxious smoke but she's a lot better today.'

'Edna is away out with Billy but she should be back very soon. She's taken him to the ice cream shop for some sweeties.'

It wasn't long before the pair returned and Edna's eyes opened in surprise when she saw Charlie sitting by the fire. Irene burst out, 'There's been a fire at the agency and Molly is in hospital. This is DS Johns and he wants to speak to you.'

While this conversation was going on, Billy stood with wide eyes at the drama unfolding before him. Edna said, 'Billy, do you want to go and play with your friend downstairs?'

'Can I take my garage and cars with me and my Meccano set?'

'No, just the Meccano set.'

When he departed quite happily to play with his pal, Charlie told the two women about the fire and how it was started deliberately. They were both shocked. 'Miss Mc-

Queen is getting home today but she needs her clothes. She told me to come and ask you if you could bring her up something to wear.'

Edna still had her coat on, so they left to go to the flat. Charlie opened the door with the key that the constable had given him. The stench of smoke was so strong that it caught their breath.

Charlie led the way up the stairs and Edna almost burst into tears when she saw the damage. The walls and ceiling were streaked by black smoke and the bedding was covered with pieces of soot. Edna went to the wardrobe but all the clothes had absorbed the smoke and were very smelly. 'Molly can't wear anything from here. I'll give her some of my clothes to get her home,' she said, going over to the chest of drawers. She didn't think Molly would want to wear her underwear so she raked about in the drawer and found some that didn't smell too badly.

Charlie said, 'I want to go and question the young lads who helped last night. Can you go to the infirmary and take Miss McQueen back to your house? I'll come there after I've seen the boys.'

The lads all lived in Nelson Street and Charlie went to the address he was given. They were all neighbours of one another and lived at the top of Nelson Street in a three-storey tenement. When he went to the first house, he found three of them playing cards and he asked if the other two could join them. The cards were put away and the small pile of money was quietly secreted into one boy's pocket.

When they were all together, he asked them about the fire the night before. They all looked at one another but the boy who had taken the money and who seemed to be the spokesman of this small group said, 'We were walking home when this woman almost fell at our feet.' He turned to his pals. 'That's right, isn't it?'

They all nodded and said, 'That's right, Ben.'

He continued, 'We could see smoke coming out of the door but she said there was a fire and pointed along Baltic Street, so Johnny, Bob and myself hurried to the close. There was quite a large pile of rubbish at the door with terrible thick black smoke pouring from it, but the flames weren't terribly high, so we put our handkerchiefs over our mouths and kicked the burning embers out into the street.'

'That's when we saw the burning tyre,' said one lad, whose name was Jeff.

'We went back to the woman,' Ben said, 'and I put my jacket over her because she was in her nightdress and it was raining and the pavement was wet. She was shivering, so I asked Jeff to go and phone for the doctor and an ambulance because she looked as if she needed a doctor.' He stopped. 'Is she all right?'

Charlie said she was.

'I ran up the Wellgate steps,' said Jeff. 'I didn't know where the nearest phone box was and, as I was busy looking for one, this policeman stopped me because he thought I looked suspicious and was having him on about the fire. But when he saw I wasn't joking, he was the one who got help for her.'

Charlie looked serious. 'Now think hard, lads. Did you see anyone other than the police constable?'

They all shook their heads. Ben said, 'There were some people in the Murraygate but we passed them and I think we were on our own at that time. When the fire brigade came, a lot of the people who live in the close opposite put their lights on and were looking out of the windows, but the street was deserted when we reached that building.'

'Where had you all been?'

Again, it was Ben who answered. 'We were at the Palais and we had met a group of girls. We walked with them to catch the last bus and then headed home.'

Then, one boy who had remained silent throughout this story spoke softly. 'I saw someone. I've just remembered it.'

His pals all looked at him. 'You never said

anything, Ian.'

He looked embarrassed. 'I've just remembered it. When you went up the steps to the phone box, Jeff, I followed because I thought we could maybe look in different directions. But you were ahead of me and as I was coming back, I bumped into an old woman who came from the direction of Meadowside. At least, she was passing McGill's shop when I saw her. I said sorry but she was really nasty and said to get out of her way.'

Charlie said, 'Now this is important, Ian, which way was she heading?'

'She was going towards Victoria Road and she looked like she was in a hurry.'

'Can you describe her?'

'Well, it was dark and rainy but she was plump and she had a hat on her head. I didn't see her face, but she was really grumpy.'

Charlie turned to Jeff. 'You didn't see her, Jeff?'

'No, but I came back to the building with the policeman before he left to go to the police box, so she must have passed when I was with him.'

This was another sighting of the elderly woman and if she was the one responsible for the fire, then she was taking risks at being found out. If it had been the police constable who saw her, then he might have questioned her as a witness. He thanked the lads for their help and said that Molly sent her sincere thanks to them all and that she would be writing to them when she felt better.

Before going back to Edna's house, he stopped at the ice cream shop on Victoria Road and bought five small tubs. Molly was sitting at the fire and didn't look too bad but when she saw the ice cream, she said, 'It's just what I need for this rawness in my throat.'

Irene was cooking the tea but Molly said she didn't want anything to eat.

Billy was eating his ice cream and Irene said, 'I think we'll have our pudding before our scrambled eggs.'

Molly wanted to go to the flat. 'I have to take my clothes to the dry cleaners tomorrow and all the bedding to the laundry, and after that I'll go and catch the Fifie.'

Charlie didn't want her to go alone. He wasn't off duty till eight o'clock but Edna said she would go to the flat with her and they would sort out all that needed doing. She said she would get her tea after helping Molly, so they set off to the office and Charlie stopped when they reached the police box. 'I'll see you tomorrow, Miss McQueen, and remember what I've told you. Be very careful.'

She promised and was amused by his formality. But he probably didn't want the staff to know they were on first name terms.

Molly was appalled when she saw the smoke damage to the flat but she said she would contact the painter in the morning and get everything back to normal. Thankfully, because the flat door had been closed, the office wasn't too bad, which meant that business would be able to go on as usual. The metal filing cabinet had protected all the paperwork so there was no problem with that, but as they took all her clothes out of the wardrobe and the drawers to put into a large suitcase, the smoky smell was obnoxious. It was the same with the bedding but they tied this up in large bundle and Molly said she would contact the laundry and they would pick it up. They also took down the curtains and Molly was dismayed to see Marigold's lovely wallpaper all streaked with black. 'Maybe it'll wash off,' said Edna.

'I hope so,' Molly replied but she wasn't confident. Whoever had done this had either wanted her dead or put under great financial and personal pressure.

An hour later, Edna went home. She had tried to persuade Molly to stay with them but Molly had said that she would have to go to her parents' house to get spare clothes anyway. 'I'll stay there until this place is cleaned up and then I'll be back.'

'Then let me walk you to the ferry.'

'No, honestly, Edna, but thank you. It's

only six o'clock, so no one is going to attack me and by the by, good luck with John tomorrow.'

Edna gave a huge grin but watched with a worried look as Molly made her way to Craig Pier. Molly wasn't feeling as chirpy as she portrayed as she walked through the wet streets. She felt strange wearing Edna's clothes and she would be glad to have a hot bath when she reached the house. The Fifie would be quiet at this time on a Sunday evening and she wasn't looking forward to crossing the river in the dark. She made up her mind that she would sit in the saloon where hopefully there would be other passengers. She didn't relish the thought of being on the deck, in case the person who was causing all this havoc had maybe followed her and was now waiting to push her overboard.

At Craig Pier, she bought a return ticket and went to wait for the ferry. Then, much to her surprise, Charlie came in. His raincoat was wet with the rain, which meant he had walked from the station. 'I can't stay long but I want you to stay with Marigold. Whoever is doing this must be watching. First Vera and Peter, then you. Try to think hard about the people you interviewed, Molly. You've opened a can of worms somewhere along the line and we have to find this person.'

'I honestly can't imagine any of them doing

this. Doctor Lowson was annoyed at me with my questions but everyone else seemed all right. I wonder if they've talked to someone we don't know about yet, but why would anyone want to hurt us? It's just a missing girl...' She stopped. 'Unless someone killed her away back then and is frightened we get to the truth.'

'I've thought of that and I'm trying to dig into their pasts, but so far everything is just as they say. I think Robina Price has a lot to answer for and I'm going to see her again tomorrow.'

'But why would she harm her sister, Peter and me?'

'Well, maybe she was the one who harmed young Etta. Who knows.'

The *BL Nairn* docked on the jetty and Molly said goodbye. 'Now watch out for yourself, Molly.'

'What happened to "Miss McQueen"?' she said with a smile.

'I'm just being discreet,' he said with a grin. He stood and watched as she hurried onto the boat and he was glad that there were a few passengers going on alongside her. The ferry slowly drew away from the pier and he hoped that this move would keep her safe.

Molly went to sit in the saloon and was pleased that three elderly women were already seated. She sat in the corner and before long they had docked at Newport. She hurried along the road to Marigold's house. When she opened the door, Marigold looked surprised. 'Molly. How nice to see you...' But her voice trailed away when Molly almost fell in the door and promptly burst into tears.

Marigold bustled about making her comfortable in one of the chairs by the fire. Sabby looked put out at this intrusion in her peaceful life and she stalked away to the kitchen with her tail swishing. Marigold came back with the teapot and a glass of sherry. 'Here, drink this, Molly.'

Molly slowly told her friend the whole story and Marigold was shocked and frightened for her. 'I know you said this could turn out to be dangerous, Marigold, but what's going on here? I'm not even on the case now.'

Marigold didn't want to frighten her but she knew how some people could be dangerous if they thought they were cornered. Molly had obviously found out something that put her at risk. 'I've only interviewed some women and one man and they couldn't tell me much, but DS Johns thinks they've mentioned it to someone else and they've been frightened by my questions.'

'I want you to stay with me, Molly, and you can have a hot bath here.'

'I have to get my clothes from next door.'

'I'll go. Just you wait here.' Marigold pulled her coat over her head and hurried out. She was just pushing open the back garden gate when she felt something hit her head. She fell to the ground and at that moment a car came along the street, illuminating the garden. Marigold vaguely saw a dark shape run off and she staggered to her feet and managed to get back home over the wet grass.

Molly was getting ready for the bath when she came in. 'Marigold, what's happened?'

Marigold took her coat off and there was a cut on her head, which thankfully was nothing more than a scalp wound. 'Someone must have thought I was you, Molly.'

Molly went to ring for the doctor but Marigold said she would clean it up with some Dettol. 'I'm glad I was wearing this coat over my head. It has a detachable quilted lining which cushioned the blow and, of course, the car coming along made the attacker run away.'

Molly dug out the card that Charlie had given her. It had his work number on it but he had also printed his home number as well. After three rings, he answered. Molly tried to be calm. 'Charlie, someone's attacked Marigold. They thought I was going into the house. It must have been someone on the boat and she will be going back that way.'

'I'll be with you as soon as I can and I'll get someone to be at the Craig Pier when it docks.'

He arrived within the hour and his face was grey with worry. Molly ran out to see him. 'Charlie, what's going on? Why is someone so set on hurting me?'

He didn't know and he was no nearer finding out. He had to get Molly and Marigold to a safer house, as this woman was becoming more deranged by the minute. Marigold said she would go to her friend Peggy's house to stay and she would take Sabby with her. Charlie went with Molly to get her clothes and they left on the return trip over the river.

At Craig Pier, two policemen had stationed themselves at the entrance and exit. No one came off the boat and the captain said that no one had boarded at Newport.

'I'm taking you to a hotel for tonight,' Charlie said. 'But we have to make sure no one is following us.' He spoke to the policemen who told him that no one had come off the last boat. Charlie had a thought and wondered if the culprit had stayed on board until the hue and cry had died away, so he told them to check on all trips right up to the final sailing. 'It might be an elderly woman, but I want all names and addresses taken from all the passengers.'

Then he made a circuitous route through the narrow streets, making sure no one was following and booked Molly into the Queen's Hotel. Before he left, he said, 'Stay in the hotel until I come and get you tomorrow.'

Molly spent another restless night in this strange bed but she fell asleep just before dawn.

45

The woman was pleased at all the mayhem she had caused but it was beginning to be wearisome. She had been surprised by the way the day had turned out. If she hadn't hung around the hospital, she would never have known about the house in Newport. Still, she had to stop now. Her revenge was over and she would soon be away from here and the police would never be able to find her. She had made all her plans and it was only a matter of days before she left.

What a pity those young lads had come along when they did. One had even bumped into her but a fat lot of good that would do with that stupid policeman. She had seen him hurrying off the boat to see how injured his Miss McQueen was and she had worked out he would put surveillance on the ferry. She had made the round trip via Perth in the car. She was too smart for them all and it was a pity it had to end, but all good things must come to a halt.

46

Molly wasn't the only one who had a sleepless night. Edna had wakened at three o'clock and hadn't been able to get back to sleep. Her mind was in turmoil over the events at the agency and she was also worried about meeting John in the morning. What if Sonia was there, still making a fuss? John had looked so frail when she had seen him in the ward and she didn't want him upset so soon after his operation. She was glad when the alarm went off at seven and she was able to get up and get Billy ready for school. She disliked the cold, dark mornings of late autumn, but at least it was dry. The wind had turned to the east and it held the sharpness of winter in its wake.

As usual, Irene was going to take Billy to school and Edna once again was grateful to have her mother staying with her, as otherwise going to work would have been impossible. She wondered how Molly was doing in Newport – she hadn't heard about the latest turn of events. How anyone could be so stupid as to put a fire beside the door was incomprehensible to her and she wondered if Molly's finances would stretch to another painter's bill.

All this was going through her head as she walked briskly up the road to John's house. The front door light was on and she saw the soft glow of the sitting room's lamps. She had to stand for a minute or two to get her courage to ring the bell, fully expecting Sonia to answer the door and not let her in. However, to her surprise, it was John who came to the door. 'Come in Edna, out of this cold wind.'

He walked with her to the front sitting room and she saw a bright fire burning in the fireplace and all his papers heaped up on the table. There was no sign of Sonia. 'I've made some coffee and warm rolls so sit down and I'll bring them through.'

When he came back, Edna thought he still looked frail and he had lost some weight, but he seemed cheerful enough as he placed the tray on the small table by the two armchairs. 'It's so good to see you again, Edna. I thought I had said something to offend you when you didn't come and see me in hospital.'

Edna started to speak but he said, 'Of course, I now know it was Sonia's doing but she told me you hadn't come back and when she inquired at the agency they told her my contract was broken.'

'She said she was engaged to you, John, and she had this marvellous diamond ring, which she flashed in front of me. Then she told me that you no longer needed me as she was to become your secretary.'

John shook his head. 'She was always devious, even as a young woman. I was actually engaged to her many years ago but I broke it off after I met her sister Kathleen, who was so different from Sonia. She took it badly and she got married almost at once but, of course, it didn't last and she blamed me for the break-up. After her divorce she went back to her maiden name.'

Edna looked at the door. 'Is she still living here?'

John laughed. 'No, she abandoned me to go and live with my brother James. He has a small flat in Arbroath, which he rents out in the summer, and she's gone to stay there. James always had a soft spot for her but I hope she doesn't ruin his life like she almost did mine.'

'Well, it's all in the past, John, and you're now back on the agency books, so where do you want to start?'

'I thought we could maybe give work a rest this morning and just sit and chat. It's so good to see you again.' He laughed once more. 'I couldn't get over your ingenuity in getting into the ward to see me. It was like some spy thriller.'

Molly explained that she had Dolly Pirie to thank for telling her about his stay in hospital. 'Her cousin's husband was in the same ward as you and she recognised you, but she couldn't understand why I never visited you. Then I tried to get in but the nurse wouldn't let me, not without a visitor's card and I knew Sonia wouldn't give me one, so Dolly and I came up with the scheme to get inside the ward. Mind you, I didn't think I was going to get over to your bed because James and Sonia didn't leave until the first bell. But I did and I'm so glad to see you're home and we're having our coffee and rolls in front of this lovely fire.'

John smiled at her and she blushed. 'I let Sonia keep Kathleen's ring and also I gave her all her jewellery, which is worth a lot of money. I hope you don't mind, Edna?'

Edna was puzzled. 'Why should I mind?'

He hesitated. 'Well, I always thought I'd like to give it all to my wife if I ever married again and I was hoping you would marry me?'

Edna was overcome with pleasure, surprise and love. 'The answer is yes, John.'

'After you've finished your coffee, we'll go down the town and get you your own engagement ring and then we'll have a celebration meal afterwards.' He brought the car around from the garage and they set off.

Edna couldn't believe how quickly everything was moving. It was only a couple of weeks ago she was in the depths of despair and now she was heading into town with the man she loved to buy a ring. She felt she had to pinch herself to make sure she wasn't dreaming.

John parked the car in Union Street and they walked to Robertson's jewellery shop. The assistant brought out a few trays of beautiful rings but Edna said she didn't want anything too large or flashy, so she settled for a small solitaire diamond. John said, 'Are you sure that's the one you want, Edna? It is one of the cheapest on that tray.'

'Yes, John. I like this one and it doesn't matter what it costs because it will always be special to me.' The young male assistant beamed at her – if he was disappointed at not selling one of the larger diamonds on show, he didn't show it.

'It's a bit early for a meal so do you want to go and see your mother and give her the news?'

Edna wanted to shout out the news to the entire world and she would gladly have hired a billboard to announce the engagement but she simply said, 'Yes, I'd like to do that.'

Irene was surprised when they both walked in the house. 'John, how lovely to see you looking so well,' she said.

'Irene, Edna and I have something to say.'

Edna held up her left hand and the diamond twinkled in the light.

'Mum, John and I are to be married, but not until the spring.' They had discussed the date after leaving the shop and springtime seemed to be the best time to arrange the marriage.

Irene began to cry and John was taken aback. She saw this and apologised. 'It's just tears of joy.'

John laughed. 'As long as it's not tears of distress at landing with this future son-in-law.'

Later, they went to the Queen's Hotel for a meal and afterwards they both went to Paradise Road to tell Billy the good news. John was a bit worried. 'What if he doesn't want me for a stepfather?'

Edna smiled. 'I think as long as he inherits all your great toys then he'll be pleased.'

When he came home from school, they waited until he had eaten before Edna said, 'Billy, John and I are going to be married in the spring. We hope you'll be happy with us both.'

Billy was playing with his cars. 'Does that mean we'll live in your house?'

When John said it would, Billy ran to get his coat and he took his granny's hand. 'Right, then, let's go.'

Edna, Irene and John laughed so much they almost cried.

47

Molly didn't want to wait on Charlie, so she left a message at the reception to say she would be at the agency. She had so much to do. The first thing was to arrange with the painter to come and paint the walls. She was determined to be back in the flat as soon as possible, as she didn't want to be in Newport and put Marigold at further risk. Molly thought whoever was watching her would know where to find her wherever she went, so at least this way there would be no danger to Marigold.

She arrived at the agency just ahead of Jean and the staff, so she was able to tell them about the fire. They were all shocked but Mary, Maisie, Alice and Deanna all said they would come back after the day's work to help clean up the flat. Molly was touched by the offer and said if they could maybe manage a couple of hours, that would let the painter make a start tomorrow.

She then made a phone call to the painter. He said he would come along later to see what needed doing. Her next call was to the laundry to come and pick up all the smoky bedclothes. Charlie arrived a few minutes later and he didn't look too pleased at her for leaving the hotel without him.

They had moved up to the flat and the damage looked worse in the daylight. Everything was dirty and she couldn't even fill the kettle without leaving greasy black stains on her hands. Charlie said, 'I think the person who's doing all this is Robina Price and I'm going to see her right away. I'll be back as soon as I've spoken to her.'

Constable Williams drove him to Elizabeth Street and they both stood outside Robina's door while Charlie knocked loudly. There was no answer and Charlie muttered loudly about the bloody woman never answering the door. He knocked again and then opened the letterbox like he did before and called in. 'It's the police, Miss Price, please open the door.' Everything was silent in the flat. 'Go and check with the neighbours and see if they have any idea where she'll be.'

The constable tried the next-door neighbour but she was also out, so he tried the two occupants downstairs. The door was opened by a young woman carrying a baby. 'We're looking for Miss Price who lives upstairs. Have you any idea where she might be?' The nameplate on the door said the occupants were called Davidson. 'Have you seen her this morning, Mrs Davidson?'

'No, I haven't seen her for a few days but she usually goes to the chapel in Forebank

Road for mass.'

PC Williams reported back to his boss and told him about the chapel. 'Right, then, let's go there and see if we can see her.'

They drove to the chapel and parked the car across the road. The chapel was quiet at this time of the morning. A few parishioners were sitting in the pews and an old woman was lighting a candle on the candleholder by the front door. Charlie quietly made his way down the aisle, trying not to make it obvious that he was looking for someone, but Miss Price was nowhere to be seen.

PC Williams said, 'Mrs Davidson told me she sometimes went to the chapel two or three times a day.'

'We'll check that out but I want to go back to speak to Mrs Davidson. Maybe Miss Price has come back by now.' Charlie doubted that, as he had a funny feeling that the woman had gone.

Back at Elizabeth Street, he tried the door again and called through the letterbox. This ploy had worked before, but either she wasn't afraid anymore that her neighbours would hear or else she had scarpered.

Mrs Davidson didn't seem to mind them coming back to her door and she asked them in. The baby was asleep in a wicker basket by the side of the fire. Charlie apologised for bothering her. 'We need to speak to Miss Price who lives up the stairs. Have you any idea where she could be?'

The woman looked thoughtful but shook her head. 'As I told the constable, the only place she usually goes during the day and early evening is the chapel.'

Charlie was puzzled by the way she inserted 'usually' into her phrasing. 'Have you ever seen her go out aside from these chapel excursions? I mean, after services would be over?'

Mrs Davidson didn't look too happy. 'I don't like to eavesdrop or be nosy with my neighbours.'

'But you have noticed some coming and going?'

'It's the baby. I have to get up late at night and sometimes during the early morning.' She blushed. 'I don't have to make up a bottle or anything like that so I usually sit in that chair by the window and give him his feed. I don't put the light on because I think it puts him to sleep quicker and over the last two or three weeks, I've noticed Miss Price coming back very late and a few times it was early in the morning. I didn't think too much about it, as I thought she was maybe visiting friends or family, especially when she was sometimes brought back by a car. I didn't hear what was said, but she would lean into the passenger door and talk quietly with the driver. She is a very private woman and keeps herself to herself. Mrs Donald, who lives next door, says she's a religious woman and her flat is like the inside of a convent; all bare white walls and very little furniture. Mrs Donald says she lives like a recluse.'

Charlie wasn't interested in finding out how Mrs Donald had managed to get into the flat. Instead, he said, 'This car, can you describe it?'

Again, she looked doubtful. 'I'm not very good with cars.' She gave this some thought. 'It was a small car and I think it was black.'

Charlie held his breath. 'Did you see the driver, Mrs Davidson?'

This time she was certain. 'No, I didn't. The car wasn't parked right by the close but diagonally across the road where the streetlight is broken. It's been like that for ages, even though Mrs Donald has reported it.' The baby began to cry and she went and picked him up.

'Thank you, Mrs Davidson, you've been a great help.' Charlie handed her a card with his phone number on it. 'I know it's asking a lot of you because you have enough to do with the baby, but is it possible to phone this number if Miss Price comes back?'

She took it with a smile. 'It's no problem. I usually go out for a walk with the pram every day and there's a phone box in Ann Street. I can phone from there if I see her.'

Charlie had to warn her. 'Please don't let

her know you've seen her at night or tell her you're phoning me.'

She gave him a worried look and held her son tightly. 'Is it something serious?'

'No, but I'm finding it hard to see her as she doesn't seem to like the police and I need to speak to her, that's all.' She looked reassured. 'I'd like to talk to this Mrs Donald. Will she be in?'

'No, she's away. She should be home next week. She has these little holidays with Gladys, her daughter. She has a house by the sea in Broughty Ferry.'

'What about Miss Price's next-door neighbour. Will they be in?'

'No, the rest of the flats in the close are rented by young married couples with no children and they are all out at work during the day.'

'Well, thank you again and that's a beautiful boy you have.'

She blushed and said she thought so as well.

When they were outside, PC Williams said, 'Do you want me to check on the chapel again, sir?'

Charlie said, 'No. We can have another look later, but I have a feeling she's gone for good, back to Ireland. We'll get onto the Irish police and they can question her.'

As they made their way back to the station, Charlie thought this move must have been planned for some time. The fire had been on Saturday night and she wouldn't have been able to clear off as quickly as this if her plans hadn't already been in place. Not unless she was hiding somewhere. Or someone was hiding her.

Later that evening, he went to see Molly to give her the latest news on the fire but he was taken aback by the amount of people in the flat; they were all busy cleaning. There were mops and buckets and pails of water and although the place still had the strong smell of smoke, it also had a whiff of vinegar like from a chip shop. This mystery was solved when Maisie emptied her bucket in the sink and refilled it with hot water and added a good measure of vinegar. She saw his look and said, 'There's nothing better for cleaning wooden furniture than a vinegar wash.'

Judging by the dirt that was on the cloths, it had been a hard night for them all. He was especially amused by Deanna, who looked like she was playing the part of the local char on the stage. She wore a frilly apron and a headscarf, tied gypsy fashion around her blonde curls. But the biggest surprise of the night was when Molly said, 'We're all congratulating Edna on becoming engaged today.'

Edna looked like she was ready to burst with pride and pleasure when Charlie congratulated her. 'Thank you,' she said. 'It's all happened so quickly that I've not really taken it in yet.'

Maisie piped up, 'Alice, Deanna and I only get other people's dirt to clean up but Edna gets a walloping diamond engagement ring. It's no' fair.' Still, this was said jokingly and everyone laughed.

Charlie asked Molly if he could see her on her own and they went downstairs to the office. As they set off downstairs, Maisie raised her eyebrows and mimed, 'Is it another engagement?'

There was still a whiff of smoke in the office but it wasn't too bad. Charlie quickly put Molly in the picture regarding Miss Price. 'It looks like she's gone back to Ireland. However, a neighbour saw her coming back late at night and in the early morning, sometimes being dropped off by car, so it looks like she's the one behind all these attacks. The problem is the car. I don't think she is the owner, as this neighbour saw her talking to someone in the driving seat. I don't even know if she can drive. I'm going to see Frances Flynn tomorrow to see if she can help with her whereabouts and answer questions about the elusive Miss Price.'

'So I can stay in the flat tonight?'

'No, I'd rather you went to see Marigold and stay at her house. Anyway, how could you possibly sleep in this place smelling like this?'

Molly was quite happy about going back to Newport tonight because she wanted to bring the car back. She had all her clothes to take to the Sixty Minute cleaners tomorrow and she could hardly stagger through the streets with her clothes. It wasn't that she owned a huge wardrobe, but everything had to be cleaned and she visualised herself dropping blouses and skirts onto the pavement as she tottered to Thorter Row. 'You'll let me know how it goes with Frances tomorrow?'

He said he would but warned her to still be careful. 'I think she's gone but in case she's not, please watch out and tell Marigold the same thing.' He said goodnight and she let him out of the office door.

Maisie's face was a picture when she returned without him. As the women hadn't been home for their evening meal, Molly and Mary went out for fish and chips while Maisie put the kettle on and Alice and Deanna set the table. Jean was finishing off cleaning the small bathroom and Edna had finished washing down the wallpapered wall. With a bit of luck, it could be saved. Everything was now ready for Ronnie and his paint pots in the morning. They all said it was a terrible shame to have happened to a lovely person like Molly, but they were all pleased by their efforts.

48

Stan had long since given up the pretence that he was just friends with Mary and to his delight, she said she felt the same. The only thing worrying them was Phil's reaction when he came home on leave. Would he think they had both betrayed him? Stan hoped not. They had been friends since their schooldays but he had to tell him. He would write to Phil and tell him how things were between Mary and him.

On the Monday night, as soon as he got back from his work and before he had his tea, he sat down and wrote a short letter. He would get his mother to post it tomorrow and then it was just a matter of time before he got an answer. 'I remember how lonely I felt when I first went into the army,' he told Mary when they were having a coffee on Saturday evening. 'A few of the guys got letters like this from their girlfriends and it was a shame to see them take it so badly. Now I'm doing the same thing and I feel terrible.'

That worried Mary. 'Do you think we should wait till Phil comes home on leave, Stan?' she asked. 'I don't want to hurt his feelings, but he did say we were just friends.'

But the letter was now written and posted. Norma came round to see Mary that Monday night and she couldn't understand why Mary had given up such a handsome man in favour of Stan. She thought Phil looked like a film star. 'If Phil had been going out with me, I would never have found someone else,' she told her. 'I mean, he's just the most gorgeous looking man in the whole wide world.'

'Well, sometimes good looks aren't everything Norma. I do like Phil, but Stan means so much more to me and I can't explain it.'

Mary was finding everything a bit stressful. The agency was all on edge with this latest and awful thing happening to Molly. She was frightened that Molly might give up and go to see her parents and sister in Australia and she might even decide to stay there. The agency was successful but there always seemed to be something happening to Molly. Last year it had been that awful job and now the same thing was happening all over again. The only bit of good news was Edna's engagement and even that had been touch and go. Edna had been in the throes of misery when she thought John cancelled the contract but it was all well now.

She was glad when Norma went away home. Even her mum sensed her apprehension. She asked her, 'Is everything going well at work, Mary?'

Mary smiled brightly. 'Yes, Mum, it is.'

Another woman was feeling the strain as well. Sandy had told Alice that the divorce papers had been served on Victor. He had been like an enraged bull at work when he got them and had told Sandy he would fight this divorce and that scheming wife of his would be sorry she ever started this. 'You've done the right thing, Alice, so don't worry. If he comes back here, don't let him in, and get Maisie to call the police. It's just as well he doesn't know I'm seeing you every night. At least this way I can listen to his threats and either tell him he's daft to act like this, or I can warn you what he's going to do.'

Alice was just beginning to enjoy life again but she couldn't relax, not with Victor on the horizon. She enjoyed her job but she had also been affected by the tension at work and she knew all the other staff felt the same. Maisie had said only yesterday, after they had helped to clean the flat, 'Somebody tried to kill her, Alice. I know the fire wasn't a huge blaze, but that smoke was a killer. Did you see how black everything was in the flat? Aye, she was a lucky woman.'

Alice wondered why life couldn't be happy with everyone getting along with one another. Earning a living was hard enough and most families were doing their best, just like she was. She looked around her house and felt so proud of what she had achieved since Victor left, but now he was like a dark shadow hanging over her. One little hope was the fact that he had joined a boxing club and Alice hoped and prayed he would get some of his anger and aggression out in the open with his opponents in the ring. At least they would give him as good as they got. She felt terrible when she realised the thought of that happening cheered her up.

49

Charlie made a late call on Frances Flynn. He was hoping to see Jimmy and his mother to see if they had any knowledge about Robina Price's movements. He waited until he thought they would be finished with their tea. Maggie Flynn answered the door and shouted for her mother. 'Mum, there's a policeman here who wants to speak to you.'

Frances looked flustered when she came to the door. 'What is it now?'

Charlie smiled. 'Just a few more questions, Mrs Flynn, I hope you don't mind.'

She gave him a sour look and said, 'Does it matter if I do mind?'

She moved aside and he went into the

living room. Jimmy and his father were busy reading the evening papers and they looked up with disinterested gazes. Maggie flounced down on the settee and looked at him with undisguised pleasure – this was something new; a real-life policeman in the house. Frances sat next to her. 'What questions do you want answered now?'

'I'm looking for Miss Price but she seems to have disappeared. I wondered if she told you what her plans were?'

As Frances shook her head no, her husband said, 'What's Vincent been up to?'

Charlie looked puzzled. Jimmy said, 'It's my dad's little joke. He thinks she looks like Vincent Price.'

Charlie nodded. 'Mrs Flynn, you knew her years ago. Do you know if she holds a driving licence, or have you ever seen her in a small black car?'

Frances shook her head. 'I don't know if she drives and no, I've never seen her in any car, black or otherwise.'

Charlie was getting nowhere. 'Did she ever mention that she was in contact with her niece Etta?'

Frances was fed up with this harping on about Etta. 'No, she never said. As I told you before, I met her last year by accident. I was at the chapel and she came and spoke to me. I was surprised that she even recognised me because I wouldn't have known her.

Mind you, the more I saw of her, the more I recognised my old teacher.'

'Did she tell you why she had the urge to come back to Dundee after years living in Ireland? I mean, did she mention her sister Vera, or Etta?'

'No. She just said she was back for a while and that she would be going back to Ireland soon. I got the impression she hadn't been very well and maybe she wanted to have a last look for her sister, but she never mentioned her name.'

Mr Flynn piped up. 'So Vincent's disappeared has she? That family seem to make a habit of vanishing and putting people like us to a lot of bother with daft questions.'

Charlie looked at Jimmy. 'How is Mr Walsh getting on?'

'He's doing fine but he won't get out of hospital for a week or so. But the good news is they've got a key for a new house just along the road from us. Donna and the girls are so pleased.'

Maggie said, 'It'll be great having Andrea and Janey living so near. I used to be pally with them when we lived in Carnegie Street.'

'Have you tried the chapel?' asked Frances. 'She seemed to spend her entire day there. Maybe Father Black will know where she is?'

Charlie nodded. 'I've had a police constable check it out but the priest doesn't know where she is. She hasn't been to the chapel since Saturday.' He got ready to leave, there wasn't anything new to be gained from questioning this family any further.

Maggie went to the door with him. 'Do you know Miss McQueen?' Charlie said he did. 'I gave her an important clue and now she says I can get a job with her agency when I leave school.'

'I don't suppose you have an important clue to give me?'

She drew herself up taller, trying to look important. 'I might have.'

Then Frances called out, 'Hurry up, Maggie. You've got to help me with the dishes.'

Charlie put his hand on her arm. 'What important clue, Maggie?'

'Well, I didn't mention it to Mum or Dad, but I saw Miss Price driving a small black car a month ago. I was coming out of Andrea's close when she passed. She was driving very slowly because it was dark. It was a Saturday night and Mum said I could get the bus to go and see Andrea. Miss Price never saw me but I watched as she drove up to the top of James Street and parked the car there, in that small piece of spare ground. She then walked back towards her house.'

Frances shouted again. 'Maggie, will you hurry up?'

Maggie hurried away and Charlie thanked her. He blessed the observance of young people who sometimes saw things older people missed. If she was correct and not lying to maybe impress him, then Miss Price could have been at the wheel of the car during the attacks.

He hurried back into town and made his way first to Elizabeth Street where he had asked the policeman on the beat to keep an eye on number ten. The window was in darkness but the other flats were showing lights. He debated about going to ask them some questions, but decided to go and look at the piece of spare ground in James Street, which was the next street. The street was crammed with crumbling tenements; some of them facing the street but others tucked away in back courtyards.

At the top of the street, he found the small bit of ground. It had been a yard for some sort of business but it now looked derelict. He shone his torch over the ground. Bits and pieces of broken wire, tin cans and other general rubbish were strewn around. There was no sign of a car but he could make out distinct tyre marks. It looked as if she had parked it out of sight of the street, definitely hidden from view at night. Come the morning, it probably could have been seen, especially by children who would use this space as a playground.

He went back to Elizabeth Street. He didn't want to bother Mrs Davidson but he had one question that he needed answered.

She came to the door and he apologised for calling so late. This didn't put her out. 'Come in, the baby is asleep and my husband is working some overtime, but he'll be home soon if you want to speak to him.'

Charlie said that wouldn't be necessary. 'Can you tell me the name of the house factor that lets out these houses?'

'Yes, it's Campbell and Cooke in Commercial Street.'

'Thank you. Well, I'll say goodnight for now, Mrs Davidson.'

'I see there's still no sign of Miss Price?'

'No, there isn't, but you'll let me know if she comes back?' She nodded and showed him to the door.

Charlie was tired. He thought about going to see Molly but she would have had the painter in today and she wouldn't be in the mood for a visitor, so he went home. Tomorrow he would get the police team to check on those tyre prints and hopefully figure out the make of the car. He would also go and see Campbell and Cooke and ask about Miss Price's tenancy. From what he had gathered, houses to rent were scarce and he wanted to know why someone from Ireland could walk into a flat right away.

One thing was clear. Miss Price had lived within the radius of all the attacks. She could easily have made her way to Peter's bike shed and cut his brakes. She could also have been Vera and Molly's attacker, nipping quickly down the street and then hugging the shadows as she made her way home – either on foot or in the car.

50

The day began with a disappointment, and a surprise. The team had gathered at the spare ground to look at the tyre prints but it had been a night of heavy rain and the ground was waterlogged into a sea of mud. A small gathering of curious residents from the surrounding houses had gathered at the edge of the pavement, wondering what the police presence was all about. Some of the women carried young children in their arms and small boys and girls stood open-mouthed and wide-eyed as the policemen skirted around the mud, looking for the tracks.

Charlie stood beside them, bitterly disappointed that the weather had turned so nasty. It had rained before, nothing as heavy as last night, but even so, the tyre tracks would have been obliterated on these nights as well, which meant the car had been parked on the spare ground on Saturday night. So where did it go to and who drove it? That was the question.

He went and spoke to some of the neighbours who were still standing and watching. No doubt this was a piece of drama in their lives. 'Has anyone seen a car parked here during the last two or three weeks?'

They stood in silence but a few shook their heads. One man said, 'I pass here every day and I've never seen a car parked here.'

That seemed to be the general consensus, which left him puzzled. If Maggie had been telling the truth, then she had seen Miss Price park the car here one Saturday evening, which meant that someone must have come to take it away before any of the neighbours noticed it. Or else that someone was already in the car. 'Are there any old garages around here where a car could be hidden?'

The same man said, 'You must be joking. Ten families share a single toilet in this close, so where's the room for garages?'

The surprise came when he left the men packing up to go back to the station. He set off for Commercial Street and the office of Campbell and Cooke. A smart young woman was typing at a desk behind the main counter but she rose to her feet when he entered. 'I'm checking on a tenant of yours. A Miss Price who lives at 10 Elizabeth Street. Can you tell me when she got the key for this property, as it seems she has not long arrived from Ireland?'

The woman excused herself and headed

into another office where he could hear a muffled conversation. After a moment or two, a small plump man appeared. He was dressed very smartly in a three-piece brown suit with an impressive watch and chain on his waistcoat. 'I'm Mr Campbell. How can I help you?'

Charlie repeated his request and added, 'It seems like rented houses are difficult to come by and I wondered how Miss Price could walk into one right after arriving from Ireland.'

It was now Mr Campbell who seemed puzzled. 'I think you're under a misapprehension. Miss Price bought that property in 1929. We look after it for her and she pays her fees half-yearly, along with her rates. She's a very religious person, I believe, and she left instructions that the chapel can use it if they need it for any reason. Should it be let to anyone, then they pay the running costs of heating and light but they don't pay any rent, which is a generous gesture from Miss Price.'

'But she's been living there for the past year, I believe?'

'Yes, she has. We got a letter from her a year ago to say she would be coming back to live in it and not to let it out again. She was in here about ten days ago to say she would be leaving to go back to Ireland and she would hand the key back to us. We haven't received it yet, but she could possibly have left it with the chapel and they just haven't had time to return it.'

Charlie didn't know what to think about this turn of events. Had she left to go back to Ireland or was she still here, perhaps lurking about the house and not answering the door?

He decided to go and see Molly. She was busy in the office and he could hear Ronnie whistling as he painted the flat upstairs. He wanted to speak to her privately but because she didn't want to get in the painter's way, they went to Wilson's café at the foot of the Wellgate. She looked tired, he thought, and with good reason. Until this woman was caught there was no telling what she might do. He told her about his fruitless search for the tyre tracks and the surprise over Miss Price. 'What I can't understand,' he said, 'is why she bought a flat if she had no intention of staying in it?'

'Do you think that's where Etta went after she disappeared? It would be the perfect hideout.'

Charlie agreed with her up to a point. 'But what would she do for money or going out for food? Anyone could have recognised her.'

'She would have had some money to tide her over, as she almost emptied her post office savings account before she went missing,' said Molly.

'Well, I suppose she could have kept her head down till all the fuss went away.' He suddenly had an idea. 'Does Mrs Barton know if her sister came back after the 1929 visit?'

'I can ask her but I'm not sure if she would know if Miss Price ever visited the flat.'

'But she must have,' said Charlie. 'Why buy the flat to leave it empty for years?'

'Well, she was letting the chapel use it. She was very religious and maybe this was what she wanted to do with her money.'

'And yet a year ago she suddenly turns up out of the blue and becomes my prime suspect for all these attacks? I can just about manage to get my mind around her harming her sister because she had done that on at least two occasions during their childhood. But why try to kill you and Peter Walsh? It doesn't make any sense.'

Molly had a headache. She took two aspirins from her bag and asked the waitress for a glass of water. She would be glad when this case was over. She had sent her bill to Vera Barton last week, and when that was paid then surely it would be all over. 'How did you find out about the car being parked in James Street?' she asked.

Charlie laughed. 'Oh, didn't I tell you? It was young Maggie Flynn. She said she had given you an important clue as well.'

'Maggie? But how did she know?'

'She said she saw her driving it.'

'Charlie, you don't think she's lying, do you?'

'It did cross my mind but she was adamant it was Miss Price and she did know the woman through her friendship with her mother.'

Molly looked doubtful. 'I just hope she's not simply trying to impress us. Young girls like getting attention.'

'Was the important clue she gave you any good or was it a false trail?'

Molly shook her head. 'Oh no, it was a great breakthrough but it just fizzled out. Etta had gone out for a few weeks with a boy called Pedro who turned out to be Peter Walsh, but he had broken up with her a few weeks earlier.'

Charlie said, 'I think Robina Price has been watching you all. First Vera, then Peter and you. For some unknown reason, she decided to attack you, but why remains a mystery. She has access to a black car and she is able to keep it somewhere, maybe a garage. Perhaps she bought the car when she arrived here or maybe she brought it over from Ireland. The other solution is that she has an accomplice, but who? It must be someone she's met through the chapel because I can't see it being anyone from the Flynn household. Those are the only two places we know she visited.'

'I've brought my father's car here and I've parked it in Paradise Road, just in case she tries to break in again and damage it.'

'How is Marigold?'

Molly laughed. 'She's great. It'll take more than an attacker to dent Marigold's courage. Sabby is a different matter. Apparently, since coming back from Peggy's, she won't eat her food or look at Marigold. Marigold thinks she's in the huff. Honestly, that cat is a prima donna.'

Charlie gave her a serious look. 'Now, I still want you to be cautious, Molly. We don't know where this woman is but hopefully I'll start getting answers to some of my inquiries.'

'Charlie, how would Robina get to Ireland? Do you think she's driven the car to Larne or Stranraer and caught the ferry? If she was seen on Saturday night by that young lad then she must have left early on Sunday morning.'

'Yes, I think she did. I made enquiries at the chapel and she didn't show for mass on Sunday, and she hasn't been back since, which isn't like her. The priest said she always went to early morning mass.' He changed the subject. 'Will you stay in the flat tonight?' he asked.

Molly said no, she would go over to Newport and stay there. There had been a lot of mail delivered and she planned to deal with it all. 'But I'll be back in my own wee corner tomorrow night.'

When he got back to the station, PC Williams came over. 'There's been no one answering to Miss Price's description on any of the ferries since Saturday. There have been a few small black cars but they have all belonged to couples with families. None of them was driven by a single lady driver.'

Charlie felt wearied by all the negatives in this case. He had nothing else planned except to have the policeman on the beat keep a beady eye on the house.

51

Molly couldn't settle when Ronnie left. He had painted most of the ceilings and walls and he was coming back to paint the doors. She had no idea how much this would cost her but she looked out her insurance policy to see if this wilful act would be covered. She decided to phone the company in the morning and find out. She had made a reasonable profit since opening last year but if these things were going to happen often, then the repairs would soon eat away at her bank balance. She didn't want her parents or Nell to know of this latest drama, and she had warned Marigold to say nothing should she write to them.

The thought of travelling over on the Fifie tonight didn't appeal to her but she couldn't stay here with the strong smell of paint everywhere. In spite of her tiredness, she was amused. Last night, the flat had smelled like a fish and chip shop and tonight, it was like a paint factory. She wondered, whatever happened to the smell of roses?

Jean was covering the typewriter, getting ready to go. She was also feeling worried about Molly. 'Come home with me and have your tea and you can easily stay the night. I've got a spare bed.'

Molly was touched by all the concern the women were showing her. Everyone had offered her a place to stay. Even Alice, who certainly didn't have a spare bed, but she was grateful. She smiled. 'Thanks, Jean, but I told DS Johns I would be going to Newport tonight. He's got the telephone number – just in case he finds out something, I asked if he would let me know.'

Jean smiled back. 'I'm glad he's on this case now. Whoever is doing this won't want to mess with him and I feel better that he's keeping an eye on you.' Molly felt the same but he wasn't with her twenty-four hours a day and she felt vulnerable when she was on her own.

After Jean left, Molly got her coat and bag and switched off the light. As she locked up, she looked over her shoulder, wondering if Robina Price was watching her from the dark abyss of a shop doorway. Charlie had said that the policeman on the beat would keep an eye on the agency, so she hoped that would prove to be a deterrent should Robina plan any more mischief. She had no idea why she should be a target for this woman's hate. Something must have happened years ago when Etta went missing. But what?

As she made her way through the town, she was too tired to think about Etta or Vera or Robina. She would go and see Marigold when she got home to see how she was after her ordeal, then she planned to have a hot bath and hopefully get a good night's sleep.

The ferry was quiet and there were hardly any passengers or vehicles. She sat in the saloon and watched to see if any elderly women were lurking around. Thankfully, there was no one who looked suspicious, not unless they were hiding on the deck. When the Fifie docked, she walked towards the house, wary of anyone walking behind her, but the only person she saw was an old man out walking with his dog. He said 'good evening' as he passed and she turned to watch his figure disappear slowly up the road.

The rain had come on again and it was

misty. The streetlights glowed hazily through the drizzle and fog and she was glad when she reached Marigold's house. The light was on in the front porch and a golden glow from the living room window seeped out onto the front garden. In contrast, her parents' house lay in darkness, with the dripping trees and shrubs making the garden into a mysterious place of menace. Molly had to give herself a good shake. She was becoming quite paranoid about shadows.

Marigold was pleased to see her. 'I've made your tea as I thought you might be hungry.'

Molly hadn't eaten much during the day and was surprised at how hungry she was. She loved being with Marigold and she thought her parents were lucky to have such a super neighbour. Once again, she felt a bit homesick. It had been her idea to have the flat renovated but she missed the warmth and homeliness of her mum and dad's house, and the company. When all the staff went home in the evening, she was on her own in the flat and although she didn't mind solitude, all this trouble had knocked the pleasure out of living on her own.

She was thinking about leaving Marigold's comfortable chair to go next door and put on the immersion heater for her bath when the phone rang. Marigold answered it and then handed it to her. 'It's DS Johns, he wants to speak to you, Molly.'

She suddenly felt cold with apprehension and she said a small prayer that the office hadn't been burnt to the ground. But it was more serious than that. Charlie didn't waste time with social chitchat. 'It's Miss Price. We've found her body in her house. It looks like she's been dead a few days.'

Molly suddenly felt faint but she gripped the receiver in her hand. 'How did she die, Charlie?'

'There will be a post-mortem done tomorrow so we'll know what happened then. I'll see you tomorrow morning. I'll come to the office but try and get a good night's sleep, Molly.'

Molly wondered if she would ever get a good night's sleep again.

52

It was snowing when she woke up and she spent a very cold half-hour crossing the river. The streets were white as she made her way to the office. The girls were coming in, dressed in warm coats and furry boots, scarves, hats and gloves. The radiator was on but it was still quite cold in the office and it would be even colder upstairs. She went to put on the electric fire so the room would be warmer for Ronnie to finish his painting. Not for the first time did Molly think longingly of the hot climate of Sydney and the wonderful blue water and white sandy beaches of Australia – especially with winter so fast approaching.

She waited for Charlie to appear but he didn't come until dinner time. They went down to Wilson's café to speak in private. The snow had turned to slush that seeped into Molly's boots and she was glad to be inside out of the cold. It was warm and muggy in the café and the air was full of cigarette smoke and the smell of wet woollen coats. However, the tea was lovely and hot.

Molly wanted to know what had happened and how the body had been found. Charlie said, 'It was the policeman on the beat. I had asked him to keep an eye on the house, just in case Miss Price came back. At about two o'clock in the morning, he thought he saw a torch shining in the house, but when he looked again a few minutes later, the house was in darkness. He thought it was the reflection of the street lamp. At the end of his shift, he thought he would go to the door. He knocked but there was no answer and he tried the handle and to his surprise, the door was unlocked. He went in and found Miss Price lying next to the bed. There were two bottles of pills on the bedside cabinet and a jug of water but there was nothing to say what she had died from. Still, we'll have the results of the post-mortem this afternoon.'

'So we're no further forward and we don't know if Miss Price is the culprit.' Molly sounded depressed.

Charlie sounded more optimistic. 'If all this stops, then we can safely assume she is, but if not...' he lapsed into silence. 'I have to leave as I want to go over the house more thoroughly and hopefully we'll have an answer to what caused her death.'

Molly was grateful that she had an assignment to go to, as it would help to take her mind off all these confusing incidents. The job was at a busy office in the town and all the normal day-to-day work was just what she needed.

Charlie made his way back to Miss Price's house. The body had been removed some hours earlier and the rooms looked neat and tidy. It was difficult to believe a person had died within these walls. The only sign that something had gone wrong was the small bedroom where a blanket had been pulled from the bed. Robina Price had been found lying on the floor by the bed and it looked like she had tried to get up before collapsing, but she was still dressed in her daytime clothes, which was a mystery. Had she come in, felt unwell and gone to lie down before trying to get up again? This seemed to be the logical explanation because of the unlocked door.

Still, he would have to wait for the result of the post-mortem. The two bottles of pills had been taken away and he looked through the bedside cabinet, but the drawer and cupboard were empty. The wardrobe held a few clothes, mostly coats and skirts in plain black styles. There was nothing fashionable here. The drawers were the same, everything serviceable and cheap. A black handbag lay at the foot of the wardrobe. It was empty apart from a purse with five-pound notes in it.

He made for the desk that lay in front of the living room window. This was the window through which the constable had thought he saw a beam from a torch. In contrast to the cheap looking clothes, the desk was of good quality. Inside, he found a few bills, a letter from Mr Campbell with a statement of the fees she had paid for the flat and a plain envelope that looked like it had been sealed but reopened. It contained her will, which was written by a solicitor and left everything to the convent in Ireland. There was also a paid-up life insurance policy with a firm in Dublin. There were no letters from her family or friends and Charlie was suddenly moved by the spartan and seemingly friendless life she had lived.

He wondered about the opened envelope that held her will. Had someone been in here last night with a torch and was this what they were looking for? And was this her original will? It had been written a few years earlier and dated 1945. Mr Campbell had said that the chapel had the use of the flat when she lived in Ireland, so it seemed quite normal for the will to be in favour of the convent. Her address at the time was the convent in Dublin and the two witnesses were clerks at the solicitor's office where the will was drawn up. Everything seemed to be in order.

He glanced around the sparsely furnished, white-walled room before slowly closing and locking the door. He would have to go and speak to Vera Barton and tell her that her sister was dead. How would she take it, he wondered? According to her, she hadn't seen her sister since 1929, but Charlie knew that death in a family could bring all sorts of hidden emotions to the surface.

But first he wanted to see Mrs Davidson, the neighbour. She answered the door right away and curiosity was written all over her face. When she spoke, she sounded breathless as if she had been running. 'I've been standing at the window watching all the activity. What's happened? Is it Miss Price?'

Charlie said it was. He asked her, 'Did you

hear anything from the flat over the last few days?'

She shook her head. 'I didn't even know she was up there and I haven't seen her for ages. Not since the night I told you about, the time she came out of the car.'

'I don't suppose you saw or heard anybody else coming in the close? Someone who doesn't live here?'

'There are a few strangers coming and going. I suppose they are friends of the people who live on the top floor but to be honest, these last few nights we've had the curtains drawn and the baby has slept right through the night, so I haven't been at the window. Anyone could have come and gone and I wouldn't have noticed.' She looked rueful. 'Sorry about that, but it's been great getting a good night's sleep.'

Charlie said it didn't matter and he hoped the baby would sleep every night.

He next made his way to the Hilltown, hoping Vera was at home. She was and looked a bit better than the last time he had seen her but she didn't ask him why he was calling. 'I've come with some bad news, Mrs Barton. I'm afraid your sister, Miss Robina Price, died a couple of days ago. Her body was found in her flat at 10 Elizabeth Street this morning.'

Vera took this news calmly. 'I wonder why she never came to see me. It was Dave who put her out of the house that day. Said he was fed up with her stories of retribution and sin and reaping what you sow, but I would have made her welcome, she knew that, so why didn't she come and see me?'

Charlie remained silent. He had no idea why the two sisters hadn't met up again after all these years. 'We're not sure what caused her death but as soon as I hear, I will let you know.'

'I'll have to make plans for her funeral. When can I do that?'

'I'll be able to tell you after the post-mortem, Mrs Barton. Is there anyone who can come and stay with you?'

She shook her head. 'No, I'll be fine, but thank you for coming to tell me and you'll let me know how she died?'

Charlie said he would and he left. Vera's flat was better furnished and more comfortable but it had the same friendless atmosphere of Robina's place. He realised there must be hundreds of lonely people all living in cells like the one at Elizabeth Street. Some would be more luxurious than others but they were still self-imposed, solitary places.

Mrs Barton had taken the news calmly, he thought, but had he gone back, he would have changed his mind. The minute he left, Vera burst into a flood of tears. She felt terrible for the wasted years with her sister, but it was too late now to remedy that. First it was Dave, then Etta and now Robina. She was the last one left in the family.

53

Stan had a letter back by return from Phil. He recognised the handwriting and the postmark. He shoved it in his pocket before leaving for work but it weighed on his mind all morning. At dinner time, he opened it. It was just one page and with Phil's usual large handwriting, there wasn't much news. He said he was glad the six-week training was nearly over and he was looking forward to coming home on leave. Stan thought he wasn't going to mention Mary but at the foot of the page he had written PTO and the letter continued:

I'm glad you and Mary like one another and I think you are both suited to each other. I'm glad to get your letter Stan because I was in a bit of a dilemma. Linda – remember the girl I used to go out with – well, she's been writing to me now and again and I look forward to her letters as she mentions all the gossip at Keiller's. She said she would like to meet up for a coffee so that I could tell her all about army life. She never said

anything about those pals of hers, so I assume it'll just be the two of us. I was gong to ask you and Mary to come as well but you'll both have plans of your own. Hopefully we'll meet up when I'm home. Regards to Mary.
Phil.

Stan had a moment of worry. What if Mary was miffed at this turnaround with Linda? But when they met up in the evening on their way to the pictures, she just smiled. As they stood in the queue at the Plaza cinema, Mary thought to herself, good for you Linda. Now keep it up.

Victor was also pleased as he left the boxing club in Lochee. The snow had started to fall again but he hardly noticed it. He still felt the warmth of the praise from the club's owner. 'You stick at this, lad, and you'll be a first-class boxer, but mind you keep the fighting in the ring and not outside it.'

So he was going to keep his nose clean and Alice could have her damned divorce. After all, he had found another girlfriend. She was a bit older than him and certainly not pretty but she looked after him and he was spending most nights with her, in her house on the Hawkhill. Yes, he would be a model citizen and a great boxer. It was a dream of his to be a champion in the ring and it looked like it might come true, so no more drinking or ending up at Arthurstone Terrace to commit a breach of the peace. The divorce would go through, the quicker the better.

Sandy could hardly wait to tell Alice and once he did, she knew her marriage would soon be a thing of the past. She had bought a lovely new rug to sit in front of the fireplace. She thought it brightened up the kitchen with its colourful pattern and after she finished paying for the three-piece suite, she intended to get a dining room suite and after that, she would furnish the bedroom. Life was looking rosy. Although she wasn't in love with Sandy, she enjoyed his company. She had been honest with him right from the start and he seemed quite content to be a friend.

54

The result of the post-mortem was in. Miss Price had died of natural causes. She had suffered a heart attack and had died within minutes. For some reason, Charlie was pleased by that small fact. She hadn't been a particularly attractive or nice woman but he was glad she hadn't suffered. He thought of the anguish she would have felt if she had been unable to summon help and had taken hours or even days to die.

He went to see Vera first to tell her the news. When she came to the door, she looked like she had just got out of bed and it was two o'clock in the afternoon. The woman was disintegrating before his eyes and he wished she had left this missing daughter in the past where she belonged. Vera looked at him with bleary eyes, almost as if she didn't recognise him. 'I've got the result of the post-mortem on your sister, Mrs Barton. Can I come in?'

She held the door open but she looked as if she didn't care whether he came in or not. She had obviously been crying, as her eyes were red and puffy and he felt so sorry for her. He came straight to the point. 'Miss Price had a heart attack but her death was quick. She wouldn't have suffered long, which is a blessing.'

Vera suddenly laughed – a deep, painful, choking laugh. 'A blessing? Well that would suit Robina. She was always very religious, you know, even as a child. My parents didn't know how to cope with her and neither did Dave and I. Because I was expecting Etta before getting married, she said my soul was dammed, and do you know something, DS Johns, she was right. I've lost everything I ever loved, so she was right about retribution.'

Charlie was alarmed by this turn of events.

Vera was becoming more depressed by the hour. He said, 'I think you should go to the doctor and get some treatment. You've had a bad shock with your sister's death. If you like, I can telephone him and get him to come and see you.'

'No, honestly, I'm fine. Just feeling a bit sorry for myself. I hardly knew Robina these past years and here I am crying for our lost lives.'

'Is there a neighbour who can come in and stay with you?'

'No, I have to arrange the funeral and after that, I might go away for a holiday.'

'I have to go and tell Mrs Flynn about your sister's death. Robina used to go and see her.'

Vera sounded bitter. 'Which was more than she did for me.'

It was teatime before he managed to get to Kirkton but he knew he wouldn't be staying very long. As before, it was Maggie who answered the door. 'Muuuuum,' she shouted along the hall, 'it's that policeman.'

Frances walked up to the door and rolled her eyes. 'What do you want now?'

Charlie apologised for calling at a mealtime. 'It's just to tell you Miss Price is dead. She suffered a heart attack.'

'Oh my God,' said Frances. 'That's awful. She was all right when she came to see me a couple of weeks ago. She looked tired and pale but she never looked healthy, not even when I was at school.'

Mr Flynn had joined them and he looked sad. 'Poor Vincent, I never liked her but we're very sorry to hear this.'

'Well, I wanted you to know. I didn't want you to read about it first in the death column of the paper.'

Charlie would be glad to be finished with bearing the sad news but he had to see Molly first. She was in the office when he arrived at the Wellgate and she smiled when he knocked at the door. 'Come in out of the cold. If you don't mind the smell of paint, we can go upstairs where it's warmer.'

The flat looked almost back to normal. Molly said not to sit on the studio couch because it had been cleaned and was still a bit damp, so they sat on the dining chairs by the table. Charlie gave her all the news about Miss Price's death and Molly said she was also glad it had been quick. 'Even though she might have tried to kill me,' she said.

Charlie nodded. 'I'm worried about Vera Barton; she seems to be depressed. She was still in her bed this afternoon and she was talking a lot of nonsense.'

'I'll go and see her tomorrow and see if she needs any help with the funeral or anything else.' Molly looked at him. 'Charlie, if Robina had heart trouble, do you think she would have been able to do all this cloak and dagger stuff? I mean, it must have taken a lot of effort to make the attacks on Vera, Peter and myself, and the weather has been cold and wet most nights.'

'I agree but she's the only suspect we've got. She lives within a half-mile radius of you and Vera and she's practically next door to Peter Walsh. Maybe she was all right these past weeks and then her heart just gave out. These things happen.'

Molly was still dubious. 'I suppose so.'

Charlie said, 'I agree with you on most things, Molly, as I don't believe she was working alone. I'm waiting on word from the car-licensing department to find out if a car was ever registered to her. I've also written to the convent in Dublin to see if she owned a car in Eire. If she did, then she could have brought it over with her when she came back here.'

'So you think the car is important?'

'It was seen by Mrs Davidson and Maggie, and a car drew out in front of Peter Walsh, making him slam on his non-existent brakes and have his accident.'

'It must be someone who knows Robina. Do you think Robina had something to do with Etta's disappearance, or knew who had and they were both trying to cover it up?'

'What I can't understand is where Etta went to on the night of her father's death.

She was seen by Mrs Pert in the evening and then, nothing. She must have had somewhere to go – either to her aunt's house in Elizabeth Street or to one of her friends. But which one?'

Molly tried to put herself in Etta's shoes. 'At the time Mrs Pert saw her Etta probably didn't know her father was dead, so she must have been planning to disappear for a while. That is why she almost emptied her savings account. But when the news of his death came out, why didn't she reappear and grieve for him? She was seemingly besotted with him, although she didn't care much for her mother.'

Charlie said, 'Even if she had already left Dundee, surely the news of his death would be in the papers and she would have come home.'

Molly ventured, 'Not unless she had somehow already found out about the accident and her distress gave her a final reason to leave forever.'

'If she stayed with someone before going, the logical person would be Frances Flynn,' said Charlie, 'but Etta didn't know about her connection with her aunt. It's not as if they have the same surname.' He suddenly had a thought. 'Unless Frances, who went to the same convent school where Miss Price was a teacher, told Etta all about her schooldays in Eire and mentioned Miss Price's name. If

Etta knew her aunt's address, then she could easily have made the connection. Then there's Doctor Lowson, who was living in Arbroath at the time.'

Molly interrupted him. 'Sasha Lowson didn't like Etta. In fact, Etta had threatened her and the doctor got the message. That's why she left the Bartons' house and got other accommodation.'

'Then let's look at the others. Anita Armstrong, the lady with the fantastic memory. She says she left with her husband the year before this all happened but what if she's lying. Maybe she became friendly with Etta and asked her to come and stay with them for a wee holiday at some point, and Etta took the chance to go there and then on to where she might be now. Then there's Vina, she was a young lass back then. Maybe Etta asked for her help and Vina knew someone she could go to, perhaps a friend or a relative.'

Molly thought there was just one flaw with all this. 'But why cover it all up? I mean, after all this time, does it matter where Etta is? And what about the attacks? Why is it worth harming people to keep her whereabouts hidden?'

Charlie shook his head and said he didn't know. 'I'll wait for the results to get back about the car and maybe that will lead to something. I hope so.' As he was leaving, he said, 'Oh, I almost forgot, the tablets in the two bottles were aspirins, so there's nothing sinister there.'

55

The woman was so pleased with herself at fooling everyone. Imagine the old bat dying like that, but that meant she was the perfect scapegoat. The police would connect her appearance with all the attacks and that suited her. All she had to do now was to keep a low profile and soon she would disappear again – this time forever. She was so full of elation that she could have danced for joy but she had to be careful now. Anyone watching her would wonder. And she didn't want that kind of scrutiny.

56

The Convent of the Holy Sisters was a beautiful building, built from a golden stone that shimmered, seemingly full of sunshine, even on a grey misty day like today. The school lay to the side of it and was a plainer building, built many, many years after the convent.

The Mother Superior sat with Sister Margaret in the small room off the chapel – a lovely place with lead windows and the ambience of a couple of centuries' mixture of beeswax and faded flowers. The Mother Superior sat with a letter in her hand. 'I have some sad news, Sister Margaret. Miss Price has died quite suddenly of a heart attack.'

Sister Margaret bowed her head. 'That is sad news, Mother Superior. I didn't think we would see her again after she left and it's God's will that we won't.'

'I have a letter from the police in Scotland. A Detective Sergeant Johns wants to know if Miss Price owned a car.'

Sister Margaret shook her head. 'No, she didn't. We all saw her off when she left and all her belongings were in one suitcase.'

The Mother Superior thought for a moment. 'Yes, that is what I thought. We will say prayers at Mass for our late companion.'

Sister Margaret nodded and left the room. The Mother Superior sat for a long time afterwards. She remembered Miss Price very well. Although she had never taken orders and become a novice nun, she had possessed a deep and strong faith. The Mother Superior had never really known the woman. She had never discussed her life with anyone, even after all the years she had spent in the school where she had been a brilliant mathematics teacher. She had been a lonely woman but the Mother Superior never doubted Miss Price's devotion to duty and to God.

Then there was the other letter, the one from the solicitor's office in Dublin. The solicitor had couched the letter in his dry and very legal way of writing, but from what she could gather, he explained that Miss Price had left her entire estate to the convent. To start with, the Mother Superior had expected a few pounds for the poor box, but her eyes widened when she read the amount. Miss Price had lived quite simply but invested her salary in the stocks and shares market. The solicitor said she had the mathematical brain of a genius and had always bought and sold at the right time. This money would do such a power of good for their work at the convent. Miss Price, who had lived with one suitcase for most of her life, had died a very wealthy woman. The Mother Superior bent her head and said a prayer for the departed soul of a lonely woman.

57

Jimmy Flynn made his way up to the infirmary to see Peter. He knew Donna and the girls were busy moving to their new house and, as it was a rotten night with snow swirling in the cold wind, he didn't think Peter would have any other visitors. Peter was beginning to get fed up in the hospital but his face brightened when Jimmy appeared. 'I should be at home helping Donna with the flitting instead of being cooped up in here.' He sounded grumpy.

Jimmy told him everything was going fine. 'Mr Cooke has arranged a couple of the vans to help her move and some of the lads are lending a hand. Of course, having Andrea there helps, as it's mostly the younger guys who volunteered.'

Peter felt tears coming into his eyes. Everyone was being so helpful and he knew he couldn't ever repay all that had been done for the family since the accident. 'As long as they don't take any liberties with her,' he said.

Jimmy laughed. 'No, they're great lads. They just like chatting to her and Janey mimics them when they go home.'

'Good old Janey,' said Peter. 'Always has an answer for everything. I often think if the Devil was stuck for an answer, then Janey would be able to set him straight.'

'She's got her jar of bath salts on the bathroom window ledge. It was the first thing to be taken inside the house,' said Jimmy. 'Donna is over the moon with the house, Peter, and you'll find it a great place as well. The girls have their own bedrooms and Donna just loves the kitchen and the bathroom. When you get back to work, there will be no more cycling, as I'll take you to the joiners' yard in the van.'

'Aye,' said Peter, lying back on his pile of pillows. '*When* I get home ... whenever that'll be.'

Jimmy was worried about broaching the subject of the dented van. So much had taken place over these last few weeks but he had to know. 'Peter, that night you borrowed the van and it got dented, how did it happen?'

Peter groaned. 'Has Mr Cooke noticed it?'

'No, but I have to know. You see, a woman got knocked down that night at the Rosebank School entrance and I want to know if it was you. I mean, you maybe didn't notice her on the road, but a lot of strange things are happening.'

To Jimmy's surprise, Peter burst out laughing. 'I was never near Rosebank

School, Jimmy. I had offered to help with old Mr and Mrs Ferguson's flitting. You don't know them, but they lived near us in Alexander Street. They had been given a key for an older house in Wedderburn Street because they couldn't afford the big rents of the new houses. Well, the removal company let them down and I said I would help. I thought of borrowing the van and doing a few runs with their stuff. They didn't own a lot as they were living in one small room in that building that's been demolished. I was almost finished when we tried to put the wardrobe in the back. The old guy's hand slipped and he dented the side of the van. I was furious but I couldn't say anything to him as he's really old. I know I haven't cleared the money with you yet, but I'll make sure I do when I'm back working. I mentioned the fence because I was worried, but I shouldn't have lied. Sorry about that.'

Jimmy let out his breath. He hadn't been aware that he had been holding it in. 'That's all right, Peter, I don't want any more money. Let's just call it quits.'

'Who is the woman who was knocked down?' Jimmy said.

'You're not going to believe this but it was Etta Barton's mother. However, she's all right. The strange thing is, she was attacked again later, in broad daylight, and we don't know what's going on. My mother is worried about all the questioning and Dad is fuming because his routine is being disrupted.'

Peter was worried. 'Are Donna and the girls safe? I don't want anything to happen to them.' Jimmy said they were fine but after he left, Peter spent a sleepless and frustrating night.

Earlier that day, Charlie had word back from the licensing department to say no car had ever been registered to a Miss Robina Price. Charlie knew that the driver of the car was still at large. But maybe they were an innocent party. Perhaps someone from the chapel had given Miss Price some lifts and he was just imagining the link to all the disturbing things that were happening.

58

Robina Price had left no special instructions for her funeral, so it was left to Vera to organise it. Father Black at the chapel in Forebank Road brought the body into the chapel for a funeral mass and afterwards she was buried at Balgay cemetery. Molly and Charlie were there, along with Vera, Mrs Davidson and the Flynn family. There were also quite a few of the parishioners from the chapel who had known the deceased woman. Molly found the service a peaceful and beautiful experience and afterwards they all went to the cemetery where it started to snow.

Molly was aware, as they all stood around the grave in a freezing cold wind, that Charlie was quietly scrutinising all the mourners. Then, afterwards, he looked at the few wreaths that had been placed on top of the grave but there were none that gave him a clue to the unknown accomplice.

Balgay cemetery was usually a quiet, green place with grass and trees and secluded benches but today the scenery was all black and white. Water dripped from tree branches now stripped of any leaves and the grey headstones looked forlorn in the overcast winter's day. Once again, Molly thought longingly of the hot sunshine of Australia and she had to mentally chide herself. This was where her life was now and it had been her choice to come back home. Still, maybe if she saved up hard enough, she would be able to have a holiday to see Nell, Terry and Molly. At least it was something to look forward to.

After the service, Frances and Mrs Davidson came to speak to them. Mrs Davidson had been crying; she felt sorry for the woman and anyway, she said, she always cried at funerals. Frances was more stoic. 'I can't say I liked the woman but I just wish she had had someone with her at the end. To die alone is a terrible thing.' Both Molly and Charlie agreed with her.

Vera had ordered a funeral tea in a private room of the Royal Hotel but Molly and Charlie didn't go back for that. Instead, they went to their favourite place at Wilson's café. Molly was chilled to the bone and glad of the hot drink. Charlie said, 'I'll still investigate this case but it looks highly unlikely that we'll ever find the accomplice. Maybe they'll continue with this vendetta against Vera, Peter and you, but hopefully it will stop. I can find no link to anyone and it seems as if Miss Price was a loner. The only person she had any dealings with was Frances Flynn and I'll keep an eye on her.'

Molly poured out more tea but Charlie said he had had enough. 'Will you be back living in the flat, Molly?'

'Yes. I can't face that river crossing every day and the smell of paint is getting fainter.'

'Be careful and keep the car in Paradise Road. I hope this has all ended but I'm not sure,' he told her.

Molly shivered and wasn't sure if it was due to the cold or the fear of another attack. 'I thought Vera looked terrible,' she said. 'I'll go and see her tomorrow and try and get her to see the doctor. I feel such a failure at not finding her daughter, but it was so long ago and people change over the years. I had to keep telling myself I wasn't looking for a young sixteen-year-old girl but a woman of forty.'

She walked back to the office alone, her hands in her pockets and her hat acting like a blinker, which meant she didn't see the woman standing in the doorway of Hunter's store. She was dressed in a long coat with a woollen hat over her hair. She looked like she was studying something in the window but her heart was filled with pleasure at the sight of Molly's sad and cold looking figure.

59

Deanna came into the office not long after Molly, beaming with good health. Her cheeks were red with the cold and she had a woollen hat pulled down over her hair. 'That's my shift finished, Molly,' she said, 'unless there is something else.'

Jean looked through the day's roster and said everything was done. 'I'll see you tomorrow then. Oh, I almost forgot, the Glencoe play is finished but I've been kept on for the next one, which is a comedy. I hope you can all come and see me.'

Molly felt guilty. 'I meant to ask everyone to come to see you but, with everything that's happened, I forgot, but we'll all be along to see this one.'

Deanna looked sad. 'Yes, you've had a rotten time of it, Molly, but you'll get a laugh at this comedy. It's really very funny. Have you ever seen the Brian Rix farces where people keep falling out of cupboards? Well, it's like that.'

When she left, Molly looked at Jean and they both burst out laughing. 'It must be good to be young and carefree and full of life,' said Molly, who suddenly felt old.

'Who on earth is Brian Rix?' asked Jean. 'And I swear that girl spends her life as if she's acting, like she's always playing a part.'

'Brian Rix is a well-known stage actor who puts on very funny plays down in one of the London theatres. I think they're very good,' said Molly, who had suddenly cheered up. 'We must ask everyone if they want to go and see Deanna at the Rep. Maybe on a Saturday night.'

Jean shook her head and laughed. 'I'll speak to the staff and see what they say.'

Edna and John were just finishing off the day's work when a car pulled up outside the door. John was standing by the window and he let out a groan of dismay. 'Here's James and Sonia. I wonder what she wants now. Do you think we can pretend to be out?'

Edna sounded doubtful. 'If you saw them through the window then they will have seen you. Better to let them in and see what they want.'

'If I know Sonia, it'll be something for her. I don't know what James sees in her but he's always had a soft spot for her. Fortunately, she went off to work in Edinburgh when I became engaged to her sister and James went off to paint in France, but now they've finally met up, and God help him is all I can say.'

However, he went to the door and because he was fond of his brother, he welcomed them with a smile. 'Come in. It's nice to see you both.'

They came into the living room and if Sonia was disappointed that all her chintzy covers had gone, she didn't show it. 'Edna, how lovely to see you,' she said, coming over to Edna like some long-lost special friend.

Edna hated to be two-faced but she managed a smile and said, 'How are you, Sonia?'

'Busy, busy, busy. James is putting on another painting exhibition and I'm organising it.' She turned to James and gave him a huge hundred-watt smile. 'It's going to be the best thing Arbroath has seen in years. The customers will be coming in their droves and he'll sell all his wonderful paintings.'

Edna remembered the last exhibition James had put on, when he had sold most of his paintings without Sonia's over-exuberant gestures. Still, James looked besotted and if he was happy, then she knew John would be pleased for his brother. James spoke for the first time. 'We've brought you both an invitation. It'll be next month at the Exclusive Gallery. We thought to hold it just before Christmas so people could maybe buy something as a gift. Sonia has managed to hire the gallery for two nights, so we are expecting great things.'

Then Sonia said, 'What a dither I am. I forgot to say congratulations on your engagement. Oh, Edna, what a lovely ring.'

After a few bits of conversation, they left. Edna felt as if a whirlwind had swept in from the north and swirled out again. Even John looked a bit shell-shocked. 'I hope James knows what he's taken on. I thought his last exhibition in his house was great and he sold most of the paintings.'

'That's what I was thinking,' said Edna.

'I mean, what is it going to cost him for two nights' rent in this Exclusive Gallery? Trust Sonia to always go overboard on everything. I think she's forgotten that her business went into the red and she had to give it up.'

Edna agreed. She liked James. He was a simple man who would be like putty in Sonia's hands.

John said, 'I expect we'll just have to let them get on with it. Maybe James will get his eyes opened with her. Now, I'll walk you back to your house.'

Edna knew that he would have liked her to stay with him until they were married in the Spring but they both understood that Irene wouldn't approve of that and, of course, they had to think about Billy. So they both set off towards Paradise Road. The snow had stopped but the park looked white and magical in the fading light. Edna felt so happy she thought she would burst with excitement. The wedding was planned for next year in March. It was going to be a simple affair, with a registry office service and a small wedding breakfast for a few close friends and family.

As they walked past the infirmary, John suddenly burst out laughing. 'What's the joke, John?' she asked him.

'Thank goodness Sonia hasn't got her hands on our wedding plans, otherwise it would have a cast of hundreds and maybe two days' hire of the Exclusive Gallery.' Edna laughed, but she didn't even want to think about it.

After James and Sonia had got into the car, she said, 'I didn't think much of Edna's engagement ring. You would have thought John would have bought something a bit more expensive looking instead of that tiny diamond.'

'Maybe that's the ring Edna wanted. After all, she would have been with him when it was bought,' he replied.

'Yes, I suppose you're right.' She felt a quick flash of jealous anger but she managed to suppress it. She was lucky to have ensnared James who was going to be a famous painter. With her help, he couldn't possibly fail.

60

Molly wasn't looking forward to seeing Vera. She got the impression the woman wanted to be left alone but this would probably be her last visit. She had paid her bill for the month's work without a murmur, although Molly knew she was deeply disappointed that there had been no result other than the violence. Vera had said that no one could blame Etta for all these attacks. It had to be someone who knew something and wanted it all hushed up. But when Molly had asked her, 'What could someone want hushed up, Vera?' she said she didn't know.

The snow had turned to a deep, dirty slush and the pavement was slippery. Molly took her time climbing up the Hill. The close was quiet. Children would be in school and it looked as if no one wanted to venture out to the shops because of the weather. When Vera answered the door, Molly thought she looked a bit better than she had yesterday. The house was tidy and Vera had dressed with some care, not like the way she had looked on Molly's previous visits. Perhaps now that Robina's funeral was over, Vera had decided to let the past go and Molly hoped this was the case.

Vera had been looking through a large photograph album. 'I'm trying to remember how Robina looked when she was young. It's hard to imagine ever being children. Robina was never a pretty child, while I was. I don't think she ever forgave me for that. Imagine, having animosity for something you can't help. I never asked to be pretty.' She sounded bitter. 'Anyway, it's all over now and she's at rest. I went to her flat this morning and everything she owned fitted in one suitcase. There are some nice pieces of furniture but they will be sold, along with the flat, and the proceeds will go to the convent in Dublin where she spent most of her adult life.'

Molly said that it probably wouldn't be a big estate. Vera explained bitterly, 'She's left £75,000 pounds in her will. She made me her executor and the solicitor in Dublin has sent me a copy of the will. There will be funeral expenses to come from it but the rest goes to the Sisters of the Poor in the convent.'

Molly could hardly take it in. 'Where did she get all that money from?'

Vera explained about her genius on the stocks and shares market. Molly suddenly felt so sad for Robina. She had lived her life in simplicity but had obviously been quite successful with the stock market. She wasn't sure if the Sisters of the Poor were allowed to gamble like this but Vera said Robina had never become a nun, and had simply been a teacher at the convent school.

Molly was about to say goodbye when Vera went to put the kettle on. 'Stay and have a coffee with me,' she said.

Out of curiosity, Molly picked up the album. Its pages were full of sepia-toned photographs but there were also a lot of black and white ones. Molly was amused by the old-fashioned clothes worn by the wives of the stiff-backed young soldiers, probably taken before the Boer War, and then there were others from the Great War. Someone had written the names of the people in the photo, the places and the dates in meticulous handwriting. Molly thought this was an excellent idea, for so often people were forgotten by the younger generation and the photos just became a collection of faces.

She was on the verge of putting the album down when one particular photo caught her eye. A man was standing beside a farm gate, a young woman by his side, and in the background loomed a large farmhouse. Molly felt herself go cold and she gasped for breath. She quickly flipped the page and came across the photo of Dave and Etta that Vera had shown her all those weeks ago. An old envelope was placed between these pages and on it was written 'Etta's birth certificate'. With shaking fingers, Molly slipped the certificate from the envelope and the truth suddenly struck her like a slap in the face. How had she managed to miss what was right in front of her?

She jumped up, giving Vera a fright. 'I have to go, Vera,' she said. 'Can I borrow these photos, please?' She didn't want to alarm her by asking for the birth certificate as well but this could be easily picked up afterwards.

Vera asked, 'What photos do you want?' She looked at the older one and said, 'Oh, that's Dave's father and my mother. My dad took that photo on Dave's uncle's farm. We lived near Dave's family in those days. That's how we met and got married.'

As Molly put her coat on, Vera said, 'I'd like the photos back, please, when you've finished with them.'

Molly promised she would look after them and return them soon. The pavement was more slippery when she reached the street but she tried to hurry as quickly as she could. She couldn't believe how stupid she had been. Before going to the office, Molly got the car from Paradise Road and parked it in Baltic Street.

Jean looked up when Molly hurried in through the door but before she could speak, Molly said, 'Jean, I want you to phone DS Johns at the police station and tell him to come to this address. Tell him it's urgent and that I've gone there to wait on him. Also, tell him I've found Dave and Etta Barton.'

She scribbled the address on Jean's pad. Jean was worried. 'Should you maybe not wait till I get in touch with him, so he can take charge of this, Molly?'

'No, I may even be too late, but I've got to try and stop her leaving.' Was that why the attacks had stopped? Because she had gone away? Molly knew if that was the case, then she would be lost forever.

The road wasn't very good. Overnight frost had left icy patches but Molly tried to keep up a reasonable speed. The hills were white with snow and a low mist was forming on the tops. It would soon be dark but Molly reckoned on having another couple of hours of daylight left. Not that there was much light to begin with because of the overcast and misty conditions.

When she reached the farm road end, she saw the 'For Sale' sign was missing. Did this mean the farm was sold? Maybe they had taken it off the market. There was a small parking space beside the track and Molly reversed into it. There was no place to hide the car but by the time Charlie arrived, there would be no more need of this pretence.

She had to watch her step as she climbed the rough track, as there were deep potholes filled with slush and water. The trees grew close to the path and their branches were white with frost. She took her time, almost expecting a car to come hurtling down towards her, but everything was quiet apart from the low sound of a tractor, which must have been in one of the fields.

The house was in darkness and as Molly skirted around it, she looked through the grimy windows to see cardboard boxes piled up, confirming that the occupants were planning a move. She found the black car in a small garage at the edge of the house. The door was open and Molly wondered if someone was inside. She crouched low and tried to make her way towards the car but she was taken suddenly by surprise by George. He was carrying a large stick and he snarled at her, 'What do you think you're doing? I'm going to get my stepfather to put the police on you. Did you think we had already left and you would steal something?' He was quite fat and had close-cropped grey hair. He wore a pair of dirty dungarees over a bulky, polo-necked jumper and mud-encrusted Wellington boots.

Molly tried to stay calm. 'I've come to see your stepfather, but I'll wait till he comes back from the field.' Molly saw the tractor on the steep hill. 'Eck's busy feeding the animals. He'll be quite a while yet, so you better come back another day. I'll tell him you called.'

'No, I'll wait,' she said.

'Then you better come inside.' He opened the door into the kitchen and the heat hit her in the face. 'We like to keep it cosy when we get in from the fields.' He shoved a chair at her. 'Sit down and make yourself welcome.'

Molly was becoming anxious. Where was Charlie? Then, she suddenly had a dreadful feeling. What if he was out on a job and didn't get the message till he came back? That could be hours? Why had she been so foolhardy in coming here without him? 'I think I will come back tomorrow to see your stepfather.'

She went to stand up but the blow hit her hard on the back of the head and she felt herself falling onto the flagstone floor.

'Oh, I don't think you will,' he said as he left the kitchen and locked the door.

Molly tried to get up but she felt sick and dizzy. She lay still for a few moments and gingerly touched the back of her head, feeling warm blood, but she had to stop them leaving the farm. She managed to drag herself to the window and she could see George's bulky figure running towards the tractor. She tried the door but it was a thick wooden one that was built to withstand fire, earthquake and flood.

The window was her best bet but she still felt woozy and faint and she had to hold onto the window ledge to let the feeling pass. The window was as strong as the door but just as she was on the point of giving up, the blue lamp of a police car lit up the yard. She knocked loudly on the window and Charlie hurried over. He had to break the window to get it open but she was soon standing outside.

Charlie was furious with her. 'I'll deal with you later, Molly,' he said angrily. He hurried after Constable Williams, who was striding up the snow-covered hill.

The car was still flashing its blue light and George seemed mesmerised by this. He stopped but shouted at his stepfather that the police were here. Molly saw the tractor wobble a little, then overturn. Charlie rushed to the scene to find Eck Barr lying beside it.

Charlie shouted to Molly, 'Phone for an ambulance. Tell them it's urgent.'

Molly went inside the house. It took her some time to find the telephone; it was in a small office at the back of the house. While she waited on it, she felt the blood on her hair becoming stiff. She now had a terrible headache but it was her own fault.

George sat in sullen silence at the other end of the table and Constable Williams, who had now come back from the hill, stood beside the door. George said, 'I didn't mean to hit her but I thought she was a thief. She was heading for the garage when I saw her.'

The policeman said nothing but continued to stand to attention. Charlie had stayed with the injured man. The ambulance didn't take long to come and he was carried off to the infirmary. 'He's still alive,' said the driver, 'but it doesn't look good.'

Molly was put in the ambulance along with Eck Barr and the police constable accompanied them. Meanwhile, Charlie took George to the station in the police car. Molly asked about her car as she stepped into the ambulance but Charlie said he would come for it later. He didn't look at Molly and she knew he was angry with her for coming on her own.

When they reached the infirmary, the injured man was whisked off for an examination while Molly had her head wound cleaned and stitched. The doctor said, 'It's not a large cut but it's deep, so I've put in a couple of stitches.' He had to cut her hair to do this and she was worried about having a bald patch but he said the rest of her hair would hide it.

Charlie arrived back at the hospital about an hour later. 'I've put George into custody, as I want to question his stepfather. Now, what's this all about, Molly?'

She took the photos from her coat pocket. 'I found these in Vera Barton's photo album.' She explained who the people were. 'Can you see the resemblance? Eck Barr is the image of Dave Barton's father. And look at the farm.'

He looked at the photos and nodded. 'Yes, I see.'

Molly explained her one and only visit to the farm. 'I met Eck but not George. I remember thinking Eck looked familiar then but I couldn't place him. George was working in the field and although he passed through the corridor, I never saw his face. And then I saw Etta's birth certificate – her full name is Georgette. I think these two people are Dave Barton and his daughter Etta.'

Charlie said he would question the man if the doctors allowed it. 'I'll have to get a message to Vera Barton to come here and identify him.' He got in touch with the station and they sent a policeman to bring Vera up to the ward.

Molly wanted to know, 'Did George say

anything when you got to the station?'

'No, she – we'd better start calling her a woman – said she didn't mean to hit you but she thought you were there to steal her car.'

The doctor appeared and said. 'It's not looking good for Mr Barr. Is there any family you can contact, as he won't last the night.'

Charlie was hoping to talk to him. 'Can I see him for a few moments, doctor?'

'Don't be too long. I don't think he'll manage to talk.'

Molly stayed at the accident and emergency room while Charlie went into the small side room. The man was lying very still. The doctor said, 'He's suffered massive internal injuries.'

Charlie sat by the side of the bed. 'Mr Barton, can you tell me why you are impersonating Lenny Barr, or "Eck" as you told Miss McQueen?'

For a minute or more there was no response, then he opened his eyes. 'It was an accident. He fell over the cliff and I tried to grab him but couldn't.'

'But why did you leave and take his identity? Surely it would have been viewed as an accident if you had told the police that at the time.'

His breathing became laboured. 'I wanted to get away ... start a new life. I never wanted Etta to come with me but she insisted, so I had to let her come along.'

'Was Etta with you that day?'

'No, I met Lenny by chance and he came with me.' He shut his eyes and the doctor said that was enough questions.

Vera arrived in a flurry of raindrops and squeaky rubber boots. She was out of breath. 'What's happened, Molly?'

By now, Charlie had joined her. 'It's your husband Dave. He's been living under an assumed identity.'

Vera let out a cry. 'It can't be Dave. He would never do this to me. I want to see him.'

Charlie put his hand on her arm. 'He's very ill and not expected to make it through the night.'

'I still want to see him.' She went into the room with Charlie following behind. She turned. 'I'd like to be alone with him if you don't mind.'

Charlie went and sat beside Molly. She now had a thumping headache and just wanted to be at home in her bed.

In the little room, Vera sat beside a husband she had long thought dead. She took his hand. 'Dave? What made you do this, and where is Etta?'

He tried to turn his head to look at her but the pain must have been too bad as a spasm showed on his face. His voice was a hoarse whisper. Vera had to lean over to him to hear what he was saying, then she nodded and held his hand. Dave Barton died at eight o'clock that night. His wife Vera was by his side and a car had brought Etta to be with him at the end.

Vera didn't recognise her daughter at first. She said, 'I've been searching for you for years. Why did you both disappear and leave me living in limbo?'

'Dad needed me more than you did so I went away with him. Lenny had an accident but Dad thought he would be blamed and put into jail.'

'But you pretended to be a lad and look at you. Your lovely hair has been chopped off and you're wearing these old muddy clothes. You always took a pride in your appearance, Etta.'

Charlie came into the waiting room where they were sitting and asked Etta to come back with him to the station. Vera said she wanted to be with her daughter, so she came as well. Charlie and PC Williams took her to the interview room. Charlie began by asking about the day of the accident. 'Were you with your father on that day in Arbroath, Etta?'

She shook her head. 'No, I wasn't. The first time I heard about it was when he came home in a terrible state and told me about the accident.'

'Why was he with Lenny Barr? It seems strange that they should both go to Arbroath, especially as your mother was ill in hospital.'

She shrugged. 'I don't know. He never spoke about it.'

'Did you know your Aunt Robina was back in Dundee?'

Etta looked surprised. 'No, I didn't. The last time I saw her was when I was about fifteen.'

'So you didn't meet up with her over these last few weeks?'

She shook her head. 'No.'

'What I would like to know is why you've pretended to be a man. You were known as a stepson. Why would you need to do that?'

Etta stared at him, her dark eyes contrasting with the grey hair. 'When Dad decided to come back here, I didn't want to be recognised by anyone, especially my mother, so I became George instead of my stupid name Georgette. Anyway, I liked being a man.'

Charlie decided to change tactics. 'Did you cut the brakes on Peter Walsh's bike, causing him to fall and have a very bad accident?'

'Who on earth is Peter Walsh?'

'He used to be a boyfriend of yours.'

'A boyfriend? I haven't had a boyfriend since I was sixteen…' She stopped. 'Oh, that Peter Walsh; he was hardly my boyfriend. We only went out together for three weeks and

I gave him up.'

'Did you work alongside your aunt in setting fire to a doorway in Baltic Street and causing the occupant to be taken to hospital? Did you attack your mother on two separate occasions by knocking her down with a car and pushing her onto the roadway? And did you damage a car in Baltic Street and steal a notebook from inside it?'

Etta became annoyed. 'No, I didn't do any of these things. Maybe my aunt did those things. She was always good on retribution.'

'Your aunt was seen on two occasions getting out of a black car and I think it's your car we're talking about.'

Etta laughed. 'Don't be daft. My car needs a new battery. If you try it, you'll find it won't start. Ask my dad if you don't believe me...' She suddenly stopped and covered her mouth with her hand. Then she began to cry. She rocked her body back and forth in the hard chair, deep sobs filling the tiny room.

Charlie stopped the interview and said she could go home. 'Your mother is waiting for you. I want you to stay with her until I finish this investigation. I'll be speaking to you again tomorrow, so don't leave the town.'

'I want to go back to the farm. It's been sold and I'll be leaving to go back to Dumfries where we stayed after leaving in 1930. My dad kept a small cottage with some land after he sold the farm down there and we always said we would retire there. So that's where I'll be going after all this is over.' She made her way to the door with the police constable walking beside her.

'I'll show you out, Miss Barton,' he said.

She gave him a strange look. 'It's been a long time since I was called that. Where can I get in touch with my aunt? I'd like to say goodbye to her before I leave.'

'Your aunt died last week from a heart attack.'

She stood with her hand on the doorknob. 'She's dead? To think I could have tried to get in touch with her but I thought she lived in Dublin. I didn't know she had moved back here.'

'Well, she did, Miss Barton, just like you did. Constable Williams will take you and your mother home and I want you to stay there.'

Charlie was standing outside the station getting some fresh air when he met Williams going to get the car. 'Where have you left them?'

'They're both sitting in the reception but not looking at nor talking to each other.'

'What do you think of her?' Charlie asked him.

'She seems genuine enough.'

Charlie didn't think so but he had no way

to prove otherwise. Dave Barton had said he was responsible for the accidental death of Lenny Barr, but why this charade? Why change your whole life when it was an accident? If, indeed, it was an accident. Perhaps there was more to it, but the main witness was dead and Etta Barton was one cool customer.

Later, when the constable came back, Charlie said, 'We're going to pick up Miss McQueen from the hospital. We'll take her home, get her car key and then you can drive me out to the farm. I want another look around out there and then I'll drive her car back.'

Molly was still in the accident and emergency room when they came to get her. She sat in silence during the ride home. She handed over her key as she was dropped off at the flat.

'Try and get a good night's sleep and I'll see you in the morning,' Charlie said.

She nodded and went upstairs. She was so exhausted and her head was throbbing. She would take a couple of aspirins and try to sleep.

Charlie and the constable reached the farm and drove into the yard. It was pitch-black but Charlie had brought a torch with him. 'I want to look at the car,' he said, moving over the rough ground to where it was parked.

He was surprised to find it unlocked and when he opened the bonnet, there was no battery in it. He scouted around the shed, almost tripping over a bale of straw. In the corner, he found the battery, placed on two bricks. So it appeared as if she had been telling the truth, but how easy would it have been to take the battery out to get it charged up? This didn't mean that she hadn't been out on the streets at night with or without her auntie. How convenient for her, or was it just luck, that the two other main suspects were now dead and Etta Barton could get away with her attacks?

The door to the farmhouse was locked but he could see the packing cases lined up against the wall. They had almost got away with the deception and no one would ever have known what happened.

After driving back into the city, he parked Molly's car in Baltic Street. When he glanced up at her window, all was in darkness.

61

Charlie went to see Molly early the next morning. He wanted to hear her side of the story before judging if he could charge Etta Barton with an assault.

Molly was still in her dressing gown when he knocked at the office door. She still had her dreadful headache and as Charlie made a pot of tea and some toast, she swallowed another two aspirins. 'Now, explain it all to me again, Molly. How exactly did you make the connection that Eck and George were Dave and Etta?'

Molly explained about going to see Vera and seeing the album lying on the sofa. 'I was just curious about all those old-fashioned photos and then I saw the one with Dave's father and Vera's mother on the farm. I recognised the gate and the house in the background immediately. Then I saw the photo of Dave and Etta that Vera had showed me at the very beginning when she first told me about the case. I thought I recognised Eck's face when I interviewed him early on in my investigation but couldn't place it, and it was only upon seeing the photo again along with the farm that I made the connection. As

I said, Dave looked like his father in the photo. Something clicked when I saw the farm as well.

'Vina's daughter Barbara was picking potatoes at the farm and she said his name was Lenny Barr. However, when he said it was Eck Barr, I never gave it another thought. He mentioned he had come from the Borders with his stepson George and I'm afraid I scratched their names out from my notebook and never followed it up. All this time, I was so certain Dave Barton was dead that my brain didn't even consider any other option. But then, when I saw the photo of Dave again and the parents standing at the farm, everything just fell into place. And then, of course, there was the birth certificate. Etta's real name was Georgette and it all just seemed to be too much of a coincidence.'

'You know, I'm furious with you for going there on your own. I think she's a very dangerous woman and you got off lightly with a scalp wound.'

'I've only got two stitches in it,' she said indignantly.

'Yes, well, you could have been badly injured or even killed.'

Molly realized that and she said, 'I'm sorry. I'll never be the tough guy investigator like in the books.'

Charlie laughed. 'That's only fiction, where a tap on the head doesn't even leave a bruise, but now you see for yourself what damage it can do. By the way, she says she was only defending her property from you as she thought you were burglar, intent on stealing her car and whatever else you could get your hands on.'

'Yes, that's what she told me.'

'Dave Barton confessed to the accidental death of Lenny Barr. He said Etta wasn't with him and she only knew when he came home in distress. He said he wanted to get away in case he was charged with murder, that he had been wanting to get away anyways and that she wanted to go with him.'

'What do you think happened, Charlie?'

'I think she was there. I'm not saying she had anything to do with the accident but she knows a lot more than she's saying, that's for sure.'

'What will happen now?'

'I'll question her again today but if she sticks to her story, then no matter what I think, I've got no proof of any wrongdoing except that she hit you, which she'll say was self-defence. She'll tell the court she came across you skulking in the yard and when she challenged you, you went to hit her. It'll be her word against yours.'

Molly was cross. 'I was not skulking in the yard. I was merely peering through the window.'

Charlie threw up his hands. 'There you go,

then. You looked like you were up to no good and she reacted. You should have left it to us, Molly.'

Molly agreed with him. 'I'm not cut out to be in this business.'

She looked so tired and downhearted that he felt sorry for being so annoyed. 'Never mind, if you hadn't found the photographs and put two and two together as quickly as you did, then they would both have disappeared again. Why they ever came back here is a mystery. They were both safe where they lived before but there's no accounting for human nature.'

'What about Robina Price? Was she involved in all of this?'

'I think she was but Etta says she didn't even know she was back in Dundee. She even asked for her address so she could go and see her and she looked so sad when I told her the woman was dead.'

'Do you think Etta will stay with her mother now that she's been found?'

Charlie looked exhausted. 'She says she's going back to the Borders where she still has a cottage and there's no word of an invite for her poor mother. Why Mrs Barton ever tried to find such a cold-hearted daughter is beyond me, for as I gather, she's always been like this towards her.'

Molly was beginning to get tired again. 'I must get dressed and go down to see Jean. I hope I don't have to go out today as I just want to sleep.' She looked at him and his eyes had dark shadows under them. 'You look like you should do the same, Charlie.'

'I wish I could, but I have to go to work. I have a desk full of reports to fill in and a huge load of crime to investigate. Not to mention questioning the fair Etta Barton again.'

They both went down the stairs just as Jean opened up the office. Her look of surprise was so comical, especially as she tried to look normal. Then, Molly realised she was still wearing her dressing gown and she blushed. Jean sat down at the desk after saying 'good morning' and kept her eyes on the typewriter.

Molly suddenly remembered something. 'I forgot to ask, when will Dave's funeral be held?'

Charlie shrugged. 'I expect Vera will have to arrange it but she did say it was to be a private affair, which I think is wise. None of the newspapers have got hold of the story, thank goodness, so I hope she organises it as quickly as possible.'

As he walked out the door into the street, he grinned. 'You know, I'll have to make an honest woman of you after being seen by Jean.'

Once again, Molly blushed and hurried inside.

62

Charlie made straight for Vera's house. The two women were sitting at the table but the atmosphere in the room was icy. He felt so sorry for the older woman. It must be heart-breaking for her to find her daughter after all these years only to be faced with this sullen silence. 'I've come to ask you again, Miss Barton, if you were with your father on the day of the accident?'

'I've already said I wasn't, so why don't you leave me alone?'

'It's just that your father's story doesn't ring true. I mean, look at it this way ... he's alone with Lenny Barr and no one sees him fall, so why all this double life? It doesn't make sense. For instance, where did he meet Lenny Barr? Why were they both together in Arbroath, especially as your mother was in hospital? You didn't visit her that afternoon, so where were you?'

'I was waiting for Dad to come back from his walk. He went out in the early morning and said he would be back by dinner time. I didn't want to leave the house without him and I thought my mother would understand when we went to the hospital for the next visiting hour.'

'Etta, did you knock your mother over with your car and then push her under a bus?' He heard Vera give a gasp of surprise. 'Did you also set a fire in the doorway of 14 Baltic Street and damage a car in the same street?'

'No, I've told you, I never came into the town as my car had no battery. It's easily seen. You don't work on a farm so you might not realise, but it's hard work from morning till night and I was always dead tired by eight o'clock and in my bed, especially as I had to get up at five.'

'Why did you almost empty your post office savings account all those years ago?'

'I needed to buy some clothes and I didn't want to bother my mother for money as she wasn't well.'

'Were these the clothes you took with you to the farm in the Borders?' She nodded. 'But you began dressing as a boy. Why would you want some pretty dresses that you would never wear?'

'I only started this as a lark when Dad bought the farm here and then realised I liked wearing men's clothes. When we were in the Borders I dressed as a girl and was known as Etta, so I wasn't committing any offence.'

Vera butted in. 'Please leave her alone. I believe her and as she says, she hasn't committed any offence. Dave told me what had happened before he died and I believe him. It was a tragic accident and although they were both stupid in running away, I do think Dave did what he thought was best.'

Charlie was getting fed up with this woman. 'Actually, Etta, you have committed a serious offence by striking Miss McQueen with a stick.'

'I didn't know who she was. When she came to the farm a few weeks ago, I didn't see her face as she was in the kitchen with Dad. I caught her peering into the house and I only meant to frighten her, not hurt her like I did. Can I say sorry to her?'

At that moment, Charlie knew he wouldn't get any more from her. She seemed grief-stricken about the assault and there was no way he was ever going to get proof of Etta's guilt.

'I want to leave after the funeral, Detective Johns. Is that all right?' she said.

'We'll have to wait and see, Miss Barton.' He looked at Vera, who was now sitting by the fire with her arms wrapped around herself as if she was cold. 'When is the funeral?'

'Not for a few days. There's to be a post-mortem, then it will be a family affair at the crematorium. Dave always said that was how he wanted to go, back in the days when we were a family.' Tears ran down her cheeks but she brushed them away while Etta moved over to the window and looked out.

When he left the house, Charlie was so angry. He wasn't the type of person to get mad very often but, on this occasion, he felt a deep resentment toward Etta Barton. Her mother had spent a lot of her savings trying to trace her, she had been knocked down and pushed under a bus, Peter Walsh was still lying in the hospital and Molly had almost been suffocated with smoke and hit over the head, and he didn't have one ounce of evidence to point the finger at her.

It could still have been Miss Price who was the culprit. After all, she had looked on innocent pleasures as sins and thought retribution was needed to cleanse the soul, but looking through her cell-like flat with its one suitcase, he got the impression she wasn't a woman of action. She may have spouted on about her religion but he couldn't see her as a person who would conduct this vendetta against innocent people. But maybe he was wrong. He would never know now.

A week later, Dave Barton was cremated, along with all his secrets. The mourners were Vera and her daughter. Charlie stood at the back of the empty crematorium chapel and watched with sadness as Vera bowed her head at another funeral. When they came out, Charlie saw that Etta was dressed in a brown pinstriped suit, which looked severe with the cropped grey hair. She looked more like a sixty-year-old than forty.

Etta marched right up to him. 'I'd like to leave now, please.'

'I would like a copy of your address, just in case some new evidence turns up,' he said. He knew he was being churlish but this woman annoyed him. She didn't even have the decency to take her mother's arm upon leaving the chapel, instead leaving that small courtesy to the minister who conducted the short service.

She handed him a copy of her address and he saw it was a small village near Dumfries. 'That's where the cottage is and I'll have a small piece of land to work. It means I can keep my hand in with growing vegetables and keeping some hens.'

'I'll come with you to the railway station tomorrow, Miss Barton, just to make sure you catch the right train.'

She laughed. 'You want to make sure I leave, don't you?'

Charlie didn't return the smile but said he would meet her when her train left at ten thirty in the morning.

Back in the house, Vera had made some dinner and tried to persuade Etta not to go. 'You can stay here and get a job. We have so much to catch up on, Etta.'

Etta wasn't in the mood for cosy chats but she didn't want her mother to be left with no hope. 'It would never work, but I'll leave my address and maybe you can come and visit any time you like.'

The next morning was cold but dry. Etta said she didn't want her mother to see her off. It was bad enough having that policeman standing watching her. Charlie got to the station early and waited till she appeared. She carried a small suitcase. When she saw him looking at it, she said, 'I've ordered a removal van to bring all the things from the house. It should arrive in a few days.' She started to walk away. 'Goodbye and please say I'm sorry to Miss McQueen for hitting her. I hope she understands it wasn't meant.'

She moved over to the ticket office and Charlie stood beside her. 'One single ticket to Dumfries, please,' she said, handing over the money.

Then she was through the barrier and onto the platform. The train was on time and arrived at the station with a huge belch of steam and various metallic noises. She stepped onto the train, giving him a small wave as she did. Then the train slowly made its way along the track. Charlie made sure she hadn't come out of her compartment and then he turned and went back to work.

The first thing he did when he reached his

desk was to phone the removal company. The young woman on the other end of the line said yes, Miss Barton's belongings would be delivered to her address in Dumfries in two days' time. There was no more he could do. He knew he was being cautious seeing her onto the train but he didn't want a repeat of the attacks on Vera, Peter and Molly. He thought about going to see Vera but she wouldn't be in the mood for more questions. It was bad enough to find your daughter only to lose her again, and Charlie was suddenly tired of this whole case. There was so much deception and he could do nothing about it – at least not at this moment.

63

Etta settled back in the carriage. Luckily she was the only occupant. She savoured the moment when she had outsmarted that policeman, although it had been touch and go for a while. She knew he suspected her but he had no proof and she had been so meek and passive when apologising to the nosy Molly McQueen. She almost burst out laughing when she recalled her actions. She had been very lucky and she knew it.

She couldn't believe her good fortune when she had accidentally met her Aunt Robina. She had been spying on Peter Walsh's movements when the older woman had approached her. 'It's Etta, isn't it?' she had said.

Etta had panicked for a moment but then she realised this woman was on her side. 'How did you recognise me, Auntie Robina?' she asked her, more in curiosity than anything else.

'You are the image of my late mother. I look like her as well, so we have that in common. What are you doing here?'

Etta decided to be truthful and she told her. Robina's face grew red and she said that sin should be punished. Etta remembered the last time she had seen her. She was fifteen and her dad had put her aunt out of the house because she had made her mother cry. She went on about paying for one's sins.

Etta didn't care about sins but she did have a deep and fervent desire for revenge that had been lying dormant for all these years. She asked if Robina would help her by scouting around and checking out Peter's movements, as well as those of her mother and that pestering woman Vera had hired to trace her.

She thought about her mother. She suspected her mum knew the truth and maybe

Dad had told her before he died. Her mother had frightened her before she left when she said quietly, 'Why was Lenny wearing Dad's watch? It was the watch that made me identify your father. He loved that watch. I don't know why he would have taken it off.'

Etta had said. 'I don't know why Lenny had it. I wasn't there.'

Her mother had remained silent and Etta knew that she had worked out the truth. But Etta wasn't worried. She knew her mother would never say a word. How fortunate she had been that Dad had confessed and then died. And Robina had died as well. What great scapegoats.

She had adored her father but recently he was beginning to annoy and worry her by always asking where she went, especially at night in the car. Lately, he had taken the battery out of it, saying it was flat, but even that had worked in her favour. She had sent the letter to her mother, knowing it was the farmers' day in the centre of the town. It was so simple to give her a hard push. Too bad the bus had managed to stop. Then that old woman who stopped to help her had made it impossible for Etta to try to finish the job, but that had also worked in her favour because the stranger would muddle the police's description of suspects.

Etta's earlier attempt to hit her mother

with the car had also failed, but she had succeeded in making Vera a nervous wreck living on sleeping pills. The fire at Molly McQueen's flat had been carefully planned but then those young lads had arrived in the nick of time. She hadn't even succeeded with Peter Walsh, though his injuries would serve as good enough punishment for the way he had treated her.

When the train reached Edinburgh, instead of staying on it, she got off and waited for the train to London. She hadn't mentioned this to the policeman but that was where she and her dad had gone when they left Dundee. There was a farm a few miles from London; Lenny had been due to start work there but they had taken his place. Luckily, her father had kept the small cottage with the two acres of ground when they sold the farm to move to the Borders.

She had been annoyed when he suggested buying Sidlaw Farm but that's when she decided to pretend to be a man. This gave her so much pleasure because she could come and go and no one was any the wiser. Once again she smiled. She could just imagine the faces of the couple who now lived in the cottage at Dumfries when the removal van turned up. The poor men wouldn't know what to do with her things and, as far as she was concerned, she didn't care what they did with it. She bought a paper from the newsagent's stall and a takeaway cup of tea from the buffet. Her train was due in ten minutes, so she sat down on a bench and waited.

64

5 October 1930

She had been sick again that morning and her dad had heard her as she retched over the bowl in the outside toilet. Of course, he knew what was wrong and she had to confess she was expecting a baby.

She had gone to see Peter. His face blanched when she told him they would have to get married. He was frightened. 'I can't get married, Etta. We're both just sixteen. And anyway, everyone knows you can't get pregnant the first time.'

But she had and it hadn't even been an enjoyable encounter. She had tried to see him twice again that week but he was dodging her. She thought her dad would go and see Peter but, instead, he suggested taking the train to Arbroath. 'The sea air will do you good, Etta.'

She wasn't fooled. He was going to see that Sasha Lowson and ask her for help in solving her problem. She had made up her mind and the last person she wanted to see was that stuck-up trainee doctor.

Then fate had stepped in on the way to the station. Standing at the entrance, looking at the departure board was Lenny Barr. Dad was so pleased to see him. 'Where are you off to then, Lenny?' said Dad, eyeing the big suitcase.

'I've got this new job on a farm near London, Dave, and I'm just checking the times of the train. I see it's nine o'clock tonight.'

'Then come with us to Arbroath. Vera's in hospital and we have to be back by one o'clock, so come along and we'll catch up with the news.'

'What about my case?' asked Lenny.

Dad said, 'Give it to me and I'll put it in the left luggage office.' He put the ticket in his pocket, meaning to give it to Lenny but the train drew in, so they hurried along the platform to catch it.

Etta was delighted to be with Lenny. Her sickness had passed but she still looked peaky. Lenny asked her how she was and if she liked her job. Etta made a face. 'Not really. In fact, I hate it.'

Lenny spoke to her father after that. 'I've landed this great job. The woman who runs the farm is needing a man to manage it.'

Dad asked if he had been down for an interview but Lenny said no, he hadn't; it had all been done by letter and a couple of phone calls. He also said he was frightened of missing his train so Dad had taken his watch off and told Lenny to wear it until they were back in Dundee.

When they reached Arbroath, they decided to walk along the cliff path to see the wonderful views. It was a cold day but it wasn't raining. Dave walked along in front while Etta kept Lenny well behind. Suddenly, Etta grabbed his hand and said she was in love with him and could he please take her away with him. Lenny was shocked. 'I can't do that, Etta. For a start, you're just a child and I'm almost twice your age.'

'But you don't look it, Lenny, and I've always been in love with you.'

Lenny glared at Etta, a look that frightened her, and sounded firm when he told her, 'I don't love you. In fact, I love someone else very much and that's why I'm leaving. She's married and she can't leave her husband and family.'

The truth had hit her right between the eyes. 'You're talking about my mother, aren't you?'

He said 'no', but he was evasive and she knew she was right. Her mother was in love with another man. A deep anger grew in her as she realised that another man was rejecting her. She swung her hand to give him a slap on the face but he grabbed it. She used her other arm to give him a shove and then, to her horror, Lenny disappeared over the edge and she heard him scream as he fell hundreds of feet into the foaming water beneath the cliffs. Her father had run back. He had taken off his jacket and he was just wearing his shirt and trousers. His face was one of horror and fright. He peered over the edge but there was no sign of Lenny. 'I must go down and see if he's lying injured,' he said, but she had cried and clung to his arm.

'It was an accident, Dad. I didn't mean to push him.'

He said it was all right. The best thing to do was for her to get the next train back and he would follow behind, after making sure there was no hope for Lenny. She did as she was told and managed to get into the house without being seen. Her dad had arrived later when it was dark and told her there was no hope of finding Lenny alive. Some other people had heard the scream and the police were out searching, but there was no sign of the body.

She then told him about Lenny and her mother. Dad went quiet, then he said, 'The police will think it was done deliberately and you'll go to jail.' Etta had howled when he said that.

Later, he decided that he would take Lenny's place on the train and when the body was found and identified, he would come back and tell them he did it and that it was an accident. Etta wanted to come as well but he had tried to dissaude her. 'Your mother needs you, Etta.'

'No she doesn't. I want to come with you.'

So they had sneaked out of the house, picked up the suitcase from the office and boarded the train to another life. Luckily, her dad had put the left luggage ticket in his pocket and Lenny had his train ticket in the suitcase. It was just a small matter of buying a train ticket to Edinburgh for Etta and they bought another one for London when they arrived there.

Dad was annoyed he had lost his treasured watch but it was a small price to pay for Etta's safety. The fact that Lenny was wearing it made her mother identify the body as Dave's. Once they had read this news and found out that Etta was presumed a runaway, they knew the truth would stay hidden.

The baby was never born. A couple of weeks into their new life, Etta suffered a miscarriage. Dad said it was probably the stress and shock of Lenny's death. That was another blessing because she knew she would have made a rotten mother.

The farm had been good for both of them. Mrs Chalmers was a bit older than Dad, but she was very good to Etta and they got along quite well. Then Dad married her but a little while later she died unexpectedly, and they were pleased to find she had left her farm to them.

65

Molly went to see Vera to return the photographs. She was sitting looking through the album when Molly arrived and she slotted them neatly back into their spaces. 'I had a happy childhood on the farm, but Robina always frightened me. She was much older than me and I think she resented me when I was born. She used to hit me when Mum and Dad weren't looking, until the day Dad saw her and told her to go and look for lodgings. That's when she went to work for the convent. Of course, that made her hate me all the more.'

Molly didn't know what to say, so she stayed silent. 'Etta told me she was full of remorse at hitting you, Molly, but she did think you were a burglar.'

Molly nodded but didn't believe a word of it. Etta had known what she was doing all right. Molly felt so sorry for Vera, though. She had found her daughter only to lose her again. 'You did a good job in finding Etta, Dave and Robina. To think they were all living near at hand and I never knew. Still, I'm planning to go and see Etta when she gets settled in her new cottage. She gave me the address.'

She showed Molly the piece of paper and Molly agreed. 'That's what you should do and through time, you can both build up your relationship again. It will just take time.'

Molly didn't want to stay, as Vera looked like she wanted to be alone with her thoughts of what might have been. She had been dealt a triple bad hand with the deaths of her sister and husband and Etta not wanting to stay with her. 'Vera, Deanna, who works at the agency, is in a play at the Rep theatre. We were all thinking of going to see her on Saturday night and I wondered if you would like to come along? It's a comedy and seemingly very funny.'

Vera shook her head. 'Thank you for asking but Mrs Jankowski has arranged a bridge night with Una and Henry and she wants me to make up the foursome. I said I would go, but I'm not looking forward to it.'

'It will get you out of the house, Vera, and do you good to meet with your friends again.'

Vera looked as if she wouldn't care if she never saw another living soul again but she said, 'I suppose so.'

Molly's head was still painful but she was getting the stitches out this afternoon and hopefully she would be able to wash her hair thoroughly. Charlie appeared at dinner time. 'I can't stay long. I had the Dumfries police check on Etta Barton and it seems she never got off that train. When they checked the cottage, they found a couple of irate removal men with a van full of furniture and nowhere to put it. The couple who live in the cottage have been there since Dave Barton sold the farm to them a year ago.'

Molly had to sit down. She was shocked. 'Where has she gone?'

'That,' said Charlie, 'is the $64,000 question.'

'I've just left Vera's house and she was planning on visiting Etta. What kind of person does this to her mother ... again?'

Charlie ran his hand through his hair. 'We'll just have to wait and see where she reappears – if she ever does.'

'If it's any comfort to the people she attacked, I don't think she'll show her face here again. She knows that we suspect her of Lenny Barr's death and all the attacks.'

'Yes, well, I have to go. I've got a desk full of paperwork to write up but I'll see you later, Molly.'

Later that afternoon, Molly went to the doctor's surgery. He snipped the stitches but it was very sore as her hair got caught up with the scissors, and not for the first time, Molly cursed Etta Barton.

When she got back to the agency, it was almost dark. Jean said that all the staff were keen to go see Deanna's play. Mary, Edna and Alice had asked if they could bring a friend. Molly looked surprised at the mention of Alice's name. Jean said yes – it was a friend called Sandy. 'You haven't seen her for a wee while but what a transformation. She's got a new hairstyle, and a new coat and dress.'

Molly was pleased. 'Good for her. I hope it lasts.' Then she added, 'Put Marigold's name down and I'll phone her.' As she went up to her flat, she felt it was a good thing to have something to look forward to. It had been a tough few weeks but hopefully it was all over.

Vera sat well into the night with her photograph album, reminiscing over happier times when Etta was a baby. Things had been less enjoyable when Dave came home from the war. It wasn't his fault, these things happened to the young men who had been traumatised with the horror and bloodshed of the trenches. He had never really settled down but there was no faulting his devotion to Etta. It was his devotion to his wife that was lacking.

She remembered Alexander Lenny Barr.

They had fallen in love almost from the first day they had met but she had refused to go off with him. She had a husband and daughter to look after. He had accepted her decision and he was the one to leave for another part of the country. What a rotten hand fate had dealt him to meet up on that awful day with Dave and Etta. All those years, when she thought Dave was dead and Lenny was still alive, she would lie awake at night and wonder where he was. She never dreamed his was the body she had identified; that horrible bloated body with no recognisable features.

However, she had to stop thinking like this. Etta was alive and although she didn't want her mother's help and love, at least she wasn't dead like her dad and Lenny. Thinking of Etta, Vera couldn't help but shudder as she thought again how alike her daughter was to her sister. She remembered that day in 1929 when Robina had arrived at their house and gone on and on about Etta being born in sin. She had said the wages of sin were death and, up to a point, that had turned out to be true. Etta had been put out to play but Vera had found her listening outside the door as Robina left and she never forgot the look on her daughter's face. Etta was mesmerised by her aunt and from that point on she seemed eager to uphold Robina's warped sense of retribution. Then, when she hit the children at school, Vera saw how alike they truly were and she had been very afraid.

She took out the piece of paper with Etta's address and threw it on the fire, where it curled up in the flames before disintegrating into ash. Just like my life, Vera thought. She knew Etta wasn't staying there. Dave had told her the true address and his final words had been, 'Forgive me, Vera, but I had to protect Etta. You do understand, don't you?'

She had nodded and said, 'Yes, I understand.' Then she held his hand till he passed away.

66

Etta boarded her train for London. No longer would she dress as a woman. Her brown pin-striped suit with a white shirt and tie looked so smart with the well-polished brogues. She was amused when she looked at her one suitcase. Like Robina who had been wealthy but lived simply, she would do the same. Dad had invested the money from the sale of the farm in her name and she was also rich.

She recalled the one time she had been in Robina's home. She had become worried after she hadn't turned up at the meeting point on the spare bit of ground near Robina's flat. That night, she decided to go and see her. Robina had given her a key. It was pitch-black and stormy and people's curtains were drawn.

To her surprise, she had found Robina lying dead. She was having a quick look in the desk, in case Robina had left any incriminating evidence, when she found the will. Everything had been left to the convent in Dublin. Like the Mother Superior, she had thought it would only be a few pounds. Then she saw the policeman looking up at the window, so she had hurried away, barely having time to shove the will back in its envelope.

That was the night her father had taken the battery from her car, when she arrived home late and covered in mud from waiting in the rain. Imagine her surprise when her mother told her it was £75,000. What a pity she hadn't left it to her niece.

She had big plans for the cottage and the grounds. She would grow all her own vegetables and keep chickens, maybe some goats and a couple of dogs, and live happily ever after. She wouldn't bother with people. The cottage lay off the beaten track and she would become a recluse and live only for her animals. She settled back in her seat with a contented sigh. She deeply regretted Lenny's death. If she hadn't been in such a rage and then heard his feelings of love for her mother, then she wouldn't have pushed him. But she had and she couldn't undo the past.

However, she had no regrets about Peter Walsh. In fact, she had hoped she had killed him but apparently he would survive. Bad luck. She was also not sorry about her mother and the McQueen woman. They had all got what they deserved. She had been rejected, lied to and had her life poked into, so she had dealt out fair retribution. She sat and watched the countryside pass by the window and closed her eyes for a sleep.

Confession is good for the soul. Now where did that thought come from?

Probably from Aunt Robina.

Hopefully the nightmares were a thing of the past and those nights when she kept falling through space onto jagged rocks and foaming waves were now in the past. No longer would she wake up covered with sweat and the intense desire for retribution for her mother.

Oh yes, from now on there would be no need for confession.

As the train sped through the countryside, she slept soundly.

67

The big night was here. Deanna was thrilled that all her friends were coming to see her. Marigold arrived in time for tea and was staying the night with Molly. 'Well, you'll be glad this case is over, Molly,' she said.

'Yes, I am. It's been a hard slog, Marigold, and all for nothing. Etta's cleared off again and Vera is back to where she started.'

Marigold was quiet for a moment and then she said, 'At least she's knows where she's staying. That's a good thing.'

'But she doesn't. Charlie said she had no intention of going to Dumfries, and goodness only knows where she is now.'

Marigold almost smiled. So it was Charlie, now, was it? 'I've said it before – it doesn't do to rake up the past, Molly. Too many dark secrets come out of the woodwork, along with the creepy crawlies. I know it's a cliché but sleeping dogs should lie and not be disturbed.'

Molly, who was determined to enjoy herself tonight said, 'Well, as you say, it's all over.'

Later, they all met in the foyer of the theatre. Charlie couldn't make it as he had to work but Alice was there with Sandy, a quiet looking man with thoughtful eyes. Edna was with John, and Molly was pleased to see them looking so happy together. Mary had a nice looking lad with her. His name was Stan and he was another quiet one. Maisie and Jean were on their own as Jean's husband was a golfer, not a theatre lover.

They had good seats and they all settled down. The play was extremely funny and Molly felt the tears running down her cheeks but there was no sign of Deanna. At the interval, Maisie said, 'Is she in this play, Molly?'

Molly nodded. 'She'll have her part in the second act.'

The actors ran about the stage in various costumes. The plot was that the main actor's wife had gone away for a week and all manner of misfortunes had befallen him since. Three minutes before the end, a maid rushed on stage. It was Deanna. 'Mr Baxter, your wife is coming up the drive.' She stood by the door while all the various actors ran about, falling over each other.

Then the wife appeared and she bellowed, 'Albert, what's the meaning of all this?'

At this point, Albert's trousers fell down and he tripped over the sofa and landed on Deanna. The audience were appreciative and they burst into a volley of applause. The actors lined up on stage and bowed. Deanna looked fabulous in her maid's costume and she got one of the loudest encores. They all gathered in the foyer and waited on Deanna to come out. When she did they all clapped and said, 'Well done.'

She tried to look modest but failed. 'I know it was a small part but I hope it'll lead to other things.'

Maisie almost had the last word. 'If it had been any smaller, Deanna, then you would have been a bloody statue.'

But it was said in fun and Deanna laughed along with them. Marigold said, 'It takes a good actress to fall on the floor elegantly and you did it superbly.'

Deanna blushed with pleasure and they all applauded her again.

Charlie sat in his office with Constable Williams. 'You have to admit it, sir, that Molly McQueen always seems to get some bizarre cases – like last year and now this one. It beats having to lock up petty thieves and shoplifters.'

He nodded. 'You're right, constable. She seems to attract trouble like a bee attracts honey.' He smiled when he thought about his meeting with the queen bee tomorrow.

Bella Jameson, a pensioner who lived in Victoria Road, threw the empty nail varnish bottle in the bin. Her granddaughter from

Canada had left it behind after her holiday in the summer. Being brought up during the war years with the motto of 'Make do and mend', Bella had been loath to throw it away. So she had spent the time painting her nails and reliving her youth when she always had red nails on her fingers and toes. She often thought of the woman who had been in the near-accident, the one whose daughter was missing, and she sometimes wondered about going into that agency place every time she passed it. However, she didn't want to ask any personal questions, she just hoped that the woman had been reunited with her girl. Thankfully, she had no idea she had once been a suspect in an attempted murder.

The publishers hope that this book has given you enjoyable reading. Large Print Books are especially designed to be as easy to see and hold as possible. If you wish a complete list of our books please ask at your local library or write directly to:

Magna Large Print Books
Magna House, Long Preston,
Skipton, North Yorkshire.
BD23 4ND